WOMEN OF WONDER

SCIENCE FICTION STORIES
BY WOMEN ABOUT WOMEN

Edited, with an
introduction and notes by

PAMELA
SARGENT

Vintage Books
A Division of Random House/New York

VINTAGE BOOKS EDITION January 1975

Library of Congress Cataloging in Publication Data

Sargent, Pamela, comp.
Women of wonder.

Includes bibliographical references.
CONTENTS: Dorman, S. The child dreams.—Merril, J.
That only a mother.—MacLean, K. Contagion. [etc.]
    1. Women's writings, American. 2. Science fiction, American.
3. Women—Fiction. I. Title.
PZ1.S18Wo [PS647.W6]   813'.0876   74–16044
ISBN 0–394–71041–X

ACKNOWL-EDGEMENTS

Dangerous Visions by permission of the author and the author's agent, Virginia Kidd.

"Vaster Than Empires and More Slow" by Ursula K. Le Guin; copyright © 1971 by Robert Silverberg. Reprinted from *New Dimensions One* by permission of the author and the author's agent, Virginia Kidd.

"False Dawn" by Chelsea Quinn Yarbro; copyright © 1972 by Random House, Inc. Reprinted from *Strange Bedfellows* by permission of the author.

"Nobody's Home" by Joanna Russ; copyright © 1972 by Robert Silverberg. Reprinted from *New Dimensions Two* by permission of the author.

"Of Mist, and Grass, and Sand" by Vonda N. McIntyre; copyright © 1973 by the Condé Nast Publications Inc. Reprinted from *Analog* by permission of the author.

I would like to thank the following people, without whose help, advice and moral support my task in putting together this anthology would have been much more difficult:

Janet Kafka
Vonda N. McIntyre
George Zebrowski
Jack Dann

For Connie and Ginny

CONTENTS

CONTENTS xii

INTRODUCTION:

WOMEN IN SCIENCE FICTION

PAMELA SARGENT

I

The story of women in science fiction clearly suggests the continuing emergence of a body of work characterized by the new-found outlook of its practitioners. This new outlook belongs naturally to good science fiction, where it has always been present to some degree, and to the new social-futurological concerns in the culture at large.

In the past, women, both as writers and as characters in sf novels and stories, were part of science fiction only sporadically. During the past twenty years, more women have entered the field. Some of them won acceptance initially by imitating the male writers, showing that they could do as well or better. Others explored the same material as male authors, but from a different perspective. There are signs that both female and male writers are beginning to work with new material and are questioning the assumptions which have dominated the field. Sci-

ence fiction as a whole, however, still reflects the
society around it.

Most science fiction has been written by men, and
they still form a majority of the writers today. About
10 to 15 percent of the writers are women. The vast
majority of the readers are male and a fair number of
them are young men or boys who stop reading sf regularly when they grow older. It is difficult to get exact
figures on this, but publications for science fiction
readers have at various times reported that most of
their subscribers are men; a readership of 90 percent
male and 10 percent female is not unusual.

This is not at all surprising when one considers the
relationship of science fiction to scientific and technical extrapolation, and the fact that science and technology are generally assumed to be masculine
domains. Women have often been discouraged from
entering scientific studies on various grounds: they
do not have the aptitude, they are essentially intuitive
rather than rational, they are concerned with triviali-
ties or the "here and now" and are inherently hostile
to any kind of intellectual exploration, being basically
conservative. Practically speaking, it no doubt seemed
unwise for a woman to invest the time and effort
required for scientific study only to be relegated to
the role of wife and mother. Women studying science
and technology have often been, and sometimes still
are, required to justify taking places that could have
gone to men. This problem occurs often enough in
other intellectual disciplines as well, but the study
of art, literature, or the social sciences can be ex-
cused if the woman does not pursue it for too long.
It might make her a better mother, a more interesting intellectual companion for her husband, or pro-

vide her with a hobby. The effort and long-term commitment that our society demands of those studying the sciences are seen as inimical to the roles women are supposed to play.

There are many scientists around who date their earliest interest in science to the time they read science fiction as boys. The writers, usually males themselves, knowing that their readership was primarily male, often wrote directly for this readership. As a consequence, young girls often found nothing of interest to them personally in science fiction. Already discouraged from having an interest in technology, many girls found little for themselves in books where men had most of the adventures and fun.

We can perhaps understand why the writers of science fiction took for granted certain presuppositions, as did almost everyone else in the society around them. Women, and racial minorities as well, suffered under these assumptions. If science was the province of males, it was also the province of white males. It is more common now to find black people and other minorities represented as characters in sf stories, although the number of black sf writers can be counted on the fingers of one hand. Women characters have been around longer but usually in unimportant roles. One can wonder why a literature that prides itself on exploring alternatives or assumptions counter to what we normally believe has not been more concerned with the roles of women in the future. There are two possible answers, although neither excludes the other. Either science fiction is not as daring or original as some of its practitioners would like to believe, this being more a worthy ideal than a reality; or this literature, designed to question our assumptions, cannot help reflecting how very deeply certain prejudices are ingrained—despite its sometimes successful efforts at imaginative liberation from time and place.

Ironically, a case can be made that the first writer of science fiction was a woman, Mary Shelley, the daughter of the eighteenth-century feminist Mary Wollstonecraft. Although influenced by the Gothic literature of the time in setting and mood, Mary Shelley's novel *Frankenstein* (1818) also reflects an awareness of new scientific discoveries at this time, the dawn of the Industrial Age. The British author and critic Brian Aldiss writes:

In . . . combining social criticism with new scientific ideas, while conveying a picture of her own day, Mary Shelley anticipates the methods of H. G. Wells when writing his own scientific romances and of some of the authors who followed him.[1]

What Aldiss calls "the first real novel of science fiction" has had an obvious and enormous influence. The story of Frankenstein is a powerful one, mirroring as it does the conflict between growing scientific knowledge and the fear that this knowledge may destroy us, as Frankenstein's monstrous creation destroyed him.

One feature of *Frankenstein* is of interest here. Ellen Moers points out that the Gothic novel in the hands of its most popular eighteenth-century practitioner, Ann Radcliffe, became "a feminine substitute for the picaresque, where heroines could enjoy all the adventures and alarms that masculine heroes had long

[1] Brian Aldiss, *Billion Year Spree* (New York, Doubleday, 1973), p. 23.

experienced, far from home, in fiction."[2] But Moers goes on to say:

> . . . what are we to make of the next major turning of the Gothic tradition that a woman brought about a generation later? Mary Shelley's *Frankenstein*, in 1818, made over the Gothic novel into what today we call science fiction. *Frankenstein* brought a new sophistication to literary terror, and it did so without a heroine, without even an important female victim.[3]

It is interesting to note the absence of important female characters in this novel, which introduced a new literary form and set the mold for later science-fiction works.

Brian Aldiss, in summing up Mary Shelley's achievement, writes:

> Overshadowed by her husband's reputation, her writing has been too greatly neglected.

> It is all too appropriate that Mary Shelley's work has been neglected. Science fiction has been similarly neglected until recently. As the standing of Mary's reputation is still in the balance, so is science fiction's.[4]

Women writers of science fiction have been in the minority since Mary Shelley's time. One nineteenth-century exception was Rhoda Broughton, the niece of fantasy writer Sheridan Le Fanu. Broughton's "Behold It Was a Dream," a story about precognition, was pub-

---

[2] Ellen Moers, "Female Gothic: The Monster's Mother," in *The New York Review of Books* (Vol. XXI, No. 4, March 21, 1974), p. 24.

[3] Moers, p. 24. In her essay, Moers makes a convincing case for *Frankenstein* being a birth myth, reflective of Mary Shelley's experience as a wife and mother.

[4] Aldiss, pp. 34, 36.

lished in 1873. In the story, a young woman, Dinah
Bellairs, visits friends and has a dream which accurately forecasts their tragic death. It was not until
the early twentieth century that another woman made
a mark in science fiction.

Francis Stevens, whose actual name was Gertrude
Barrows, was born in 1884. Her first published work,
"The Nightmare," appeared in 1917. Widowed and
responsible for the support of her mother and child,
she made part of her living through the writing of
fiction, much of it fantasy. A science fiction novel, *The
Heads of Cerberus*, was published in 1919 as a serial
in Street & Smith's *The Thrill Book*; it was later re-
issued by Polaris Press in 1953 in a limited edition.

The Heads of Cerberus may be the first work of
science fiction to use the concept of parallel time, in
which it is assumed that there are parallel worlds
which have developed differently from our own as a
result of different choices, circumstances and historical
developments. This theme has been used fairly often
in sf ever since.[5] In Stevens's novel, Robert Drayton,
his friend Terence Trenmore, and Trenmore's sister
Viola journey to a future Philadelphia in a parallel
world. Viola Trenmore, who fulfills the traditional role
of love interest in the story, is also depicted as a
courageous and determined woman.

The end of Francis Stevens's life is as mysterious as
some of her fiction. After moving to California, she
simply disappeared. A letter sent to her by her daughter in 1939 was returned and all attempts to trace her
were unsuccessful. To this day, no one knows what
became of her.

---

[5] One excellent example is Philip K. Dick's *The Man in the
High Castle* (New York, Putnam's, 1962), which shows us a
world in which Japan and Germany won World War II.

Another gifted writer of science fiction and fantasy is C. L. Moore. Catherine Moore began writing during the 1930s, and the best of her work has a brooding, hypnotic atmosphere. Moore was adept at writing from the male point of view, a necessity for anyone who wished to publish in the pulp magazines which had dominated American sf since the 1920s. A number of her stories dealt with the adventures of Northwest Smith, a rugged soldier of fortune who traveled throughout the solar system. But Moore also wrote fantasy stories with a female heroine, Jirel of Joiry, a strong Amazonian figure.

One of Moore's finest efforts is the short novel *No Woman Born* (1944). The heroine, a dancer named Deirdre, has her brain transplanted into a robotic body after nearly dying in a fire. In spite of her metal body, she is determined to dance again. The men in the story, anxious to protect her, want to prevent her from returning to the stage. Maltzer, the scientist who has given Deirdre her new body, fears that audiences will hate and resent the dancer. But Deirdre persists, gives a successful performance and points out to Maltzer how important it is for her to continue her contact with humanity through dance.

Moore's story is an important one for several reasons. It is an interesting example of an sf story which relies for its tension not on the mechanics of an adventure plot, but on the interaction between characters. More important, it is one of the earliest thoughtful treatments of the cyborg, a person who is partly or mostly machine. Deirdre, in her metal body, has gained new senses to replace the ones she lost (smell, taste and touch), and she recognizes that she could easily become alienated from the human beings around her. She thinks she can prevent this from happening by using the contact with her audiences provided by dancing. The men in the story feel sorry for her, seeing her somehow as trapped and cut off in her mechanical body. Deirdre, however, finds a new perceptual world opening up to her, and succeeds in creating a new style of dance as well.

C. L. Moore married another science fiction writer, Henry Kuttner, in 1940, and the two began to collaborate on much of their work. Sf writer and critic Damon Knight commented on the marriage of these two different talents:

> Kuttner's previous stories had been superficial and clever, well constructed but without much content or conviction; Moore had written moody fantasies, meaningful but a little thin. In the forties, working together, they began to turn out stories in which the practical solidity of Kuttner's plots seemed to provide a vessel for Moore's poetic imagination.[6]

One of these collaborations, "Vintage Season," an atmospheric story about visitors from the future in search of some enjoyment at the expense of the twentieth-century protagonist, is widely regarded as a classic in the field. This team of writers continued to write stories together and separately until Kuttner's sudden death in 1958.

Leigh Brackett, who began writing sf during the 1940s, became a prolific writer of entertaining stories and novels and is still writing today. Her most recent credits include screenplays (*Rio Bravo, The Long Goodbye*) as well as sf. Her work is characterized by plenty of action, he-man protagonists and toughness. In a way, Brackett exemplifies the supposed

---

[6] Damon Knight, *In Search of Wonder* (Chicago, Advent, 1967), p. 144.

compliment, "she writes as well as a man"; in fact she writes exactly like a man steeped in *machismo*. Her vivid stories are fairly popular and are generally better written than many similar works.

One of Brackett's stories, "The Halfling" (1943), provides an interesting example of her work. Its hero, "Jade" Greene, is the cynical owner of a carnival featuring performers from various planets. He becomes involved with a young woman named Laura Darrow who, unknown to Jade, is an alien sent by her tribe to kill renegades on other worlds. When Jade realizes that Laura is an assassin responsible for the murder of two of his performers, he kills her in self-defense during a final confrontation. Although the characters are stereotypes, Brackett hints at an underlying sensitivity in Jade and makes Laura a good deal tougher than one might expect a female character to be. But the story, which might have been an interesting study of the relationship between man and alien and the conflict between their very different cultures, is marred by the emphasis on action and the hardness, approaching brutality, of the hero.

The character of Laura no doubt personifies some of the attitudes toward women held by many sf readers. She is a beautiful creature, but extremely dangerous and full of guile and deception. Another female character, a human named Sindi who suspects that Laura is an alien, is treated as a jealous woman by Jade. When Sindi objects to Jade's hiring Laura as a dancer, he tells her, "Just like a dame. Why can't you be a good loser?"[7]

A very different writer, Wilmar Shiras, began her sf

---

[7] Leigh Brackett, "The Halfling," in *The Halfling and Other Stories* by Leigh Brackett (New York, Ace, 1973), p. 15.

career with a story, "In Hiding," published in *Astounding* in 1948. In this story, a psychiatrist, Peter Welles, meets a seemingly average boy who has been sent to Welles by a schoolteacher. The boy, Timothy, is not doing anything overtly wrong, but the teacher suspects him of hiding something and believes he might be disturbed. Welles befriends the boy and discovers that Timothy is in fact a genius, capable of pursuing many different studies. Timothy has already published books under pseudonyms and has been doing work in genetics and linguistics. The boy is a mutant whose parents worked in an atomic-energy plant at the time of an accident. Born after the accident, Timothy was genetically changed. Two years after the accident his parents suddenly died, as did others who had worked in the atomic plant. Welles and Timothy resolve to find the other orphaned children of such workers and help them.

In a second story, "Opening Doors" (1949), Welles and Timothy find another genetically altered child genius, Elsie Lambeth. Elsie has lived in a mental hospital for years, unable to play the role of a "normal" child. She has adjusted to the hospital and is relatively free to do what she wants there. She finds it easier to live in the institution than in a world suspicious of an inquisitive and brilliant child. Welles and Timothy must try to convince Elsie that she has made the wrong kind of adjustment.

Shiras went on to write a novel about these children and others, *Children of the Atom* (Gnome Press, 1953). This thoughtful work does not present the children as frightening threats but as interesting and concerned individuals, and it raises some ethical questions. How can the children best use their gifts for the benefit of humanity? Should they remain in the special school they and their adult friends and relatives plan, or should they go out into the world and associate with other children not so gifted? How will they deal with the suspicion and hatred others might feel toward them? In the problems of these mutant children, we can see reflections of the problems of all children; minority children, those who do not fit in, those whose dreams are discouraged or ridiculed, rejected children, idealistic children. In the situation of Elsie Lambeth and others, women might recognize some of the compromises and adjustments they have had to make in a world which often places a low value on their intellectual accomplishments.

In the late 1940s another writer, Judith Merril, published her first science fiction story, "That Only a Mother," about the aftermath of an atomic war. She went on to write several novels and stories, but became even more renowned for her editing, which has included many volumes of the year's best of stories, published annually throughout the fifties and early sixties. In these collections Merril showed a talent for selecting fine stories which also represented the various directions science fiction was taking.

The 1950s saw another development in science fiction which accurately reflected the attitudes of the time. Many stories, often written by women, featured housewife heroines. These characters were usually passive or addlebrained and solved problems inadvertently, through ineptitude, or in the course of fulfilling their assigned roles in society. Often they, unlike the reader, never really understood what was going on, even by the end of the story. These stories showed women as child-raisers (whose children were generally a good deal more gifted than they were), as consumers of goods (often in a future world where advertising and the free-enterprise system had run wild), or as wives trying to hold their families together after an atomic holocaust or a similar disaster.

One example of this kind of story is Ann Warren Griffith's "Captive Audience" (1953), in which the heroine lives in a world taken over by advertising. The cereal boxes, cans, and packages in her pantry are constantly booming out commercial messages of all kinds.

In Mildred Clingerman's "Minister Without Portfolio" (1951), the central character is a kindly grandmother who meets some visiting aliens in a park. The old woman does not realize who or what the aliens are, makes friends with them and exchanges photographs, thus ensuring interstellar harmony and peace between the two races. Although the story is clever and well written, and the grandmother believably portrayed, it follows the pattern of relying on the ignorance of its main female character to make its point. How valuable are these little things that women do!

"Created He Them" by Alice Eleanor Jones (1954) shows us a future housewife from an interesting perspective. Ann Crothers is literally a slave to her husband Henry, an ill-tempered man dissatisfied with nearly everything Ann does. She is miserable with Henry, but goes out of her way to hold the marriage together. We might wonder why she bothers, until we find out that Ann's world is a post-holocaust world contaminated by radioactive fallout. Few people can have children who are not monstrosities, but Ann and Henry "breed true" to produce healthy children and are therefore condemned to a loveless life together for the sake of future generations.

Henry Crothers is a boor. When Ann announces that she is pregnant for the eighth time, Henry says, "Oh, God, now you'll be sick all the time, and there's no living with you when you're sick."[8] He criticizes her when she cries, hates her because she is big and he has always liked small women. Ann's only purpose in life is to bear healthy children. Her only pleasure is in getting difficult-to-obtain consumer goods with the bonuses granted to those who have healthy children. This bitter and horrifying picture of a future marriage is, either consciously or inadvertently, a condemnation of the form marriage has taken for many in our own time. It is Ann who must make all concessions, must care for the children (until they are taken from her by the government at the age of three), must give up her own needs and desires. In the passive Ann Crothers we see the archetypical figure of woman as sufferer, bringing forth children in pain for humanity's bene-fit—but never for her own.

Other writers of the fifties departed from this pat-tern. Katherine MacLean, author of many fine stories, often used male protagonists but also wrote stories featuring female scientists or wives who were be-lievably characterized. MacLean's stories rely on scientific and social extrapolations combined with sound characterization.

Margaret St. Clair, a prolific writer of stories under her own name as well as under the pseudonym Idris Seabright, specialized in short, sharp, elegant fantasies often containing a dark side. In one of her stories, "Short in the Chest," published in 1954 under the Sea-bright nom de plume, St. Clair writes about a milita-ristic world in which a malfunctioning robot psychia-trist gives advice to a young female marine calculated

---

[8] Alice Eleanor Jones, "Created He Them," in *The Best from Fantasy and Science Fiction*, Fifth Series, ed. Anthony Boucher (New York, Doubleday, 1956), p. 134.

to bring about a disastrous conflict. The story, which mentions sexuality, had some difficulty finding publication in a market that regarded the subject as too daring.

Zenna Henderson, another writer who came to prominence in the fifties, produced a series of stories about "The People," a group of humanlike aliens who have settled in an isolated area on Earth. These "people" are a gentle group with extrasensory powers. The first story of the series (later made into a movie for television) deals with the problems a young schoolteacher has with her alien students. These stories were later published in two volumes, *Pilgrimage* (Doubleday, 1961) and *The People: No Different Flesh* (Doubleday, 1967).

Another very talented writer, Andre Norton, began writing during the 1950s and became known as the author of many science fiction novels for younger readers. Often neglected by sf critics, who dismiss her books perhaps because they are for the young reader, Norton is in fact a gifted writer who in her best work shows a talent for vivid description, great feeling for her characters and detailed depiction of alien peoples, ways, and settings. In several novels she uses American Indians as protagonists (this in a field not noted, even today, for its use of minority characters). In *The Beast Master* (Harcourt, Brace and Co., 1959), Hosteen Storm, a young Navajo, must make an alien world his new home. He is one of only a few survivors of an Earth completely destroyed in an interstellar war. Hosteen Storm's exile takes on added meaning when we consider that he is the descendant of those who have had their homeland taken from them centuries before. In *The Sioux Spaceman* (Ace, 1960), Kade Whitehawk, a member of an Indian culture on

Earth which has once again become strong and powerful, is sent to an alien world. There his gift for communicating with animals, taught to him by his culture, is again needed. *Star Man's Son 2250 A.D.* (Harcourt, Brace and World, 1952), shows us the diverse and multiracial cultures that have developed after an atomic war. One culture guards old scientific knowledge; another creates artifacts and has preserved old crafts; a third has resumed the life of the Plains Indians. This novel, which holds out the hope that different cultures can work together peacefully without sacrificing their distinctive ways, remains one of Norton's best and most popular books. Norton often uses male protagonists in her novels, but a young girl transformed into an alien inhabitant of a forest world plays a central role in *Judgment on Janus* (Harcourt, Brace and World, 1963) and *Victory on Janus* (Harcourt, Brace and World, 1966). A recent novel, *Forerunner Foray* (Viking, 1973), has as its main character Ziantha, a young woman who can read minds.

The late 1950s and the early 1960s saw the entrance of more women writers into the field. Perhaps not coincidentally, science fiction writers and readers were at the same time reexamining the assumptions and the style of much science fiction. Several British writers, publishing in the English magazine *New Worlds* under the editorship of Michael Moorcock, experimented with literary forms and different subject matter. Many American writers were also influenced by this development.

Among the writers who first became known during the sixties were the British writers Hilary Bailey and Josephine Saxton, the Canadian Phyllis Gotlieb, and the Americans Joanna Russ, Carol Emshwiller, Kit

Reed, Sonya Dorman and Pamela Zoline. Many of their stories, instead of dealing with the traditional "hardware" of science fiction, concentrated on the effects that different societies or perceptions would have on individual characters.

One of the most interesting of the stories published by *New Worlds* at this time is Pamela Zoline's "The Heat Death of the Universe" (1967). Written in a fragmented style, the story is about a California housewife, Sarah Boyle. The entropic decline of the universe becomes a metaphor for the state of Sarah's mind. Trapped in a role made obsolete by technology, Sarah is breaking down; this breakdown is underscored by the accumulating dust in her house, her fear that the sugary breakfast cereal her children love to eat might produce a virulent form of cancer as well as tooth decay, the chaotic birthday party she puts on for her children and their friends. Sarah's husband is a dim figure never seen onstage, and she is not sure how many children she has. The story is related to the "silly housewife" sf stories of the fifties, but Sarah Boyle's problems are not resolved in any way. She continues to decline, as does the universe around her.

Josephine Saxton's work, which includes a novel, *Group Feast* (Doubleday, 1971), and several stories, often relies on fantasy rather than explicitly science-fictional elements. But in "The Power of Time" (1971), she writes movingly about a British housewife who wins a trip to New York, her love for a Mohawk man she meets there, and the events of a far future in which the woman's descendant, with the help of a Mohawk chief, utilizes the power of an advanced technology to move all of New York City to the English Midlands. The present and future worlds are skillfully welded together in this story. The present-day love affair ends sadly; the moving of New York to England ends in disaster.

Anne McCaffrey is another writer who came to prominence during the sixties. Her work relies on more traditional science-fictional elements, but female characters are prominent. An early novel, *Restoree* (Ballantine, 1967), has a female protagonist and caused some controversy when it was first published, female protagonists being rare. Two novels that are part of a series, *Dragonflight* (Ballantine, 1968) and *Dragonquest* (Ballantine, 1971), deal with a distant planet where the inhabitants have a telepathic link with the dragonlike creatures there. If there is a flaw in McCaffrey's work, it is that some of it is overly romantic and sentimental, but in a genre dominated by rugged he-men and overly intellectual scientific sorts, this occasional romanticism provides a welcome change. At its best, McCaffrey's writing shows us believable human characters interacting in realistically portrayed alien and future settings.

Kate Wilhelm also makes use of traditional elements in her work, but often questions the presuppositions of science and technology. In "The Planners" (1968), a scientist, Darin, who is working on the chemical basis of memory, is beginning to have doubts about the ethics of his experimentation, which involves the use of convicts and a severely disturbed boy. Darin cannot admit these doubts to himself and his mind begins to externalize them in the form of a young girl, Rae, who criticizes Darin's belief that he is only interested in furthering knowledge. This complex story demonstrates a belief that scientific thought cannot be considered independently of ethical considerations. In a longer story, "Somerset Dreams" (1969), research into dreams is going on in a town inhabited mostly by

old people. Here Wilhelm writes about a doctor and
the conflict she feels between her professional obliga-
tions and her responsibilities to her aging parents. In
"The Village" (1973), Wilhelm paints a horrifying
picture of a Florida town transformed into a My Lai
by a group of American soldiers. The story is a vivid
picture of a military system out of control and is a suitable antidote to the glorification of military virtues
found in so much science fiction. Wilhelm's female
characters sometimes appear in the familiar role of
housewife but they are complex individuals, often
quite different from what the men around them perceive them to be.

Joanna Russ is another major talent who began writing during the sixties. Her work is marked by a carefully crafted prose. Her first novel, *Picnic on Paradise*
(Ace, 1968), has as its main character Alyx, a tough
young woman of the distant past brought to the
future, who must guide a somewhat frivolous group of
tourists to safety on a recreational planet. Alyx was
also the subject of short stories, among them "The
Barbarian" (1968) and "The Adventuress" (1967).
Russ's novelette "The Second Inquisition" (1969)
is about a young girl who is visited by her time-
traveling descendant. In *And Chaos Died* (Ace,
1970), a complex novel based on Taoist thought,
Russ's Earthman hero comes in contact with a culture
gifted with parapsychological abilities.

Ursula K. Le Guin, one of the most important con-
temporary science-fiction writers, also began writing
during the sixties. She is the author of several novels
and short stories. Among the stories, "Nine Lives"
(1969) is one of the best. It is about ten members of a
clone, individuals produced from the genetic material
of one person who are identical twins of that per-

son. These ten people are sympathetically and carefully drawn; when nine of them die in a mining accident, the tenth, used to being with people exactly like himself, must adjust to being with more disparate human beings.

Le Guin's *The Left Hand of Darkness* (Walker, 1969) is deservedly regarded as one of the best novels in the field. The human narrator, a man named Genly Ai, is sent as an envoy to the Gethenians, inhabitants of the planet Winter. The Gethenians are neuter, but are subject to a monthly fertile season, called kemmer. Each Gethenians finds a partner; hormonal secretions make one Gethenian either male or female. The other then becomes a member of the opposite sex and they mate. No Gethenian knows which sex "he" will become during kemmer.

Genly Ai, the Earthman, considers the implications of this physiological development: rape is not possible, since all sex must be by mutual consent. Since the Gethenians are neuter most of the time, sex plays no role in their daily lives except during kemmer, when everything else is subordinated to it. In the words of Genly Ai and Le Guin:

Consider: Anyone can turn his hand to anything. This sounds very simple, but its psychological effects are incalculable. The fact that everyone between seventeen and thirty-five or so is liable to be (as Nim put it) "tied down to childbearing" implies that no one is quite so thoroughly "tied down" here as women, elsewhere, are likely to be—psychologically or physically. Burden and privilege are shared out pretty equally; everybody has the same risk to run or choice to make. Therefore nobody here is quite so free as a free male anywhere else.

Consider: there is no division of humanity into strong and weak halves, protective/protected, dominant/submissive, owner/chattel, active/passive. In fact the whole tendency to dualism that pervades human thinking may be found to be lessened, or changed, on Winter.

The following must go into my finished Directives: When you meet a Gethenian you cannot and must not do what a bisexual naturally does, which is to cast him in the role of Man or Woman, while adopting toward him a corresponding role dependent on your expectations of the patterned or possible interactions between persons of the same or the opposite sex.

One is respected and judged only as a human being. It is an appalling experience.[9]

Genly Ai manages to achieve a close personal relationship with one of Winter's inhabitants, and sees his own race of humans as alien at the end of the novel; two different species, almost repellent. In showing us Winter, Le Guin manages to give us some insight into human culture as well.[10]

---

[9] Ursula K. Le Guin, *The Left Hand of Darkness* (New York, Walker, 1969), pp. 68–69.

[10] An interesting discussion about *The Left Hand of Darkness* took place between Ms. Le Guin and the distinguished Polish sf writer Stanisław Lem in the pages of *SF Commentary,* an Australian publication edited by Bruce R. Gillespie. In an essay entitled "Lost Opportunities," Lem makes the following remarks:

> Although her anthropological understanding is very good, her psychological insight, on the other hand, is only sufficient and sometimes even insufficient. Mrs. Le Guin invents a biologically plausible and fictionally valuable creation. She invents "other humans" who not only become sexual beings periodically (we find such things in sf, including bisexuality) but who [also] become periodically male *or* female during their "kemmer" period (sexual period). Not only this, but also they do not know beforehand which sexual incarnation they will experience next time.
>
> The author would not create, could not create, or did

The 1970s have seen the first published works of a new generation of women sf writers; among them are Vonda N. McIntyre, Ruth Berman, Chelsea Quinn Yarbro, Raylyn Moore, Lisa Tuttle, Grania Davis, Joan Bernott, Suzette Hadin Elgin, Carol Carr, Doris

---

not know how to create the cruel harshness of the individual's destiny in such a system. She gives us some hints in discursively developed chapters, but she does not transform this anthropological material into the shapes of individual lives.

However, let us imagine ourselves in the situation of the people in this novel. Two questions about basic existence force themselves upon our minds:

(i) Who will I become during the next "kemmer" (sexual) period, male or female? Contrary to all stereotyped opinions, the normal uncertainty of our lives, already well-known to us, becomes painfully extended by this sexual indeterminism. We wouldn't need to worry merely about the trivial question of whether next month we impregnate or get impregnated, but we would face a whole new class of psychic problems about the roles which await us at the two poles of the sexual alternative.

(ii) From a circle of totally indifferent people, to whom will we feel erotically attracted during the next "kemmer"? For the time being, everybody else is a neuter as well, and so we can never determine our biological future. The changing pattern of sexual relationships will always surprise us with new and always doubtful changes within the already known environment . . .

But consider the cruel irony of fate: Let's assume that a person as a male happened to love somebody else as a female during the "kemmer" period, and that after some months both became "women" or "men." Can we believe that both will then simply search for biologically suitable (heterosexual) partners? If we answered "yes" to this question, then not only would we speak nonsense, but we would also tell a flat lie, because we know more clearly how the power of cultural-psychological conditioning may form our inner lives in defiance of our biological instincts.

Therefore, Winter's people must experience a lot of un-

Piserchia, Lin Nielson, Maggie Nadler, Phyllis Mac-
Lennan, Suzy McKee Charnas and others. Among the
writers specializing in fantasy are Phyllis Eisenstein,
Katherine Kurtz (author of *Deryni Rising*, 1970,
Deryni Checkmate, 1972 and *High Deryni*, 1973, all

---

happiness and grief, as well as a lot of "perversion," as
"past" males remain more strongly attracted by their "past"
female partners—perhaps now neuters or males—than to
those people who, because of the dictates of their glands,
are now prepared to play the female role. What cruel,
bizarre, even hellish possibilities may an author find here!
These possibilities hide within them the roots of a malig-
nancy that would strike us as openly hellish and inten-
tional . . .

I take from the novel the truth about me (i.e. about all
human beings) that however painful our sexual lives may
be, the limitation of our sexual unequivocality is a blessing,
and not a curse. Of course, the Karhider [Gethenian] *must*
think quite differently from us, and think of us as abnormal,
as Mrs. Le Guin rightly shows . . .

Now back to the novel. Stylistically, it is very well
written. Also it contains the richness and variety of the
mores and customs of an alien civilization, although it is
not wholly consistent. Whatever the author may try to
tell us, she has written about a planet where there are no
women, but only men—not in the sexual, but in the social
sense—because Karhider garments, manners of speech, mores,
and behaviour, are masculine. In the social realm, the male
element has remained victorious over the female one. [*SF
Commentary* 24, November 1971, pp. 22–24. The original
essay was published in the German publication *Quarber
Merkur* no. 25. Translated from the German by Franz
Rottensteiner and revised by Bruce Gillespie.]

In a later issue Ms. Le Guin responded to Lem's remarks:

Stanisław Lem's projected novel . . . is fascinating, as
tantalising as one of Borges' hints-for-stories. I wish that
Lem would write it. I couldn't, partly because the phys-

published by Ballantine), Sanders Anne Laubenthal (author of *Excalibur,* Ballantine, 1973) and Joy Chant (author of *Red Moon and Black Mountain,* Ballantine, 1970). Some of these women, and others in the years to come, may be important authors of science

---

iology of "my" Gethenians is not as Lem reads it. The tragedies that he calls for are obviated by the "differentiating" mechanism which provides that the second or slower of a pair which enter kemmer will *always* develop the opposite sex to the first or earlier. . . . The entrance-door for tragedy, I think, is rather the strong likelihood that two long-term lovers might drift out of synchronisation, as it were: a few hours' difference in the length of their somer-kemmer periods would do it within a year. This difficulty I evaded shamelessly, and only provided a sophisticated pharmacopeia and highly refined techniques of body control to the Gethenians, so that some solution of such latent disasters was imaginable.

Lem is not the first to accuse the Gethenians of being all, or 90%, male. . . . Will he, or anyone else, please point out one passage or speech in which Estraven [a Gethenian character] does or says something that *only a man* could or would do or say?

Is it possible that we tend to insist that Estraven and the other Gethenians are men, because most of us are unwilling or unable to imagine women as scheming prime ministers, haulers of sledges across icy wastes, etc.?

I know that the use of the masculine pronoun influences the reader's imagination, perhaps decisively . . . Alexei Panshin and others have demanded an invented neuter pronoun. I did consider this carefully, and I decided against it. The experiment was tried by Lindsay in *A Voyage To Arcturus,* and it is to my ears a failure, an exasperating preciosity; three hundred pages of it would be intolerable. The intransigence of the medium is, after all, the joy of it. Though you can do more with English, perhaps, than with any language that any artist was ever lucky enough to speak, you cannot do anything you like with it. . . .

. . . You refer to their dress as masculine. What do people in really cold climates wear? I took the Eskimos

fiction. They will undoubtedly bring a new perspective and new materials to the field, and should help
dispel the notion that science fiction is primarily for
men.

II

It might be useful to look at how some male sf
writers have dealt with women. A Swedish writer and
critic, Sam J. Lundwall, says:

> The sex roles in science fiction are as unyielding as the
> metal in the space ship's hull; emancipation is an un-
> known word.

> The holy cry seems to be "Woman, know thy place!"
> and even though women are usually present in the space-
> ships, they are generally treated like some kind of inferior
> creature.[11]

No doubt some of this has its roots in the pulp
origins of American sf (as opposed to serious world

---

as models. They—men and women—wear tunics and trousers,
of course. Did *you* ever try to wear a skirt—long or short—
in a wind at 20° F in deep snow?

I did want a "normal," and male, Terran observer as narrator, because I thought that people would have trouble
to identify emotionally with Gethenians. Indeed, I thought
that many people, especially men, would find them repul-
sive. I was wrong, and I should have had more courage.
None the less I still believe that one can convey more in-
directly than directly, unless one simply delivers a message.
I am a novelist, not a telegraph office. . . . What I had to
say about Gethenians was intended to rouse the reader's
own imagination. . . . [*SF Commentary* 26, April 1972, pp.
90–92.]

11 Sam J. Lundwall, *Science Fiction: What It's All About*
(New York, Ace, 1971), pp. 145, 144.

sf), designed, for all its scientific pretensions, as primarily an escapist literature for men and boys.[12] Science fiction provided a world in which a male could experience high adventure and the interplay of scientific ideas and technological gadgets free from the interference of females. Sf became the neighborhood clubhouse where the boys could get together away from the girls (or parents, or the short-sighted culture at large), who were a nuisance anyway. They got in the way in the clubhouse; they got in the way of the stories too, unless they stayed in their assigned domain.

Women, in their limited roles, served a practical function for the writer. In his story he could have a character explain the workings of a gadget or a scientific principle to an ignorant girl or woman, and by extension to the reader. Women could also serve as rewards for some heroic deed, could be rescued from danger, could sometimes be dangerous (or devious) enemies that the hero had to defeat, or could adorn the covers of magazines, which often showed them dressed in revealing and impractical outfits.

But women were ignored in sf before Hugo Gernsback, the so-called father of science fiction, founded the pulp magazine *Amazing* in 1926. The two major nineteenth-century figures in science fiction, Jules Verne and H. G. Wells, who influenced much of the sf to follow, paid little attention to women.

Mary Shelley, as we have seen, laid some of the groundwork by leaving out important female figures. Jules Verne, in his adventurous and entertaining

---

[12] One must remember that science fiction is not homogeneous anywhere. It is written at every level of quality, as is all fiction. This is an obvious point, but one many people forget.

novels, left out female characters entirely, or else cast them in the roles of endangered women for the heroes to rescue, or as relations of protagonists, there to provide a love interest. Verne was an enormously popular author in his own time and films based on his work (*Twenty Thousand Leagues under the Sea, A Journey to the Centre of the Earth, Around the World in Eighty Days* and others) continue to entertain us today. But more important, his influence is still present in sf novels which rely heavily on adventure and gadgetry rather than on a serious exploration of the social consequences of new discoveries. Verne's characters were nineteenth-century men, essentially unchanged by exciting adventures, strange new devices or the discovery of other worlds. Modern-day authors who follow this example present unchanged twentieth-century men and twentieth-century sex roles. Occasionally some variety is provided by allowing the hero to go to bed with a woman, or several women. "Liberated women" in this context are ones who will sleep with the hero at little or no provocation.

H. G. Wells, who wrote most of his science fiction in the late nineteenth century, can be considered the forerunner of science fiction that deals seriously with change. Socially committed, Wells was very much interested in the rights of women, among other issues; yet this interest is absent from his science fiction. His protagonists are male, and the women who appear do not seem different from what we might expect. Wells's concern for women was expressed instead in non-science-fictional works.

Wells remains the classic sf author. Books such as *The Time Machine, The Invisible Man* and *The War of the Worlds* are examples of sf at its best. It is interesting to speculate on what might have happened in the field if Wells had dealt more completely with women.[13]

Many major sf writers have what at best could be called an ambivalent attitude toward women. One story considered a classic in the field, "Helen O'Loy" by Lester del Rey (1938), concerns a man who builds a robot and programs her to be the perfect wife. Helen, the completely devoted robot, immerses herself in housewifely duties, and chooses to die with her inventor, even though her metal body makes her virtually immortal. At the end of the story, the inventor's friend bemoans the fact that there was only one Helen. Sf reviewer and critic Beverly Friend writes:

> Frankly, one in sf is too many: another blatant statement of woman as mere appendage to man—a walking, talking doll who performs better as an android than she could possibly do as a woman.[14]

Isaac Asimov, in his "robot" stories published during the forties in *Astounding* and still regarded as some of the best stories in the field, produced a major

---

[13] One interesting female character in Wells's work is Weena, the woman the Time Traveler meets on his journey. Weena is helpless and weak, but so are all her people, men and women alike. They are the Eloi, the childlike far-future descendants of the human race.

[14] Beverly Friend, "Virgin Territory: Women and Sex in Science Fiction," in *Extrapolation* (Vol. 14, No. 1, December 1972), p. 49. Ms. Friend has some interesting comments about Philip José Farmer and Theodore Sturgeon, two writers who have pioneered in speculating about sex in their sf stories and novels. Of particular interest is Sturgeon's *Venus Plus X* (New York, Pyramid, 1960), which is about a single-sexed culture and a man's reaction to it.

female character, Dr. Susan Calvin. Susan Calvin is an intelligent and extremely rational expert on robots, who is often called in to solve problems during the course of the series. But she is also an individual who prefers robots to people, who has never married, who is, in short, peculiar from the viewpoint of most people.[15] Although Asimov is clearly sympathetic to Calvin and her work, the reader is free to draw the conclusion that Susan Calvin is a frustrated "old maid" who has never really fulfilled herself. In most of Asimov's other work, the women are either in traditional roles or work only when single; the scientific realm is predominantly male. In his classic sf-mystery novel, *The Caves of Steel* (first published in *Galaxy* magazine in 1953), the hero, Lije Baley, is a detective in a future New York which is part of an overpopulated world. Baley's wife, Jessie, is a housewife who worked as a dietician in one of the communal kitchens before her marriage. In his latest novel, *The Gods Themselves* (Doubleday, 1972), Asimov implies that males are rational, females intuitive. Although he does not assign values to these functions and seems to feel that they are both necessary, one wonders about the assumption. It is, however, interesting to note that the alien species dealt with in this novel is three-sexed, and that the member of the triad who cares for the children is referred to with the masculine pronoun.

Robert Heinlein, one of the most popular novelists

---

[15] Although Dr. Calvin prefers robots to people, there is a logical reason for her preference. Asimov's ethical and endearing robots *are* better than people. The "robot" stories were eventually published in two volumes, *I, Robot* (New York, Gnome Press, 1950) and *The Rest of the Robots* (New York, Doubleday, 1964). The second volume also contains two novels, *The Caves of Steel* and *The Naked Sun*.

of science fiction, presents a complex case. Heinlein's novels are populated with women and girls who join the army, pilot spaceships, are engineers or doctors, or are familiar with higher mathematics. As early as 1941, in a speech at a science-fiction convention, Heinlein spoke of how valuable it is for a person to use the scientific method in dealing with people:

> . . . he can't hate all women—you can't be a woman-hater, not if you use the scientific method, you can't possibly—you don't know all women . . . you don't even know a large enough percentage of the group to be able to form an opinion on what the whole group may be![16]

He has also gone on record publicly in favor of women's rights. In a recent interview, Heinlein said:

> If you want my personal opinion . . . women haven't been invited into the space program because the people who set up the rules are prejudiced. I would like to see some qualified women hit NASA under the Civil Rights Act of 1964. They're entitled to go; they're paying half the taxes; it's just as much their program as ours. How in God's name NASA could fail to notice that half the human race is female, I don't know.[17]

Yet many of Heinlein's female characters act in an inexplicable manner for people who are supposedly so gifted. In *Tunnel in the Sky* (Scribner's, 1955), an entertaining and well-written novel for young readers,

---

[16] Robert A. Heinlein and Forrest J. Ackerman, "Heinlein On Science Fiction," in *Vertex* (Vol. 1, No. 1, April 1973), p. 96. This article is the text of a speech entitled "The Discovery of the Future" given by Heinlein at the 3rd World Science Fiction Convention in Denver in 1941. The speech was transcribed for *Vertex* by Forrest J. Ackerman.

[17] Frank Robinson, "Conversation With Robert Heinlein," in *Oui* (Vol. 1, No. 3, December 1972), p. 112.

the hero's sister is a member of the armed services, but her only real desire is to marry almost any man she can find (women outnumber men in this future world) and settle down to raise children. In *Citizen of the Galaxy* (Scribner's, 1957), the young hero meets a girl who is gifted in mathematics but pretends she is ignorant to hold his interest. In *Podkayne of Mars* (Putnam's, 1963), a novel in which a teen-aged girl is the central figure, Heinlein portrays her as an adolescent Doris Day, constantly flirting with men, disguising the fact that she is bright, and making use of "feminine wiles." Podkayne soon decides that raising children and being a pediatrician are much more exciting than being a spaceship captain, her previous goal. *Have Spacesuit, Will Travel* (Scribner's, 1958) shows us a heroine who is neither silly nor unintelligent, but that is probably because she is a little girl and has not been socially conditioned as yet; *The Star Beast* (Scribner's, 1954) has a young female character who has divorced her parents and lives in a youth hostel.

Heinlein may represent an advance over much previous sf; he at least concedes the fact that women are capable of courageous deeds and intellectual activity. But he is apparently uncomfortable with women who are not at some point subordinate to men. No matter how capable, gifted or adventurous she is, a woman's main interest is in bearing children to a robust and worthy male.

Heinlein often presents societies which have quite different bases than ours, but the sex roles do not vary. In *Podkayne of Mars*, for example, women bear their children in youth; then the newly born infants are "frozen" cryonically. After mother and father have established themselves in their careers, the babies are "thawed out" or revived, and raised when the parents have the time. One would think that this development alone would alter the family structure, but women are still seen as primarily responsible for child care. In *The Moon Is a Harsh Mistress* (Putnam's, 1966), the inhabitants of the moon are the descendants of a penal colony, of criminals exiled from Earth. Heinlein speculates on the different forms marriage has taken in this world where men outnumber women, but the women are generally responsible for domestic life.

Oddly enough, when sex started to become a more acceptable part of science fiction in the 1960s (it still remains out of bounds to some readers and magazines), this did little to aid Heinlein's characterizations of women. In *Stranger in a Strange Land* (Putnam's, 1961), an immensely popular and much reprinted Heinlein novel, the women characters have regressed to being nothing more than beautiful sex objects. *I Will Fear No Evil* (Putnam's, 1970) has a very silly heroine whose body is used to house the brain of an old and dying man. In fact, Heinlein's female characters seem to have become more one-dimensional in later works. The use of sex in science fiction, for many other writers as well, seemed to mean only one thing: the role of woman as sex object could be added to the traditional ones of housewife, child-raiser, damsel in distress and scientist's daughter.[18]

---

[18] Robert Heinlein has been severely criticized by many sf critics and reviewers for his depictions of female characters. Sam J. Lundwall stated that Heinlein "still firmly believes that women are fit only for the harem." Others have objected to the fact that many Heinlein heroines are as preoccupied with cosmetics, flirtations, child-bearing or "holding their men" as they are with science or higher mathematics. Still others have complained that they are not "feminine" *enough.*

It is true that many of his women characters would not be

In other stories and novels, we see a world in which gadgets have usurped most of the household tasks commonly done by women. In "With Folded Hands" (1954) by Jack Williamson, a thoughtful story about the consequences of making machines the guardians

---

out of place in a harem or its modern-day equivalent; this is especially true of the women in his most recent work. We can speculate on the reasons for this:

(1) Heinlein's novels are another case of "cultural spillage," of the culture around the author spilling into what should be a speculative work about the future and affecting the author's assumptions. Cultural spillage does not have to be a bad thing. The assumptions or concerns of the culture at large can be used to inform or improve a science fiction novel or story, and have been used successfully at times. But a science-fiction writer, because of the distinctive nature of his or her work, must be on guard and ready to assume a skeptical or questioning attitude if he or she is to be truly speculative.

(2) Heinlein may be assuming that it is a *real possibility* that women will in the future, in spite of increased opportunities, choose to be flirts, mothers or wives. As a matter of fact, Heinlein's female characters *choose* their fates to a certain extent. They are generally not passive creatures but strong-willed sorts who make up their own minds about what they want. Even the sex objects in his novels often initiate the action. Those who become mothers resemble "professional parents" more than put-upon housewives, and parenthood is respected and honored. It seems that Heinlein genuinely believes that parenthood is an exciting occupation and as fulfilling as anything else might be. This is a good and defensible position.

One can still ask, however, why men in Heinlein's novels don't also choose so-called feminine occupations. Of course, a society of the future need not be rational and sf authors do not have to write normatively (although because sf has a strong didactic strain, one often feels that authors are prescribing as well as speculating, and some of them undoubtedly are).

Perhaps Heinlein, like most of us, believes different things at different times. If he emphasizes the wonders of parenthood and family life in many books, he also shows us a girl "divorcing" her parents (in *The Star Beast*). If he shows us female

of humanity, robots do the housework and can even handle child care. Yet the hero's wife apparently does nothing outside the home. As it turns out, there is a logical reason for this, as the robots are soon trying to prevent everyone from working, but this is not the case at the beginning of the story. In *The Age of the*

---

sex objects in later works, he also shows us a married couple who are good friends as well as lovers and who function as a team, with no apparent desire for children (in "The Unpleasant Profession of Jonathan Hoag," 1942). In *The Rolling Stones* (New York, Scribner's, 1952), the hero's mother is a physician who has given up her practice for full-time motherhood. In spite of this lapse, she acts much more rationally than her husband in an emergency situation. Ignoring her husband's objections and his desire to protect his wife from infection, the doctor boards a stranded spaceship with sick passengers in need of medical assistance. Women are shown in positions of power in some early works, and it is not too unusual for Heinlein to imply that they are more knowledgeable or rational than men.

Heinlein as a person appears to have a strong libertarian streak and has publicly denounced any form of coercion (including prisons and the military draft). It is difficult to believe that he would have any desire to keep women "in their place." Yet he still seems to believe, consciously or unconsciously, that women are sometimes in need of protection or wish to fulfill themselves primarily as wives or mothers (usually, however, after expressing themselves in other areas). It may be that Heinlein sincerely believes that being a mother is superior to anything men can do. But because this belief is often used as a rationalization by others to limit women's lives, Heinlein has been criticized for it.

Heinlein's novels present an informative and sometimes contradictory picture of the various ways in which men have viewed women and might view them in the future. It is interesting to think about what might happen if Heinlein took more care with his female characterizations. Obviously he is a complex case and it is difficult to make a definitive comment about him or where he stands.

Pussyfoot by Frederik Pohl (Ballantine, 1969), we see
a future world in which death has been conquered,
boring tasks are automated, and people use personal
computers for everyday decisions. Joanna Russ comments:

> But if you look more closely at this weird world you
> find that it practices a laissez-faire capitalism, one even
> freer than our own; that men make more money than
> women; that men have the better jobs (the book's heroine
> is the equivalent of a consumer-research guinea pig); and
> that children are raised at home by their mothers.[19]

Often the treatment of women in sf is rationalized
by setting the story on a far planet where the characters are colonists or are accidentally stranded. Stories
of people colonizing or accidentally landing on alien
worlds are a popular subject in science fiction for
obvious reasons. The alien setting, with its unusual
flora and fauna and its unknown dangers, provides
adventurous escape reading. It allows the author to
use his or her imagination in the creation of such a
world. At its best such a story can also provide a
setting for the thoughtful exploration of the problems
involved in confronting an alien world and the ways in
which humans might deal with the new planet.

Unfortunately, much of this type of science fiction
assigns women to the traditional roles of bearing and
caring for children and the home, on the grounds that
the primary duty of the colonists is to procreate. Normally the women agree to this necessity; those who
do not usually find fulfillment, as the novel pro-

---

[19] Joanna Russ, "The Image of Women in Science Fiction,"
in *Vertex* (Vol. 1, No. 6, February 1974), p. 54.

gresses, in their "natural" function. This type of sf presents a problem. Our roles are, after all, often dictated by the surroundings in which we find ourselves. Yet it is surprising that the colonists do not experiment more with social structures and that reluctant women trapped in the constraints of certain roles are not treated more sympathetically.[20] Occasionally the colonists abandon monogamy, on the grounds that the future society will be healthier with as many different genetic combinations as possible. This may be perfectly true, but it still leaves the women in the position of brood mares.

One might wonder why women would abandon Earth for such restrictive roles. The fact is that usually their lives on Earth are depicted as equally restricted, if not more so. The Earth they leave behind is decadent, totalitarian, overpopulated, dull, or all of these and more. Sometimes there is a shortage of "husband material," and it is often assumed that a woman's primary desire is finding a husband. In other novels the Earth has, through war or some other disaster, become unable to sustain life. Occasionally the women simply follow their men. Poul Anderson, a gifted and

---

[20] It would be interesting, for example, to show the conflict in a woman character between the role demanded by physical necessity and her desire to use her other abilities. It would be even more interesting to resolve the problem, and not simply by having the woman find fulfillment as a mother.

To make an obvious point, women, like men, are more than just their bodily equipment. Male colonists in sf novels are valued for their abilities and for their genes. Women, however talented or well-educated, are often valued *only* for the genes they will pass on to succeeding generations. The frequency with which writers insist on bodily basics is greater than the truth demands.

prolific author of science fiction, describes such a woman in his novel *Orbit Unlimited:*

> She still hadn't asked him what it was [a plan one character has just mentioned]. But that was typical of her. Like most women, she kept her warmth for human things and left the abstractions to her husband. He often thought she had come to Rustum less for her beliefs than for him.[21]

Often the reasons for the colonization of other worlds rest on an assumption not unlike the popular nineteenth-century notion of "manifest destiny." Humanity must have new frontiers if it is to survive and prosper; nature has made us extremely fertile and will not be thwarted in her aim; therefore we must find new worlds and settle them. These assumptions have been questioned in the past by some sf writers and are being questioned today.

But the old cultural assumptions say a lot about how women have been regarded in sf. Man is seen as aggressive and driven outward in his explorations. Woman follows, a satellite in his shadow, rarely initiating any action of her own. There are surely other alternatives. We need not so ruin the Earth that we are forced off it. We need not regard other worlds as ours if we happen to be stronger than their inhabitants. It should be possible for us, men and women, to explore other worlds together and perhaps to learn more about them, and ourselves.

---

[21] Poul Anderson, *Orbit Unlimited* (New York, Pyramid, 1961), p. 89. Anderson later, in *Tau Zero* (New York, Doubleday, 1970), depicted women who want to explore space for the same reasons the men do, although they are ready to begin the customary breeding at the end of the novel. One female character, Ingrid Lindgren, shows considerable strength. When the starship's captain becomes unable to function, she takes over most of his tasks.

III

In spite of the fact that women have either been ignored or assigned traditional roles in most sf, there is a small branch of sf specifically about women. Sam Moskowitz writes:

> . . . there is one theme spotlighting the female sex which, since the beginning, has been regarded as legitimately within the province of science fiction—that is the extrapolation of the woman dominant: the female of the species completely independent of or ruling over the male.[22]

Among the works Moskowitz cites as examples of this genre are *The Coming Race* by Edward Bulwer-Lytton (1874), *Mizora* by Mary E. Lane (under the pseudonym Princess Vera Zaravitch), published in 1890, and "The Revolt of the ———" by Robert Barr (1894).

Most of these works dealing with matriarchies, however, are more a reflection of the fears or wishes of their authors than serious extrapolations. Many of them simply involve role-reversal (in which men do housework and women hold power) or they depict faraway or future states in which the women are portrayed as more barbaric than men might be in similar circumstances (male children are killed; a few men are kept or captured for breeding). Sometimes the stories end with a battle scene; some of the

---

[22] Sam Moskowitz, "When Women Rule," in *When Women Rule* (New York, Walker, 1972) ed. Sam Moskowitz, p. 1. This interesting anthology contains an informative essay by Moskowitz and several little-known stories on the theme of dominant women.

surviving women decide to mate with men and begin a more "natural" cycle.

The theme of dominant women is present in some twentieth-century sf as well. In John Wyndham's "Consider Her Ways" (1956), a woman of the twentieth century visits the future and finds a matriarchy; men are extinct. This future society is antlike. The idea that a female society would be static and much like an insect society is one that others besides Wyndham have held. He does, however, include several passages condemning the role assigned to twentieth-century women.

In A. M. Lightner's *The Day of the Drones* (New York, Norton, 1969), a novel for young readers, an expedition from Africa journeys to Britain five hundred years after an atomic holocaust. The expedition believes that only black Africans have survived the disaster, but in Britain it soon meets a woman-dominated society modeled on insect life. The Africans, coming from a society in which men and women are treated equally, are appalled at the cruelty present in the British society. But the Africans also realize that their own society, rigidly stratified and prejudiced against those with lighter skins, has its cruel tendencies as well. In her novel, Lightner has used her female-dominant society to enlighten the reader, pointing out that male-dominant societies were equally cruel. She has also provided a logical reason for the development of the matriarchy. Insect life is the only form of animal life to have survived on the British Isles; the human survivors have accordingly modeled their society on it.

Some science fiction and fantasy prefers to deal with the possibility that women are already dominant in some way, disguising this dominance with a mask of submission. One brilliant example of this kind of story is Fritz Leiber's *Conjure Wife* (first published in 1943 and reprinted in *Witches Three,* Twayne, 1952), in which the women are in fact witches, protecting and guiding the lives of their men with spells and incantations. The heroine's husband is skeptical of his wife's "superstitions" and forces her to dispose of her charms and amulets, not realizing that she has been protecting him from harm. The novel takes place at a small New England college and the interdepartmental faculty politics are realistically portrayed.

A variation on this theme can be found in "The Misogynist" by James Gunn (1952). This story advances the assumption that women are in fact aliens from another world. One male character cites as evidence the "facts" that wives can easily find objects their husbands misplace, that women furnish homes with all kinds of purposeless devices, that their thought processes are alien to men, that women have cold and clammy feet at night in bed, and that women are uninterested in sports, intellectual matters and other such things. These "alien" women are in fact controlling things. They are seen as parasites with few abilities of their own except a talent for living off of hard-working, creative and adventurous men. This ambivalent story has apparently struck a resonant chord in some readers. It has been reprinted many times, once as recently as 1974.

Poul Anderson, in *Virgin Planet* (Bouregy & Co., 1959), set his satirical story on an alien world where only the female descendants of an Earth colony have survived. A man lands there and finds these women very curious about his penis. The women have been praying that a group of men would join them.

A more serious exploration of this theme appeared

in Philip Wylie's *The Disappearance* (Holt, Rinehart, 1951), in which each sex mysteriously disappears and both men and women find themselves in a world populated entirely by their own sex. Four years pass before men and women are reunited; during that time, each sex begins to explore the mixed feelings it has toward the other. One character, Paula Gaunt, says:

They sent you to school and made you work and told you good marks meant everything . . . You went to college. You studied. You earned degrees. You married. And then—*what?* You had to learn a lot of new things about running a house and raising babies . . .

We were forever told we were equal—and forever being kept from behaving equally. We were brought up to think of ourselves as independent—and then forced into dependence.[23]

Paula's husband, Bill Gaunt, also has time in his male world to do some thinking:

In the demeaning of woman *man has demeaned himself.* His chivalry, his mother reverence, are but sickly pretenses to hide his ageless, vile convictions. What would we say of any other beast that held its mate in secret revulsion? What do we feel of the spider that copulates and then devours its mate? Let *that* be said of humanity![24]

By the time the two sexes are reunited, there is some hope that humanity will not repeat the mistakes of the past.

During 1972, two more examples of the dominant-woman theme appeared: *Regiment of Women,* by Thomas Berger (Simon & Schuster) and "When It Changed," by Joanna Russ. Berger's novel was an-

23 Philip Wylie, *The Disappearance* (New York, Pocket Books, 1966), p. 273.

24 Wylie, pp. 246–247.

other "role-reversal" story. Although it makes some good points about the silliness of sex-role stereotyping (football, for instance, is considered too dangerous for men to play, because it is difficult to protect their genitals), it is basically a skillful reworking of some very old ground.

Russ's story is a departure from the usual way of treating dominant women. Her women characters, the descendants of an Earth colony stranded on a planet called Whileaway, are depicted as sensible, fairly normal people instead of as super-Amazonian warriors, barbarians, or an antlike hive. The women have been able, with the aid of their scientific equipment, to breed parthenogenetically; all men died shortly after the expedition arrived.

The descendants of the expedition live in a society where each woman does what best suits her, unencumbered by imposed roles. Lesbian relationships are formed and the culture is a viable one. When men from Earth arrive, they appear alien to these women. The daughter of one character expresses amusement at the notion that anyone would desire a man sexually. The men, all of whom profess their belief in women's equality, are actually surprised that the women have survived and soon begin to adopt "protective" and "chivalrous" attitudes toward them.

"When It Changed" won the Nebula Award, given annually by the members of the Science Fiction Writers of America. Yet it was also severely criticized in some science-fiction publications. It is a bit odd that readers should feel threatened by a story in which well-characterized, likable women can get along without men, when there is such an abundance of science fiction in which well-characterized, likable men get along without women.

The theme of dominant women in science fiction is an interesting one, but it has never played a very large role in the genre. It has tended, consciously or unconsciously, to reflect the belief that the sexes are at war with each other and that peace can be bought only with the dominance of one sex over the other. It has often been propagandistic rather than truly extrapolative. The notion that the sexes could live and work together harmoniously, in an equal fashion, was rarely considered and is still being questioned.

IV

It is a popular idea that technological developments have taken place with such rapidity that they seem to have outrun our capacity for dealing with them. Despite the ongoing changes in our customs, ethical systems and societal structures, we are still largely living in ways that either do not take account of our technological tools or are allowing the technology to rule us, deciding things for us as nature has done in the past.

We have arrived at one of the crucial periods of history where the decisions we make (or refuse to make) will have drastic consequences. We may inadvertently be forced to return to former ways of life, and our former roles, if complex technological and ecological systems collapse. The options for women, and indeed for all human beings, would accordingly decrease. We may continue to allow our technology to develop in an unplanned way, with unforeseen consequences not easily reversed or remedied. This situation is likely to develop if we do not begin to consider our goals, our priorities, and possible or present scientific developments which may help us to achieve them.

It will not help any of us to reject technology and scientific research out of hand. It is easy to understand why this is the path some might wish to take; it is even easier to understand why women in particular might view technology with alarm. Women have had little to say about how science and technology should be used, and they have had even less to do with research and the development of new tools. They may view technology as one of the tools of male dominance, and scientific research as a robber of funds that might have been better spent. But this is a mistaken view. Science is, after all, only a tool. It has no values, save one: an imperative to learn as much about our universe as we can know. Science and her handmaiden, technology, can only show us what is possible, what is known and what is left to be learned. They pose questions. It is up to all of us to decide how to use them to further those aspects of human life that we decide are valuable and necessary.

Norman Mailer, in *The Prisoner of Sex,* has written:

. . . if past revolutions had been the attempt of the exploited to define themselves as men, and present attempts (since power was now technological) were to achieve command of techniques, then the female revolution, Women's Liberation itself, would have an inbuilt tendency to technologize women . . .

. . . technology, by extending man's power over nature, reduced him before women . . .

Indeed, in a technological time when the historical tendency was to homogenize the work-and-leisure patterns of men and women (because that made it easier to design the world's oncoming social machine) so a time might arrive which would be relatively free of cultural conditioning, and then males and females might virtually cease to exist.[25]

   . . . there was a technology which looked to manipulate the genes . . . —more than one piece of engineering would yet take up squatter's rights in the ovum. The extra-uterine womb, which he had assumed in his innocence was the end of the road, was only the road which led to the theater where they were looking to operate on the Lord, yes, genetic engineering "could conceivably be used in the distant future to create a whole new breed of man—man capable of changing sex after birth and changing it repeatedly."[26]

There is some truth in Mailer's statements. There is also, however, an almost morbid fear of technology interwoven with Mailer's idiosyncratic metaphysical views. Technology has altered our living patterns and promises to do so in the future. Medical and agricultural advances in particular have produced a situation in which the world has become overpopulated, thereby making motherhood, a primary occupation for women, not only unnecessary to some degree but socially irresponsible when unplanned or carried to excess. We must begin to consider not only the proper and constructive uses of science and technology, but also social experimentation. Astronomer-exobiologist Carl Sagan writes:

We should be encouraging social, economic, and political experimentation on a massive scale in all countries. Instead, the opposite seems to be occurring. . . .

---

[25] Norman Mailer, *The Prisoner of Sex* (Boston, Little, Brown, 1971), pp. 67, 127, 169.

[26] Mailer, p. 214. Mailer is quoting from David M. Rorvik's *Your Baby's Sex: Now You Can Choose* (New York, Bantam, 1971).

We should not be surprised . . . if experimental communities fail. Only a small fraction of mutations succeed. But the advantage social mutations have over biological mutations is that individuals learn; the participants in unsuccessful communal experiments are able to assess the reasons for failure and can participate in later experiments that attempt to avoid the consequences of initial failure.

There should be not only popular approval for such experiments, but also official government support for them. Volunteers for such experiments in utopia—facing long odds for the benefit of society as a whole—will, I hope, be thought of as men and women of exemplary courage. They are the cutting edge of the future.[27]

Such experimental communities offer many possibilities for women, and some women are already living in such communities. Aided by the thoughtful use of scientific tools, such experiments may open the way to new experiences for all people.

But what is the role of science fiction in such explorations? Science fiction can be seen as a part of futurological research. Futurological institutes and futurologists allied with educational institutions are actively engaged in thinking about the future. They look for social trends, possible and probable technological developments and their uses, and in some cases they affect the present and the future by the kinds of advice they give to groups and businesses that use their services.[28] Individuals in various disciplines,

---

[27] Carl Sagan, *The Cosmic Connection* (New York, Doubleday-Anchor Press, 1973), p. 38.

[28] The advice given by some "think tanks" to the military during American involvement in the Vietnamese war is one unfortunate example, and points out the necessity for considering priorities and values in the use we make of such work. The "think tanks" simply discuss what is possible in both the

such as city planning, sociology, law and engineering, among others, are exploring possible future developments in their fields. Journalists and scientists are exploring the future in speculative works written for the general public.[29]

Thoughtful science fiction can present speculative ideas in a way these nonfiction works cannot. It can show us the future as it might be *experienced* by its inhabitants. It can show us how different developments might affect individuals and their customs, problems that could arise, and how the future might *feel*. It can also aid us in questioning our own ideas and assumptions by giving us a different perspective.

All women and indeed all people should seek to familiarize themselves with these futurological explorations. An acquaintance with scientific advances and their possible results is important if we are to make informed decisions about our society's future. We can no longer think only in terms of what will happen in the next ten years, or even in our own lifetimes. The world is changing too rapidly for that. We must examine our values in the context of these changes.

---

present and the future. It is up to us to decide how to use such advice. Herman Kahn's assessment of the probable results of nuclear warfare, as hideous and dehumanizing as it seems, may have helped in making the thought of such warfare unthinkable.

[29] Among them are *The Biological Time Bomb* by Gordon Rattray Taylor (New York, New American Library, 1968), *Future Shock* by Alvin Toffler (New York, Random House, 1970), *Man Into Superman* by R. C. W. Ettinger (New York, St. Martin's, 1972), *The Future of the Future* by John McHale (New York, Ballantine, 1969), *The Prometheus Project* by Gerald Feinberg (New York, Doubleday-Anchor, 1969), and *An Inquiry Into the Human Prospect* by Robert L. Heilbroner (New York, Norton, 1974).

People who believe they are not gifted in scientific thought or intellectual discipline (and most often such preconceptions are culturally induced) can, and should, take part in such explorations. Science, after all, begins with the asking of questions and the desire to learn. This is a quality all people share, not only the "intellectually gifted" or "educated." If women do not want men to make their future for them, they must explore these problems. Science fiction is one tool for doing this.

Science fiction opens the mind. Even the worst sf, with its old-fashioned adventure and stereotyped characters, can sometimes serve this purpose. Much genre sf contains bad writing, stereotyped heroes, heroines and villains. But it also provides the reader with some understanding of the immensity of our universe. The aliens in these novels, whose ways of thinking are completely different from ours, can give the reader an understanding of what it might be like to deal with intelligent beings who do not have our preconceptions.

At its best, science fiction can also provide a new and different literary experience. This fact has often been obscured by the pulp origins of the genre in the United States. To this day much sf, still influenced by these origins, seems to be primarily escapist adventure, saturated with male-oriented power fantasies. But writers such as Gene Wolfe, Robert Silverberg, Ursula K. Le Guin, Stanisław Lem, Carol Emshwiller, Thomas M. Disch, Kate Wilhelm, Barry Malzberg and R. A. Lafferty, among others, have brought literary skill and a deeper exploration of ideas to their science fiction. Newer writers such as George R. R. Martin, Vonda N. McIntyre, James Tiptree, Jr., Gardner R. Dozois, Jack Dann, Chelsea Quinn Yarbro, Geo.

Alec Effinger, Doris Piserchia, Joe W. Haldeman, Joan D. Vinge, George Zebrowski, Gregory Benford and Edward Bryant show great promise in developing both literary skills and original ideas in their science fiction.

Science fiction can provide women with possible scenarios for their own future development. Other literature can show us women imprisoned by attitudes toward them, at odds with what is expected of them, or making the best of their situation in present or past societies. The branch of popular literature written explicitly for women, the "gothic," limits women to primarily passive, victimlike roles. *Only sf and fantasy literature can show us women in entirely new or strange surroundings. It can explore what we might become if and when the present restrictions on our lives vanish, or show us new problems and restrictions that might arise.* It can show us the remarkable woman as normal where past literature shows her as the exception. Will we become more like men, ultimately indistinguishable from them with all their faults and virtues, or will we bring new concerns and values to society, perhaps changing men in the process? How will biological advances, and the greater control they will bring us over our bodies, affect us? What might happen if women in the future are thrown back into a situation in which male dominance might reassert itself? What might actually happen if women were dominant? How might future economic systems affect our societal roles? These are only a few of the questions that can be explored fictionally by sf writers. Even unpretentious and lively adventure novels can explore these issues in the ways in which they make use of their female, male and alien characters.

A whole essay could be written about innovative sf works dealing with women. Sexual equality was an ideal in E. E. Smith's "Lensmen" series, published during the 1930s and '40s. A memorable female character dominates Stanley Weinbaum's novel *The Black Flame* (Fantasy Press, 1948). A. E. van Vogt has portrayed impressive, almost frightening, women, notably the Empress Innelda in the "weapons shop" stories. Philip K. Dick has included many important female characters in his works, among them judo instructor Juliana Frink (in *The Man in the High Castle*) and Ella Runciter, whose husband depends on her to aid him in business decisions (in *Ubik*, Doubleday, 1969). I suspect that women may play an important role in the futures depicted in foreign science fiction, one obvious example being Ivan Yefremov's *Andromeda* (Moscow, Foreign Languages Publishing House, 1959).

Science fiction at its best could be seen as superior to the culture around it in its attitudes toward human rights, despite the crudities which can be found in genre sf. A body of better works by male authors exhibit sane and sometimes innovative attitudes. Thus we see the culture at large affecting a forward-looking literature and deforming it to a degree, much in the same way as pulp-genre strictures have deformed sf. If we limit ourselves to the best non-genre sf, the effects would be less apparent, while they would become more visible if we looked at larger samples of lesser, repetitiously patterned works which make up what we mean by a genre. I have been interested in pointing out serious lacks, however, rather than in writing an appreciation of virtues.

Science-fiction novels for young adults and children can also offer role models for younger readers. This has happened often enough in the past for boys, as I pointed out earlier. There is no reason why this cannot be true for girls as well. Novels for young readers by Andre Norton, Ursula K. Le Guin, A. M. Lightner and Robert Heinlein (who, in spite of the faults of some of his female characters, has a talent for writing engrossing stories with realistic details) can, like all good children's literature, be enjoyed by adults as well.

It should be noted that much of the truly innovative work in science fiction still remains to be done. There are, however, signs that the field is changing. Part of this is due to the growing numbers of women entering the field as writers, and to the changing views of some of the male writers. One well-known author and editor, Harlan Ellison, has said:

> . . . **women are writing many of the things male sf writers thought could never be written; they are opening up whole new areas to us; they are making us examine tenets and shibboleths we thought were immutable. The mightily thewed warrior trip is one of these. People like Ursula Le Guin, Joanna Russ, Kate Wilhelm, and Doris Piserchia are making that seem hideously ridiculous.**[30]

But real changes in the genre are also dependent on the readers. Much of science fiction is a popular literature, and much of it is likely to remain so. It must satisfy and entertain its readership. This does not mean, however, that it must be simple-minded or cater only to those desiring good escapist reading. (It

---

[30] Arthur Byron Cover, "*Vertex* Interviews Harlan Ellison," in *Vertex* (Vol. 2, No. 1, April 1974), p. 37. Ellison was responsible for the publication of "When It Changed" by Joanna Russ in his anthology *Again, Dangerous Visions* (New York, Doubleday, 1972).

also does not mean that serious works are not entertaining. Some of the best and most serious sf is also the most entertaining.) If more women begin to take an interest in sf and the scientific and futurological ideas involved, publishers will have an interest in publishing and writers in writing novels exploring such ideas from different perspectives. If, however, publishers and writers can do better with the old stereotypes and have little reason to believe that readers want anything else, women will remain minor characters, and familiar roles and prejudices will be a major part of the literature. Only dedicated writers and publishers willing to take a risk would then provide more thoughtful works.

It is up to us, both as writers and as readers, to begin exploring the unfamiliar, to acquaint ourselves with scientific and futurological concerns, and to give serious thought to what we are and what we would like to become.

A few words about this anthology: My primary concern was to present entertaining, thoughtful and well-written science-fiction stories by women, in which women characters play important roles. The number of stories I could include was necessarily limited, partly by considerations of space and partly because of my own limitations on the kind of story I wanted for the book. There were others, equally as fine and engrossing, that I could have chosen, but some were too long and others too much like stories I had already decided to include. I have tried to give the reader as many different kinds of stories as I could. The reader unfamiliar with science fiction should gain some understanding of the many different types of stories sf can present and the kinds of ideas explored in them. The reader familiar with science fiction should recognize some old friends in these pages, and may be drawn to consider the literature and its ideas from another perspective.

WOMEN OF WONDER

THE CHILD DREAMS

The child dreams that her dream
is faster than light, because
we promised her that's how death
would come for her. Queen of the sky,
she will slip away at her own speed,
and dreams of rockets big enough
to lift above the oceans.

She soars through the universe,
leaving cliffs where her family
hangs; she will not be Andromeda,
bound to a rock until the prince
comes, but fly on her own
from our stifling kitchens.

The prince is a figment
of our boring legends, he is
the gravity her sleep-ship
may escape from. Dressed
in a red shift, she's always
a world ahead of his weight.

—Sonya Dorman

THAT ONLY A MOTHER

JUDITH MERRIL

Judith Merril was born in New York City, the daughter of a playwright and critic in the Yiddish theater. She has written adventure, western and suspense fiction, but she is best known for her writing and editing in science fiction. Her novels include **Shadow on the Hearth** (Doubleday), **The Tomorrow People** (Pyramid), **Mars Child** (Abelard) and **Gunner Cade** (Simon & Schuster), the last two written with C. M. Kornbluth under the joint pseudonym Cyril Judd. Her story collections include **Out of Bounds** (Pyramid), **The Daughters of Earth** (Dell), and **Survival Ship and Other Stories** (Kakabeka).

As an editor, Ms. Merril's influence on the field has been of great importance. Throughout the late fifties and early sixties, she edited annual collections of the best sf stories of the year, in addition to such anthologies as **Beyond the Barriers of Space and Time** (Random House) and **England Swings SF** (Doubleday). She was one of those responsible for bringing British science fiction, with its experimentation in form and subject matter during the early 1960s, to the attention of American readers. She now lives in Canada.

"That Only a Mother" was Judith Merril's first science-fiction story. Published in **Astounding** magazine in 1948, it reflects a concern with atomic weapons and shows us a world which they might have given us. The story is a warning; it is also a moving tale about a mother, her child, and the effect of atomic war on them. Such wars, we see, can never really be over.

Margaret reached over to the other side of the bed where Hank should have been. Her hand patted the empty pillow, and then she came altogether awake, wondering that the old habit should remain after so many months. She tried to curl up, cat-style, to hoard her own warmth, found she couldn't do it any more, and climbed out of bed with a pleased awareness of her increasingly clumsy bulkiness.

Morning motions were automatic. On the way through the kitchenette, she pressed the button that would start breakfast cooking—the doctor had said to eat as much breakfast as she could—and tore the paper out of the facsimile machine. She folded the long sheet carefully to the "National News" section, and propped it on the bathroom shelf to scan while she brushed her teeth.

No accidents. No direct hits. At least none that had been officially released for publication. *Now, Maggie, don't get started on that. No accidents. No hits. Take the nice newspaper's word for it.*

The three clear chimes from the kitchen announced that breakfast was ready. She set a bright napkin and cheerful colored dishes on the table in a futile attempt to appeal to a faulty morning appetite. Then, when there was nothing more to prepare, she went for the mail, allowing herself the full pleasure of prolonged anticipation, because today there would *surely* be a letter.

There was. There were. Two bills and a worried note from her mother: "Darling. Why didn't you write and tell me sooner? I'm thrilled, of course, but, well, one hates to mention these things, but are you *certain* the doctor was right? Hank's been around all that uranium or thorium or whatever it is all these years, and I know you say he's a designer, not a technician, and he doesn't get near anything that might be dangerous, but you know he used to, back at Oak Ridge. Don't you think . . . well, of course, I'm just being a foolish old woman, and I don't want you to get upset. You know much more about it than I do, and I'm sure your doctor was right. He *should* know . . ."

Margaret made a face over the excellent coffee, and caught herself refolding the paper to the medical news.

Stop it, Maggie, stop it! The radiologist said Hank's job couldn't have exposed him. And the bombed area we drove past . . . No, no. Stop it, now! Read the social notes or the recipes, Maggie girl.

A well-known geneticist, in the medical news, said that it was possible to tell with absolute certainty, at five months, whether the child would be normal, or at least whether the mutation was likely to produce anything freakish. The worst cases, at any rate, could be prevented. Minor mutations, of course, displacements in facial features, or changes in brain structure could not be detected. And there had been some cases recently, of normal embryos with atrophied limbs that did not develop beyond the seventh or eight month. But, the doctor concluded cheerfully, the *worst* cases could now be predicted and prevented.

"Predicted and prevented." We predicted it, didn't we? Hank and the others, they predicted it. But we didn't prevent it. We could have stopped it in '46 and '47. Now . . .

Margaret decided against the breakfast. Coffee had been enough for her in the morning for ten years; it would have to do for today. She buttoned herself into interminable folds of material that, the salesgirl had assured her, was the *only* comfortable thing to wear during the last few months. With a surge of pure pleasure, the letter and newspaper forgotten, she realized she was on the next to the last button. It wouldn't be long now.

The city in the early morning had always been a special kind of excitement for her. Last night it had rained, and the sidewalks were still damp-gray instead of dusty. The air smelled the fresher, to a city-bred woman, for the occasional pungency of acrid factory smoke. She walked the six blocks to work, watching the lights go out in the all-night hamburger joints, where the plate-glass walls were already catching the sun, and the lights go on in the dim interiors of cigar stores and dry-cleaning establishments.

The office was in a new Government building. In the rolovator, on the way up, she felt, as always, like a frankfurter roll in the ascending half of an old-style rotary toasting machine. She abandoned the air-foam cushioning gratefully at the fourteenth floor, and settled down behind her desk, at the rear of a long row of identical desks.

Each morning the pile of papers that greeted her was a little higher. These were, as everyone knew, the decisive months. The war might be won or lost on these calculations as well as any others. The manpower office had switched her here when her old expediter's job got to be too strenuous. The computer was easy to operate, and the work was absorbing, if not as exciting as the old job. But you didn't just stop working these days. Everyone who could do anything at all was needed.

And—she remembered the interview with the psychologist—*I'm probably the unstable type. Wonder what sort of neurosis I'd get sitting home reading that sensational paper* . . .

She plunged into the work without pursuing the thought.

February 18.

Hank darling,

Just a note—from the hospital, no less. I had a dizzy spell at work, and the doctor took it to heart. Blessed if I know what I'll do with myself lying in bed for weeks, just waiting —but Dr. Boyer seems to think it may not be so long.

There are too many newspapers around here. More infanticides all the time, and they can't seem to get a jury to convict any of them. It's the fathers who do it. Lucky thing you're not around, in case—

Oh, darling, that wasn't a very *funny* joke, was it? Write as often as you can, will you? I have too much time to think. But there really isn't anything wrong, and nothing to worry about.

Write often, and remember I love you.

Maggie.

SPECIAL SERVICE TELEGRAM

FEBRUARY 21, 1953
22:04 LK37G

FROM: TECH. LIEUT. H. MARVELL
X47–016 GCNY
TO: MRS. H. MARVELL
WOMEN'S HOSPITAL
NEW YORK CITY

HAD DOCTOR'S GRAM STOP WILL ARRIVE FOUR OH TEN STOP SHORT LEAVE STOP YOU DID IT MAGGIE STOP LOVE HANK

February 25.

Hank dear,

So you didn't see the baby either? You'd think a place this size would at least have visiplates on the incubators, so the fathers could get a look, even if the poor benighted mommas can't. They tell me I won't see her for another week, or maybe more—but of course, mother always warned me if I didn't slow my pace, I'd probably even have my babies too fast. Why must she *always* be right?

Did you meet that battle-ax of a nurse they put on here? I imagine they save her for people who've already had theirs, and don't let her get too near the prospectives —but a woman like that simply shouldn't be allowed in a maternity ward. She's obsessed with mutations, can't seem to talk about anything else. Oh, well, *ours* is all right, even if it was in an unholy hurry.

I'm tired. They warned me not to sit up so soon, but I *had* to write you. All my love, darling,

Maggie.

February 29.

Darling,

I finally got to see her! It's all true, what they say about new babies and the face that only a mother could love— but it's all there, darling, eyes, ears, and noses—no, only one!—all in the right places. We're so *lucky*, Hank.

I'm afraid I've been a rambunctious patient. I kept telling that hatchet-faced female with the mutation mania that I wanted to *see* the baby. Finally the doctor came in to "explain" everything to me, and talked a lot of nonsense, most of which I'm sure no one could have understood, any more than I did. The only thing I got out of it was that she didn't actually *have* to stay in the incubator; they just thought it was "wiser."

I think I got a little hysterical at that point. Guess I was more worried than I was willing to admit, but I threw a small fit about it. The whole business wound up with one of those hushed medical conferences outside the door, and finally the Woman in White said: "Well, we might as well. Maybe it'll work out better that way."

I'd heard about the way doctors and nurses in these places develop a God complex, and believe me it is as true figuratively as it is literally that a mother hasn't got a leg to stand on around here.

I *am* awfully weak, still. I'll write again soon. Love,

Maggie.

March 8.

Dearest Hank,

Well, the nurse was wrong if she told you that. She's an idiot anyhow. It's a girl. It's easier to tell with babies than with cats, and *I know*. How about Henrietta?

I'm home again, and busier than a betatron. They got *everything* mixed up at the hospital, and I had to teach myself how to bathe her and do just about everything else. She's getting prettier, too. When can you get a leave, a *real* leave?

Love,
Maggie.

May 26.

Hank dear,

You should see her now—and you shall. I'm sending along a reel of color movie. My mother sent her those nighties with drawstrings all over. I put one on, and right now she looks like a snow-white potato sack with that beautiful, beautiful flower-face blooming on top. Is that *me* talking? Am I a doting mother? But wait till you *see* her!

July 10.

. . . Believe it or not, as you like, but your daughter can talk, and I don't mean baby talk. Alice discovered it— she's a dental assistant in the WACs, you know—and when she heard the baby giving out what I thought was a string of gibberish, she said the kid knew words and sentences, but couldn't say them clearly because she has no teeth yet. I'm taking her to a speech specialist.

September 13.

. . . We have a prodigy for real! Now that all her front teeth are in, her speech is perfectly clear and—a new talent now—she can sing! I mean really carry a tune! At seven months! Darling my world would be perfect if you could only get home.

November 19.

. . . at last. The little goon was so busy being clever, it took her all this time to learn to crawl. The doctor says development in these cases is always erratic . . .

SPECIAL SERVICE TELEGRAM
DECEMBER 1, 1953
08:47 LK59F

FROM: TECH. LIEUT. H. MARVELL
    X47–016 GCNY
      TO: MRS. H. MARVELL
        APT. K-17
        504 E. 19 ST.
        N.Y. N.Y.

WEEK'S LEAVE STARTS TOMORROW STOP WILL ARRIVE AIRPORT TEN OH FIVE STOP DON'T MEET ME STOP LOVE LOVE LOVE HANK

Margaret let the water run out of the bathinette until only a few inches were left, and then loosed her hold on the wriggling baby.

"I think it was better when you were retarded, young woman," she informed her daughter happily. "You *can't* crawl in a bathinette, you know."

"Then why can't I go in the bathtub?" Margaret was used to her child's volubility by now, but every now and then it caught her unawares. She swooped the resistant mass of pink flesh into a towel, and began to rub.

"Because you're too little, and your head is very soft, and bathtubs are very hard."

"Oh. Then when can I go in the bathtub?"

"When the outside of your head is as hard as the inside, brainchild." She reached toward a pile of fresh clothing. "I cannot understand," she added, pinning a square of cloth through the nightgown, "why a child of your intelligence can't learn to keep a diaper on the way other babies do. They've been used for centuries, you know, with perfectly satisfactory results."

The child disdained to reply; she had heard it too often. She waited patiently until she had been tucked, clean and sweet-smelling, into a white-painted crib. Then she favored her mother with a smile that inevitably made Margaret think of the first golden edge of the sun bursting into a rosy predawn. She remembered Hank's reaction to the color pictures of his beautiful daughter, and with the thought, realized how late it was.

"Go to sleep, puss. When you wake up, you know, your *daddy* will be here."

"Why?" asked the four-year-old mind, waging a losing battle to keep the ten-month-old body awake.

Margaret went into the kitchenette and set the timer for the roast. She examined the table, and got her clothes from the closet, new dress, new shoes, new slip, new everything, bought weeks before and saved for the day Hank's telegram came. She stopped to pull a paper from the facsimile, and, with clothes and news, went into the bathroom, and lowered herself gingerly into the steaming luxury of a scented tub.

She glanced through the paper with indifferent interest. Today at least there was no need to read the national news. There was an article by a geneticist. The same geneticist. Mutations, he said, were increasing disproportionately. It was too soon for recessives;

even the first mutants, born near Hiroshima and Nagasaki in 1946 and 1947 were not old enough yet to breed. *But my baby's all right.* Apparently, there was some degree of free radiation from atomic explosions causing the trouble. *My baby's fine. Precocious, but normal.* If more attention had been paid to the first Japanese mutations, he said . . .

There was that little notice in the paper in the spring of '47. That was when Hank quit at Oak Ridge. "Only 2 or 3 percent of those guilty of infanticide are being caught and punished in Japan today . . ." *But* MY BABY's *all right.*

She was dressed, combed, and ready to the last light brush-on of lip paste, when the door chime sounded. She dashed for the door, and heard for the first time in eighteen months the almost-forgotten sound of a key turning in the lock before the chime had quite died away.

"Hank!"

"Maggie!"

And then there was nothing to say. So many days, so many months, of small news piling up, so many things to tell him, and now she just stood there, staring at a khaki uniform and a stranger's pale face. She traced the features with the finger of memory. The same high-bridged nose, wide-set eyes, fine feathery brows; the same long jaw, the hair a little farther back now on the high forehead, the same tilted curve to his mouth. Pale . . . Of course, he'd been underground all this time. And strange, stranger because of lost familiarity than any newcomer's face could be.

She had time to think all that before his hand reached out to touch her, and spanned the gap of eighteen months. Now, again, there was nothing to say, because there was no need. They were together, and for the moment that was enough.

"Where's the baby?"

"Sleeping. She'll be up any minute."

No urgency. Their voices were as casual as though it were a daily exchange, as though war and separation did not exist. Margaret picked up the coat he'd thrown on the chair near the door, and hung it carefully in the hall closet. She went to check the roast, leaving him to wander through the rooms by himself, remembering and coming back. She found him, finally, standing over the baby's crib.

She couldn't see his face, but she had no need to.

"I think we can wake her just this once." Margaret pulled the covers down and lifted the white bundle from the bed. Sleepy lids pulled back heavily from smoky brown eyes.

"Hello." Hank's voice was tentative.

"Hello." The baby's assurance was more pronounced.

He had heard about it, of course, but that wasn't the same as hearing it. He turned eagerly to Margaret. "She really can—?"

"Of course she can, darling. But what's more important, she can even do nice normal things like other babies do, even stupid ones. Watch her crawl!" Margaret set the baby on the big bed.

For a moment young Henrietta lay and eyed her parents dubiously.

"Crawl?" she asked.

"That's the idea. Your daddy is new around here, you know. He wants to see you show off."

"Then put me on my tummy."

"Oh, of course." Margaret obligingly rolled the baby over.

"What's the matter?" Hank's voice was still casual, but an undercurrent in it began to charge the air of the room. "I thought they turned over first."

"This baby"—Margaret would not notice the tension—"*This* baby does things when she wants to."

This baby's father watched with softening eyes while the head advanced and the body hunched up propelling itself across the bed.

"Why, the little rascal." He burst into relieved laughter. "She looks like one of those potato-sack racers they used to have on picnics. Got her arms pulled out of the sleeves already." He reached over and grabbed the knot at the bottom of the long nightie.

"I'll do it, darling." Margaret tried to get there first.

"Don't be silly, Maggie. This may be *your* first baby, but *I* had five kid brothers." He laughed her away, and reached with his other hand for the string that closed one sleeve. He opened the sleeve bow, and groped for an arm.

"The way you wriggle," he addressed his child sternly, as his hand touched a moving knob of flesh at the shoulder, "anyone might think you are a worm, using your tummy to crawl on, instead of your hands and feet."

Margaret stood and watched, smiling. "Wait till you hear her sing, darling—"

His right hand traveled down from the shoulder to where he thought an arm would be, traveled down, and straight down, over firm small muscles that writhed in an attempt to move against the pressure of his hand. He let his fingers drift up again to the shoulder. With infinite care he opened the knot at the bottom of the nightgown. His wife was standing by the bed, saying, "She can do 'Jingle Bells,' and—"

His left hand felt along the soft knitted fabric of the gown, up toward the diaper that folded, flat and smooth, across the bottom end of his child. No wrinkles. No kicking. *No . . .*

"Maggie." He tried to pull his hands from the neat fold in the diaper, from the wriggling body. "Maggie." His throat was dry; words came hard, low and grating. He spoke very slowly, thinking the sound of each word to make himself say it. His head was spinning, but he had to *know* before he let it go. "Maggie, why . . . didn't you . . . tell me?"

"Tell you what, darling?" Margaret's poise was the immemorial patience of woman confronted with man's childish impetuosity. Her sudden laugh sounded fantastically easy and natural in that room; it was all clear to her now. "Is she wet? I didn't know."

She didn't know. His hands, beyond control, ran up and down the soft-skinned baby body, the sinuous, limbless body. *Oh God, dear God*—his head shook and his muscles contracted in a bitter spasm of hysteria. His fingers tightened on his child— *Oh God, she didn't know . . .*

CONTAGION

KATHERINE MACLEAN

Katherine MacLean began reading science fiction at an early age and at fifteen was offered a laboratory to do a neural synaptic pathways experiment by the American Association for the Advancement of Science. Instead, she temporarily dropped out of science and studied at Barnard College, where she received her B.A. in economics. She has worked as a technician in various hospitals and laboratories, and presently teaches English at the University of Maine as a part-time lecturer. She spends much of her time learning new skills and researching her ideas thoroughly, and her science fiction is marked by careful attention to both character and detail. Her stories have been published in various magazines and anthologies, as well as in a collection, **The Diploids** (Manor Books). Her novella, "The Missing Man," won the 1972 Nebula Award, given annually by the Science Fiction Writers of America.

Women have often found their self-esteem or lack of it tied to societal standards of beauty; it is safe to say that for many women, their physical appearance probably determined their lives and the ways in which other people thought of them, as well as their attitudes toward themselves.

"Contagion" is, on one level, a story about a group of people who must deal with a rather unusual biological phenomenon on another world. But it is also about physical appearance and its relationship to our personal identity, as well as to our feelings about others.

It was like an Earth forest in the fall, but it was not fall. The forest leaves were green and copper and purple and fiery red, and a wind sent patches of bright greenish sunlight dancing among the leaf shadows.

The hunt party of the *Explorer* filed along the narrow trail, guns ready, walking carefully, listening to the distant, half-familiar cries of strange birds.

A faint crackle of static in their earphones indicated that a gun had been fired.

"Got anything?" asked June Walton. The helmet intercom carried her voice to the ears of the others without breaking the stillness of the forest.

"Took a shot at something," explained George Barton's cheerful voice in her earphones. She rounded a bend of the trail and came upon Barton standing peering up into the trees, his gun still raised. "It looked like a duck."

"This isn't Central Park," said Hal Barton, his brother, coming into sight. His green spacesuit struck an incongruous note against the bronze and red forest. "They won't all be ducks," he said soberly.

"Maybe some will be dragons. Don't get eaten by a dragon, June," came Max's voice quietly into her earphones. "Not while I still love you." He came out of the trees carrying the blood-sample kit, and touched her glove with his, the grin on his ugly beloved face barely visible in the mingled light and shade. A patch of sunlight struck a greenish glint from his fishbowl helmet.

They walked on. A quarter of a mile back, the space ship *Explorer* towered over the forest like a tapering skyscraper, and the people of the ship looked out of the viewplates at fresh winds and sunlight and clouds, and they longed to be outside.

But the likeness to Earth was danger, and the cool wind might be death, for if the animals were like Earth animals, their diseases might be like Earth diseases, alike enough to be contagious, different enough to be impossible to treat. There was warning enough in the past. Colonies had vanished, and traveled spaceways drifted with the corpses of ships which had touched on some plague planet.

The people of the ship waited while their doctors, in airtight spacesuits, hunted animals to test them for contagion.

The four medicos, for June Walton was also a doctor, filed through the alien homelike forest, walking softly, watching for motion among the copper and purple shadows.

They saw it suddenly, a lighter, moving, copper patch among the darker browns. Reflex action swung June's gun into line, and behind her someone's gun went off with a faint crackle of static, and made a hole in the leaves beside the specimen. Then for a while no one moved.

This one looked like a man, a magnificently muscled, leanly graceful, humanlike animal. Even in its callused bare feet, it was a head taller than any of them. Red-haired, hawk-faced and darkly tanned, it stood breathing heavily, looking at them without expression. At its side hung a sheath knife, and a crossbow was slung across one wide shoulder.

They lowered their guns.

"It needs a shave," Max said reasonably in their earphones, and he reached up to his helmet and flipped the switch that let his voice be heard. "Something we could do for you, Mac?"

The friendly drawl was the first voice that had broken the forest sounds. June smiled suddenly. He was right. The strict logic of evolution did not demand beards; therefore a non-human would not be wearing a three-day growth of red stubble.

Still panting, the tall figure licked dry lips and spoke. "Welcome to Minos. The mayor sends greetings from Alexandria."

"English?" gasped June.

"We were afraid you would take off again before I could bring word to you . . . It's three hundred miles . . . We saw your scout plane pass twice, but we couldn't attract its attention."

June looked in stunned silence at the stranger leaning against the tree. Thirty-six light years—thirty-six times six trillion miles of monotonous space travel—to be told that the planet was already settled! "We didn't know there was a colony here," she said. "It's not on the map."

"We were afraid of that," the tall bronze man answered soberly. "We have been here three generations and no traders have come."

Max shifted the kit strap on his shoulder and offered a hand. "My name is Max Stark, M.D. This is June Walton, M.D., Hal Barton, M.D., and George Barton, Hal's brother, also M.D."

"Patrick Mead is the name." The man smiled, shaking hands casually. "Just a hunter and bridge carpenter myself. Never met any medicos before."

The grip was effortless, but even through her airproofed glove June could feel that the fingers that touched hers were as hard as padded steel.

"What—what is the population of Minos?" she asked.

He looked down at her curiously for a moment before answering. "Only one hundred and fifty." He smiled. "Don't worry, this isn't a city planet yet.

There's room for a few more people." He shook hands with the Bartons quickly. "That is—you are people, aren't you?" he asked startlingly.

"Why not?" said Max with a poise that June admired.

"Well, you are all so—so—" Patrick Mead's eyes roamed across the faces of the group. "So varied."

They could find no meaning in that, and stood puzzled.

"I mean," Patrick Mead said into the silence, "all these—interesting different hair colors and face shapes and so forth—" He made a vague wave with one hand as if he had run out of words or was anxious not to insult them.

"Joke?" Max asked, bewildered.

June laid a hand on his arm. "No harm meant," she said to him over the intercom. "We're just as much of a shock to him as he is to us."

She addressed a question to the tall colonist on outside sound. "What should a person look like, Mr. Mead?"

He indicated her with a smile. "Like you."

June stepped closer and stood looking up at him, considering her own description. She was tall and tanned, like him; had a few freckles, like him; and wavy red hair, like his. She ignored the brightly humorous blue eyes.

"In other words," she said, "everyone on the planet looks like you and me?"

Patrick Mead took another look at their four faces and began to grin. "Like me, I guess. But I hadn't thought of it before, that people could have different colored hair or that noses could fit so many ways onto faces. Judging by my own appearance, I suppose any fool can walk on his hands and say the world is upside down!" He laughed and sobered. "But then why wear spacesuits? The air is breathable."

"For safety," June told him. "We can't take any chances on plague."

Pat Mead was wearing nothing but his weapons, and the wind ruffled his hair. He looked comfortable, and they longed to take off the stuffy spacesuits and feel the wind against their own skins. Minos was like home, like Earth . . . But they were strangers.

"Plague," Pat Mead said thoughtfully. "We had one here. It came two years after the colony arrived and killed everyone except the Mead families. They were immune. I guess we look alike because we're all related, and that's why I grew up thinking that it is the only way people can look."

Plague. "What was the disease?" Hal Barton asked.

"Pretty gruesome, according to my father. They called it the melting sickness. The doctors died too soon to find out what it was or what to do about it."

"You should have trained more doctors, or sent to civilization for some." A trace of impatience was in George Barton's voice.

Pat Mead explained patiently, "Our ship, with the power plant and all the books we needed, went off into the sky to avoid the contagion, and never came back. The crew must have died." Long years of hardship were indicated by that statement, a colony with electric power gone and machinery stilled, with key technicians dead and no way to replace them. June realized then the full meaning of the primitive sheath knife and bow.

"Any recurrence of melting sickness?" asked Hal Barton.

"No."

"Any other diseases?"

"Not a one."

Max was eying the bronze red-headed figure with something approaching awe. "Do you think all the Meads look like that?" he said to June on the intercom. "I wouldn't mind being a Mead myself!"

Their job had been made easy by the coming of Pat. They went back to the ship laughing, exchanging anecdotes with him. There was nothing now to keep Minos from being the home they wanted except the melting sickness, and forewarned against it, they could take precautions.

The polished silver and black column of the *Explorer* seemed to rise higher and higher over the trees as they neared it. Then its symmetry blurred all sense of specific size as they stepped out from among the trees and stood on the edge of the meadow, looking up.

"Nice!" said Pat. "Beautiful!" The admiration in his voice was warming.

"It was a yacht," Max said, still looking up, "secondhand, an old-time beauty without a sign of wear. Synthetic diamond-studded control board and murals on the walls. It doesn't have the new speed drives, but it brought us thirty-six light years in one and a half subjective years. Plenty good enough."

The tall tanned man looked faintly wistful, and June realized that he had never had access to a film library, never seen a movie, never experienced luxury. He had been born and raised on Minos without electricity.

"May I go aboard?" Pat asked hopefully.

Max unslung the specimen kit from his shoulder,

laid it on the carpet of plants that covered the ground, and began to open it.

"Tests first," Hal Barton said. "We have to find out if you people still carry this so-called melting sickness. We'll have to de-microbe you and take specimens before we let you on board. Once on, you'll be no good as a check for what the other Meads might have."

Max was taking out a rack and a stand of preservative bottles and hypodermics.

"Are you going to jab me with those?" Pat asked with alarm.

"You're just a specimen animal to me, bud!" Max grinned at Pat Mead, and Pat grinned back. June saw that they were friends already, the tall pantherish colonist and the wry, black-haired doctor. She felt a stab of guilt because she loved Max and yet could pity him for being smaller and frailer than Pat Mead.

"Lie down," Max told him, "and hold still. We need two spinal-fluid samples from the back, a body-cavity one in front, and another from the arm."

Pat lay down obediently. Max knelt, and as he spoke, expertly swabbed and inserted needles with the smooth speed that had made him a fine nerve surgeon on Earth.

High above them the scout helioplane came out of an opening in the ship and angled off toward the west, its buzz diminishing. Then, suddenly, it veered and headed back, and Reno Ulrich's voice came tinnily from their earphones.

"What's that you've got? Hey, what are you docs doing down there?" He banked again and came to a stop, hovering fifty feet away. June could see his startled face looking through the glass at Pat.

Hal Barton switched to a narrow radio beam, explained rapidly and pointed in the direction of Alexandria. Reno's plane lifted and flew away over the odd-colored forest.

"The plane will drop a note on your town, telling them you got through to us," Hal Barton told Pat, who was sitting up watching Max dexterously put the blood and spinal fluids into the right bottles without exposing them to air.

"We won't be free to contact your people until we know if they still carry melting sickness," Max added. "You might be immune so it doesn't show on you, but still carry enough germs—if that's what caused it—to wipe out a planet."

"If you do carry melting sickness," said Hal Barton, "we won't be able to mingle with your people until we've cleared them of the disease."

"Starting with me?" Pat asked.

"Starting with you," Max told him ruefully, "as soon as you step on board."

"More needles?"

"Yes, and a few little extras thrown in."

"Rough?"

"It isn't easy."

A few minutes later, standing in the stalls for space-suit decontamination, being buffeted by jets of hot disinfectant, bathed in glares of sterilizing ultraviolet radiation, June remembered that and compared Pat Mead's treatment to theirs.

In the *Explorer,* stored carefully in sealed tanks and containers, was the ultimate, multipurpose cureall. It was a solution of enzymes so like the key catalysts of the human cell nucleus that it caused chemical derangement and disintegration in any nonhuman cell. Nothing could live in contact with it but human cells;

any alien intruder to the body would die. Nucleocat Cureall was its trade name.

But the cureall alone was not enough for complete safety. Plagues had been known to slay too rapidly and universally to be checked by human treatment. Doctors are not reliable; they die. Therefore spaceways and interplanetary health law demanded that ship equipment for guarding against disease be totally mechanical in operation, rapid and efficient.

Somewhere near them, in a series of stalls which led around and around like a rabbit maze, Pat was being herded from stall to stall by peremptory mechanical voices, directed to soap and shower, ordered to insert his arm into a slot which took a sample of his blood, given solutions to drink, bathed in germicidal ultraviolet, shaken by sonic blasts, breathing air thick with sprays of germicidal mists, being directed to put his arms into other slots where they were anesthetized and injected with various immunizing solutions.

Finally, he would be put in a room of high temperature and extreme dryness, and instructed to sit for half an hour while more fluids were dripped into his veins through long thin tubes.

All legal spaceships were built for safety. No chance was taken of allowing a suspected carrier to bring an infection on board with him.

June stepped from the last shower stall into the locker room, zipped off her spacesuit with a sigh of relief, and contemplated herself in a wall mirror. Red hair, dark blue eyes, tall . . .

"I've got a good figure," she said thoughtfully.

Max turned at the door. "Why this sudden interest in your looks?" he asked suspiciously. "Do we stand here and admire you, or do we finally get something to eat?"

"Wait a minute." She went to a wall phone and dialed it carefully, using a combination from the ship's directory. "How're you doing, Pat?"

The phone picked up a hissing of water or spray. There was a startled chuckle. "Voices, too! Hello, June. How do you tell a machine to go spray itself?"

"Are you hungry?"

"No food since yesterday."

"We'll have a banquet ready for you when you get out," she told Pat and hung up, smiling. Pat Mead's voice had a vitality and enjoyment which made shipboard talk sound like sad artificial gaiety in contrast.

They looked into the nearby small laboratory where twelve squealing hamsters were protestingly submitting to a small injection each of Pat's blood. In most of them the injection was followed by one of antihistaminics and adaptives. Otherwise the hamster defense system would treat all nonhamster cells as enemies, even the harmless human blood cells, and fight back against them violently.

One hamster, the twelfth, was given an extra-large dose of adaptive so that if there were a disease, he would not fight it or the human cells, and thus succumb more rapidly.

"How ya doing, George?" Max asked.

"Routine," George Barton grunted absently.

On the way up the long spiral ramps to the dining hall, they passed a viewplate. It showed a long scene of mountains in the distance on the horizon, and between them, rising step by step as they grew farther away, the low rolling hills, bronze and red with patches of clear green where there were fields.

Someone was looking out, standing very still, as if

she had been there a long time—Bess St. Clair, a Canadian woman. "It looks like Winnipeg," she told them as they paused. "When are you doctors going to let us out of this barberpole? Look." She pointed. "See that patch of field on the south hillside, with the brook winding through it? I've staked that hillside for our house. When do we get out?"

Reno Ulrich's tiny scout plane buzzed slowly in from the distance and began circling lazily.

"Sooner than you think," Max told her. "We've discovered a castaway colony on the planet. They've done our tests for us by just living here. If there's anything here to catch, they've caught it."

"People on Minos?" Bess's handsome ruddy face grew alive with excitement.

"One of them is down in the medical department," June said. "He'll be out in twenty minutes."

"May I go see him?"

"Sure," said Max. "Show him the way to the dining hall when he gets out. Tell him we sent you."

"Right!" She turned and ran down the ramp like a small girl going to a firc. Max grinned at June and she grinned back. After a year and a half of isolation in space, everyone was hungry for the sight of new faces, the sound of unfamiliar voices.

They climbed the last two turns to the cafeteria and entered to a rich subdued blend of soft music and quiet conversation. The cafeteria was a section of the old dining room, left when the rest of the ship had been converted to living and working quarters, and it still had the original finely grained wood of the ceiling and walls, the sound absorbency, the soft-music spools and the intimate small light at each table where people leisurely ate and talked.

They stood in line at the hot foods counter, and

behind her June could hear a girl's voice talking excitedly through the murmur of conversation.

"—new man, honest! I saw him through the viewplate when they came in. He's down in the medical department. A real frontiersman."

The line drew abreast of the counters, and she and Max chose three heaping trays, starting with hydroponic mushroom steak, raised in the growing trays of water and chemicals; sharp salad bowl with rose tomatoes and aromatic peppers; tank-grown fish with special sauce; four different desserts, and assorted beverages.

Presently they had three tottering trays successfully maneuvered to a table. Brant St. Clair came over. "I beg your pardon, Max, but they are saying something about Reno carrying messages to a colony of savages for the medical department. Will he be back soon, do you know?"

Max smiled up at him, his square face affectionate. Everyone liked the shy Canadian. "He's back already. We just saw him come in."

"Oh, fine." St. Clair beamed. "I had an appointment with him to go out and confirm what looks like a nice vein of iron to the northeast. Have you seen Bess? Oh—there she is." He turned swiftly and hurried away.

A very tall man with fiery red hair came in surrounded by an eagerly talking crowd of ship people. It was Pat Mead. He stood in the doorway alertly scanning the dining room. Sheer vitality made him seem even larger than he was. Sighting June, he smiled and began to thread toward their table.

"Look!" said someone. "There's the colonist!" Sheila, a pretty, jeweled woman, followed and caught his arm. "Did you *really* swim across a river to come here?"

Overflowing with good will and curiosity, people approached from all directions. "Did you actually walk three hundred miles? Come, eat with us. Let me help choose your tray."

Everyone wanted him to eat at their table, everyone was a specialist and wanted data about Minos. They all wanted anecdotes about hunting wild animals with a bow and arrow.

"He needs to be rescued," Max said. "He won't have a chance to eat."

June and Max got up firmly, edged through the crowd, captured Pat and escorted him back to their table. June found herself pleased to be claiming the hero of the hour.

Pat sat in the simple, subtly designed chair and leaned back almost voluptuously, testing the way it gave and fitted itself to him. He ran his eyes over the bright tableware and heaped plates. He looked around at the rich grained walls and soft lights at each table. He said nothing, just looking and feeling and experiencing.

"When we build our town and leave the ship," June explained, "we will turn all the staterooms back into the lounges and ballrooms and cocktail bars that used to be inside. Then it will be beautiful."

Pat smiled, cocked his head to the music, and tried to locate its source. "It's good enough now. We only play music tapes once a week in city hall."

They ate, Pat beginning the first meal he had had in more than a day.

Most of the other diners finished when they were halfway through, and began walking over, diffidently at first, then in another wave of smiling faces, handshakes, and introductions. Pat was asked about crops, about farming methods, about rainfall and floods, about farm animals and plant breeding, about the compatibility of imported Earth seeds with local ground, about mines and strata.

There was no need to protect him. He leaned back in his chair and drawled answers with the lazy ease of a panther; where he could think of no statistics, he would fill the gap with an anecdote. It showed that he enjoyed spinning campfire yarns and being the center of interest.

Between bouts of questions, he ate and listened to the music.

June noticed that the female specialists were prolonging the questions more than they needed, clustering around the table laughing at his jokes, until presently Pat was almost surrounded by pretty faces, eager questions, and chiming laughs. Sheila the beautiful laughed most chimingly of all.

June nudged Max, and Max shrugged indifferently. It wasn't anything a man would pay attention to, perhaps. But June watched Pat for a moment more, then glanced uneasily back to Max. He was eating and listening to Pat's answers and did not feel her gaze. For some reason Max looked almost shrunken to her. He was shorter than she had realized; she had forgotten that he was only the same height as herself. She was aware of the clear lilting chatter of female voices increasing at Pat's end of the table.

"That guy's a menace," Max said, and laughed to himself, cutting another slice of hydroponic mushroom steak. "What's got you?" he added, glancing aside at her when he noticed her sudden stillness.

"Nothing," she said hastily, but she did not turn back to watching Pat Mead. She felt disloyal. Pat was only a superb animal. Max was the man she loved. Or—was he? Of course he was, she told herself angrily. They had gone colonizing together because they wanted to spend their lives together; she had never thought of marrying any other man. Yet the sense of dissatisfaction persisted, and along with it a feeling of guilt.

Len Marlow, the protein tank-culture technician responsible for the mushroom steaks, had wormed his way into the group and asked Pat a question. Now he was saying, "I don't dig you, Pat. It sounds like you're putting the people into the tanks instead of the vegetables!" He glanced at them, looking puzzled. "See if you two can make anything of this. It sounds medical to me."

Pat leaned back and smiled, sipping a glass of hydroponic burgundy. "Wonderful stuff. You'll have to show us how to make it."

Len turned back to him. "You people live off the country, right? You hunt and bring in steaks and eat them, right? Well, say I have one of those steaks right here and I want to eat it, what happens?"

"Go ahead and eat it. It just wouldn't digest. You'd stay hungry."

"Why?" Len was aggrieved.

"Chemical differences in the basic protoplasm of Minos. Different amino linkages, left-handed instead of right-handed molecules in the carbohydrates, things like that. Nothing will be digestible here until you are adapted chemically by a little test-tube evolution. Till then you'd starve to death on a full stomach."

Pat's side of the table had been loaded with the

dishes from two trays, but it was almost clear now and the dishes were stacked neatly to one side. He started on three desserts, thoughtfully tasting each in turn.

"Test-tube evolution?" Max repeated. "What's that? I thought you people had no doctors."

"It's a story." Pat leaned back again. "Alexander P. Mead, the head of the Mead clan, was a plant geneticist, a very determined personality and no man to argue with. He didn't want us to go through the struggle of killing off all Minos plants and putting in our own, spoiling the face of the planet and upsetting the balance of its ecology. He decided that he would adapt our genes to this planet or kill us trying. He did it, all right."

"Did which?" asked June, suddenly feeling a sourceless prickle of fear.

"Adapted us to Minos. He took human cells—"

She listened intently, trying to find a reason for fear in the explanation. It would have taken many human generations to adapt to Minos by ordinary evolution, and that only at a heavy toll of death and hunger which evolution exacts. There was a shorter way: Human cells have the ability to return to their primeval condition of independence, hunting, eating and reproducing alone.

Alexander P. Mead took human cells and made them into phagocytes. He put them through the hard savage school of evolution—a thousand generations of multiplication, hardship and hunger, with the alien indigestible food always present, offering its reward of plenty to the cell that reluctantly learned to absorb it.

"Leucocytes can run through several thousand generations of evolution in six months," Pat Mead finished. "When they reached a point where they would absorb Minos food, he planted them back in the people he had taken them from."

"What was supposed to happen then?" Max asked, leaning forward.

"I don't know exactly how it worked. He never told anybody much about it, and when I was a little boy he had gone loco and was wandering ha-ha-ing around waving a test tube. Fell down a ravine and broke his neck at the age of eighty."

"A character," Max said.

Why was she afraid? "It worked, then?"

"Yes. He tried it on all the Meads the first year. The other settlers didn't want to be experimented on until they saw how it worked out. It worked. The Meads could hunt and plant while the other settlers were still eating out of hydroponics tanks."

"It worked," said Max to Len. "You're a plant geneticist and a tank-culture expert. There's a job for you."

"Uh-*uh!*" Len backed away. "It sounds like a medical problem to me. Human cell control—right up your alley."

"It is a one-way street," Pat warned. "Once it is done, you won't be able to digest ship food. I'll get no good from this protein. I ate it just for the taste."

Hal Barton appeared quietly beside the table. "Three of the twelve test hamsters have died," he reported, and turned to Pat. "Your people carry the germs of melting sickness, as you call it. The dead hamsters were injected with blood taken from you before you were de-infected. We can't settle here unless we de-infect everybody on Minos. Would they object?"

"We wouldn't want to give you folks germs." Pat smiled. "Anything for safety. But there'll have to be a vote on it first."

The doctors went to Reno Ulrich's table and walked with him to the hangar, explaining. He was to carry the proposal to Alexandria, mingle with the people, be persuasive and wait for them to vote before returning. He was to give himself shots of cureall every two hours on the hour or run the risk of disease.

Reno was pleased. He had dabbled in sociology before retraining as a mechanic for the expedition. "This gives me a chance to study their mores." He winked wickedly. "I may not be back for several nights." They watched through the viewplate as he took off, and then went over to the laboratory for a look at the hamsters.

Three were alive and healthy, munching lettuce. One was the control; the other two had been given shots of Pat's blood from before he entered the ship, but with no additional treatment. Apparently a hamster could fight off melting sickness easily if left alone. Three were still feverish and ruffled, with a low red blood count, but recovering. The three dead ones had been given strong shots of adaptive and counter-histamine, so their bodies had not fought back against the attack.

June glanced at the dead animals hastily and looked away again. They lay twisted with a strange semi-fluid limpness, as if ready to dissolve. The last hamster, which had been given the heaviest dose of adaptive, had apparently lost all its hair before death. It was hairless and pink, like a stillborn baby.

"We can find no microorganisms," George Barton said. "None at all. Nothing in the body that should not be there. Leucosis and anemia. Fever only for the ones that fought it off." He handed Max some temperature charts and graphs of blood counts.

June wandered out into the hall. Pediatrics and obstetrics were her field; she left the cellular research to Max, and just helped him with laboratory routine. The strange mood followed her out into the hall, then abruptly lightened.

Coming toward her, busily telling a tale of adventure to the gorgeous Sheila Davenport, was a tall, red-headed, magnificently handsome man. It was his handsomeness which made Pat such a pleasure to look upon and talk with, she guiltily told herself, and it was his tremendous vitality . . . It was like meeting a movie hero in the flesh, or a hero out of the pages of a book—Deerslayer, John Clayton, Lord Greystoke.

She waited in the doorway to the laboratory and made no move to join them, merely acknowledged the two with a nod and a smile and a casual lift of the hand. They nodded and smiled back.

"Hello, June," said Pat and continued telling his tale, but as they passed he lightly touched her arm.

"You Tarzan?" she said mockingly and softly to his passing profile, and knew that he had heard.

That night she had a nightmare. She was running down a long corridor looking for Max, but every man she came to was a big bronze man with red hair and bright-blue eyes who touched her arm.

The pink hamster! She woke suddenly, feeling as if alarm bells had been ringing, and listened carefully, but there was no sound. She had had a nightmare, she told herself, but alarm bells were still ringing in her unconscious. Something was wrong.

Lying still and trying to preserve the images, she groped for a meaning, but the mood faded under the cold touch of reason. Damn intuitive thinking! A pink hamster! Why did the unconscious have to be so vague? She fell asleep again and forgot.

They had lunch with Pat Mead that day, and after it was over, Pat delayed June with a hand on her shoulder and looked down at her.

"Me Tarzan, you Jane," he said and then turned away, answering the hails of a party at another table as if he had not spoken. She stood shaken, and then walked to the door where Max waited.

She was particularly affectionate with Max the rest of the day, and it pleased him. He would not have been if he had known why. She tried to forget Pat's reply.

June was in the laboratory with Max, watching the growth of a small tank culture of the alien protoplasm from a Minos weed, and listening to Len Marlow pour out his troubles.

"And Elsie tags around after that big goof all day, listening to his stories. And then she tells me I'm just jealous, I'm imagining things!" He passed his hand across his eyes. "I came away from Earth to be with Elsie. . . . I'm getting a headache. Look, can't you persuade Pat to cut it out, June? You and Max are his friends."

"Here, have an aspirin," June said. "We'll see what we can do."

"Thanks." Len picked up his tank culture and went out, not at all cheered.

Max sat brooding over the dials and meters at his end of the laboratory, apparently sunk in thought. When Len had gone, he spoke almost harshly. "Why encourage the guy? Why let him hope?"

"Found out anything about the differences in proto-plasm?" she evaded.

"Why let him kid himself? What chance has he got against that hunk of muscle and smooth talk?"

"But Pat isn't after Elsie," she protested.

"Every scatterbrained woman on this ship is trailing after Pat with her tongue hanging out. Brant St. Clair is in the bar right now. He doesn't say what he is drinking about, but do you think Pat is resisting all these women crowding down on him?"

"There are other things besides looks and charm," she said, grimly trying to concentrate on a slide under her binocular microscope.

"Yeah, and whatever they are, Pat has them, too. Who's more competent to support a woman and a family on a frontier planet than a handsome bruiser who was born here?"

"I meant"—June spun around on her stool with unexpected passion—"there is old friendship, and there's loyalty and memories, and personality!" She was half shouting.

"They're not worth much on the secondhand market," Max said. He was sitting slumped on his lab stool, looking dully at his dials. "Now *I'm* getting a headache!" He smiled ruefully. "No kidding, a real headache. And over other people's troubles, yet!"

Other people's troubles . . . She got up and wandered out into the long curving halls. "Me Tarzan, you Jane," Pat's voice repeated in her mind. Why did the man have to be so overpoweringly attractive, so glaring a contrast to Max? Why couldn't the universe manage to run on without generating troublesome love triangles?

She walked up the curving ramps to the dining hall where they had eaten and drunk and talked yesterday. It was empty except for one couple talking forehead to forehead over cold coffee.

She turned and wandered down the long easy spiral of corridor to the pharmacy and dispensary. It was empty. George was probably in the test lab next door, where he could hear if he was wanted. The automatic vendor of harmless euphorics, stimulants and opiates stood in the corner, brightly decorated in pastel abstract designs, with its automatic tabulator graph glowing above it.

Max had a headache, she remembered. She recorded her thumbprint in the machine and pushed the plunger for a box of aspirins, trying to focus her attention on the problem of adapting the people of the ship to the planet Minos. An aquarium tank with a faint solution of histamine would be enough to convert a piece of human skin into a community of voracious active phagocytes individually seeking something to devour, but could they eat enough to live away from the rich sustaining plasma of human blood?

After the aspirins, she pushed another plunger for something for herself. Then she stood looking at it, a small box with three pills in her hand—Theobromine, a heart strengthener and a confidence-giving euphoric all in one, something to steady shaky nerves. She had used it before only in emergency. She extended a hand an looked at it. It was trembling. Damn triangles!

While she was looking at her hand, there was a click from the automatic drug vendor. It summed the morning use of each drug in the vendors throughout the ship, and recorded it in a neat addition to the end of each graph line. For a moment she could not find the green line for anodynes and the red line for stimulants, and then she saw that they went almost straight up.

There were too many being used—far too many to be explained by jealousy or psychosomatic peevishness. This was an epidemic, and only one disease was possible!

The disinfecting of Pat had not succeeded. Nucleocat Cureall, killer of all infections, had not cured! Pat had brought melting sickness into the ship with him!

Who had it?

The drugs vendor glowed cheerfully, uncommunicative. She opened a panel in its side and looked in on restless interlacing cogs, and on the inside of the door she saw printed some directions . . . "To remove or examine records before reaching end of the reel—"

After a few fumbling minutes she had the answer. In the cafeteria at breakfast and lunch, thirty-eight men out of the forty-eight aboard ship had taken more than his norm of stimulant. Twenty-one had taken aspirin as well. The only woman who had made an unusual purchase was herself!

She remembered the hamsters that had thrown off the infection with a short sharp fever, and checked back in the records to the day before. There was a short rise in aspirin sales to women at late afternoon. The women were safe.

It was the men who had melting sickness!

Melting sickness killed in hours, according to Pat Mead. How long had the men been sick?

As she was leaving, Jerry came into the pharmacy, recorded his thumbprint and took a box of aspirin from the machine.

She felt all right. Self-control was working well, and it was possible still to walk down the corridor smiling at the people who passed. She took the emergency elevator to the control room and showed her credentials to the technician on watch.

"Medical Emergency." At a small control panel in the corner was a large red button, precisely labeled. She considered it and picked up the control-room phone. This was the hard part, telling someone, especially someone who had it—Max.

She dialed, and when the click on the end of the line showed he had picked up the phone, she told Max what she had seen.

"No women, just the men," he repeated. "That right?"

"Yes."

"Probably it's chemically alien, inhibited by one of the female hormones. We'll try sex hormone shots, if we have to. Where are you calling from?"

She told him.

"That's right. Give Nucleocat Cureall another chance. It might work this time. Push that button."

She went to the panel and pushed the large red button. Through the long height of the *Explorer,* bells woke to life and began to ring in frightened clangor, emergency doors thumped shut, mechanical apparatus hummed into life and canned voices began to give rapid urgent directions.

A plague had come.

She obeyed the mechanical orders, went out into the hall and walked in line with the others. The captain walked ahead of her and the gorgeous Sheila Davenport fell into step beside her. "I look like a positive hag this morning. Does that mean I'm sick? Are we all sick?"

June shrugged, unwilling to say what she knew.

Others came out of all rooms into the corridor, thickening the line. They could hear each room lock as the last person left it, and then, faintly, the hiss of disinfectant spray. Behind them, on the heels of the last person in line, segments of the ship slammed off and began to hiss.

They wound down the spiral corridor until they reached the medical-treatment section again, and there they waited in line.

"It won't scar my arms, will it?" asked Sheila apprehensively, glancing at her smooth, lovely arms.

The mechanical voice said, "Next. Step inside, please, and stand clear of the door."

"Not a bit," June reassured Sheila, and stepped into the cubicle.

Inside, she was directed from cubicle to cubicle and given the usual buffeting by sprays and radiation, had blood samples taken and was injected with Nucleocat and a series of other protectives. At last she was directed through another door into a tiny cubicle with a chair.

"You are to wait here," commanded the recorded voice metallically. "In twenty minutes the door will unlock and you may then leave. All people now treated may visit all parts of the ship which have been protected. It is forbidden to visit any quarantined or unsterile part of the ship without permission from the medical officers."

Presently the door unlocked and she emerged into bright lights again, feeling slightly battered.

She was in the clinic. A few men sat on the edge of beds and looked sick. One was lying down. Brant and Bess St. Clair sat near each other, not speaking.

Approaching her was George Barton, reading a thermometer with a puzzled expression.

"What is it, George?" she asked anxiously.

"Some of the women have a slight fever, but it's going down. None of the fellows have any—but their white count is way up, their red count is way down, and they look sick to me."

She approached St. Clair. His usually ruddy cheeks were pale, his pulse was light and too fast, and his skin felt clammy. "How's the headache? Did the Nucleocat treatment help?"

"I feel worse, if anything."

"Better set up beds," she told George. "Get everyone back into the clinic."

"We're doing that," George assured her. "That's what Hal is doing."

She went back to the laboratory. Max was pacing up and down, absently running his hands through his black hair until it stood straight up. He stopped when he saw her face, and scowled thoughtfully. "They are still sick?" It was more a statement than a question.

She nodded.

"The Cureall didn't cure this time," he muttered. "That leaves it up to us. We have melting sickness and according to Pat and the hamsters, that leaves us less than a day to find out what it is and learn how to stop it."

Suddenly an idea for another test struck him and he moved to the work table to set it up. He worked rapidly, with an occasional uncoordinated movement breaking his usual efficiency.

It was strange to see Max troubled and afraid.

She put on a laboratory smock and began to work. She worked in silence. The mechanicals had failed. Hal and George Barton were busy staving off death from the weaker cases and trying to gain time for Max and her to work. The problem of the plague had to be solved by the two of them alone. It was in their hands.

Another test, no results. Another test, no results.

Max's hands were shaking and he stopped a moment to take stimulants.

She went into the ward for a moment, found Bess and warned her quietly to tell the other women to be ready to take over if the men became too sick to go on. "But tell them calmly. We don't want to frighten the men." She lingered in the ward long enough to see the word spread among the women in a widening wave of paler faces and compressed lips; then she went back to the laboratory.

Another test. There was no sign of a microorganism in anyone's blood, merely a growing horde of leucocytes and phagocytes, prowling as if mobilized to repel invasion.

Len Marlow was wheeled in unconscious, with Hal Barton's written comments and conclusions pinned to the blanket.

"I don't feel so well myself," the assistant complained. "The air feels thick. I can't breathe."

June saw that his lips were blue. "Oxygen short," she told Max.

"Low red-corpuscle count," Max answered. "Look into a drop and see what's going on. Use mine; I feel the same way he does." She took two drops of Max's blood. The count was low, falling too fast.

Breathing is useless without the proper minimum of red corpuscles in the blood. People below that minimum die of asphyxiation although their lungs are full of pure air. The red-corpuscle count was falling too fast. The time she and Max had to work in was too short.

"Pump some more CO_2 into the air system," Max said urgently over the phone. "Get some into the men's end of the ward."

She looked through the microscope at the live sample of blood. It was a dark clear field and bright moving things spun and swirled through it, but she could see nothing that did not belong there.

"Hal," Max called over the general speaker system, "cut the other treatments, check for accelerating anemia. Treat it like monoxide poisoning—CO_2 and oxygen."

She reached into a cupboard under the work table, located two cylinders of oxygen, cracked the valves and handed one to Max and one to the assistant. Some of the bluish tint left the assistant's face as he breathed, and he went over to the patient with re-awakened concern.

"Not breathing, Doc!"

Max was working at the desk, muttering equations of hemoglobin catalysis.

"Len's gone, Doc," the assistant said more loudly.

"Artificial respiration and get him into a regeneration tank," said June, not moving from the microscope. "Hurry! Hal will show you how. The oxidation and mechanical heart action in the tank will keep him going. Put anyone in a tank who seems to be dying. Get some women to help you. Give them Hal's instructions."

The tanks were ordinarily used to suspend animation in a nutrient bath during the regrowth of any diseased organ. They could preserve life in an almost totally destroyed body during the usual disintegration and regrowth treatments for cancer and old age, and they could encourage healing as destruction continued . . . but they could not prevent ultimate death as long as the disease was not conquered.

The drop of blood in June's microscope was a great dark field, and in the foreground, brought to gargantuan solidity by the stereo effect, drifted neat saucer shapes of red blood cells. They turned end for end, floating by the humped misty mass of a leucocyte which was crawling on the cover glass. There were not enough red corpuscles, and she felt that they grew fewer as she watched.

She fixed her eye on one, not blinking in fear that she would miss what might happen. It was a tidy red button, and it spun as it drifted, the current moving it aside in a curve as it passed by the leucocyte.

Then, abruptly, the cell vanished.

June stared numbly at the place where it had been. Where had it gone?

Behind her, Max was calling over the speaker system again: "Dr. Stark speaking. Any technician who knows anything about the life tanks, start bringing more out of storage and set them up. Emergency."

"We may need forty-seven," June said quietly. There were forty-seven men.

"We may need forty-seven," Max repeated to the ship in general. His voice did not falter. "Set them up along the corridor. Hook them in on extension lines."

His voice filtered back from the empty floors above in a series of dim echoes. What he had said meant that every man on board might be on the point of heart stoppage.

June looked blindly through the binocular microscope, trying to think. Out of the corner of her eye she could see that Max was wavering and breathing more and more frequently of the pure, cold, burning oxygen of the cylinders. In the microscope she could see that there were fewer red cells left alive in the drop of his blood. The rate of fall was accelerating.

She didn't have to glance at Max to know how he would look—skin pale, black eyebrows and keen brown eyes slightly squinted in thought, a faint ironical grin twisting the bluing lips. Intelligent, thin, sensitive, his face was part of her mind. It was inconceivable that Max could die. He couldn't die. He couldn't leave her alone.

She forced her mind back to the problem. All the men of the *Explorer* were at the same point, wherever they were. Somehow losing blood, dying.

Moving to Max's desk, she spoke into the intercom system. "Bess, send a couple of women to look through the ship, room by room, with a stretcher. Make sure all the men are down here." She remembered Reno. "Sparks, heard anything from Reno? Is he back?"

Sparks replied weakly after a lag. "The last I heard from Reno was a call this morning. He was raving about mirrors, and Pat Mead's folks not being real people, just carbon copies, and claiming he was crazy; and I should send him the psychiatrist. I thought he was kidding. He didn't call back."

"Thanks, Sparks." Reno was dead.

Max dialed and spoke gasping over the phone. "Are you okay up there? Forget about engineering controls. Drop everything and head for the tanks while you can still walk. If your tank's not done, lie down next to it."

June went back to the work table and whispered into her own phone. "Bess, send up a stretcher for Max. He looks pretty bad."

There had to be a solution. The life tanks could sustain life in a damaged body, encouraging it to regrow more rapidly, but they merely slowed death as long as the disease was not checked. The postponement could not last long, for destruction could go on steadily in the tanks until the nutritive solution would hold no life except the triumphant microscopic killers that caused melting sickness.

There were very few red blood corpuscles in the microscope field now, incredibly few. She tipped the microscope and they began to drift, spinning slowly. A lone corpuscle floated through the center. She watched it as the current swept it in an arc past the dim off-focus bulk of the leucocyte. There was a sweep of motion and it vanished.

For a moment it meant nothing to her; then she lifted her head from the microscope and looked around. Max sat at his desk, head in hand, his rumpled short black hair sticking out between his fingers at odd angles. A pencil and a pad scrawled with formulas lay on the desk before him. She could see his concentration in the rigid set of his shoulders. He was still thinking; he had not given up.

"Max, I just saw a leucocyte grab a red blood corpuscle. It was unbelievably fast."

"Leukemia," muttered Max without moving. "Galloping leukemia yet! That comes under the heading of cancer. Well, that's part of the answer. It might be all we need." He grinned feebly and reached for the speaker set. "Anybody still on his feet in there?" he muttered into it, and the question was amplified to a booming voice throughout the ship. "Hal, are you still going? Look, Hal, change all the dials, change the dials, set them to deep melt and regeneration. One week. This is like leukemia. Got it? This is like leukemia."

June rose. It was time for her to take over the job. She leaned across his desk and spoke into the speaker system. "Doctor Walton talking," she said. "This is to the women. Don't let any of the men work any more; they'll kill themselves. See that they all go into the tanks right away. Set the tank dials for deep regeneration. You can see how from the ones that are set."

Two exhausted and frightened women clattered in the doorway with a stretcher. Their hands were scratched and oily from helping to set up tanks.

"That order includes you," she told Max sternly and caught him as he swayed.

Max saw the stretcher bearers and struggled upright. "Ten more minutes," he said clearly. "Might think of an idea. Something not right in this setup. I have to figure how to prevent a relapse, how the thing started."

He knew more bacteriology than she did; she had to help him think. She motioned the bearers to wait, fixed a breathing mask for Max from a cylinder of CO_2 and one of oxygen. Max went back to his desk.

She walked up and down, trying to think, remembering the hamsters. The melting sickness, it was called. Melting. She struggled with an impulse to open a tank which held one of the men. She wanted to look in, see if that would explain the name.

Melting sickness . . .

Footsteps came and Pat Mead stood uncertainly in the doorway. Tall, handsome, rugged, a pioneer. "Anything I can do?" he asked.

She barely looked at him. "You can stay out of our way. We're busy."

"I'd like to help," he said.

"Very funny." She was vicious, enjoying the whip of her words. "Every man is dying because you're a carrier, and you want to help."

He stood nervously clenching and unclenching his hands. "A guinea pig, maybe. I'm immune. All the Meads are."

"Go away." God, why couldn't she think? What makes a Mead immune?

"Aw, let 'im alone," Max muttered. "Pat hasn't done anything." He went waveringly to the microscope, took a tiny sliver from his finger, suspended it in a slide and slipped it under the lens with detached habitual dexterity. "Something funny going on," he said to June. "Symptoms don't feel right."

After a moment he straightened and motioned for her to look. "Leucocytes, phagocytes—" He was bewildered. "My own—"

She looked in, and then looked back at Pat in a growing wave of horror. "They're not your own, Max!" she whispered.

Max rested a hand on the table to brace himself, put his eye to the microscope, and looked again. June knew what he saw. Phagocytes, leucocytes, attacking and devouring his tissues in a growing incredible horde, multiplying insanely.

Not his phagocytes! Pat Mead's! The Meads' evolved cells had learned too much. They were contagious. And Pat Mead's . . . How much alike *were* the Meads? . . . Mead cells contagious from one to another, not a disease attacking or being fought, but acting as normal leucocytes in whatever body they were in! The leucocytes of tall, red-headed people, finding no strangeness in the bloodstream of any of the tall, red-headed people. No strangeness . . . A toti-potent leucocyte finding its way into cellular wombs.

The womblike life tanks. For the men of the *Explorer*, a week's cure with deep melting to de-differentiate the leucocytes and turn them back to normal tissue, then regrowth and reforming from the cells that were there. From the cells that *were* there. *From the cells that were there* . . .

"Pat, the germs are your cells!"

Crazily, Pat began to laugh, his face twisted with sudden understanding. "I understand. I get it. I'm a contagious personality. That's funny, isn't it?"

Max rose suddenly from the microscope and lurched. Pat caught him as he fell, and the bewildered stretcher bearers carried him out to the tanks.

For a week June tended the tanks. The other women volunteered to help, but she refused. She said nothing, hoping her guess would not be true.

"Is everything all right?" Elsie asked her anxiously. "How is Len coming along?" Elsie looked haggard and worn, like all the women, from doing the work that the men had always done, and their own work too.

"He's fine," June said tonelessly, shutting tight the door of the tank room. "They're all fine."

"That's good," Elsie said, but she looked more frightened than before.

June firmly locked the tank room door and the girl went away.

The other women had been listening, and now they wandered back to their jobs, unsatisfied by June's answer, but not daring to ask for the truth. They were there whenever June went into the tank room, and they were still there—or relieved by others, June was not sure—when she came out. And always some one of them asked the unvarying question for all the others, and June gave the unvarying answer. But she kept the key. No woman but herself knew what was going on in the life tanks.

Then the day of completion came. June told no one

of the hour. She went into the room as on the other days, locked the door behind her, and there was the nightmare again. This time it was reality and she wandered down a path between long rows of coffin-like tanks, calling, "Max! Max!" silently and looking into each one as it opened.

But each face she looked at was the same. Watching them dissolve and regrow in the nutrient solution, she had only been able to guess at the horror of what was happening. Now she knew.

They were all the same lean-boned, blond-skinned face, with a pin-feather growth of reddish down on cheeks and scalp. All horribly—and handsomely—the same.

A medical kit lay carelessly on the floor beside Max's tank. She stood near the bag. "Max," she said, and found her throat closing. The canned voice of the mechanical apparatus mocked her, speaking glibly about waking and sitting up. "I'm sorry, Max . . ."

The tall man with rugged features and bright blue eyes sat up sleepily and lifted an eyebrow at her, and ran his hand over his red-fuzzed head in a gesture of bewilderment. "What's the matter, June?" he asked drowsily.

She gripped his arm. "Max—"

He compared the relative size of his arm with her hand and said wonderingly, "You shrank."

"I know, Max. I know."

He turned his head and looked at his arms and legs, pale blond arms and legs with a down of red hair. He touched the thick left arm, squeezed a pinch of hard flesh. "It isn't mine," he said, surprised. "But I can feel it."

Watching his face was like watching a stranger mimicking and distorting Max's expressions. Max in fear. Max trying to understand what had happened to him, looking around at the other men sitting up in their tanks. Max feeling the terror that was in herself and all the men as they stared at themselves and their friends and saw what they had become.

"We're all Pat Mead," he said harshly. "All the Meads are Pat Mead. That's why he was surprised to see people who didn't look like himself."

"Yes, Max."

"Max," he repeated. "It's me, all right. The nervous system didn't change." His new blue eyes held hers. "I'm me inside. Do you love me, June?"

But she couldn't know yet. She had loved Max with the thin, ironic face, the rumpled black hair and the twisted smile that never really hid his quick sympathy. Now he was Pat Mead. Could he also be Max? "Of course I still love you, darling."

He grinned. It was still the wry smile of Max, though fitting strangely on the handsome new blond face. "Then it isn't so bad. It might even be pretty good. I envied him this big, muscular body. If Pat or any of these Meads so much as looks at you, I'm going to knock his block off. Now I can do it."

She laughed and couldn't stop. It wasn't that funny. But it was still Max, trying to be unafraid, drawing on humor. Maybe the rest of the men would also be their old selves, enough so the women would not feel that their men were strangers.

Behind her, male voices spoke characteristically. She did not have to turn to know which was which: "This is one way to keep a guy from stealing your girl," that was Len Marlow; "I've got to write down reactions," Hal Barton; "Now I can really work that hillside vein of metal," St. Clair. Then others complaining, swearing, laughing bitterly at the trick that had been played on them and their flirting, tempted women. She knew who they were. Their women would know them apart too.

"We'll go outside," Max said. "You and I. Maybe the shock won't be so bad to the women after they see me." He paused. "You didn't tell them, did you?"

"I couldn't. I wasn't sure. I—was hoping I was wrong."

She opened the door and closed it quickly. There was a small crowd on the other side.

"Hello, Pat," Elsie said uncertainly, trying to look past them into the tank room before the door shut.

"I'm not Pat, I'm Max," said the tall man with the blue eyes and the fuzz-reddened skull. "Listen—"

"Good heavens, Pat, what happened to your hair?" Sheila asked.

"I'm Max," insisted the man with the handsome face and the sharp blue eyes. "Don't you get it? I'm Max Stark. The melting sickness is Mead cells. We caught them from Pat. They adapted us to Minos. They also changed us all into Pat Mead."

The women stared at him, at each other. They shook their heads.

"They don't understand," June said. "I couldn't have if I hadn't seen it happening, Max."

"It's Pat," said Sheila, dazedly stubborn. "He shaved off his hair. It's some kind of joke."

Max shook her shoulders, glaring down at her face. "I'm Max. Max Stark. They all look like me. Do you hear? It's funny, but it's not a joke. Laugh for us, for God's sake!"

"It's too much," said June. "They'll have to see."

She opened the door and let them in. They hurried past her to the tanks, looking at forty-six identical blond faces, beginning to call in frightened voices:

"Jerry!"

"Harry!"

"Lee, where are you, sweetheart—"

June shut the door on the voices that were growing hysterical, the women terrified and helpless, the men shouting to let the women know who they were.

"It isn't easy," said Max, looking down at his own thick muscles. "But you aren't changed and the other girls aren't. That helps."

Through the muffled noise and hysteria, a bell was ringing.

"It's the airlock," June said.

Peering in the viewplate were nine Meads from Alexandria. To all appearances, eight of them were Pat Mead at various ages, from fifteen to fifty, and the other was a handsome, leggy, red-headed girl who could have been his sister.

Regretfully, they explained through the voice tube that they had walked over from Alexandria to bring news that the plane pilot had contracted melting sickness there and had died.

They wanted to come in.

June and Max told them to wait and returned to the tank room. The men were enjoying their new height and strength, and the women were bewilderedly learning that they could tell one Pat Mead from another by voice, by gesture of face or hand. The panic was gone. In its place was acceptance of the fantastic situation.

Max called for attention. "There are nine Meads outside who want to come in. They have different names, but they're all Pat Mead."

They frowned or looked blank, and George Barton asked, "Why didn't you let them in? I don't see any problem."

"One of them," said Max soberly, "is a girl. *Patricia* Mead. The girl wants to come in."

There was a long silence while the implication settled to the fear center of the women's minds. Sheila the beautiful felt it first. She cried, "No! Please don't let her in!" There was real fright in her tone and the women caught it quickly.

Elsie clung to Len, begging, "You don't want me to change, do you, Len? You like me the way I am! Tell me you do!"

The other girls backed away. It was illogical, but it was human. June felt terror rising in herself. She held up her hand for quiet, and presented the necessity to the group.

"Only half of us can leave Minos," she said. "The men cannot eat ship food; they've been conditioned to this planet. We women can go, but we would have to go without our men. We can't go outside without contagion, and we can't spend the rest of our lives in quarantine inside the ship. George Barton is right— there is no problem."

"But we'd be changed!" Sheila shrilled. "I don't want to become a Mead! I don't want to be somebody else!"

She ran to the inner wall of the corridor. There was a brief hesitation, and then, one by one, the women fled to that side, until there were only Bess, June and four others left.

"See!" cried Sheila. "A vote! We can't let the girl in!"

No one spoke. To change, to be someone else—the idea was strange and horrifying. The men stood uneasily glancing at each other, as if looking into mirrors, and against the wall of the corridor the women watched in fear and huddled together, staring at the men. One man in forty-seven poses. One of them made a beseeching move toward Elsie and she shrank away.

"No, Len! I won't let you change me!"

Max stirred restlessly, the ironic smile that made his new face his own unconsciously twisting into a grimace of pity. "We men can't leave, and you women can't stay," he said bluntly. "Why not let Patricia Mead in. Get it over with!"

June took a small mirror from her belt pouch and studied her own face, aware of Max talking forcefully, the men standing silent, the women pleading. Her face . . . her own face with its dark-blue eyes, small nose, long mobile lips . . . the mind and the body are inseparable; the shape of a face is part of the mind. She put the mirror back.

"I'd kill myself!" Sheila was sobbing. "I'd rather die!"

"You won't die," Max was saying. "Can't you see there's only one solution—"

They were looking at Max. June stepped silently out of the tank room, and then turned and went to the airlock. She opened the valves that would let in Pat Mead's sister.

THE WIND PEOPLE

MARION ZIMMER BRADLEY

Marion Zimmer Bradley has been writing science fiction since 1953, and was an active reader of sf before that time. She is best known for her series of books about the planet Darkover. She is the author of **Sword of Aldones** (Ace), a runner-up for the 1963 Hugo Award, an award named after editor Hugo Gernsback and given by members of the World Science Fiction Convention held each year. Her novels include **The World Wreckers** (Ace), **The Bloody Sun** (Ace), **Hunters of the Red Moon** (DAW Books), **Darkover Landfall** (DAW Books) and **Spell-Sword** (DAW Books). Most of her time is devoted to writing, but she is also a member of the Tolkien Society and is a semi-professional composer and singer. She lives in California.

"The Wind People," first published in **If** magazine, is a haunting story about a woman who chooses to remain on an alien world with her son. Moving and mysterious, it allows various interpretations of its ultimately tragic outcome.

It had been a long layover for the *Starholm's* crew, hunting heavy elements for fuel—eight months, on an idyllic green paradise of a planet; a soft, windy, whispering world, inhabited only by trees and winds. But in the end it presented its own unique problem.

Specifically, it presented Captain Merrihew with the

problem of Robin, male, father unknown, who had been born the day before, and a month prematurely, to Dr. Helen Murray.

Merrihew found her lying abed in the laboratory shelter, pale and calm, with the child beside her.

The little shelter, constructed roughly of green planks, looked out on the clearing which the *Starholm* had used as a base of operations during the layover; a beautiful place at the bottom of a wide valley, in the curve of a broad, deep-flowing river. The crew, tired of being shipbound, had built half a dozen such huts and shacks in these eight months.

Merrihew glared down at Helen. He snorted, "This is a fine situation. You, of all the people in the whole damned crew—the ship's doctor! It's—it's—" Inarticulate with rage, he fell back on a ridiculously inadequate phrase. "It's—criminal carelessness!"

"I know." Helen Murray, too young and far too lovely for a ship's officer on a ten-year cruise, still looked weak and white, and her voice was a gentle shadow of its crisp self. "I'm afraid four years in space made me careless."

Merrihew brooded, looking down at her. Something about ship-gravity conditions, while not affecting potency, made conception impossible; no child had ever been conceived in space and none ever would. On planet layovers, the effect wore off very slowly; only after three months aground had Dr. Murray started routine administration of anticeptin to the twenty-two women of the crew, herself included. At that time she had been still unaware that she herself was already carrying a child.

Outside, the leafy forest whispered and rustled, and Merrihew knew Helen had forgotten his existence again. The day-old child was tucked up in one of her rolled coveralls at her side. To Merrihew, he looked like a skinned monkey, but Helen's eyes smoldered as her hands moved gently over the tiny round head.

He stood and listened to the winds and said at random, "These shacks will fall to pieces in another month. It doesn't matter, we'll have taken off by then."

Dr. Chao Lin came into the shack, an angular woman of thirty-five. She said, "Company, Helen? Well, it's about time. Here, let me take Robin."

Helen said in weak protest, "You're spoiling me, Lin."

"It will do you good," Chao Lin returned. Merrihew, in a sudden surge of fury and frustration, exploded, "Damn it, Lin, you're making it all worse. He'll die when we go into overdrive, you know as well as I do!"

Helen sat up, clutching Robin protectively. "Are you proposing to drown him like a kitten?"

"Helen, I'm not proposing anything. I'm stating a fact."

"But it's not a fact. He won't die in overdrive because he won't be aboard when we go into overdrive!"

Merrihew looked at Lin helplessly, but his face softened. "Shall we—put him to sleep and bury him here?"

The woman's face turned white. "No!" she cried in passionate protest, and Lin bent to disengage her frantic grip.

"Helen, you'll hurt him. Put him down. There."

Merrihew looked down at her, troubled, and said, "We can't just abandon him to die slowly, Helen—"

"Who says I'm going to abandon him?"

Merrihew asked slowly, "Are you planning to desert?" He added, after a minute, "There's a chance he'll survive. After all, his very birth was against all medical precedent. Maybe—"

"Captain"—Helen's voice sounded desperate—"even drugged, no child under ten has ever endured the shift into hyperspace drive. A newborn would die in seconds." She clasped Robin to her again and said, "It's the only way—you have Lin for a doctor, Reynolds can handle my collateral duties. This planet is uninhabited, the climate is mild, we couldn't possibly starve." Her face, so gentle, was suddenly like rock. "Enter my death in the log, if you want to."

Merrihew looked from Helen to Lin, and said, "Helen, you're insane!"

She said, "Even if I'm sane now, I wouldn't be long if I had to abandon Robin." The wild note had died out of her voice, and she spoke rationally, but inflexibly. "Captain Merrihew, to get me aboard the *Starholm*, you will have to have me drugged or taken by force; I promise you I won't go any other way. And if you do that—and if Robin is left behind, or dies in overdrive, just so you will have my services as a doctor—then I solemnly swear that I will kill myself at the first opportunity."

"My God," said Merrihew, "you *are* insane!"

Helen gave a very tiny shrug. "Do you want a madwoman aboard?"

Chao Lin said quietly, "Captain, I don't see any other way. We would have had to arrange it that way if Helen had actually died in childbirth. Of two unsatisfactory solutions, we must choose the less harmful." And Merrihew knew that he had no real choice.

"I still think you're both crazy," he blustered, but it was surrender, and Helen knew it.

Ten days after the *Starholm* took off, young Colin Reynolds, technician, committed suicide by the messy procedure of slicing his jugular vein, which—in zero gravity—distributed several quarts of blood in big round globules all over his cabin. He left an incoherent note.

Merrihew put the note in the disposal and Chao Lin put the blood in the ship's blood bank for surgery, and they hushed it up as an accident; but Merrihew had the unpleasant feeling that the layover on the green and windy planet was going to become a legend, spread in whispers by the crew. And it did, but that is another story.

Robin was two years old when he first heard the voices in the wind. He pulled at his mother's arm and crooned softly, in imitation.

"What is it, lovey?"

"Pretty." He crooned again to the distant murmuring sound.

Helen smiled vaguely and patted the round cheek. Robin, his infant imagination suddenly distracted, said, "Hungry. Robin hungry. Berries."

"Berries after you eat," Helen promised absently, and picked him up. Robin tugged at her arm.

"Mommy pretty, too!"

She laughed, a rosy and smiling young Diana. She was happy on the solitary planet; they lived quite comfortably in one of the larger shacks, and only a little frown line between her eyes bore witness to the terror which had closed down on her in the first months, when every new day had been some new struggle—against weakness, against unfamiliar sounds, against loneliness and dread. Nights when she lay wakeful, sweating with terror while the winds rose and fell again and her imagination gave them voices, bleak days when she wandered dazedly around the shack or stared moodily at Robin. There had been moments—only fleeting, and penanced with hours of shame and regret—when she thought that even the horror of losing Robin in those first days would have been less than the horror of spending the rest of her life alone here, when she had wondered why Merrihew had not realized that she was unbalanced, and forced her to go with them; by now, Robin would have been only a moment's painful memory.

Still not strong, knowing she had to be strong for Robin or he would die as surely as if she had abandoned him, she had spent the first months in a somnambulistic dream. Sometimes she had walked for days at a time in that dream; she would wake to find food that she could not remember gathering. Somehow, pervasive, the dream voices had taken over; the whispering winds had been full of voices and even hands.

She had fallen ill and lain for days sick and delirious, and had heard a voice which hardly seemed to be her own, saying that if she died the wind voices would care for Robin . . . and then the shock and irrationality of that had startled her out of delirium, agonized and trembling, and she pulled herself upright and cried out, "No!"

And the shimmer of eyes and voices had faded again into vague echoes, until there was only the stir of sunlight on the leaves, and Robin, chubby and naked, kicking in the sunlight, cooing with his hands outstretched to the rustle of leaves and shadows.

She had known, then, that she had to get well. She had never heard the wind voices again, and her crisp, scientific mind rejected the fanciful theory that if she only believed in the wind voices she would see their forms and hear their words clearly. And she rejected them so thoroughly that when she heard them speak, she shut them away from her mind, and after a time heard them no longer, except in restless dreams.

By now she had accepted the isolation and the beauty of their world, and begun to make a happy life for Robin.

For lack of other occupation last summer—though the winter was mild and there was no lack of fruits and roots even then—Helen had patiently snared male and female of small animals like rabbits, and now she had a pen of them. They provided a change of diet, and after a few smelly unsuccessful experiments she had devised a way to supple their fur pelts. She made no effort at gardening, though when Robin was older she might try that. For the moment, it was enough that they were healthy and safe and protected.

Robin was *listening* again. Helen bent her ear, sharpened by the silence, but heard only the rustle of wind and leaves; saw only falling brightness along a silvered tree-trunk.

Wind? When there were no branches stirring?

"Ridiculous," she said sharply, then snatched up the baby boy and squeezed him before hoisting him astride her hip. "Mommy doesn't mean *you*, Robin. Let's look for berries."

But soon she realized that his head was tipped back and that he was listening, again, to some sound she could not hear.

On what she said was Robin's fifth birthday, Helen had made a special bed for him in another room of the building. He missed the warmth of Helen's body, and the comforting sound of her breathing; for Robin, since birth, had been a wakeful child.

Yet, on the first night alone, Robin felt curiously

freed. He did something he had never dared do before, for fear of waking Helen; he slipped from his bed and stood in the doorway, looking into the forest.

The forest was closer to the doorway now; Robin could fuzzily remember when the clearing had been wider. Now, slowly, beyond the garden patch which Helen kept cleared, the underbrush and saplings were growing back, and even what Robin called "the burned place" was covered with new sparse grass.

Robin was accustomed to being alone during the day—even in his first year, Helen had had to leave him alone, securely fastened in the house, or inside a little tight-fenced yard. But he was not used to being alone at night.

Far off in the forest, he could hear the whispers of the other people. Helen said there were no other people, but Robin knew better, because he could hear their voices on the wind, like fragments of the songs Helen sang at bedtime. And sometimes he could almost see them in the shadowy spots.

Once when Helen had been sick, a long time ago, and Robin had run helplessly from the fenced yard to the inside room and back again, hungry and dirty and furious because Helen only slept on the bed with her eyes closed, rousing up now and then to whimper like he did when he fell down and skinned his knee, the winds and voices had come into the very house; Robin had hazy memories of soothing voices, of hands that touched him more softly than Helen's hands. But he could not quite remember.

Now that he could hear them so clearly, he would go and find the other people. And then if Helen was sick again, there would be someone else to play with him and look after him. He thought gleefully, *Won't Helen be surprised?* and darted off across the clearing.

Helen woke, roused not by a sound but by a silence. She no longer heard Robin's soft breaths from the alcove, and after a moment she realized something else:

The winds were silent.

Perhaps, she thought, a storm was coming. Some change in air pressure could cause this stillness—but Robin? She tiptoed to the alcove; as she had suspected, his bed was empty.

Where could he be? In the clearing? With a storm coming? She slid her feet into handmade sandals and ran outside, her quivering call ringing out through the silent forest:

"Robin—oh, Robin!"

Silence. And far away a little ominous whisper. And for the first time since that first frightening year of loneliness, she felt lost, deserted in an alien world. She ran across the clearing, looking around wildly, trying to decide which way he could have wandered. Into the forest? What if he had strayed toward the riverbank? There was a place where the bank crumbled away, down toward the rapids—her throat closed convulsively, and her call was almost a shriek:

"Oh, Robin! Robin, darling! Robin!"

She ran through the paths worn by their feet, hearing snatches of rustle, winds and leaves suddenly vocal in the cold moonlight around her. It was the first time since the spaceship left them that Helen had ventured out into the night of their world. She called again, her voice cracking in panic.

"Ro-bin!"

A sudden stray gleam revealed a glint of white, and a child stood in the middle of the path. Helen gasped with relief and ran to snatch up her son—then fell back in dismay. It was not Robin who stood there.

The child was naked, about a head shorter than Robin, and female.

There was something curious about the bare and gleaming flesh, as if she could see the child only in the full flush of the moonlight. A round, almost expressionless face was surrounded by a mass of colorless streaming hair, the exact color of the moonlight. Helen's audible gasp startled her to a stop: she shut her eyes convulsively, and when she opened them the path was black and empty and Robin was running down the track toward her.

Helen caught him up, with a strangled cry, and ran, clasping him to her breast, back down the path to their shack. Inside, she barred the door and laid Robin down in her own bed, and threw herself down shivering, too shaken to speak, too shaken to scold him, curiously afraid to question. I had a hallucination, she told herself, a hallucination, another dream, a dream . . .

A dream, like the other Dream. She dignified it to herself as The Dream because it was not like any other dream she had ever had. She had dreamed it first before Robin's birth, and been ashamed to speak of it to Chao Lin, fearing the common-sense skepticism of the older woman.

On their tenth night on the green planet (the *Starholm* was a dim recollection now), when Merrihew's scientists had been convinced that the little world was safe, without wild beasts or diseases or savage natives, the crew had requested permission to camp in the valley clearing beside the river. Permission granted, they had gone apart in couples almost as usual, and even those who had no enduring liaison at the moment had found a partner for the night.

It must have been that night . . .

Colin Reynolds was two years younger than Helen, and their attachment, enduring over a few months of shiptime, was based less on mutual passion than on a sort of boyish need in him, a sort of impersonal feminine solicitude in Helen. All her affairs had been like that, companionable, comfortable, but never passionate. Curiously enough, Helen was a woman capable of passion, of great depths of devotion; but no man had ever roused it and now no man ever would. Only Robin's birth had touched her deeply pent emotions.

But that night, when Colin Reynolds was sleeping, Helen stayed restlessly awake, hearing the unquiet stirring of wind on the leaves. After a time she wandered down to the water's edge, staying a cautious distance from the shore—for the cliff crumbled dangerously—and stretched herself out to listen to the wind-voices. And after a time she fell asleep, and had The Dream, which was to return to her again and again.

Helen thought of herself as a scientist, without room for fantasies, and that was why she called it, fiercely, a dream; a dream born of some undiagnosed conflict in her. Even to herself Helen would not recall it in full.

There had been a man, and to her it seemed that he was part of the green and windy world, and he had found her sleeping by the river. Even in her drowsy state, Helen had suspected that perhaps one of the other crew members, like herself sleepless and drawn to the shining water, had happened upon her there; such things were not impossible, manners and mores being what they were among starship crews.

But to her, half dreaming, there had been some strangeness about him, which prevented her from seeing him too clearly even in the brilliant green moonlight. No dream and no man had ever seemed so living to her; and it was her fierce rationalization of the dream which kept her silent, months later, when she discovered (to her horror and secret despair) that she was with child. She had felt that she would lose the haze and secret delight of the dream if she openly acknowledged that Colin had fathered her child.

But at first—in the cool green morning that followed—she had not been at all sure it was a dream. Seeing only sunlight and leaves, she had held back from speaking, not wanting ridicule; could she have asked each man of the *Starholm,* "Was it you who came to me last night? Because if it was not, there are other men on this world, men who cannot be clearly seen even by moonlight."

Severely she reminded herself, Merrihew's men had pronounced the world uninhabited, and uninhabited it must be. Five years later, hugging her sleeping son close, Helen remembered the dream, examined the content of her fantasy, and once again, shivering, repeated, "I had a hallucination. It was only a dream. A dream, because I was alone . . ."

When Robin was fourteen years old, Helen told him the story of his birth, and of the ship.

He was a tall, silent boy, strong and hardy but not talkative; he heard the story almost in silence, and looked at Helen for a long time in silence afterward. He finally said in a whisper, "You could have died—you gave up a lot for me, Helen, didn't you?" He knelt and took her face in his hands.

She smiled and drew a little away from him. "Why are you looking at me like that, Robin?"

The boy could not put instant words to his thoughts; emotions were not in his vocabulary. Helen had taught him everything she knew, but she had always concealed her feelings from her son. He asked at last, "Why didn't my father stay with you?"

"I don't suppose it entered his head," Helen said. "He was needed on the ship. Losing me was bad enough."

Robin said passionately, "I'd have stayed!"

The woman found herself laughing. "Well—you did stay, Robin."

He asked, "Am I like my father?"

Helen looked gravely at her son, trying to see the half-forgotten features of young Reynolds in the boy's face. No, Robin did not look like Colin Reynolds, nor like Helen herself. She picked up his hand in hers; despite his robust health, Robin never tanned; his skin was pearly pale, so that in the green sunlight it blended into the forest almost invisibly. His hand lay in Helen's palm like a shadow. She said at last, "No, nothing like him. But under this sun, that's to be expected."

Robin said confidently, "I'm like the *other* people."

"The ones on the ship? They—"

"No," Robin interrupted, "you always said when I was older you'd tell me about the other people. I mean the other people *here*. The ones in the woods. The ones you can't see."

Helen stared at the boy in blank disbelief. "What do you mean? There are no other people, just us." Then she recalled that every imaginative child invents playmates. *Alone*, she thought, *Robin's always alone, no other children, no wonder he's a little—strange*. She said quietly, "You dreamed it, Robin."

The boy only stared at her in bleak, blank alienation. "You mean," he said, "you can't *hear* them, either?" He got up and walked out of the hut. Helen called, but he didn't turn back. She ran after him, catching at his arm, stopping him almost by force. She whispered, "Robin, Robin, tell me what you mean! There isn't anyone here. Once or twice I thought I had seen—something, by moonlight, only it was a dream. Please, Robin—please—"

"If it's only a dream, why are you frightened?" Robin asked, through a curious constriction in his throat. "If they've never hurt you . . ."

No, they had never hurt her. Even if, in her long-ago dream, one of them had come to her. *And the sons of God saw the daughters of men that they were fair*—a scrap of memory from a vanished life on another world sang in Helen's thoughts. She looked up at the pale, impatient face of her son, and swallowed hard.

Her voice was husky when she spoke. "Did I ever tell you about rationalization—when you want something to be true so much that you can make it sound right to yourself?"

"Couldn't that also happen to something you wanted *not* to be true?" Robin retorted with a mutinous curl of his mouth.

Helen would not let go his arm. She begged, "Robin, no, you'll only waste your life and break your heart looking for something that doesn't exist."

The boy looked down into her shaken face, and suddenly a new emotion welled up in him and he dropped to his knees beside her and buried his face against her breast. He whispered, "Helen, I'll never leave you, I'll never do anything you don't want me to do, I don't want anyone but you."

And for the first time in many years, Helen broke into wild and uncontrollable crying, without knowing why she wept.

Robin did not speak again of his quest in the forest. For many months he was quiet and subdued, staying near the clearing, hovering near Helen for days at a time, then disappearing into the forest at dusk. He heard the winds numbly, deaf to their promise and their call.

Helen too was quiet and withdrawn, feeling Robin's alienation through his submissive mood. She found herself speaking to him sharply for being always underfoot; yet, on the rare days when he vanished into the forest and did not return until after sunset, she felt a restless unease that set her wandering the paths herself, not following him, but simply uneasy unless she knew he was within call.

Once, in the shadows just before sunset, she thought she saw a man moving through the trees, and for an instant, as he turned toward her, she saw that he was naked. She had seen him only for a second or two, and after he had slipped between the shadows again common sense told her it was Robin. She was vaguely shocked and annoyed; she firmly intended to speak to him, perhaps to scold him for running about naked and slipping away like that; then, in a sort of remote embarrassment, she forbore to mention it. But after that, she kept out of the forest.

Robin had been vaguely aware of her surveillance and knew when it ceased. But he did not give up his own pointless rambles, although even to himself he no longer spoke of searching, or of any dreamlike inhabitants of the woods. At times it still seemed that some shadow concealed a half-seen form, and the distant murmur grew into a voice that mocked him; a white arm, the shadow of a face, until he lifted his head and stared straight at it.

One evening toward twilight he saw a sudden

shimmer in the trees, and he stood, fixedly, as the stray glint resolved itself first into a white face with shadowy eyes, then into a translucent flicker of bare arms, and then into the form of a woman, arrested for an instant with her hand on the bole of a tree. In the shadowy spot, filled only with the last ray of a cloudy sunset, she was very clear; not cloudy or unreal, but so distinct that he could see even a small smudge or bramble scratch on her shoulder, and a fallen leaf tangled in her colorless hair. Robin, paralyzed, watched her pause, and turn, and smile, and then she melted into the shadows.

He stood with his heart pounding for a second after she had gone; then whirled, bursting with the excitement of his discovery, and ran down the path toward home. Suddenly he stopped short, the world tilting and reeling, and fell on his face in a bed of dry leaves.

He was still ignorant of the nature of the emotion in him. He felt only intolerable misery and the conviction that he must never, never speak to Helen of what he had seen or felt.

He lay there, his burning face pressed into the leaves, unaware of the rising wind, the little flurry of blown leaves, the growing darkness and distant thunder. At last an icy spatter of rain aroused him, and cold, numbed, he made his way slowly homeward. Over his head the boughs creaked woodenly, and Robin, under the driving whips of the rain, felt their tumult only echoed his own voiceless agony.

He was drenched by the time he pushed the door of the shack open and stumbled blindly toward the fire, only hoping that Helen would be sleeping. But she started up from beside the hearth they had built together last summer.

"Robin?"

Deathly weary, the boy snapped, "Who *else* would it be?"

Helen didn't answer. She came to him, a small swift-moving figure in the firelight, and drew him into the warmth. She said, almost humbly, "I was afraid—the storm—Robin, you're all wet, come to the fire and dry out."

Robin yielded, his twitching nerves partly soothed by her voice. *How tiny Helen is,* he thought, *and I can remember that she used to carry me around on one arm; now she hardly comes to my shoulder.* She brought him food and he ate wolfishly, listening to the steady pouring rain, uncomfortable under Helen's watching eyes. Before his own eyes there was the clear memory of the woman in the wood, and so vivid was Robin's imagination, heightened by loneliness and undiluted by any random impressions, that it seemed to him Helen must see her too. And when she came to stand beside him, the picture grew so keen in his thoughts that he actually pulled himself free of her.

The next day dawned gray and still, beaten with long needles of rain. They stayed indoors by the smoldering fire; Robin, half sick and feverish from his drenching, sprawled by the hearth too indolent to move, watching Helen's comings and goings about the room; not realizing why the sight of her slight, quick form against the gray light filled him with such pain and melancholy.

The storm lasted four days. Helen exhausted her household tasks and sat restlessly thumbing through the few books she knew by heart—they had allowed her to remove all her personal possessions, all the things she had chosen on a forgotten and faraway Earth for a ten-year star cruise. For the first time in years, Helen was thinking again of the life, the civilization she had thrown away, for Robin who had been a pink scrap in the circle of her arm and now lay sullen on the hearth, not speaking, aimlessly whittling a stick with the knife (found discarded in a heap of rubbish from the *Starholm*) which was his dearest possession. Helen felt slow horror closing in on her. *What world, what heritage did I give him, in my madness? This world has driven us both insane. Robin and I are both a little mad, by Earth's standards. And when I die, and I will die first, what then?* At that moment Helen would have given her life to believe in his old dream of strange people in the wood.

She flung her book restlessly away, and Robin, as if waiting for that signal, sat upright and said almost eagerly, "Helen—"

Grateful that he had broken the silence of days, she gave him an encouraging smile.

"I've been reading your books," he began diffidently, "and I read about the sun you came from. It's different from this one. Suppose—suppose there were actually a kind of people here, and something in this light, or in your eyes, made them invisible to you."

Helen said, "Have you been seeing them again?"

He flinched at her ironical tone, and she asked, somewhat more gently, "It's a theory, Robin, but it wouldn't explain, then, why *you* see them."

"Maybe I'm—more used to this light," he said gropingly. "And anyway, you said you thought you'd seen them and thought it was only a dream."

Halfway between exasperation and a deep pity, Helen found herself arguing, "If these other people of yours really exist, why haven't they made themselves known in sixteen years?"

The eagerness with which he answered was almost frightening. "I think they only come out at night,

they're what your book calls a primitive civilization."
He spoke the words he had read, but never heard,
with an odd hesitation. "They're not really a civilization at all, I think, they're like—part of the woods."

"A forest people," Helen mused, impressed in spite
of herself, "and nocturnal. It's always moonlight or
dusky when you see them—"

"Then you *do* believe me—oh, Helen," Robin cried,
and suddenly found himself pouring out the story of
what he had seen, in incoherent words, concluding,
"and by daylight I can hear them, but I can't see
them. Helen, Helen, you have to believe it now, you'll
have to let me try to find them and learn to talk to
them . . ."

Helen listened with a sinking heart. She knew they
should not discuss it now, when five days of enforced
housebound proximity had set their nerves and
tempers on edge, but some unknown tension hurled
her sharp words at Robin. "You saw a woman, and
I—a man. These things are only dreams. Do I have to
explain more to you?"

Robin flung his knife sullenly aside. "You're so
blind, so stubborn."

"I think you are feverish again." Helen rose to go.

He said wrathfully, "You treat me like a child!"

"Because you act like one, with your fairy tales of
women in the wind."

Suddenly Robin's agony overflowed and he caught
at her, holding her around the knees, clinging to her as
he had not done since he was a small child, his words
stumbling and rushing over one another.

"Helen, Helen darling, don't be angry with me," he
begged, and caught her in a blind embrace that pulled
her off her feet. She had never guessed how strong he
was; but he seemed very like a little boy, and she

hugged him quickly as he began to cover her face with childish kisses.

"Don't cry, Robin, my baby, it's all right," she murmured, kneeling close to him. Gradually the wildness of his passionate crying abated; she touched his forehead with her cheek to see if it was heated with fever, and he reached up and held her there. Helen let him lie against her shoulder, feeling that perhaps after the violence of his outburst he would fall asleep, and she was half-asleep herself when a sudden shock of realization darted through her; quickly she tried to free herself from Robin's entangling arms.

"Robin, let me go."

He clung to her, not understanding. "Don't let go of me, Helen. Darling, stay here beside me," he begged, and pressed a kiss into her throat.

Helen, her blood icing over, realized that unless she freed herself very quickly now, she would be fighting against a strong, aroused young man not clearly aware of what he was doing. She took refuge in the sharp maternal note of ten years ago, almost vanished in the closer, more equal companionship of the time between: "No, Robin. Stop it at once, do you hear?"

Automatically he let her go, and she rolled quickly away, out of his reach, and got to her feet. Robin, too intelligent to be unaware of her anger and too naïve to know its cause, suddenly dropped his head and wept, wholly unstrung. "Why are you angry?" he blurted out. "I was only loving you."

And at the phrase of the five-year-old child, Helen felt her throat would burst with its ache. She managed to choke out, "I'm not angry, Robin—we'll talk about this later, I promise," and then, her own control vanishing, turned and fled precipitately into the pouring rain.

She plunged through the familiar woods for a long time, in a daze of unthinking misery. She did not even fully realize that she was sobbing and muttering aloud, "No, no, no, no!"

She must have wandered for several hours. The rain had stopped and the darkness was lifting before she began to grow calmer and to think more clearly.

She had been blind not to foresee this day when Robin was a child; only if her child had been a daughter could it have been avoided. Or—she was shocked at the hysterical sound of her own laughter —if Colin had stayed and they had raised a family like Adam and Eve!

But what now? Robin was sixteen; she was not yet forty. Helen caught at vanishing memories of society; taboos so deeply rooted that for Helen they were instinctual and impregnable. Yet for Robin nothing existed except this little patch of forest and Helen herself—the only person in his world, more specifically at the moment the only woman in his world. *So much,* she thought bitterly, *for instinct. But have I the right to begin this all over again? Worse; have I the right to deny its existence and, when I die, leave Robin alone?*

She had stumbled and paused for breath, realizing that she had wandered in circles and that she was at a familiar point on the riverbank which she had avoided for sixteen years. On the heels of this realization she became aware that for only the second time in memory, the winds were wholly stilled.

Her eyes, swollen with crying, ached as she tried to pierce the gloom of the mist, lilac-tinted with the approaching sunrise, which hung around the water. Through the dispersing mist she made out, dimly, the form of a man.

He was tall, and his pale skin shone with misty

white colors. Helen sat frozen, her mouth open, and for the space of several seconds he looked down at her without moving. His eyes, dark splashes in the pale face, had an air of infinite sadness and compassion, and she thought his lips moved in speech, but she heard only a thin familiar rustle of wind.

Behind him, mere flickers, she seemed to make out the ghosts of other faces, tips of fingers of invisible hands, eyes, the outline of a woman's breast, the curve of a child's foot. For a minute, in Helen's weary numbed state, all her defenses went down and she thought: *Then I'm not mad and it wasn't a dream and Robin isn't Reynolds' son at all. His father was this— one of these—and they've been watching me and Robin, Robin has seen them, he doesn't know he's one of them, but they know. They know and I've kept Robin from them all these sixteen years.*

The man took two steps toward her, the translucent body shifting to a dozen colors before her blurred eyes. His face had a curious familiarity—*familiarity*— and in a sudden spasm of terror Helen thought, "I'm going mad, it's Robin, *it's Robin!*"

His hand was actually outstretched to touch her when her scream cut icy lashes through the forest, stirring wild echoes in the wind-voices, and she whirled and ran blindly toward the treacherous, crumbling bank. Behind her came steps, a voice, a cry—Robin, the strange dryad-man, she could not guess. The horror of incest, the son the father the lover suddenly melting into one, overwhelmed her reeling brain and she fled insanely to the brink. She felt a masculine hand actually gripping her shoulder, she might have been pulled back even then, but she twisted free blindly, shrieking, "No, Robin, no, no—" and flung herself down the steep bank, to slip and hurl downward and whirl around in the raging current to spinning oblivion and death . . .

Many years later, Merrihew, grown old in the Space Service, falsified a log entry to send his ship for a little while into the orbit of the tiny green planet he had named Robin's World. The old buildings had fallen into rotted timbers, and Merrihew quartered the little world for two months from pole to pole but found nothing. Nothing but shadows and whispers and the unending voices of the wind. Finally, he lifted his ship and went away.

THE SHIP WHO SANG

ANNE McCAFFREY

Anne McCaffrey studied at Radcliffe College, where she received a degree in Slavonic Languages and Literature. She is the author of several novels, among them **Restoree, Decision at Doona, Dragonflight** and **Dragonquest** (all published by Ballantine). She is also the editor of an anthology, **Alchemy & Academe** (Doubleday), and a cookbook, **Cooking Out of This World** (Ballantine), a collection of recipes by science-fiction writers. She won the Hugo Award for her novella "Weyr Search" and the Nebula for her novella "Dragonrider"; she was the first woman to receive both awards. Ms. McCaffrey lives in Ireland with her three children, a gray Irish horse, a dog and a cat.

The cyborg, a person who is part human, part machine, is the subject of many science-fiction stories. The cyborg is often sympathetically portrayed, sometimes alienated from unchanged people, sometimes seeking to reconcile his human and mechanical selves. Helva, the female cyborg in "The Ship Who Sang," is a spaceship, but her thoughts and emotions are still recognizably human. Her feelings of helplessness and despair are feelings most women have had to conquer; in this character, we see a little of ourselves.

She was born a thing and as such would be condemned if she failed to pass the encephalograph test required of all newborn babies. There was always the possibility that though the limbs were twisted, the mind was not, that though the ears would hear only dimly, the eyes see vaguely, the mind behind them was receptive and alert.

The electroencephalogram was entirely favorable, unexpectedly so, and the news was brought to the waiting, grieving parents. There was the final, harsh decision: to give their child euthanasia or permit it to become an encapsulated "brain," a guiding mechanism in any one of a number of curious professions. As such, their offspring would suffer no pain, live a comfortable existence in a metal shell for several centuries, performing unusual service to Central Worlds.

She lived and was given a name, Helva. For her first three vegetable months she waved her crabbed claws, kicked weakly with her clubbed feet and enjoyed the usual routine of the infant. She was not alone, for there were three other such children in the big city's special nursery. Soon they all were removed to Central Laboratory School, where their delicate transformation began.

One of the babies died in the initial transferral, but of Helva's "class," seventeen thrived in the metal shells. Instead of kicking feet, Helva's neural responses started her wheels; instead of grabbing with hands, she manipulated mechanical extensions. As she matured, more and more neural synapses would be adjusted to operate other mechanisms that went into the maintenance and running of a spaceship. For Helva was destined to be the "brain" half of a scout ship, partnered with a man or a woman, whichever she chose, as the mobile half. She would be among the elite of her kind. Her initial intelligence tests registered above normal and her adaptation index was unusually high. As long as her development within her shell lived up to expectations, and there were no side-effects from the pituitary tinkering, Helva would live a rewarding, rich and unusual life, a far cry from what she would have faced as an ordinary, "normal" being.

However, no diagram of her brain patterns, no early IQ tests recorded certain essential facts about Helva that Central must eventually learn. They would have to bide their official time and see, trusting that the massive doses of shell-psychology would suffice her, too, as the necessary bulwark against her unusual confinement and the pressures of her profession. A ship run by a human brain could not run rogue or insane with the power and resources Central had to build into their scout ships. Brain ships were, of course, long past the experimental stages. Most babies survived the perfected techniques of pituitary manipulation that kept their bodies small, eliminating the necessity of transfers from smaller to larger shells. And very, very few were lost when the final connection was made to the control panels of ship or industrial combine. Shell-people resembled mature dwarfs in size whatever their natal deformities were, but the well-oriented brain would not have changed places with the most perfect body in the Universe.

So, for happy years, Helva scooted around in her shell with her classmates, playing such games as Stall, Power-Seek, studying her lessons in trajectory, propulsion techniques, computation, logistics, mental hygiene, basic alien psychology, philology, space history, law, traffic, codes: all the et ceteras that eventually became compounded into a reasoning, logical, informed citizen. Not so obvious to her, but of more importance to her teachers, Helva ingested the precepts of her conditioning as easily as she absorbed her nutrient fluid. She would one day be grateful to the patient drone of the subconscious-level instruction.

Helva's civilization was not without busy, do-good associations, exploring possible inhumanities to terrestrial as well as extraterrestrial citizens. One such group—Society for the Preservation of the Rights of Intelligent Minorities—got all incensed over shelled "children" when Helva was just turning fourteen. When they were forced to, Central Worlds shrugged its shoulders, arranged a tour of the Laboratory Schools and set the tour off to a big start by showing the members case histories, complete with photographs. Very few committees ever looked past the first few photos. Most of their original objections about "shells" were overridden by the relief that these hideous (to them) bodies *were* mercifully concealed.

Helva's class was doing fine arts, a selective subject in her crowded program. She had activated one of her microscopic tools which she would later use for minute repairs to various parts of her control panel. Her subject was large—a copy of "The Last Supper"—and her canvas, small—the head of a tiny screw. She had tuned her sight to the proper degree. As she worked she absentmindedly crooned, producing a curious sound. Shell-people used their own vocal chords and diaphragms, but sound issued through microphones rather than mouths. Helva's hum, then, had a curious vibrancy, a warm, dulcet quality even in its aimless chromatic wanderings.

"Why, what a lovely voice you have," said one of the female visitors.

Helva "looked" up and caught a fascinating panorama of regular, dirty craters on a flaky pink surface. Her hum became a gurgle of surprise. She instinctively regulated her "sight" until the skin lost it cratered look and the pores assumed normal proportions.

"Yes, we have quite a few years of voice training, madam," remarked Helva calmly. "Vocal peculiarities often become excessively irritating during prolonged interstellar distances and must be eliminated. I enjoyed my lessons."

Although this was the first time that Helva had seen unshelled people, she took this experience calmly. Any other reaction would have been reported instantly.

"I meant that you have a nice singing voice . . . dear," the lady said.

"Thank you. Would you like to see my work?" Helva asked politely. She instinctively sheered away from personal discussions, but she filed the comment away for further meditation.

"Work?" asked the lady.

"I am currently reproducing 'The Last Supper' on the head of a screw."

"Oh, I say," the lady twittered.

Helva turned her vision back to magnification and surveyed her copy critically. "Of course, some of my color values do not match the old Master's and the perspective is faulty, but I believe it to be a fair copy."

The lady's eyes, unmagnified, bugged out.

"Oh, I forget," and Helva's voice was really contrite. If she could have blushed, she would have. "You people don't have adjustable vision."

The monitor of this discourse grinned with pride and amusement as Helva's tone indicated pity for the unfortunate.

"Here, this will help," said Helva, substituting a magnifying device in one extension and holding it over the picture.

⇥ In a kind of shock, the ladies and gentlemen of the committee bent to observe the incredibly copied and brilliantly executed Last Supper on the head of a screw.

"Well," remarked one gentleman who had been forced to accompany his wife, "the good Lord can eat where angels fear to tread."

"Are you referring, sir," asked Helva politely, "to the Dark Age discussions of the number of angels who could stand on the head of a pin?"

"I had that in mind."

"If you substitute 'atom' for 'angel,' the problem is not insoluble, given the metallic content of the pin in question."

"Which you are programmed to compute?"

"Of course."

"Did they remember to program a sense of humor, as well, young lady?"

"We are directed to develop a sense of proportion, sir, which contributes the same effect."

The good man chortled appreciatively and decided the trip was worth his time.

If the investigation committee spent months digesting the thoughtful food served them at the Laboratory School, they left Helva with a morsel as well.

"Singing" as applicable to herself required research. She had, of course, been exposed to and enjoyed a music-appreciation course that had included the better-known classical works, such as *Tristan und Isolde, Candide, Oklahoma,* and *Nozze diFigaro,* along with the atomic-age singers, Birgit Nilsson, Bob Dylan, and Geraldine Todd, as well as the curious rhythmic progressions of the Venusians, Capellan visual chromatics, the sonic concerti of the Altairians and Reticulan croons. But "singing" for any shell-person posed considerable technical difficulties. Shell-people were schooled to examine every aspect of a problem or situation before making a prognosis. Balanced properly between optimism and practicality, the nondefeatist attitude of the shell-people led them to extricate themselves, their ships, and personnel, from bizarre situations. Therefore to Helva, the problem that she couldn't open her mouth to sing, among other restrictions, did not bother her. She would work out a method, by-passing her limitations, whereby she could sing.

She approached the problem by investigating the methods of sound reproduction through the centuries, human and instrumental. Her own sound-production equipment was essentially more instrumental than vocal. Breath control and the proper enunciation of vowel sounds within the oral cavity appeared to require the most development and practice. Shell-people did not, strictly speaking, breathe. For their purposes, oxygen and other gases were not drawn from the surrounding atmosphere through the medium of lungs but sustained artificially by solution in their shells. After experimentation, Helva discovered that she could manipulate her diaphragmic unit to sustain tone. By relaxing the throat muscles and expanding the oral cavity well into the frontal sinuses, she could direct the vowel sounds into the most felicitous position for proper reproduction through her throat microphone. She compared the results with tape recordings of modern singers and was not unpleased, although her own tapes had a peculiar quality about them, not at all unharmonious, merely unique. Acquiring a repertoire from the Laboratory library was no problem to one trained to perfect recall. She found herself able to sing any role and any song which struck her fancy. It would not have occurred to her that it was curious for a female to sing bass, baritone, tenor, mezzo, soprano, and coloratura as she pleased. It was, to Helva, only a matter of the correct reproduction and diaphragmatic control required by the music attempted.

If the authorities remarked on her curious avocation, they did so among themselves. Shell-people were encouraged to develop a hobby so long as they maintained proficiency in their technical work.

On the anniversary of her sixteenth year, Helva was unconditionally graduated and installed in her ship, the XH-834. Her permanent titanium shell was recessed behind an even more indestructible barrier in the central shaft of the scout ship. The neural, audio, visual, and sensory connections were made and sealed. Her extendibles were diverted, connected or augmented and the final, delicate-beyond-description brain taps were completed while Helva remained anesthetically unaware of the proceedings. When she woke, she *was* the ship. Her brain and intelligence controlled every function from navigation to such loading as a scout ship of her class needed. She could take care of herself and her ambulatory half in any situation already recorded in the annals of Central Worlds and any situation its most fertile minds could imagine.

Her first actual flight, for she and her kind had made mock flights on dummy panels since she was eight, showed her to be a complete master of the techniques of her profession. She was ready for her great adventures and the arrival of her mobile partner.

There were nine qualified scouts sitting around collecting base pay the day Helva reported for active duty. There were several missions that demanded instant attention, but Helva had been of interest to several department heads in Central for some time and each bureau chief was determined to have her assigned to *his* section. No one had remembered to introduce Helva to the prospective partners. The ship always chose its own partner. Had there been another "brain" ship at the base at the moment, Helva would have been guided to make the first move. As it was, while Central wrangled among itself, Robert Tanner sneaked out of the pilots' barracks, out to the field and over to Helva's slim metal hull.

"Hello, anyone at home?" Tanner said.

"Of course," replied Helva, activating her outside scanners. "Are you my partner?" she asked hopefully, as she recognized the Scout Service uniform.

"All you have to do is ask," he retorted in a wistful tone.

"No one has come. I thought perhaps there were no partners available and I've had no directives from Central."

Even to herself Helva sounded a little self-pitying, but the truth was she was lonely, sitting on the darkened field. She had always had the company of other shells and more recently, technicians by the score. The sudden solitude had lost its momentary charm and become oppressive.

"No directives from Central is scarcely a cause for regret, but there happen to be eight other guys biting their fingernails to the quick just waiting for an invitation to board you, you beautiful thing."

Tanner was inside the central cabin as he said this, running appreciative fingers over her panel, the scout's gravity-chair, poking his head into the cabins, the galley, the head, the pressured-storage compartments.

"Now, if you want to goose Central and do *us* a

favor all in one, call up the barracks and let's have a ship-warming partner-picking party. Hmmmm?"

Helva chuckled to herself. He was so completely different from the occasional visitors or the various Laboratory technicians she had encountered. He was so gay, so assured, and she was delighted by his suggestion of a partner-picking party. Certainly it was not against anything in her understanding of regulations.

"Cencom, this is XH-834. Connect me with Pilot Barracks."

"Visual?"

"Please."

A picture of lounging men in various attitudes of boredom came on her screen.

"This is XH-834. Would the unassigned scouts do me the favor of coming aboard?"

Eight figures were galvanized into action, grabbing pieces of wearing apparel, disengaging tape mechanisms, disentangling themselves from bedsheets and towels.

Helva dissolved the connection while Tanner chuckled gleefully and settled down to await their arrival.

Helva was engulfed in an unshell-like flurry of anticipation. No actress on her opening night could have been more apprehensive, fearful or breathless. Unlike the actress, she could throw no hysterics, china *objets d'art* or grease paint to relieve her tension. She could, of course, check her stores for edibles and drinks, which she did, serving Tanner from the virgin selection of her commissary.

Scouts were colloquially known as "brawns" as opposed to their ship "brains." They had to pass as rigorous a training program as the brains and only the top 1 percent of each contributory world's highest scholars were admitted to Central Worlds Scout Training Program. Consequently the eight young men who came pounding up the gantry into Helva's hospitable lock were unusually fine looking, intelligent, well-coordinated and well-adjusted young men, looking forward to a slightly drunken evening, Helva permitting, and all quite willing to do each other dirt to get possession of her.

Such a human invasion left Helva mentally breathless, a luxury she thoroughly enjoyed for the brief time she felt she should permit it.

She sorted out the young men. Tanner's opportunism amused but did not specifically attract her; the blond Nordsen seemed too simple; dark-haired Alatpay had a kind of obstinacy for which she felt no compassion; Mir-Ahnin's bitterness hinted an inner darkness she did not wish to lighten, although he made the biggest outward play for her attention. Hers was a curious courtship—this would be only the first of several marriages for her, for brawns retired after seventy-five years of service, or earlier if they were unlucky. Brains, their bodies safe from any deterioration, were indestructible. In theory, once a shell-person had paid off the massive debt of early care, surgical adaptation and maintenance charges, he or she was free to seek employment elsewhere. In practice, shell-people remained in the Service until they chose to self-destruct or died in line of duty. Helva had actually spoken to one shell-person 322 years old. She had been so awed by the contact she hadn't presumed to ask the personal questions she had wanted to.

Her choice of a brawn did not stand out from the others until Tanner started to sing a scout ditty, recounting the misadventures of the bold, dense, painfully inept Billy Brawn. An attempt at harmony resulted in cacophony and Tanner wagged his arms wildly for silence.

"What we need is a roaring good lead tenor. Jennan, besides palming aces, what do you sing?"

"Sharp," Jennan replied with easy good humor.

"If a tenor is absolutely necessary, I'll attempt it," Helva volunteered.

"My good *woman*," Tanner protested.

"Sound your 'A,'" said Jennan, laughing.

Into the stunned silence that followed the rich, clear, high "A," Jennan remarked quietly, "Such an 'A' Caruso would have given the rest of his notes to sing."

It did not take them long to discover her full range.

"All Tanner asked for was one roaring good lead tenor," Jennan said jokingly, "and our sweet mistress supplied us an entire repertory company. The boy who gets this ship will go far, far, far."

"To the Horsehead Nebula?" asked Nordsen, quoting an old Central saw.

"To the Horsehead Nebula and back, we shall make beautiful music," said Helva, chuckling.

"Together," Jennan said. "Only you'd better make the music and, with my voice, I'd better listen."

"I rather imagined it would be I who listened," suggested Helva.

Jennan executed a stately bow with an intricate flourish of his crush-brimmed hat. He directed his bow toward the central control pillar where Helva *was*. Her own personal preference crystallized at that precise moment and for that particular reason: Jennan, alone of the men, had addressed his remarks directly at her physical presence, regardless of the fact that he knew she could pick up his image wherever he was in the ship and regardless of the fact that her body was behind massive metal walls. Throughout their partnership, Jennan never failed to turn his head in her direction no matter where he was in relation to her. In response to this personalization, Helva at that moment and from then on always spoke to Jennan only through her central mike, even though that was not always the most efficient method.

Helva didn't know that she fell in love with Jennan that evening. As she had never been exposed to love or affection, only the drier cousins, respect and admiration, she could scarcely have recognized her reaction to the warmth of his personality and thoughtfulness. As a shell-person, she considered herself remote from emotions largely connected with physical desires.

"Well, Helva, it's been swell meeting you," said Tanner suddenly as she and Jennan were arguing about the baroque quality of "Come All Ye Sons of Art." "See you in space sometime, you lucky dog, Jennan. Thanks for the party, Helva."

"You don't have to go so soon?" asked Helva, realizing belatedly that she and Jennan had been excluding the others from this discussion.

"Best man won," Tanner said wryly. "Guess I'd better go get a tape on love ditties. Might need 'em for the next ship, if there're any more at home like you."

Helva and Jennan watched them leave, both a little confused.

"Perhaps Tanner's jumping to conclusions?" Jennan asked.

Helva regarded him as he slouched against the console, facing her shell directly. His arms were crossed on his chest and the glass he held had been empty for some time. He was handsome, they all were; but his watchful eyes were unwary, his mouth assumed a smile easily, his voice (to which Helva was particularly drawn) was resonant, deep, and without unpleasant overtones or accent.

"Sleep on it, at any rate, Helva. Call me in the morning if it's your opt."

She called him at breakfast, after she had checked her choice through Central. Jennan moved his things aboard, received their joint commission, had his personality and experience file locked into her reviewer, gave her the coordinates of their first mission. The XH-834 officially became the JH-834.

Their first mission was a dull but necessary crash priority (Medical got Helva), rushing a vaccine to a distant system plagued with a virulent spore disease. They had only to get to Spica as fast as possible.

After the initial, thrilling forward surge at her maximum speed, Helva realized her muscles were to be given less of a workout than her brawn on this tedious mission. But they did have plenty of time for exploring each other's personalities. Jennan, of course, knew what Helva was capable of as a ship and partner, just as she knew what she could expect from him. But these were only facts and Helva looked forward eagerly to learning that human side of her partner which could not be reduced to a series of symbols. Nor could the give and take of two personalities be learned from a book. It had to be experienced.

"My father was a scout, too, or is that programmed?" began Jennan their third day out.

"Naturally."

"Unfair, you know. You've got all my family history and I don't know one blamed thing about yours."

"I've never known either," Helva said. "Until I read

yours, it hadn't occurred to me I must have one, too, someplace in Central's files."

Jennan snorted. "Shell psychology!"

Helva laughed. "Yes, and I'm even programmed against curiosity about it. You'd better be, too."

Jennan ordered a drink, slouched into the gravity couch opposite her, put his feet on the bumpers, turning himself idly from side to side on the gimbals.

"Helva—a made-up name . . ."

"With a Scandinavian sound."

"You aren't blond," Jennan said positively.

"Well, then, there're dark Swedes."

"And blond Turks and this one's harem is limited to one."

"Your woman in purdah, yes, but you can comb the pleasure houses—" Helva found herself aghast at the edge to her carefully trained voice.

"You know," Jennan interrupted her, deep in some thought of his own, "my father gave me the impression he was a lot more married to his ship, the Silvia, than to my mother. I know I used to think Silvia was my grandmother. She was a low number, so she must have been a great-great-grandmother at least. I used to talk to her for hours."

"Her registry?" asked Helva, unwittingly jealous of everyone and anyone who had shared his hours.

"422. I think she's TS now. I ran into Tom Burgess once."

Jennan's father had died of a planetary disease, the vaccine for which his ship had used up in curing the local citizens.

"Tom said she'd got mighty tough and salty. You lose your sweetness and I'll come back and haunt you, girl," Jennan threatened.

Helva laughed. He startled her by stamping up to

the column panel, touching it with light, tender fingers.

"I *wonder* what you look like," he said softly, wistfully.

Helva had been briefed about this natural curiosity of scouts. She didn't know anything about herself and neither of them ever would or could.

"Pick any form, shape, and shade and I'll be yours obliging," she countered, as training suggested.

"Iron Maiden, I fancy blondes with long tresses," and Jennan pantomimed Lady Godiva–like tresses. "Since you're immolated in titanium, I'll call you Brunehilde, my dear," and he made his bow.

With a chortle, Helva launched into the appropriate aria just as Spica made contact.

"What'n'ell's that yelling about? Who are you? And unless you're Central Worlds Medical, go away. We've got a plague. No visiting privileges."

"My ship is singing, we're the JH-834 of Worlds and we've got your vaccine. What are our landing coordinates?"

"Your *ship* is singing?"

"The greatest S.A.T.B. in organized space. Any request?"

The JH-834 delivered the vaccine but no more arias and received immediate orders to proceed to Leviticus IV. By the time they got there, Jennan found a reputation awaiting him and was forced to defend the 834's virgin honor.

"I'll stop singing," murmured Helva contritely as she ordered up poultices for his third black eye in a week.

"You will not," Jennan said through gritted teeth. "If I have to black eyes from here to the Horsehead to keep the snicker out of the title, we'll be the ship who sings."

After the "ship who sings" tangled with a minor but vicious narcotic ring in the Lesser Magellanics, the title became definitely respectful. Central was aware of each episode and punched out a "special interest" key on JH-834's file. A first-rate team was shaking down well.

Jennan and Helva considered themselves a first-rate team, too, after their tidy arrest.

"Of all the vices in the universe, I *hate* drug addiction," Jennan remarked as they headed back to Central Base. "People can go to hell quick enough without that kind of help."

"Is that why you volunteered for Scout Service? To redirect traffic?"

"I'll bet my official answer's on your review."

"In far too flowery wording. 'Carrying on the traditions of my family, which has been proud of four generations in Service,' if I may quote you your own words."

Jennan groaned. "I was *very* young when I wrote that. I certainly hadn't been through Final Training. And once I was in Final Training, my pride wouldn't let me fail . . .

"As I mentioned, I used to visit Dad on board the Silvia and I've a very good idea she might have had her eye on me as a replacement for my father because I had had massive doses of scout-oriented propaganda. It took. From the time I was seven, I was going to be a scout or else." He shrugged as if deprecating a youthful determination that had taken a great deal of mature application to bring to fruition.

"Ah, so? Scout Sahir Silan on the JS-422 penetrating into the Horsehead Nebula?"

Jennan chose to ignore her sarcasm.

"With *you*, I may even get that far. But even with

Silvia's nudging *I* never daydreamed myself *that* kind of glory in my wildest flights of fancy. I'll leave the whoppers to your agile brain henceforth. I have in mind a smaller contribution to space history."

"So modest?"

"No. Practical. We also serve, et cetera." He placed a dramatic hand on his heart.

"Glory hound!" scoffed Helva.

"Look who's talking, my Nebula-bound friend. At least I'm not greedy. There'll only be one hero like my dad at Parsaea, but I *would* like to be remembered for some kudos. Everyone does. Why else do or die?"

"Your father died on his way back from Parsaea, if I may point out a few cogent facts. So he could never have known he was a hero for damming the flood with his ship. Which kept the Parsaean colony from being abandoned. Which gave them a chance to discover the antiparalytic qualities of Parsaea. Which *he* never knew."

"I know," said Jennan softly.

Helva was immediately sorry for the tone of her rebuttal. She knew very well how deep Jennan's attachment to his father had been. On his review a note was made that he had rationalized his father's loss with the unexpected and welcome outcome of the Affair at Parsaea.

"Facts are not human, Helva. My father was and so am I. And *basically,* so are you. Check over your dial, 834. Amid all the wires attached to you is a heart, an underdeveloped human heart. Obviously!"

"I apologize, Jennan," she said.

Jennan hesitated a moment, threw out his hands in acceptance and then tapped her shell affectionately.

"If they ever take us off the milkruns, we'll make a stab at the Nebula, huh?"

As so frequently happened in the Scout Service, within the next hour they had orders to change course, not to the Nebula, but to a recently colonized system with two habitable planets, one tropical, one glacial. The sun, named Ravel, had become unstable; the spectrum was that of a rapidly expanding shell, with absorption lines rapidly displacing toward violet. The augmented heat of the primary had already forced evacuation of the nearer world, Daphnis. The pattern of spectral emissions gave indication that the sun would sear Chloe as well. All ships in the immediate spatial vicinity were to report to Disaster Headquarters on Chloe to effect removal of the remaining colonists.

The JH-834 obediently presented itself and was sent to outlying areas on Chloe to pick up scattered settlers who did not appear to appreciate the urgency of the situation. Chloe, indeed, was enjoying the first temperatures above freezing since it had been flung out of its parent. Since many of the colonists were religious fanatics who had settled on rigorous Chloe to fit themselves for a life of pious reflection, Chloe's abrupt thaw was attributed to sources other than a rampaging sun.

Jennan had to spend so much time countering specious arguments that he and Helva were behind schedule on their way to the fourth and last settlement.

Helva jumped over the high range of jagged peaks that surrounded and sheltered the valley from the former raging snows as well as the present heat. The violent sun with its flaring corona was just beginning to brighten the deep valley as Helva dropped down to a landing.

"They'd better grab their toothbrushes and hop aboard," Helva said. "HQ says speed it up."

"All women," remarked Jennan in surprise as he walked down to meet them. "Unless the men on Chloe wear furred skirts."

"Charm 'em but pare the routine to the bare essentials. And turn on your two-way private."

Jennan advanced smiling, but his explanation of his mission was met with absolute incredulity and considerable doubt as to his authenticity. He groaned inwardly as the matriarch paraphrased previous explanations of the warming sun.

"Revered mother, there's been an overload on that prayer circuit and the sun is blowing itself up in one obliging burst. I'm here to take you to the spaceport at Rosary—"

"That Sodom?" The worthy woman glowered and shuddered disdainfully at his suggestion. "We thank you for your warning but we have no wish to leave our cloister for the rude world. We must go about our morning meditation which has been interrupted—"

"It'll be permanently interrupted when that sun starts broiling you. You must come now," Jennan said firmly.

"Madame," said Helva, realizing that perhaps a female voice might carry more weight in this instance than Jennan's very masculine charm.

"Who spoke?" cried the nun, startled by the bodiless voice.

"I, Helva, the ship. Under my protection you and your sisters-in-faith may enter safely and be unprofaned by association with a male. I will guard you and take you safely to a place prepared for you."

The matriarch peered cautiously into the ship's

open port. "Since only Central Worlds is permitted the use of such ships, I acknowledge that you are not trifling with us, young man. However, we are in no danger here."

"The temperature at Rosary is now 99 degrees," said Helva. "As soon as the sun's rays penetrate directly into this valley, it will also be 99 degrees, and it is due to climb to approximately 180 degrees today. I notice your buildings are made of wood with moss chinking. Dry moss. It should fire around noontime."

The sunlight was beginning to slant into the valley through the peaks, and the fierce rays warmed the restless group behind the matriarch. Several opened the throats of their furry parkas.

"Jennan," said Helva privately to him, "our time is very short."

"I can't leave them, Helva. Some of those girls are barely out of their teens."

"Pretty, too. No wonder the matriarch doesn't want to get in."

"Helva."

"It will be the Lord's will," said the matriarch stoutly and turned her back squarely on rescue.

"To burn to death?" shouted Jennan as she threaded her way through her murmuring disciples.

"They want to be martyrs? Their opt, Jennan," said Helva dispassionately, "We must leave and that is no longer a matter of option."

"How can I leave, Helva?"

"Parsaea?" Helva asked tauntingly as he stepped forward to grab one of the women. "You can't drag them *all* aboard and we don't have time to fight it out. Get on board, Jennan, or I'll have you on report."

"They'll die," muttered Jennan dejectedly as he reluctantly turned to climb on board.

"You can risk only so much," Helva said sympathetically. "As it is we'll just have time to make a rendezvous. Lab reports a critical speedup in spectral evolution."

Jennan was already in the airlock when one of the younger women, screaming, rushed to squeeze in the closing port. Her action set off the others. They stampeded through the narrow opening. Even crammed back to breast, there was not enough room inside for all the women. Jennan broke out spacesuits for the three who would have to remain with him in the airlock. He wasted valuable time explaining to the matriarch that she must put on the suit because the airlock had no independent oxygen or cooling units.

"We'll be caught," said Helva in a grim tone to Jennan on their private connection. "We've lost eighteen minutes in this last-minute rush. I am now overloaded for maximum speed and I must attain maximum speed to outrun the heat wave."

"Can you lift? We're suited."

"Lift? Yes," she said, doing so. "Run? I stagger."

Jennan, bracing himself and the women, could feel her sluggishness as she blasted upward. Heartlessly, Helva applied thrust as long as she could, despite the fact that the gravitational force mashed her cabin passengers brutally and crushed two fatally. It was a question of saving as many as possible. The only one for whom she had any concern was Jennan and she was in desperate terror about his safety. Airless and uncooled, protected by only one layer of metal, not three, the airlock was not going to be safe for the four trapped there, despite their spacesuits. These were only the standard models, not built to withstand the excessive heat to which the ship would be subjected.

Helva ran as fast as she could but the incredible

wave of heat from the explosive sun caught them halfway to cold safety.

She paid no heed to the cries, moans, pleas, and prayers in her cabin. She listened only to Jennan's tortured breathing, to the missing throb in his suit's purifying system and the sucking of the overloaded cooling unit. Helpless, she heard the hysterical screams of his three companions as they writhed in the awful heat. Vainly, Jennan tried to calm them, tried to explain they would soon be safe and cool if they could be still and endure the heat. Undisciplined by their terror and torment, they tried to strike out at him despite the close quarters. One flailing arm became entangled in the leads to his power pack and the damage was quickly done. A connection, weakened by heat and the dead weight of the arm, broke.

For all the power at her disposal, Helva was helpless. She watched as Jennan fought for his breath, as he turned his head beseechingly toward *her,* and died.

Only the iron conditioning of her training prevented Helva from swinging around and plunging back into the cleansing heart of the exploding sun. Numbly she made rendezvous with the refugee convoy. She obediently transferred her burned, heat-prostrated passengers to the assigned transport.

"I will retain the body of my scout and proceed to the nearest base for burial," she informed Central dully.

"You will be provided escort," was the reply.

"I have no need of escort."

"Escort is provided, XH-834," she was told curtly. The shock of hearing Jennan's initial severed from her call number cut off her half-formed protest. Stunned, she waited by the transport until her screens showed the arrival of two other slim brain ships. The cortege proceeded homeward at unfunereal speeds.

"834? The ship who sings?"

"I have no more songs."

"Your scout was Jennan."

"I do not wish to communicate."

"I'm 422."

"Silvia?"

"Silvia died a long time ago. I'm 422. Currently MS," the ship rejoined curtly. "AH-640 is our other friend, but Henry's not listening in. Just as well—he wouldn't understand it if you wanted to turn rogue. But I'd stop *him* if he tried to deter you."

"Rogue?" The term snapped Helva out of her apathy.

"Sure. You're young. You've got power for years. Skip. Others have done it. 732 went rogue twenty years ago after she lost her scout on a mission to that white dwarf. Hasn't been seen since."

"I never heard about rogues."

"As it's exactly the thing we're conditioned against, you sure wouldn't hear about it in school, my dear," 422 said.

"Break conditioning?" cried Helva, anguished, thinking longingly of the white, white furious hot heart of the sun she had just left.

"For you I don't think it would be hard at the moment," 422 said quietly, her voice devoid of her earlier cynicism. "The stars are out there, winking."

"Alone?" cried Helva from her heart.

"Alone!" 422 confirmed bleakly.

Alone with all of space and time. Even the Horsehead Nebula would not be far enough away to daunt her. Alone with a hundred years to live with her memories and nothing . . . nothing more.

"Was Parsaea worth it?" she asked 422 softly.

"Parsaea?" 422 repeated, surprised. "With his father? Yes. We were there, at Parsaea when we were needed. Just as you . . . and his son . . . were at Chloe. When you were needed. The crime is not knowing where need is and not being there."

"But *I* need *him*. Who will supply my need?" said Helva bitterly . . .

"834," said 422 after a day's silent speeding, "Central wishes your report. A replacement awaits your opt at Regulus Base. Change course accordingly."

"A replacement?" That was certainly not what she needed . . . a reminder inadequately filling the void Jennan left. Why, her hull was barely cool of Chloe's heat. Atavistically, Helva wanted time to morn Jennan.

"Oh, none of them are impossible if *you're* a good ship," 422 remarked philosophically. "And it is just what you need. The sooner the better."

"You told them I wouldn't go rogue, didn't you?" Helva said.

"The moment passed you even as it passed me after Parsaea, and before that, after Glen Arthur, and Betelgeuse."

"We're conditioned to go on, aren't we? We *can't* go rogue. You were testing."

"Had to. Orders. Not even Psych knows why a rogue occurs. Central's very worried, and so, daughter, are your sister ships. I asked to be your escort. I . . . don't want to lose you both."

In her emotional nadir, Helva could feel a flood of gratitude for Silvia's rough sympathy.

"We've all known this grief, Helva. It's no consolation, but if we couldn't feel with our scouts, we'd only be machines wired for sound."

Helva looked at Jennan's still form stretched before her in its shroud and heard the echo of his rich voice in the quiet cabin.

"Silvia! I *couldn't* help him," she cried from her soul.

"Yes, dear, I know," 422 murmured gently and then was quiet.

The three ships sped on, wordless, to the great Central Worlds base at Regulus. Helva broke silence to acknowledge landing instructions and the officially tendered regrets.

The three ships set down simultaneously at the wooded edge where Regulus' gigantic blue trees stood sentinel over the sleeping dead in the small Service cemetery. The entire Base complement approached with measured step and formed an aisle from Helva to the burial ground. The honor detail, out of step, walked slowly into her cabin. Reverently they placed the body of her dead love on the wheeled bier, covered it honorably with the deep-blue, star-splashed flag of the Service. She watched as it was driven slowly down the living aisle which closed in behind the bier in last escort.

Then, as the simple words of interment were spoken, as the atmosphere planes dipped in tribute over the open grave, Helva found voice for her lonely farewell.

Softly, barely audible at first, the strains of the ancient song of evening and requiem swelled to the final poignant measure until black space itself echoed back the sound of the song the ship sang.

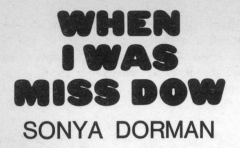

WHEN I WAS MISS DOW

SONYA DORMAN

Sonya Dorman grew up and was educated in New England. Her prose and poetry have appeared in **Cavalier, Galaxy, The Saturday Evening Post, The Magazine of Fantasy & Science Fiction, Redbook** and **Orbit.** She raises and shows Akita dogs and has been a receptionist, a flamenco dancer and a riding instructor.

Science fiction writers have often written of how humans might look to aliens. Such stories not only give us imaginative glimpses of beings and societies unlike our own, but also give us a different perspective on our own species. In "When I was Miss Dow," we see humanity from the viewpoint of an alien who has become a woman; this being's transformation mirrors our own experience of a role most women have had to play.

These hungry, mother-haunted people come and find us living in what they like to call crystal palaces, though really we live in glass places, some of them highly ornamented and others plain as paper. They come first as explorers, and perhaps realize we are a race of one sex only, rather amorphous beings of proteide; and we, even baby I, are Protean also, being able to take various shapes at will. One sex, one brain lobe, we live in more or less glass bridges over the humanoid chasm, eating, recreating, attending races and playing other games like most living creatures.

Eventually, we're all dumped into the cell banks and reproduced once more.

After the explorers comes the colony of miners and scientists; the Warden and some of the other elders put on faces to greet them, agreeing to help with the mining of some ores, even giving them a koota or two as they become interested in our racing dogs. They set up their places of life, pop up their machines, bang-bang, chug-chug; we put on our faces, forms, smiles and costumes. I am old enough to learn to change my shape too.

The Warden says to me, "It's about time you made a change, yourself. Some of your friends are already working for these people, bringing home credits and sulfas."

My Uncle (by the Warden's fourth conjunction) made himself over at the start, being one of the first to realize how it could profit us.

I protest to the Warden, "I'm educated and trained as a scholar. You always say I must remain deep in my mathematics and other studies."

My Uncle says, "You have to do it. There's only one way for us to get along with them," and he runs his fingers through his long blond hair. My Uncle's not an educated person, but highly placed politically, and while Captain Dow is around, my Uncle retains this particular shape. The captain is shipping out soon, then Uncle will find some other features, because he's already warned it's unseemly for him to be chasing around in the face of a girl after the half-bearded boys from the spaceships. I don't want to do this myself, wasting so much time, when the fourteen decimals even now are clicking on my mirrors.

The Warden says, "We have a pattern from a female botanist, she ought to do for you. But before we put you into the pattern tank, you'll have to approximate another brain lobe. They have two."

"I know," I say sulkily. A botanist. A she.

"Into the tank," the Warden says to me without mercy, and I am his to use as he believes proper.

I spend four days in the tank absorbing the female Terran pattern. When I'm released, the Warden tells me, "Your job is waiting for you. We went to a lot of trouble to arrange it." He sounds brusque, but perhaps this is because he hasn't conjoined for a long time. The responsibilities of being Warden of Mines and Seeds come first, long before any social engagement.

I run my fingers through my brunette curls and notice my Uncle is looking critically at me. "Haven't you made yourself rather old?" he asks.

"Oh, he's all right," the Warden says. "Thirty-three isn't badly matched to the Doctor, as I understand it."

Dr. Arnold Proctor, the colony's head biologist, is busy making radiograph pictures (with his primitive x-rays) of skeletal structures: murger birds, rodents, and our pets and racers, the kootas. Dogs, to the Terrans, who are fascinated by them. We breed them primarily for speed and stamina, but some of them carry a gene for an inherited structural defect which cripples them, and they have to be destroyed before they are full grown. The Doctor is making a special study of kootas.

He gets up from his chair when I enter the office. "I'm Miss Dow, your new assistant," I say, hoping my long fingernails will stand up to the pressure of punchkeys on the computer, since I haven't had much practice in retaining foreign shapes. I'm still in uncertain balance between myself and Martha Dow, who is also myself. But one does not have two lobes for nothing, I discover.

"Good morning. I'm glad you're here," the Doctor says.

He is a nice, pink man with silver hair, soft-spoken, intelligent. I'm pleased, as we work along, to find he doesn't joke and wisecrack like so many of the Terrans, though I am sometimes whimsical, I like music and banquets as well as my studies.

Though absorbed in his work, Dr. Proctor isn't rude to interrupters. A man of unusual balance, coming as he does from a culture which sends out scientific parties that are 90 percent of one sex, when their species provides them with two. At first meeting he is dedicated but agreeable, and I'm charmed.

"Dr. Proctor," I ask him one morning, "is it possible for you to radiograph my koota? She's very fine, from the fastest stock available, and I'd like to breed her."

"Yes, yes, of course," he promises with his quick, often absent smile. "By all means. You wish to breed only the best." It's typical of him to assume we're all as dedicated as he.

My Uncle's not pleased. "There's nothing wrong with your koota," he says. "What do you want to x-ray her for? Suppose he finds something is wrong? You'll be afraid to race or breed her, and she won't be replaced. Besides, your interest in her may make him suspicious."

"Suspicious of what?" I ask, but my Uncle won't say, so I ask him, "Suppose she's bred and her pups are cripples?"

The Warden says, "You're supposed to have your mind on your work, not on racing. The koota was just to amuse you when you were younger."

I lean down and stroke her head, which is beautiful, and she breathes a deep and gentle breath in response.

"Oh, let him go," my Uncle says wearily. He's getting disgusted because they didn't intend for me to bury myself in a laboratory or a computer room without making more important contacts. But a scholar is born with a certain temperament and has an introspective nature, and as I'm destined eventually to replace the Warden, naturally I prefer the life of the mind.

"I must say," my Uncle remarks, "you look the image of a Terran female. Is the work interesting?"

"Oh, yes, fascinating," I reply, and he snorts at my lie, since we both know it's dull and routine, and most of my time is spent working out the connections between my two brain lobes, which still present me with some difficulty.

My koota bitch is subjected to a pelvic radiograph. Afterward, I stand on my heels in the small, darkened cubicle, looking at the film on the viewing screen. There he stands too, with his cheekbones emerald in the peculiar light, and his hair, which is silver in daylight, looks phosphorescent. I resist this. I am resisting this Doctor with the x-ray eyes who can examine my marrow with ease. He sees Martha's marrow, every perfect corpuscle of it.

You can't imagine how comforting it is to be so transparent. There's no need to pretend, adjust, advance, retreat or discuss the oddities of my planet. We are looking at the x-ray film of my prized racer and companion to determine the soundness of her hip joints, yet I suspect the doctor, platinum-green and tall as a tower, is piercing my reality with his educated gaze. He can see the blood flushing my surfaces. I don't need to do a thing but stand up straight so the crease of fat at my waist won't distort my belly button, the center of it all.

"You see?" he says. I do see, looking at the film in this darkness where perfection or disaster may be viewed, and I'm twined in the paradox which confronts me here. The darker the room, the brighter the screen and the clearer the picture. Less light! and the truth becomes more evident. Either the koota is properly jointed and may be bred without danger of passing the gene on to her young, or she is not properly jointed, and cannot be used. Less light, more truth! And the Doctor is green sculpture—a little darker and he would be a bronze—but his natural color is pink alabaster.

"You see," the Doctor says, and I do try to see. He points his wax pencil at one hip joint on the film, and says, "A certain amount of osteoarthritic build-up is already evident. The cranial rim is wearing down, she may go lame. She'll certainly pass the defect on to some of her pups, if she's bred."

This koota has been my playmate and friend for a long time. She retains a single form, that of koota, full of love and beautiful speed; she has been a source of pleasure and pride.

Dr. Proctor, of the pewter hair, will discuss the anatomical defects of the koota in a gentle and cultivated voice. I am disturbed. There shouldn't be any need to explain the truth, which is evident. Yet it seems that to comprehend the exposures, I require a special education. It's said that the more you have seen, the quicker you are to sort the eternal verities into one pile and the dismal illusions into another. How is it that sometimes the Doctor wears a head which resembles that of a koota, with a splendid muzzle and noble brow?

Suddenly, he gives a little laugh and points the end of the wax pencil at my navel, announcing, "There. There, it is essential that the belly button onto the pelvis, or you'll bear no children." Thoughts of off-spring had occurred to me. But weren't we discussing my racer? The radiograph film is still clipped to the view screen, and upon it, spread-eagled, appears the bony Rorschach of my koota bitch, her hip joints expressing doom.

I wish the Doctor would put on the daylight. I come to the conclusion that there's a limit to how much truth I can examine, and the more I submit to the conditions necessary for examining it, the more unhappy I become.

Dr. Proctor is a man of such perfect integrity that he continues to talk about bones and muscles until I'm ready to scream for mercy. He has done something unusual and probably prohibited, but he's not aware of it. I mean it must be prohibited in his culture, where it seems they play on each other, but not with each other. I'm uneasy, fluctuating.

He snaps two switches. Out goes the film and on goes the sun, making my eyes stream with grateful tears, although he's so adjusted to these contrasts he doesn't so much as blink. Floating in the sunshine, I've become opaque; he can't see anything but my surface tensions, and I wonder what he does in his spare time. A part of me seems to tilt, or slide.

"There, there, oh dear, Miss Dow," he says, patting my back, rubbing my shoulder blades. His forearms and fingers extend gingerly. "You do want to breed only the best, don't you?" he asks. I begin within me a compulsive ritual of counting the elements; it's all I can do to keep communications open between my brain lobes. I'm suffering from eclipses; one goes dark, the other lights up like a new saloon, that one goes dark, the other goes nova.

"There, there," the Doctor says, distressed because I'm quivering and trying to keep the connections open; I have never felt clogged before. They may have to put me back into the pattern tank.

Profoundly disturbed, I lift my face, and he gives me a kiss. Then I'm all right, balanced again, one lobe composing a concerto for virtix flute, the other one projecting, "Oh Arnie, oh Arnie." Yes, I'm okay for the shape I'm in. He's marking off my joints with his wax pencil (the marks of which can be easily erased from the film surface) and he's mumbling, "It's essential, oh yes, it's essential."

Finally, he says, "I guess all of us colonists are lonely here," and I say, "Oh yes, aren't we," before I realize the enormity of the Warden's manipulations, and what a lot I have to learn. Evidently the Warden triple-carded me through the Colony Punch Center as a Terran. I lie and say, "Oh yes, yes. Oh Arnie, put out the light," for we may find some more truth.

"Not here," Arnie says, and of course he's right, this is a room for study, for cataloging obvious facts, not a place for carnival. There are not many places for it, I discover with surprise. Having lived in glass all my life, I expect everyone else to be as comfortable there as I am. But this isn't so.

Just the same we find his quarters, after dark, to be comfortable and free of embarrassment. You wouldn't think a dedicated man of his age would be so vigorous, but I find out he spends his weekends at the recreation center hitting a ball with his hand. The ball bounces back off a wall and he hits it and hits it.

Though he's given that up now because we're together on weekends.

"You're more than an old bachelor like me deserves," he tells me.

"Why are you an old bachelor?" I ask him. I do wonder why, if it's something not to be.

He tries to explain it to me. "I'm not a young man. I wouldn't make a good husband, I'm afraid. I like to work late, to be undisturbed. In my leisure time, I like to make wood carvings. Sometimes I go to bed with the sun and sometimes I'm up working all night. And then children. No. I'm lucky to be an old bachelor," he says.

Arnie carves kaku wood, which has a brilliant grain and is soft enough to permit easy carving. He's working on a figure of a murger bird, whittling lengthwise down the wood so the grain, wavy, full of flowing, wedge-shaped lines, will represent the feathers. The lamplight shines on his hair and the crinkle of his eyelids as he looks down, and carves, whittles, turns. He's absorbed in what he doesn't see there, but he's projecting what he wants to see. It's the reverse of what he must do in the viewing room. I begin to suffer a peculiar pain, located in the nerve cluster between my lungs. He's not talking to me. He's not caressing me. He's forgotten I'm here, and like a false projection, I'm beginning to fade. In another hour perhaps the film will become blank. If he doesn't see me, then am I here?

He's doing just what I do when busy with one of my own projects, and I admire the intensity with which he works: it's magnificent. Yes, I'm jealous of it, I burn with rage and jealousy, he has abandoned me to be Martha and I wish I were myself again, free in shape and single in mind. Not this sack of mud clinging to another. Yet he's teaching me that it's good to cling to another. I'm exhausted from strange disciplines. Perhaps he's tired too; I see that sometimes he kneads the muscles of his stomach with his hands, and closes his eyes.

The Warden sits me down on one of my rare evenings home, and talks angrily. "You're making a mistake," he says. "If the Doctor finds out what you are, you'll lose your job with the Colony. Besides, we never supposed you'd have a liaison with only one man. You were supposed to start with the Doctor, and go on from there. We need every credit you can bring in. And by the way, you haven't done well on that score lately. Is he stingy?"

"Of course he isn't."

"But all you bring home in credits is your pay."

I can think of no reply. It's true the Warden has a right to use me in whatever capacity will serve us all best, as I will use others when I'm a Warden, but he and my Uncle spend half the credits from my job on sulfadiazole, to which they've become addicted.

"You've no sense of responsibility," the Warden says. Perhaps he's coming close to time for conjunction again, and this makes him more concerned about my stability.

My Uncle says, "Oh, he's young, leave him alone. As long as he turns over most of those pay credits to us. Though what he uses the remainder for, I'll never know."

I use it for clothes at the Colony Exchange. Sometimes Arnie takes me out for an evening, usually to the Laugh Tree Bar, where the space crews, too, like to relax. The bar is the place to find joy babies; young, pretty, planet-born girls who work at the Colony Punch Center during the day and spend their evenings here competing for the attention of the officers. Sitting here with Arnie, I can't distinguish a colonist's daughter from one of my friends or relatives. They wouldn't know me, either.

Once, at home, I try to talk with a few of these friends about my feelings. But I discover that whatever female patterns they've borrowed are superficial ones; none of them bother to grow an extra lobe, but merely tuck the Terran pattern into a corner of their own for handy reference. They are most of them on sulfas. Hard and shiny toys, they skip like pebbles over the surface of the colonists' lives.

Then they go home, revert to their own free forms, and enjoy their mathematics, colors, compositions and seedings.

"Why me?" I demand of the Warden. "Why two lobes? Why me?"

"We felt you'd be more efficient," he answers. "And while you're here, which you seldom are these days, you'd better revert to other shapes. Your particles may be damaged if you hold that female form too long."

Oh, but you don't know, I want to tell him. You don't know I'll hold it forever. If I'm damaged or dead, you'll put me into the cell banks, and you'll be amazed, astonished, terrified, to discover that I come out complete, all Martha. I can't be changed.

"You little lump of protagon," my Uncle mumbles bitterly. "You'll never amount to anything, you'll never be a Warden. Have you done any of your own work recently?"

I say, "Yes, I've done some crystal divisions, and regrown them in nonestablished patterns." My Uncle's

in a bad mood, as he's kicking sulfa and his nerve
tissue is addled. I'm wise to speak quietly to him, but
he still grumbles.

"I can't understand why you like being a two-lobed
pack of giggles. I couldn't wait to get out of it. And
you were so dead against it to begin with."

"Well, I have learned," I start to say, but can't
explain what it is I'm still learning, and close my eyes.
Part of it is that on the line between the darkness and
the brightness it's easiest to float. I've never wanted to
practice only easy things. My balance is damaged. I
never had to balance. It's not a term or concept I
understand even now, at home, in free form. Some
impress of Martha's pattern lies on my own brain cells.
I suspect it's permanent damage, which gives me joy.
That's what I mean about not understanding it; I am
taught to strive for perfection, how can I be pleased
with this, which may be a catastrophe?

Arnie carves on a breadth of kaku wood, bringing
out to the surface a seascape. Knots become clots of
spray, a flaw becomes wind-blown spume. I want to
be Martha. I'd like to go to the Laugh Tree with
Arnie, for a good time, I'd like to learn to play cards
with him.

You see what happens: Arnie is, in his way, like my
original self, and I hate that part of him, since I've
given it up to be Martha. Martha makes him happy,
she is chocolate to his appetite, pillow for his
weariness.

I turn for company to my koota. She's the color of
morning, her chest juts out like an axe blade, her ribs
spring up and back like wings, her eyes are large and
clear as she returns my gaze. Yet she's beyond hope; in
a little time, she'll be lame; she can't race any more,
she must not mother a litter. I turn to her and she

gazes back into my eyes, dreaming of speed and wind on the sandy beaches where she has run.

"Why don't you read some tapes?" Arnie suggests to me, because I'm restless and I disturb him. The koota lies at my feet. I read tapes. Every evening in his quarters Arnie carves, I read tapes, the broken racer lies at my feet. I pass through Terran history this way. When the clown tumbles into the tub, I laugh. Terran history is full of clowns and tubs; at first it seems that's all there is, but you learn to see beneath the comic costumes.

While I float on that taut line, the horizon between light and dark, where it's so easy, I begin to sense what is under the costumes: staggering down the street dead drunk on a sunny afternoon with everyone laughing at you; hiding under the veranda because you made blood come out of Pa's face; kicking a man when he's in the gutter because you've been kicked and have to pass it on. Terrans have something called tragedy. It's what one of them called being a poet in the body of a cockroach.

"Have you heard the rumor?" Arnie asks, putting down the whittling tool. "Have you heard that some of the personnel in Punch Center aren't really humans?"

"Not really?" I ask, putting away the tape. We have no tragedy. In my species, family relationships are based only on related gene patterns; they are finally dumped into the family bank and a new relative is created from the old. It's one form of ancient history multiplying itself, but it isn't tragic. The koota, her utility destroyed by a recessive gene, lies sleeping at my feet. Is this tragedy? But she is a single form, she can't regenerate a lost limb, or exfoliate brain tissue. She can only return my gaze with her steadfast and affectionate one.

"What are they, then?" I ask Arnie. "If they're not human?"

"The story is that the local life forms aren't as we really see them. They've put on faces, like ours, to deal with us. And some of them have filtered into personnel."

Filtered! As if I were a virus.

I say, "But they must be harmless. No harm has come to anyone."

"We don't know that for a fact," Arnie replies.

"You look tired," I say, and he comes to me to be soothed, to be loved in his flesh, his single form, his search for the truth in the darkness of the viewing cubicle. At present he's doing studies of murger birds. Their spinal cavities are large, air-filled ovals, and their bone is extremely porous, which permits them to soar to great heights.

The koota no longer races on the windblown beaches; she lies at our feet, looking into the distance. The wall must be transparent to her eyes, I feel that beyond it she sees clearly how the racers go, down the long, bright curve of sand in the morning sun. She sighs, and lays her head down on her narrow, delicate paws.

Arnie says, "I seem to be tired all the time," and kneads the muscles of his chest. He puts his head down on my breasts. "I don't think the food's agreeing with me lately."

"Do you suffer pains?" I ask curiously.

"Suffer," he says, "what kind of nonsense is that, with analgesics. No. I don't suffer. I just don't feel well."

He's absorbed in murger birds, kaku wood, he descends into the darks and rises up like a rocket across the horizon into the thin clarity above. While I float. I no longer dare to breathe, I'm afraid of disturbing everything. I do not want anything. His head lies on my breast and I will not disturb him.

"Oh. My God," Arnie says, and I know what it's come to, even before he begins to choke, and his muscles leap although I hold him in my arms. I know his heart is choking on massive doses of blood; the brilliance fades from his eyes and they begin to go dark while I tightly hold him. If he doesn't see me as he dies, will I be here?

I can feel, under my fingers, how rapidly his skin cools. I must put him down, here with his carvings and his papers, and I must go home. But I lift Arnie in my arms, and call the koota, who gets up rather stiffly. It's long after dark, and I carry him slowly, carefully, home to what he called a crystal palace, where the Warden and my Uncle are teaching each other to play chess with a set some space captain gave them in exchange for seed crystals. They sit in a bloom of light, sparkling, their old brains bent over the chessmen, as I breathe open the door and carry Arnie in.

First, my Uncle gives me just a glance, but then another glance, and a hard stare. "Is that the Doctor?" he asks.

I put Arnie down and hold one of his cold hands. "Warden," I say, on my knees, on eye level with the chess board and its carved men. "Warden, can you put him in one of the banks?"

The Warden turns to look at me, as hard as my Uncle. "You've become deranged, trying to maintain two lobes," he says. "You cannot reconstitute or recreate a Terran by our methods, and you must know it."

"Over the edge, over the edge," my Uncle says, now a blond, six-foot, hearty male Terran, often at the

Laugh Tree with one of the joy babies. He enjoys life, his own or someone else's. I have too, I suppose. Am I fading? I am, really, just one of Arnie's projections, a form on a screen in his mind. I am not, really, Martha. Though I tried.

"We can't have him here," the Warden says. "You'd better get him out of here. You couldn't explain a corpse like that to the colonists, if they came looking for him. They'll think we did something to him. It's nearly time for my next conjunction, do you want your nephew to arrive in disgrace? The Uncles will drain his bank."

The Warden gets up and comes over to me. He takes hold of my dark curls and pulls me to my feet. It hurts my physical me, which is Martha, God knows, Arnie, I'm Martha, it seems to me. "Take him back to his quarters," the Warden says to me. "And come back here immediately. I'll try to see you back to your own pattern, but it may be too late. In part, I blame myself. If you must know. So I will try."

Yes, yes, I want to say to him; as I was, dedicated, free; turn me back into myself, I never wanted to be anyone else, and now I don't know if I am anyone at all. The light's gone from his eyes and he doesn't see me.

I pick him up and breathe the door out, and go back through the night to his quarters, where the lamp still burns. I'm going to leave him here, where he belongs. Before I go, I pick up the small carving of the murger bird and take it with me, home to my glass bridge where at the edge of the mirrors the decimals are still clicking perfectly, clicking out known facts; an octagon can be reduced, the planet turns at such a degree on its axis, to see the truth you must have light of some sort, but to see the light you must have darkness of some sort. I can no longer float on the horizon between the two because that horizon has disappeared. I've learned to descend, and to rise, and descend again.

I'm able to revert without help to my own free form, to reabsorb the extra brain tissue. The sun comes up and it's bright. The night comes down and it's dark. I'm becoming somber, and a brilliant student. Even my Uncle says I'll be a good Warden, when the time comes.

The Warden goes to conjunction; from the cell banks a nephew is lifted out. The koota lies dreaming of races she has run in the wind. It is our life, and it goes on, like the life of other creatures.

THE FOOD FARM

KIT REED

Kit Reed was born in California and educated at the College of Notre Dame of Maryland. She has worked as a reporter and television editor and was New England Newspaperwoman of the Year in both 1954 and 1958. Her stories have appeared in **Cosmopolitan, Redbook, Transatlantic Review, Ladies' Home Journal** and **The Magazine of Fantasy & Science Fiction,** as well as in the anthologies **Orbit** and **Bad Moon Rising.** Her novels include **Armed Camps, Cry of the Daughter** and **Tiger Rag** (all published by Dutton), and a short-story collection, **Mister Da V. and Other Stories** (Berkley Books), was published in 1973. She was awarded a Guggenheim Fellowship in 1964 and was the first American recipient of a five-year literary grant from the Abraham Woursell Foundation. She was a Visiting Professor of English at Wesleyan University in the spring of 1974.

"The Food Farm" contains some familiar images of adolescence: the overweight girl, shielding herself from others under a protective layer of fat; the distressed and puzzled parents; the popular and worshiped male singer; the institution that houses those who do not meet their parents', and society's, expectations. These elements are skillfully woven together in an imaginative fantasy that reflects pieces of our own early lives and feelings.

So here I am, warden-in-charge, fattening them up for our leader, Tommy Fango; here I am laying on the banana pudding and the milkshakes and the cream-and-brandy cocktails, going about like a technician, gauging their effect on haunch and thigh when all the time it is I who love him, I who could have pleased him eternally if only life had broken differently. But I am scrawny now, I am swept like a leaf around corners, battered by the slightest wind. My elbows rattle against my ribs and I have to spend half the day in bed so a gram or two of what I eat will stay with me, for if I do not, the fats and creams will vanish, burned up in my own insatiable furnace, and what little flesh I have will melt away.

Cruel as it may sound, I know where to place the blame.

It was vanity, all vanity, and I hate them most for that. It was not my vanity, for I have always been a simple soul; I reconciled myself early to reenforced chairs and loose garments, to the spattering of remarks. Instead of heeding them I plugged in, and I would have been happy to let it go at that, going through life with my radio in my bodice, for while I never drew cries of admiration, no one ever blanched and turned away.

But they were vain and in their vanity my frail father, my pale, scrawny mother saw me not as an entity but as a reflection on themselves. I flush with shame to remember the excuses they made for me. "She takes after May's side of the family," my father would say, denying any responsibility. "It's only baby fat," my mother would say, jabbing her elbow into my soft flank. "Nelly is big for her age." Then she would jerk furiously, pulling my voluminous smock down to cover my knees. That was when they still consented to be seen with me. In that period they would stuff me with pies and roasts before we went anywhere, filling me up so I would not gorge myself in public. Even so I had to take thirds, fourths, fifths and so I was a humiliation to them.

In time I was too much for them and they stopped taking me out; they made no more attempts to explain. Instead they tried to think of ways to make me look better; the doctors tried the fool's poor battery of pills; they tried to make me join a club. For a while my mother and I did exercises; we would sit on the floor, she in a black leotard, I in my smock. Then she would do the brisk one-two, one-two and I would make a few passes at my toes. But I had to listen, I had to plug in, and after I was plugged in, naturally I had to find something to eat; Tommy might sing and I always ate when Tommy sang, and so I would leave her there on the floor, still going one-two, one-two. For a while after that they tried locking up the food. Then they began to cut into my meals.

That was the cruelest time. They would refuse me bread, they would plead and cry, plying me with lettuce and telling me it was all for my own good. My own good. Couldn't they hear my vitals crying out? I fought, I screamed, and when that failed I suffered in silent obedience until finally hunger drove me into the streets. I would lie in bed, made brave by the Monets and Barry Arkin and the Philadons coming in over the radio, and Tommy (there was never enough; I heard him a hundred times a day and it was never enough; how bitter that seems now!). I would hear them and then when my parents were asleep I would unplug and go out into the neighborhood. The first few nights I begged, throwing myself on the mercy of passers-by and then plunging into the bakery, bringing home everything I didn't eat right there in the shop. I got money quickly enough; I didn't even have to ask. Per-

haps it was my bulk, perhaps it was my desperate
subverbal cry of hunger; I found I had only to ap-
proach and the money was mine. As soon as they saw
me, people would whirl and bolt, hurling a purse or
wallet into my path as if to slow me in my pursuit;
they would be gone before I could even express my
thanks. Once I was shot at. Once a stone lodged itself
in my flesh.

At home my parents continued with their tears and
pleas. They persisted with their skim milk and their
chops, ignorant of the life I lived by night. In the
daytime I was complaisant, dozing between snacks,
feeding on the sounds which played in my ear, coming
from the radio concealed in my dress. Then, when
night fell, I unplugged; it gave a certain edge to
things, knowing I would not plug in again until I was
ready to eat. Some nights this only meant going to one
of the caches in my room, bringing forth bottles and
cartons and cans. On other nights I had to go into the
streets, finding money where I could. Then I would
lay in a new supply of cakes and rolls and baloney
from the delicatessen and several cans of ready-made
frosting and perhaps a flitch of bacon or some ham; I
would toss in a basket of oranges to ward off scurvy
and a carton of candy bars for quick energy. Once I
had enough I would go back to my room, concealing
food here and there, rearranging my nest of pillows
and comforters. I would open the first pie or the first
half-gallon of ice cream and then, as I began, I would
plug in.

You had to plug in; everybody that mattered was
plugged in. It was our bond, our solace and our
power, and it wasn't a matter of being distracted, or
occupying time. The sound was what mattered, that
and the fact that fat or thin, asleep or awake, you

were important when you plugged in, and you knew that through fire and flood and adversity, through contumely and hard times there was this single bond, this common heritage; strong or weak, eternally gifted or wretched and ill-loved, we were all plugged in.

Tommy, beautiful Tommy Fango, the others paled to nothing next to him. Everybody heard him in those days; they played him two or three times an hour, but you never knew when it would be, so you were plugged in and listening hard every living moment; you ate, you slept, you drew breath for the moment when they would put on one of Tommy's records, you waited for his voice to fill the room. Cold cuts and cupcakes and game hens came and went during that period in my life, but one thing was constant: I always had a cream pie thawing and when they played the first bars of "When a Widow" and Tommy's voice first flexed and uncurled, I was ready, I would eat the cream pie during Tommy's midnight show. The whole world waited in those days; we waited through endless sunlight, through nights of drumbeats and monotony, we all waited for Tommy Fango's records, and we waited for that whole unbroken hour of Tommy, his midnight show. He came on live at midnight in those days; he sang, broadcasting from the Hotel Riverside, and that was beautiful, but more important, he talked, and while he was talking he made everything all right. Nobody was lonely when Tommy talked; he brought us all together on that midnight show, he talked and made us powerful, he talked and finally he sang. You have to imagine what it was like, me in the night, Tommy, the pie. In a while I would go to a place where I had to live on Tommy and only Tommy, to a time when hearing Tommy would bring back the pie, all the poor lost pies . . .

Tommy's records, his show, the pie . . . that was perhaps the happiest period of my life. I would sit and listen and I would eat and eat and eat. So great was my bliss that it became torture to put away the food at daybreak; it grew harder and harder for me to hide the cartons and the cans and the bottles, all the residue of my happiness. Perhaps a bit of bacon fell into the register; perhaps an egg rolled under the bed and began to smell. All right, perhaps I did become careless, continuing my revels into the morning, or I may have been thoughtless enough to leave a jelly roll unfinished on the rug. I became aware that they were watching, lurking just outside my door, plotting as I ate. In time they broke in on me, weeping and plead-ing, lamenting over every ice cream carton and crumb of pie; then they threatened. Finally they restored the food they had taken from me in the daytime, thinking to curtail my eating at night. Folly. By that time I needed it all, I shut myself in with it and would not listen. I ignored their cries of hurt pride, their out-pourings of wounded vanity, their puny little threats. Even if I had listened, I could not have forestalled what happened next.

I was so happy that last day. There was a Smithfield ham, mine, and I remember a jar of cherry preserves, mine, and I remember bacon, pale and white on Italian bread. I remember sounds downstairs and before I could take warning, an assault, a company of uniformed attendants, the sting of a hypodermic gun. Then the ten of them closed in and grappled me into a sling, or net, and heaving and straining, they bore me down the stairs. I'll never forgive you, I cried, as they bundled me into the ambulance. I'll never forgive you, I bellowed, as my mother in a last betrayal took away my radio, and I cried out one last time, as my father removed a hambone from my breast: I'll never forgive you. And I never have.

It is painful to describe what happened next. I remember three days of horror and agony, of being too weak, finally, to cry out or claw the walls. Then at last I was quiet and they moved me into a sunny, pastel, chintz-bedizened room. I remember that there were flowers on the dresser and someone watching me.

"What are you in for?" she said.

I could barely speak for weakness. "Despair."

"Hell with that," she said, chewing. "You're in for food."

"What are you eating?" I tried to raise my head.

"Chewing. Inside of the mouth. It helps."

"I'm going to die."

"Everybody thinks that at first. I did." She tilted her head in an attitude of grace. "You know, this is a very exclusive school."

Her name was Ramona, and as I wept silently, she filled me in. This was a last resort for the few who could afford to send their children here. They prettied it up with a schedule of therapy, exercise, massage; we would wear dainty pink smocks and talk of art and theater; from time to time we would attend classes in elocution and hygiene. Our parents would say with pride that we were away at Faircrest, an elegant finishing school; we knew better—it was a prison and we were being starved.

"It's a world I never made," said Ramona, and I knew that her parents were to blame, even as mine were. Her mother liked to take the children into hotels and casinos, wearing her thin daughters like a garland of jewels. Her father followed the sun on his private yacht, with the pennants flying and his children on the fantail, lithe and tanned. He would pat his flat, tanned belly and look at Ramona in disgust. When it was no longer possible to hide her, he gave in to blind pride. One night they came in a launch and took her away. She had been here six months now, and had lost almost a hundred pounds. She must have been monumental in her prime; she was still huge.

"We live from day to day," she said. "But you don't know the worst."

"My radio," I said in a spasm of fear. "They took away my radio."

"There is a reason," she said. "They call it therapy."

I was mumbling in my throat, in a minute I would scream.

"Wait." With ceremony, she pushed aside a picture and touched a tiny switch and then, like sweet balm for my panic, Tommy's voice flowed into the room.

When I was quiet she said, "You only hear him once a day."

"No."

"But you can hear him any time you want to. You hear him when you need him most."

But we were missing the first few bars and so we shut up and listened, and after "When a Widow" was over we sat quietly for a moment, her resigned, me weeping, and then Ramona threw another switch and the Sound filtered into the room, and it was almost like being plugged in.

"Try not to think about it."

"I'll die."

"If you think about it you *will* die. You have to learn to use it instead. In a minute they will come with lunch," Ramona said and as The Screamers sang sweet background, she went on in a monotone: "A chop. One lousy chop with a piece of lettuce and maybe some gluten bread. I pretend it's a leg of lamb, that works if you eat very, very slowly and think about Tommy the whole time; then if you look at your picture of Tommy you can turn the lettuce into anything you want, Caesar salad or a whole smorgasbord, and if you say his name over and over you can pretend a whole bombe or torte if you want to and . . ."

"I'm going to pretend a ham and kidney pie and a watermelon filled with chopped fruits and Tommy and I are in the Rainbow Room and we're going to finish up with Fudge Royale . . ." I almost drowned in my own saliva; in the background I could almost hear Tommy, and I could hear Ramona saying, "Capon, Tommy would like capon, canard à l'orange, Napoleons, tomorrow we will save Tommy for lunch and listen while we eat . . ." and I thought about that, I thought about listening and imagining whole cream pies and I went on, ". . . lemon pie, rice pudding, a whole Edam cheese . . . I think I'm going to live."

The matron came in the next morning at breakfast, and stood as she would every day, tapping red fingernails on one svelte hip, looking on in revulsion as we fell on the glass of orange juice and the hard-boiled egg. I was too weak to control myself; I heard a shrill sniveling sound and realized only from her expression that it was my own voice: "Please, just some bread, a stick of butter, anything, I could lick the dishes if you'd let me, only please don't leave me like this, please . . ." I can still see her sneer as she turned her back.

I felt Ramona's loyal hand on my shoulder. "There's always toothpaste, but don't use too much at once or they'll come and take it away from you."

I was too weak to rise and so she brought it and we shared the tube and talked about all the banquets we had ever known, and when we got tired of that, we talked about Tommy, and when that failed, Ramona went to the switch and we heard "When a Widow," and that helped for a while, and then we decided that tomorrow we would put off "When a Widow" until bedtime because then we would have something to look forward to all day. Then lunch came and we both wept.

It was not just hunger: after a while the stomach begins to devour itself and the few grams you toss it at mealtimes assuage it, so that in time the appetite itself begins to fail. After hunger comes depression. I lay there, still too weak to get about, and in my misery I realized that they could bring me roast pork and watermelon and Boston cream pie without ceasing; they could gratify all my dreams and I would only weep helplessly, because I no longer had the strength to eat. Even then, when I thought I had reached rock bottom, I had not comprehended the worst. I noticed it first in Ramona. Watching her at the mirror, I said, in fear, "You're thinner."

She turned with tears in her eyes. "Nelly, I'm not the only one."

I looked around at my own arms and saw that she was right: there was one less fold of flesh above the elbow; there was one less wrinkle at the wrist. I turned my face to the wall and all Ramona's talk of food and Tommy did not comfort me. In desperation she turned on Tommy's voice, but as he sang I lay back and contemplated the melting of my own flesh.

"If we stole a radio we could hear him again," Ramona said, trying to soothe me. "We could hear him when he sings tonight."

Tommy came to Faircrest on a visit two days later, for reasons that I could not then understand. All the other girls lumbered into the assembly hall to see him, thousands of pounds of agitated flesh. It was that morning that I discovered I could walk again, and I was on my feet, struggling into the pink tent in a fury to get to Tommy, when the matron intercepted me.

"Not you, Nelly."

"I have to get to Tommy. I have to hear him sing."

"Next time, maybe." With a look of naked cruelty she added, "You're a disgrace. You're still too gross."

I lunged, but it was too late; she had already shot the bolt. And so I sat in the midst of my diminishing body, suffering while every other girl in the place listened to him sing. I knew then that I had to act; I would regain myself somehow, I would find food and regain my flesh and then I would go to Tommy. I would use force if I had to, but I would hear him sing. I raged through the room all that morning, hearing the shrieks of five hundred girls, the thunder of their feet, but even when I pressed myself against the wall I could not hear Tommy's voice.

Yet Ramona, when she came back to the room, said the most interesting thing. It was some time before she could speak at all, but in her generosity she played "When a Widow" while she regained herself, and then she spoke: "He came for something, Nelly. He came for something he didn't find."

"Tell about what he was wearing. Tell what his throat did when he sang."

"He looked at all the *before* pictures, Nelly. The matron was trying to make him look at the *afters,* but he kept looking at the *befores* and shaking his head and then he found one and put it in his pocket and if he hadn't found it, he wasn't going to sing."

I could feel my spine stiffen. "Ramona, you've got to help me. I must go to him."

That night we staged a daring break. We clubbed the attendant when he brought dinner, and once we had him under the bed we ate all the chops and gluten bread on his cart and then we went down the corridor, lifting bolts, and when we were a hundred strong we locked the matron in her office and raided the dining hall, howling and eating everything we could find. I ate that night, how I ate, but even as I ate I was aware of a fatal lightness in my bones, a failure in capacity, and so they found me in the frozen-food locker, weeping over a chain of link sausage, inconsolable because I understood that they had spoiled it for me, they with their chops and their gluten bread; I could never eat as I once had, I would never be myself again.

In my fury I went after the matron with a ham hock, and when I had them all at bay I took a loin of pork for sustenance and I broke out of that place. I had to get to Tommy before I got any thinner; I had to try. Outside the gate I stopped a car and hit the driver with the loin of pork and then I drove to the Hotel Riverside, where Tommy always stayed. I made my way up the fire stairs on little cat feet and when the valet went to his suite with one of his velveteen suits I followed, quick as a tigress, and the next moment I was inside. When all was quiet I tiptoed to his door and stepped inside.

He was magnificent. He stood at the window, gaunt and beautiful; his blond hair fell to his waist and his shoulders shriveled under a heartbreaking double-breasted pea-green velvet suit. He did not see me at first; I drank in his image and then, delicately, cleared my throat. In the second that he turned and saw me, everything seemed possible.

"It's you." His voice throbbed.

"I had to come."

Our eyes fused and in that moment I believed that we two could meet, burning as a single, lambent flame, but in the next second his face had crumpled in disappointment; he brought a picture from his pocket, a fingered, cracked photograph, and he looked from it to me and back at the photograph, saying, "My darling, you've fallen off."

"Maybe it's not too late," I cried, but we both knew I would fail.

And fail I did, even though I ate for days, for five desperate, heroic weeks; I threw pies into the breech, fresh hams and whole sides of beef, but those sad days at the food farm, the starvation and the drugs have so upset my chemistry that it cannot be restored; no matter what I eat I fall off and I continue to fall off; my body is a halfway house for foods I can no longer assimilate. Tommy watches, and because he knows he almost had me, huge and round and beautiful, Tommy mourns. He eats less and less now. He eats like a bird and lately he has refused to sing; strangely, his records have begun to disappear.

And so a whole nation waits.

"I almost had her," he says, when they beg him to resume his midnight shows; he will not sing, he won't talk, but his hands describe the mountain of woman he has longed for all his life.

And so I have lost Tommy, and he has lost me, but I am doing my best to make it up to him. I own Faircrest now, and in the place where Ramona and I once suffered I use my skills on the girls Tommy wants me to cultivate. I can put twenty pounds on a girl in a couple of weeks and I don't mean bloat, I mean solid fat. Ramona and I feed them up and once a week we weigh and I poke the upper arm with a special stick and I will not be satisfied until the stick goes in and does not rebound because all resiliency is gone. Each week I bring out my best and Tommy shakes his head in misery because the best is not yet good enough, none of them are what I once was. But one day the time and the girl will be right—would that it were me—the time and the girl will be right and Tommy will sing again. In the meantime, the whole world waits; in the meantime, in a private wing well away from the others, I keep my special cases; the matron, who grows fatter as I watch her. And Mom. And Dad.

BABY, YOU WERE GREAT

KATE WILHELM

Kate Wilhelm is the author of science fiction stories published in **Orbit, Again Dangerous Visions, Quark** and **The Magazine of Fantasy & Science Fiction.** Her novels include **The Killer Thing** (Doubleday), **Let the Fire Fall** (Doubleday), **Margaret and I** (Little, Brown) and **City of Cain** (Little, Brown). She has also written two novels with sf author Ted Thomas, **The Clone** and **Year of the Cloud** (both published by Doubleday), and has published two short-story collections, **The Downstairs Room** (Doubleday) and **The Mile-Long Spaceship** (Berkley). Her short story "The Planners" won the Nebula Award in 1968, and she is the editor of **Nebula Award Stories Nine** (Harper & Row). She is married to sf author, editor and critic Damon Knight and lives in Florida.

We have all admired celebrities, who set our fashions and through whom we sometimes live vicariously. Anne Beaumont, one of the characters in this story, is such a glamorous figure, exploited with the use of an electronic implant. The world we see in "Baby, You Were Great" is a world we shall have the ability to create, and is an extension of our own society.

John Lewisohn thought that if one more door slammed, or one more bell rang, or one more voice asked if he was all right, his head would explode.

Leaving his laboratories, he walked through the carpeted hall to the elevator that slid wide to admit him noiselessly, was lowered, gently, two floors, where there were more carpeted halls. The door he shoved open bore a neat sign, AUDITIONING STUDIO. Inside he was waved on through the reception room by three girls who knew better than to speak to him unless he spoke first. They were surprised to see him; it was his first visit there in seven or eight months. The inner room where he stopped was darkened, at first glance appearing empty, revealing another occupant only after his eyes had time to adjust to the dim lighting.

John sat in the chair next to Herb Javits, still without speaking. Herb was wearing the helmet and gazing at a wide screen that was actually a one-way glass panel permitting him to view the audition going on in the adjacent room. John lowered a second helmet to his head. It fit snugly and immediately made contact with the eight prepared spots on his skull. As soon as he turned it on, the helmet itself was forgotten.

A girl had entered the other room. She was breathtakingly lovely, a long-legged honey blonde with slanting green eyes and apricot skin. The room was furnished as a sitting room with two couches, some chairs, end tables and a coffee table, all tasteful and lifeless, like an ad in a furniture-trade publication. The girl stopped at the doorway, and John felt her indecision heavily tempered with nervousness and fear. Outwardly she appeared poised and expectant, her smooth face betraying none of the emotions. She took a hesitant step toward the couch, and a wire showed trailing behind her. It was attached to her head. At the same time a second door opened. A young man ran inside, slamming the door behind him;

he looked wild and frantic. The girl registered surprise, mounting nervousness; she felt behind her for the door handle, found it and tried to open the door again. It was locked. John could hear nothing that was being said in the room; he only felt the girl's reaction to the unexpected interruption. The wild-eyed man was approaching her, his hands slashing through the air, his eyes darting glances all about them constantly. Suddenly he pounced on her and pulled her to him, kissing her face and neck roughly. She seemed paralyzed with fear for several seconds, then there was something else, a bland nothing kind of feeling that accompanied boredom sometimes, or too complete self-assurance. As the man's hands fastened on her blouse in the back and ripped it, she threw her arms about him, her face showing passion that was not felt anywhere in her mind or in her blood.

"Cut!" Herb Javits said quietly.

The man stepped back from the girl and left her without a word. She looked about blankly, her blouse torn, hanging about her hips, one shoulder strap gone. She was very beautiful. The audition manager entered, followed by a dresser with a gown that he threw about her shoulders. She looked startled; waves of anger mounted to fury as she was drawn from the room, leaving it empty. The two watching men removed their helmets.

"Fourth one so far," Herb grunted. "Sixteen yesterday; twenty the day before . . . all nothing." He gave John a curious look. "What's got you stirred out of your lab?"

"Anne's had it this time," John said. "She's been on the phone all night and all morning."

"What now?"

"Those damn sharks! I told you that was too much on top of the airplane crash last week. She can't take much more of it."

"Hold it a minute, Johnny," Herb said. "Let's finish off the next three girls and then talk." He pressed a button on the arm of his chair and the room beyond the screen took their attention again.

This time the girl was slightly less beautiful, shorter, a dimply sort of brunette with laughing blue eyes and an upturned nose. John liked her. He adjusted his helmet and felt with her.

She was excited; the audition always excited them. There was some fear and nervousness, not too much. Curious about how the audition would go, probably. The wild young man ran into the room, and her face paled. Nothing else changed. Her nervousness increased, not uncomfortably. When he grabbed her, the only emotion she registered was the nervousness.

"Cut," Herb said.

The next girl was brunette, with gorgeously elongated legs. She was very cool, a real professional. Her mobile face reflected the range of emotions to be expected as the scene played through again, but nothing inside her was touched. She was a million miles away from it all.

The next one caught John with a slam. She entered the room slowly, looking about with curiosity, nervous, as they all were. She was younger than the other girls had been, less poised. She had pale-gold hair piled in an elaborate mound of waves on top of her head. Her eyes were brown, her skin nicely tanned. When the man entered, her emotion changed quickly to fear, and then to terror. John didn't know when he closed his eyes. He was the girl, filled with unspeakable terror; his heart pounded, adrenalin pumped into his system; he wanted to scream but could not. From the dim unreachable depths of his psyche there came something else, in waves, so mixed with terror that the two merged and became one emotion that pulsed and throbbed and demanded. With a jerk he opened his eyes and stared at the window. The girl had been thrown down to one of the couches, and the man was kneeling on the floor beside her, his hands playing over her bare body, his face pressed against her skin.

"Cut!" Herb said. His voice was shaken. "Hire her," he said. The man rose, glanced at the girl, sobbing now, and then quickly bent over and kissed her cheek. Her sobs increased. Her golden hair was down, framing her face; she looked like a child. John tore off the helmet. He was perspiring.

Herb got up, turned on the lights in the room, and the window blanked out, blending with the wall, making it invisible. He didn't look at John. When he wiped his face, his hand was shaking. He rammed it in his pocket.

"When did you start auditions like that?" John asked, after a few moments of silence.

"Couple of months ago. I told you about it. Hell, we had to, Johnny. That's the six-hundred-nineteenth girl we've tried out! Six hundred nineteen! All phonies but one! Dead from the neck up. Do you have any idea how long it was taking us to find that out? Hours for each one. Now it's a matter of minutes."

John Lewisohn sighed. He knew. He had suggested it, actually, when he had said, "Find a basic anxiety situation for the test." He hadn't wanted to know what Herb had come up with.

He said, "Okay, but she's only a kid. What about her parents, legal rights, all that?"

"We'll fix it. Don't worry. What about Anne?"

"She's called me five times since yesterday. The sharks were too much. She wants to see us, both of us, this afternoon."

"You're kidding! I can't leave here now!"

"Nope. Kidding I'm not. She says no plug up if we don't show. She'll take pills and sleep until we get there."

"Good Lord! She wouldn't dare!"

"I've booked seats. We take off at twelve thirty-five." They stared at one another silently for another moment, then Herb shrugged. He was a short man, not heavy but solid. John was over six feet, muscular, with a temper that he knew he had to control. Others suspected that when he did let it go, there would be bodies lying around afterward, but he controlled it.

Once it had been a physical act, an effort of body and will to master that temper; now it was done so automatically that he couldn't recall occasions when it even threatened to flare any more.

"Look, Johnny, when we see Anne, let me handle it. Right?" Herb said. "I'll make it short."

"What are you going to do?"

"Give her an earful. If she's going to start pulling temperament on me, I'll slap her down so hard she'll bounce a week." He grinned happily. "She's had it all her way up to now. She knew there wasn't a replacement if she got bitchy. Let her try it now. Just let her try." Herb was pacing back and forth with quick, jerky steps.

John realized with a shock that he hated the stocky, red-faced man. The feeling was new, it was almost as if he could taste the hatred he felt, and the taste was unfamiliar and pleasant.

Herb stopped pacing and stared at him for a moment. "Why'd she call you? Why does she want you

down, too? She knows you're not mixed up with this
end of it."

"She knows I'm a full partner, anyway," John said.

"Yeah, but that's not it." Herb's face twisted in a
grin. "She thinks you're still hot for her, doesn't she?
She knows you tumbled once, in the beginning, when
you were working on her, getting the gimmick working right." The grin reflected no humor then. "Is she
right, Johnny, baby? Is that it?"

"We made a deal," John said coldly. "You run your
end, I run mine. She wants me along because she
doesn't trust you, or believe anything you tell her any
more. She wants a witness."

"Yeah, Johnny. But you be sure you remember our
agreement." Suddenly Herb laughed. "You know what
it was like, Johnny, seeing you and her? Like a flame
trying to snuggle up to an icicle."

At three-thirty they were in Anne's suite in the Sky-
line Hotel in Grand Bahama. Herb had a reservation
to fly back to New York on the six P.M. flight. Anne
would not be off until four, so they made themselves
comfortable in her rooms and waited. Herb turned her
screen on, offered a helmet to John, who shook his
head, and they both seated themselves. John watched
the screen for several minutes; then he too put on a
helmet.

Anne was looking at the waves far out at sea where
they were long, green, undulating; then she brought
her gaze in closer, to the blue-green and quick seas,
and finally in to where they stumbled on the sand
bars, breaking into foam that looked solid enough to
walk on. She was peaceful, swaying with the motion
of the boat, the sun hot on her back, the fishing rod
heavy in her hands. It was like being an indolent
animal at peace with the world, at home in the world,

being one with it. After a few seconds she put down the rod and turned, looking at a tall smiling man in swimming trunks. He held out his hand and she took it. They entered the cabin of the boat, where drinks were waiting. Her mood of serenity and happiness ended abruptly, to be replaced by shocked disbelief and a start of fear.

"What the hell . . . ?" John muttered, adjusting the audio. You seldom needed audio when Anne was on.

". . . Captain Brothers had to let them go. After all, they've done nothing yet . . .," the man was saying soberly.

"But why do you think they'll try to rob me?"

"Who else is here with a million dollars' worth of jewels?"

John turned it off and said to Herb, "You're a fool! You can't get away with something like that!"

Herb stood up and crossed the room to stand before a window wall that was open to the stretch of glistening blue ocean beyond the brilliant white beaches. "You know what every woman wants? To own something worth stealing." He chuckled, a low throaty sound that was without mirth. "Among other things, that is. They want to be roughed up once or twice, and forced to kneel . . . Our new psychologist is pretty good, you know? Hasn't steered us wrong yet. Anne might kick some, but it'll go over great."

"She won't stand for an actual robbery." Louder, emphasizing it, he added, "I won't stand for that."

"We can dub it," Herb said. "That's all we need, Johnny, plant the idea, and then dub the rest."

John stared at his back. He wanted to believe that. He needed to believe it. His voice showed no trace of emotion when he said, "It didn't start like this, Herb. What happened?"

Herb turned then. His face was dark against the glare of light behind him. "Okay, Johnny, it didn't start like this. Things accelerate, that's all. You thought of a gimmick, and the way we planned it, it sounded great, but it didn't last. We gave them the feeling of gambling, of learning to ski, of automobile racing, everything we could dream of, and it wasn't enough. How many times can you take the first ski jump of your life? After a while you want new thrills, you know? For you it's been great, hasn't it? You bought yourself a shining new lab and pulled the cover over you and it. You bought yourself time and equipment, and when things didn't go right you could toss it out and start over, and nobody gave a damn. Think of what it's been like for me, kid! I gotta keep coming up with something new, something that'll give Anne a jolt and, through her, all those nice little people who aren't even alive unless they're plugged in. You think it's been easy? Anne was a green kid. For her everything was new and exciting, but it isn't like that now, boy. You better believe it is *not* like that now. You know what she told me last month? She's sick and tired of men. Our little hot-box Annie! Tired of men!"

John crossed to him and pulled him around. "Why didn't you tell me?"

"Why, Johnny? What would you have done that I didn't do? *I* looked harder for the right guy for her. What would you do for a new thrill for her? I worked for them, kid. Right from the start you said for me to leave you alone. Okay. I left you alone. You ever read any of the memos I sent? You initialed them, kiddo. Everything that's been done, we both signed. Don't give me any of that why-didn't-I-tell-you stuff. It won't work!" His face was ugly red and a vein bulged in his neck. John wondered if he had high blood pressure, if he would die of a stroke during one of his flash rages.

John left him at the window. He had read the memos. Herb knew he had. Herb was right; all he had wanted was to be left alone. It had been his idea; after twelve years of work in a laboratory on prototypes he had shown his . . . gimmick . . . to Herb Javits. Herb was one of the biggest producers on television then; now he was the biggest producer in the world.

The gimmick was fairly simple. A person fitted with electrodes in his brain could transmit his emotions, which in turn could be broadcast and picked up by the helmets to be felt by the audience. No words or thoughts went out, only basic emotions . . . fear, love, anger, hatred . . . That, tied in with a camera showing what the person saw, with a voice dubbed in, and you were the person having the experience, with one important difference, you could turn it off if it got to be too much. The "actor" couldn't. A simple gimmick. You didn't really need the camera and the soundtrack; many users never turned them on at all, but let their own imagination fill in to fit the emotional broadcast.

The helmets were not sold, only rented after a short, easy fitting session. Rent of one dollar a month was collected on the first of the month, and there were over thirty-seven million subscribers. Herb had bought his own network after the second month when the demand for more hours barred him from regular television. From a one-hour weekly show it had gone to one hour nightly, and now it was on the air eight hours a day live, with another eight hours of taped programing.

What had started out as A DAY IN THE LIFE OF ANNE

BEAUMONT was now a life in the life of Anne Beaumont, and the audience was insatiable.

Anne came in then, surrounded by the throng of hangers-on that mobbed her daily—hairdressers, masseurs, fitters, script men . . . She looked tired. She waved the crowd out when she saw John and Herb were there. "Hello, John," she said, "Herb."

"Anne, baby, you're looking great!" Herb said. He took her in his arms and kissed her solidly. She stood still, her hands at her sides.

She was tall, very slender, with wheat-colored hair and gray eyes. Her cheekbones were wide and high, her mouth firm and almost too large. Against her deep red-gold sun tan her teeth looked whiter than John remembered them. Although too firm and strong ever to be thought of as pretty, she was a very beautiful woman. After Herb released her, she turned to John, hesitated only a moment, and then extended a slim, sun-browned hand. It was cool and dry in his.

"How have you been, John? It's been a long time."

He was very glad she didn't kiss him or call him darling. She smiled only slightly and gently removed her hand from his. He moved to the bar as she turned to Herb.

"I'm through, Herb," she said. Her voice was too quiet. She accepted a whiskey sour from John, but kept her gaze on Herb.

"What's the matter, honey? I was just watching you, baby. You were great today, like always. You've still got it, kid. It's coming through like always."

"What about this robbery? You must be out of your mind . . ."

"Yeah, that. Listen, Anne baby, I swear to you I don't know a thing about it. Laughton must have been telling you the straight goods on that. You know we agreed that the rest of this week you just have a good time, remember? That comes over too, baby. When you have a good time and relax, thirty-seven million people are enjoying life and relaxing. That's good. They can't be stimulated all the time. They like the variety . . ." Wordlessly John held out a glass, Scotch and water. Herb took it without looking.

Anne was watching him coldly. Suddenly she laughed. It was a cynical, bitter sound. "You're not a damn fool, Herb. Don't try to act like one." She sipped her drink again, continuing to stare at him over the rim of the glass. "I am warning you, if anyone shows here to rob me, I'm going to treat him like a real burglar. I bought a gun after today's broadcast, and I learned how to shoot when I was only nine or ten. I still know how. I'll kill him, Herb, whoever it is."

"Baby," Herb started, but she cut him short.

"And this is my last week. As of Saturday, I'm through."

"You can't do that, Anne," Herb said. John watched him closely, searching for a sign of weakness, anything; he saw nothing. Herb exuded confidence. "Look around, Anne, at this room, your clothes, everything . . . You are the richest woman in the world, having the time of your life, able to go anywhere, do anything . . ."

"While the whole world watches . . ."

"So what? It doesn't stop you, does it?" Herb started to pace, his steps jerky and quick. "You knew that when you signed the contract. You're a rare girl, Anne, beautiful, emotional, intelligent. Think of all those women who've got nothing but you. If you quit them, what do they do? Die? They might, you know. For the first time in their lives they are able to feel like they're living. You're giving them what no one ever did before, what was only hinted at in books and films in the old days. Suddenly they know what it feels like to face excitement, to experience love, to feel contented and peaceful. Think of them, Anne, empty, with nothing in their lives but you, what you're able to give them. Thirty-seven million drabs, Anne, who never felt anything but boredom and frustration until you gave them life. What do they have? Work, kids, bills. You've given them the world, baby! Without you they wouldn't even want to live any more."

She wasn't listening. Almost dreamily she said, "I talked to my lawyers, Herb, and the contract is meaningless. You've already broken it countless times by insisting on adding to the original agreement. I agreed to learn a lot of new things, so they could feel them with me. I did. My God! I've climbed mountains, hunted lions, learned to ski and water ski, but now you want me to die a little bit each week . . . that airplane crash, not bad, just enough to terrify me. Then the sharks. I really do think it was having sharks brought in when I was skiing that did it, Herb. You see, you will kill me. It will happen, and you won't be able to top it, Herb. Not ever."

There was a hard, waiting silence following her words. "No!" John shouted, soundlessly, the words not leaving his mouth. He was looking at Herb. He had stopped pacing when she started to talk. Something flicked across his face, surprise, fear, something not readily identifiable. Then his face went completely blank and he raised his glass and finished the Scotch and water, replacing the glass on the bar. When he turned again, he was smiling with disbelief.

"What's really bugging you, Anne? There have been plants before. You knew about them. Those lions didn't just happen by, you know. And the avalanche needed a nudge from someone. You know that. What else is bugging you?"

"I'm in love, Herb. I want out now before you manage to kill me." Herb waved that aside impatiently.

"Have you ever watched your own show, Anne?" She shook her head. "I thought not. So you wouldn't know about the expansion that took place last month, after we planted that new transmitter in your head. Johnny boy here's been busy, Anne. You know these scientist types, never satisfied, always improving, changing. Where's the camera, Anne? Do you ever know where it is any more? Have you even seen a camera in the past couple of weeks, or a recorder of any sort? You have not, and you won't again. You're on now, honey." His voice was quite low, amused almost. "In fact the only time you aren't on is when you're sleeping. I know you're in love; I know who he is; I know how he makes you feel; I even know how much money he makes per week. I should know, Anne baby. I pay him." He had come closer to her with each word, finishing with his face only inches from hers. He didn't have a chance to duck the flashing slap that jerked his head around, and before either of them realized it, he had hit her back. Anne fell back to the chair, too stunned to speak for a moment.

The silence grew, became something ugly and heavy, as if words were being born and dying without utterance because they were too brutal for the human spirit to bear. There was a spot of blood on Herb's mouth where her diamond ring had cut him. He touched it and looked at his finger. "It's all being taped now, honey, even this," he said. He returned to the bar, turning his back on her.

There was a large red print on her cheek. Her gray

eyes had turned black with rage; she didn't take her gaze from him.

"Honey, relax," Herb said after a moment, his voice soft and easy again. "It won't make any difference to you, in what you do, or anything like that. You know we can't use most of the stuff, but it gives the editors a bigger variety to pick from. It was getting to the point where most of the interesting stuff was going on after you were off. Like buying the gun. That's great stuff there, baby. You weren't blanketing a single thing, and it'll all come through like pure gold." He finished mixing his drink, tasted it, and then swallowed most of it. "How many women have to go out and buy a gun to protect themselves? Think of them all, feeling that gun, feeling the things you felt when you picked it up, looked at it . . ."

"How long have you been tuning in all the time?" she asked. John felt a stirring along his spine, a tingle of excitement. He knew what was going out over the miniature transmitter, the rising crests of emotion she was feeling. Only a trace of them showed on her smooth face, but the raging interior torment was being recorded faithfully. Her quiet voice and quiet body were lies; only the tapes never lied.

Herb felt it too, a storm behind her quietude. He put his glass down and went to her, kneeling by the chair, taking her hand in both of his. "Anne, please, don't be that angry with me. I was desperate for new material. When Johnny got this last wrinkle out, and we knew we could record around the clock, we had to try it, and it wouldn't have been any good if you had known. That's no way to test anything. You knew we were planting the transmitter . . ."

"How long?"

"Not quite a month."

"And Stuart? He's one of your men? He is transmitting also? You hired him to . . . to make love to me? Is that right?"

Herb nodded. She pulled her hand free and averted her face, not willing to see him any longer. He got up then and went to the window. "But what difference does it make?" he shouted. "If I introduced the two of you at a party, you wouldn't think anything of it. What difference if I did it this way? I knew you'd like each other. He's bright, like you, likes the same sort of things you do. Comes from a poor family, like yours . . . Everything said you'd get along . . ."

"Oh, yes," she said almost absently. "We get along." She was feeling in her hair, her fingers searching for the scars.

"It's all healed by now," John said. She looked at him as if she had forgotten he was there.

"I'll find a surgeon," she said, standing up, her fingers white on her glass. "A brain surgeon . . ."

"It's a new process," John said slowly. "It would be dangerous to go in after them . . ."

She looked at him for a long time. "Dangerous?"

He nodded.

"You could take it back out . . ."

He remembered the beginning, how he had quieted her fear of the electrodes and the wires. Her fear was that of a child for the unknown and the unknowable. Time and again he had proven to her that she could trust him, that he wouldn't lie to her. He hadn't lied to her, then. There was the same trust in her eyes, the same unshakable faith. She would believe him. She would accept without question whatever he said. Herb had called him an icicle, but that was wrong. An icicle would have melted in her fires. More like a

stalactite, shaped by centuries of civilization, layer by
layer he had been formed until he had forgotten how
to bend, forgotten how to find release for the stirrings
he felt somewhere in the hollow, rigid core of himself.
She had tried and, frustrated, she had turned from
him, hurt, but unable not to trust one she had loved.
Now she waited. He could free her, and lose her
again, this time irrevocably. Or he could hold her as
long as she lived.

Her lovely gray eyes were shadowed with fear and
the trust that he had given to her. Slowly he shook his
head.

"I can't," he said. "No one can."

"I see," she murmured, the black filling her eyes.
"I'd die, wouldn't I? Then you'd have a lovely se-
quence, wouldn't you, Herb?" She swung around,
away from John. "You'd have to fake the story line, of
course, but you are so good at that. An accident,
emergency brain surgery needed, everything I feel
going out to the poor little drabs who never will have
brain surgery done. It's very good," she said admir-
ingly. Her eyes were very black. "In fact, anything I
do from now on, you'll use, won't you? If I kill you,
that will simply be material for your editors to pick
over. Trial, prison, very dramatic . . . On the other
hand, if I kill myself . . ."

John felt chilled; a cold, hard weight seemed to be
filling him. Herb laughed. "The story line will be
something like this," he said. "Anne has fallen in love
with a stranger, deeply, sincerely in love with him.
Everyone knows how deep that love is; they've all felt
it, too, you know. She finds him raping a child, a
lovely little girl in her early teens. Stuart tells her
they're through. He loves the little nymph. In a

passion she kills herself. You are broadcasting a real storm of passion, right now, aren't you, honey? Never mind, when I run through this scene, I'll find out." She hurled her glass at him, ice cubes and orange sections leaving a trail across the room. Herb ducked, grinning.

"That's awfully good, baby. Corny, but after all, they can't get too much corn, can they? They'll love it, after they get over the shock of losing you. And they will get over it, you know. They always do. Wonder if it's true about what happens to someone experiencing a violent death?" Anne's teeth bit down on her lip, and slowly she sat down again, her eyes closed tight. Herb watched her for a moment, then said, even more cheerfully, "We've got the kid already. If you give them a death, you've got to give them a new life. Finish one with a bang. Start one with a bang. We'll name the kid Cindy, a real Cinderella story after that. They'll love her, too."

Anne opened her eyes, black dulled now; she was so tight with tension that John felt his own muscles contract and become taut. He wondered if he would be able to stand the tape she was transmitting. A wave of excitement swept him and he knew he would play it all, feel it all, the incredibly contained rage, fear, the horror of giving a death to them to gloat over, and finally, anguish. He would know them all. Watching Anne, he wished she would break then, with him there. She didn't. She stood up stiffly, her back rigid, a muscle hard and ridged in her jaw. Her voice was flat when she said, "Stuart is due in half an hour. I have to dress." She left them without looking back.

Herb winked at John and motioned toward the door. "Want to take me to the plane, kid?" In the cab he said, "Stick close to her for a couple of days,

Johnny. There might be an even bigger reaction later when she really understands just how hooked she is." He chuckled again. "By God! It's a good thing she trusts you, Johnny, boy!"

As they waited in the chrome-and-marble terminal for the liner to unload its passengers, John said, "Do you think she'll be any good after this?"

"She can't help herself. She's too life oriented to deliberately choose to die. She's like a jungle inside, raw, wild, untouched by that smooth layer of civilization she shows on the outside. It's a thin layer, kid, real thin. She'll fight to stay alive. She'll become more wary, more alert to danger, more excited and exciting . . . She'll really go to pieces when he touches her tonight. She's primed real good. Might even have to do some editing, tone it down a little." His voice was very happy. "He touches her where she lives, and she reacts. A real wild one. She's one; the new kid's one; Stuart . . . They're few and far apart, Johnny. It's up to us to find them. God knows we're going to need all of them we can get." His face became thoughtful and withdrawn. "You know, that really wasn't such a bad idea of mine about rape and the kid. Who ever dreamed we'd get that kind of a reaction from her? With the right sort of buildup . . ." He had to run to catch his plane.

John hurried back to the hotel, to be near Anne if she needed him. He hoped she would leave him alone. His fingers shook as he turned on his screen; suddenly he had a clear memory of the child who had wept, and he hoped Stuart would hurt Anne just a little. The tremor in his fingers increased; Stuart was on from six until twelve, and he already had missed almost an hour of the show. He adjusted the helmet and sank back into a deep chair. He left the audio off, letting his own words form, letting his own thoughts fill in the spaces.

Anne was leaning toward him, sparkling champagne raised to her lips, her eyes large and soft. She was speaking, talking to him, John, calling him by name. He felt a tingle start somewhere deep inside him, and his glance was lowered to rest on her tanned hand in his, sending electricity through him. Her hand trembled when he ran his fingers up her palm, to her wrist where a blue vein throbbed. The slight throb became a pounding that grew, and when he looked again into her eyes, they were dark and very deep. They danced and he felt her body against his, yielding, pleading. The room darkened and she was an outline against the window, her gown floating down about her. The darkness grew denser, or he closed his eyes, and this time when her body pressed against his, there was nothing between them, and the pounding was everywhere.

In the deep chair, with the helmet on his head, John's hands clenched, opened, clenched, again and again.

SEX AND/OR MR. MORRISON

CAROL EMSHWILLER

Carol Emshwiller attended art school at the University of Michigan and received a Fulbright Scholarship to study in France. Her stories have appeared in science-fiction magazines and in the anthologies **Bad Moon Rising, Orbit** and **Showcase,** among others. She is also the author of **Joy in Our Cause** (Harper & Row). She is married to artist and film maker Ed Emshwiller.

The sexes are differentiated by their reproductive organs. This difference is ultimately the basis of all the codes and attitudes that have governed the behavior of the sexes toward each other, ignoring the much greater number of similarities between them. These restrictive attitudes may also be at the root of our ambivalent and sometimes hateful feelings about our own genitals.

When "Sex and/or Mr. Morrison" first appeared in Harlan Ellison's anthology **Dangerous Visions,** Ms. Emshwiller wrote in her afterword to the story: "It would be nice to live in a society where the genitals were really considered Beauty. It seems to me any other way of seeing is obscene."

I can set my clock by Mr. Morrison's step upon the stairs, not that he is that accurate, but accurate enough for me. Eight thirty thereabouts. (My clock runs fast anyway.) Each day he comes clumping down and I set it back ten minutes, or eight minutes

159

or seven. I suppose I could just as well do it without him, but it seems a shame to waste all that heavy treading and those puffs and sighs of expending energy on only getting downstairs, so I have timed my life to this morning beat. Funereal tempo, one might well call it, but it is funereal only because Mr. Morrison is fat and therefore slow. Actually he's a very nice man as men go. He always smiles.

I wait downstairs, sometimes looking up and sometimes holding my alarm clock. I smile a smile I hope is not as wistful as his. Mr. Morrison's moonface has something of the Mona Lisa to it. Certainly he must have secrets.

"I'm setting my clock by you, Mr. M."

"Heh, heh . . . my, my," grunt, breath. "Well," heave the stomach to the right, "I hope . . ."

"Oh, you're on time enough for *me*."

"Heh, heh. Oh. Oh, yes." The weight of the world is certainly upon him or perhaps he's crushed and flattened by a hundred miles of air. How many pounds per square inch weighing him down? He hasn't the inner energy to push back. All his muscles spread like jelly under his skin.

"No time to talk," he says. (He never has time.) Off he goes. I like him and his clipped little Boston accent, but I know he's too proud ever to be friendly. Proud is the wrong word, so is shy. Well, I'll leave it at that.

He turns back, pouting, and then winks at me as a kind of softening of it. Perhaps it's just a twitch. He thinks, if he thinks of me at all: What can she say and what can I say talking to her? What can she possibly know that I don't know already? And so he duck-walks, knock-kneed, out the door.

And now the day begins.

There are really quite a number of things that I can

do. I often spend time in the park. Sometimes I rent a
boat there and row myself about and feed the ducks. I
love museums and there are all those free art galleries
and there's window-shopping, and if I'm very careful
with my budget, now and then I can squeeze in a
matinée. But I don't like to be out after Mr. Morrison
comes back. I wonder if he keeps his room locked
while he's off at work?

His room is directly over mine and he's too big to be
a quiet man. The house groans with him and settles
when he steps out of bed. The floor creaks under his
feet. Even the walls rustle and the wallpaper clicks its
dried paste. But don't think I'm complaining of the
noise. I keep track of him this way. Sometimes, here
underneath, I ape his movements, bed to dresser, step,
clump, dresser to closet and back again. I imagine him
there, flat-footed. Imagine him. Just imagine those
great legs sliding into pants, their godlike width (for
no mere man could have legs like that), those Thor-
legs into pants holes wide as caves. Imagine those two
landscapes, sparsely fuzzed in a faint, wheat-colored
brush finding their way blindly into the waist-wide
skirt-things of brown wool that are still damp from
yesterday. Ooo. Ugh. Up go the suspenders. I think I
can hear him breathe from here.

I can comb my hair three times to his once and I
can be out and waiting at the bottom step by the time
he opens his door.

"I'm setting my clock by you, Mr. M."

"No time. No time. I'm off. Well . . ." and he shuts
the front door so gently one would think he is afraid
of his own fat hands.

And so, as I said, the day begins.

The question is (and perhaps it is the question for
today): Who is he really, one of the Normals or one of

the Others? It's not going to be so easy to find out with someone so fat. I wonder if I'm up to it. Still, I'm willing to go to certain lengths and I'm nimble yet. All that rowing and all that walking up and down and then, recently, I've spent all night huddled under a bush in Central Park and twice I've crawled out on the fire escape and climbed to the roof and back again (but I haven't seen much and I can't be sure of the Others yet).

I don't think the closet will do because there's no keyhole, though I could open the door a crack and maybe wedge my shoe there. (It's double A.) He might not notice it. Or there's the bed to get under. While it's true that I am thin and small, almost child-sized, one might say, still it will not be so easy, but then neither has it been easy to look for lovers on the roof.

Sometimes I wish I were a little, fast-moving lizard, dull-green or a yellowish brown. I could scamper in under his stomach when he opened the door and he'd never see me, though his eyes are as quick as his feet are clumsy. Still I would be quicker. I would skitter off behind the bookcase or back of his desk or maybe even just lie very still in a corner, for surely he does not see the floor so much. His room is no larger than mine and his presence must fill it, or rather his stomach fills it and his giant legs. He sees the ceiling and the pictures on the wall, the surfaces of night table, desk and bureau, but the floor and the lower halves of everything would be safe for me. No, I won't even have to regret not being a lizard, except for getting in. But if he doesn't lock his room it will be no problem and I can spend all day scouting out my hiding places. I'd best take a snack with me too if I decide this is the night for it. No crackers and no nuts, but noiseless things like cheese and fig newtons.

It seems to me, now that I think about it, that I was rather saving Mr. Morrison for last, as a child saves the frosting of the cake to eat after the cake part is finished. But I see that I have been foolish, for, since he is really one of the most likely prospects, he should have been first.

And so today the day begins with a gathering of supplies and an exploratory trip upstairs.

The room is cluttered. There is no bookcase but there are books and magazines by the hundreds. I check behind the piles. I check the closet, full of drooping, giant suit coats I can easily hide in. Just see how the shoulders extend over the ordinary hangers. I check under the bed and the kneehole of the desk. I squat under the night table. I nestle among the dirty shirts and socks tossed in the corner. Oh, it's better than Central Park for hiding places. I decide to use them all.

There's something very nice about being here, for I do like Mr. Morrison. Even just his size is comforting; he's big enough to be everybody's father. His room reassures with all his father-sized things in it. I feel lazy and young here.

I eat a few fig newtons while I sit on his shoes in the closet, soft, wide shoes with their edges all collapsed and all of them shaped more like cushions than shoes. Then I take a nap in the dirty shirts. It looks like fifteen or so but there are only seven and some socks. After that I hunch down in the kneehole of the desk, hugging my knees, and I wait and I begin to have doubts. That pendulous stomach, I can already tell, will be larger than all my expectations. There will certainly be nothing it cannot overshadow or conceal, so why do I crouch here clicking my fingernails against the desk leg when I might be out feeding pigeons? Leave now, I tell myself. Are you actually going to spend the whole day, and maybe night too, cramped and confined in here? Yet haven't I done it plenty of times lately and always for nothing too? Why not one more try? For Mr. Morrison is surely the most promising of all. His eyes, the way the fat pushes up his cheeks under them, look almost Chinese. His nose is Roman and in an ordinary face it would be overpowering, but here it is lost. Dwarfed. "Save me," cries the nose, "I'm sinking." I would try, but I will have other more important duties, after Mr. Morrison comes back. Duty it is, too, for the good of all and I do mean *all*, but do not think that I am the least bit prejudiced in this.

You see, I did go to a matinée a few weeks ago. I saw the Royal Ballet dance *The Rite of Spring* and it occurred to me then . . . Well, what would *you* think if you saw them wearing their suits that were supposed to be bare skin? Naked suits, I called them. And all those well-dressed, cultured people clapping at them, accepting even though they knew perfectly well . . . like a sort of Emperor's New Clothes in reverse. Now just think, there are only two sexes and every one of us *is* one of those and certainly, presumably that is, knows something of the other. But then that may be where I have been making my mistake. You'd think . . . why, just what I *did* start thinking: that there must be Others among us.

But it is not out of fear or disgust that I am looking for them. I am open and unprejudiced. You can see that I am when I say that I've never seen (and doesn't this seem strange?) the very organs of my own conception, neither my father nor my mother. Goodness knows what *they* were and what this might make me?

So I wait here, tapping my toes inside my slippers and chewing hangnails off my fingers. I contemplate the unvarnished underside of the desk top. I ridge it with my thumbnail. I eat more cookies and think whether I should make his bed for him or not but decide not to. I suck my arm until it is red in the soft crook opposite the elbow. Time jerks ahead as slowly as a school clock, and I crawl across the floor and stretch out behind the books and magazines. I read first paragraphs of dozens of them. What with the dust back here and lying in the shirts and socks before, I'm getting a certain smell and a sort of gray, animal fuzz that makes me feel safer, as though I really did belong in this room and could actually creep around and not be noticed by Mr. Morrison at all except perhaps for a pat on the head as I pass him.

Thump . . . pause. Clump . . . pause. One can't miss his step. The house shouts his presence. The floors wake up squeaking and lean toward the stairway. The banister slides away from his slippery ham-hands. The wallpaper seems suddenly full of bugs. He must think: Well, this time she isn't peeking out of her doorway at me. A relief. I can concentrate completely on climbing up. Lift the legs against the pressure. Ooo. Ump. Pause and seem to be looking at the picture on the wall.

I skitter back under the desk.

It's strange that the first thing he does is to put his newspaper on the desk and sit down with his knees next to my nose, regular walls, furnaces of knees, exuding heat and dampness, throwing off a miasma delicately scented of wet wool and sweat. What a

wide roundness they have to them, those knees.
Mother's breasts pressing toward me. Probably as soft.
Why can't I put my cheek against them? Observe how
he can sit so still with no toe tapping, no rhythmic
tensing of the thigh. He's not like the rest of us, but
could a man like this do *little* things?

How the circumstantial evidence piles up, but that
is all I've had so far and it is time for something concrete. One thing, just one fact, is all I need.

He reads and adjusts the clothing at his crotch and
reads again. He breathes out winds of sausages and
garlic and I remember that it is after supper and I
take out my cheese and eat it as slowly as possible in
little rabbit bites. I make a little piece last a half an
hour.

At last he goes down the hall to the bathroom and I
shift back under the shirts and socks and stretch my
legs. What if he undresses like my grandmother did,
under a nightgown? under, for him, some giant,
double-bed-sized thing?

But he doesn't. He hangs his coat on the little
hanger and his tie on the closet doorknob. I receive his
shirt and have to make myself another spy hole. Then
off with the shoes, then socks. Off come the huge
pants with slow, unseeing effort (he stares out the
window). He begins on his yellowed undershorts,
scratching himself first behind and starting earth-
quakes across his buttocks.

Where could he have bought those elephantine
undershorts? In what store were they once folded on
the shelf? In what factory did women sit at sewing
machines and put out one after another after another
of those otherworldly items? Mars? Venus? Saturn,
more likely. Or perhaps, instead, a tiny place, some

moon of Jupiter with less air per square inch upon the skin and less gravity, where Mr. Morrison can take the stairs three at a time and jump the fences (for surely he's not particularly old) and dance all night with girls his own size.

He squints his oriental eyes toward the ceiling light and takes off the shorts, lets them fall loosely to the floor. I see Alleghenies of thigh and buttock. How does a man like that stand naked even before a small-sized mirror? I lose myself, hypnotized. Impossible to tell the color of his skin, just as it is with blue-gray eyes or the ocean. How tan, pink, olive and red and sometimes a bruised elephant-gray. His eyes must be used to multiplicities like this, and to plethoras, conglomerations, to an opulence of self, to an intemperant exuberance, to the universal, the astronomical.

I find myself completely tamed. I lie in my cocoon of shirts not even shivering. My eyes do not take in what they see. He is utterly beyond my comprehension. Can you imagine how thin my wrists must seem to him? He is thinking (if he thinks of me at all), he thinks: She might be from another world. How alien her ankles and leg bones. How her eyes do stand out. How green her complexion in the shadows at the edges of her face. (For I must admit that perhaps I may be as far along the scale at my end of humanity as he is at his.)

Suddenly I feel like singing. My breath purrs in my throat in hymns as slow as Mr. Morrison himself would sing. Can this be love, I wonder? My first *real* love? But haven't I always been passionately interested in people? Or rather in those who caught my fancy? But isn't this feeling different? Can love really have come to me this late in life? (La, la, lee la from whom all blessings flow.) I shut my eyes and duck my head into the shirts. I grin into the dirty socks. Can you imagine *him* making love to *me!*

Well below his abstracted, ceilingward gazes, I crawl on elbows and knees back behind the old books. A safer place to shake out the silliness. Why, I'm old enough for him to be (had I ever married) my youngest son of all. Yet if he were a son of mine, how he would have grown beyond me. I see that I cannot ever follow him (as with all sons). I must love him as a mouse might love the hand that cleans the cage, and as uncomprehendingly too, for surely I see only a part of him here. I sense more. I sense deeper largenesses. I sense excesses of bulk I cannot yet imagine. Rounded afterimages linger on my eyeballs. There seems to be a mysterious darkness in the corners of the room and his shadow covers, at the same time, the window on one wall and the mirror on the other. Certainly he is like an iceberg, seven-eighths submerged.

But now he has turned toward me. I peep from the books holding a magazine over my head as one does when it rains. I do so more to shield myself from too much of him all at once than to hide.

And there we are, confronting each other eye to eye. We stare and he cannot seem to comprehend me any more than I can comprehend him, and yet usually his mind is ahead of mine, jumping away on unfinished phrases. His eyes are not even wistful and not yet surprised. But his belly button, that is another story. Here is the eye of God at last. It nestles in a vast, bland sky like a sun on the curve of the universe flashing me a wink of heat, a benign, fat wink. The stomach eye accepts and understands. The stomach eye recognizes me and looks at me as I've always wished to be looked at. (Yea, though I walk through the valley of the shadow of death.) I see you now.

But I see him now. The skin hangs in loose, plastic folds just there, and there is a little copper-colored circle like a fifty-cent piece made out of pennies. There's a hole in the center and it is corroded green at the edges. This must be a kind of "naked suit" and whatever the sex organs may be, they are hidden behind this hot, pocked and pitted imitation skin.

I look up into those girlish eyes of his and they are as blank as though the eyeballs were all whites, as blank as having no sex at all, eggs without yolks, like being built like a boy-doll with a round hole for the water to empty out.

God, I think. I am not religious but I think, My God, and then I stand up and somehow, in a limping run, I get out of there and down the stairs as though I fly. I slam the door of my room and slide in under my bed. The most obvious of hiding places, but after I am there I can't bear to move out. I lie and listen for his thunder on the stairs, the roar of his feet splintering the steps, his hand tossing away the banister.

I know what I'll say. "I accept. I accept," I'll say. "I will love, I love already, whatever you are."

I lie listening, watching the hanging edges of my bedspread in the absolute silence of the house. Can there be anyone here at all in such a strange quietness? Must I doubt even my own existence?

"Goodness knows," I'll say, "if I'm normal myself." (How is one to know such things when everything is hidden?) "Tell all of them that we accept. Tell them it's the naked suits that are ugly. Your dingles, your dangles, wrinkles, ruts, bumps and humps, we accept whatever there is. Your loops, strings, worms, buttons, figs, cherries, flower petals, your soft little toad-shapes, warty and greenish, your cat's tongues or rat's tails, your oysters, one-eyed between your legs, garter snakes, snails, we accept. We think the truth is lovable."

But what a long silence this is. Where is he? for he must (mustn't he?) come after me for what I saw. But where has he gone? Perhaps he thinks I've locked my door, but I haven't. I haven't.

Why doesn't he come?

VASTER THAN EMPIRES AND MORE SLOW

URSULA K. Le GUIN

Ursula K. Le Guin was born in California. She is the daughter of anthropologist A. L. Kroeber and writer Theodora Kroeber. She received her B.A. from Radcliffe College, where she was elected to Phi Beta Kappa, and earned her M.A. at Columbia University. She also studied in Paris on a Fulbright Scholarship. She is the author of stories which have appeared in **Again Dangerous Visions, New Dimensions, Orbit** and **Galaxy.** Among her novels are **The Wizard of Earthsea** (Parnassus Press), winner of the Boston Globe–Horn Book Award in 1969, **The Tombs of Atuan** (Atheneum), a Newbery Honor Book in 1972, and **The Farthest Shore** (Atheneum), all part of a trilogy. **The Farthest Shore** received the National Book Award for Children's Literature in 1973. Her novel **The Left Hand of Darkness** (Walker) won both the Hugo and Nebula Awards and her novella, "The Word for World is Forest," won the Hugo Award in 1973. Her most recent novels are **The Lathe of Heaven** (Scribner's) and **The Dispossessed** (Harper & Row). She is married to historian and professor Charles Le Guin and lives in Oregon.

"Vaster Than Empires and More Slow" deals with extrasensory perception and the unusual members of an interstellar expedition. These perceptual powers highlight the interpersonal relationships of the crew as they travel to a fascinating alien planet.

You're looking at a clock. It has hands, and figures arranged in a circle. The hands move. You can't tell if they move at the same rate, or if one moves faster than the other. What does *than* mean? There is a relationship between the hands and the circle of figures, and the name of this relationship is on the tip of your tongue; the hands are . . . something-or-other, at the figures. Or is it the figures that . . . at the hands? What does *at* mean? They are figures—your vocabulary hasn't shrunk at all—and of course you can count, one two three four etc., but the trouble is you can't tell which one is one. Each one is one: itself. Where do you begin? Each one being one, there is no, what's the word, I had it just now, something-ship, between the ones. There is no between. There is only here and here, one and one. There is no there. Maya has fallen. All is here now one. But if all is now and all here and one all, there is no end. It did not begin so it cannot end. Oh God, here now One get me out of this—

I'm trying to describe the sensations of the average person in NAFAL flight. It can be much worse than this for some, whose time-sense is acute. For others it is restful, like a drug-haze freeing the mind from the tyranny of hours. And for a few the experience is certainly mystical; the collapse of time and relation leading them directly to intuition of the eternal. But the mystic is a rare bird, and the nearest most people get to God in paradoxical time is by inarticulate and anguished prayer for release.

They used to drug people for the long jumps, but stopped the practice when they realized its effects. What happens to a drugged, or ill, or wounded person during near-lightspeed flight is, of course, indeterminable. A jump of ten lightyears should logically make no difference to a victim of measles or gunshot. The body ages only a few minutes; why is the measles patient carried out of the ship a leper, and the wounded man a corpse? Nobody knows, except perhaps the body, which keeps the logic of the flesh, and knows it has lain festering, bleeding, or drugged into mindlessness for ten years. Many imbeciles having been produced, the Fisher King Effect was established as fact, and they stopped using drugs and transporting the ill, the damaged and the pregnant. You have to be in common health to go NAFAL, and you have to take it straight.

But you don't have to be sane.

It was only during the earliest decades of the League that Earthmen, perhaps trying to bolster their battered collective ego, sent out ships on enormously long voyages, beyond the pale, over the stars and far away. They were seeking for worlds that had not, like all the known worlds, been settled or seeded by the Founders on Hain, truly alien worlds; and all the crews of these Extreme Surveys were of unsound mind. Who else would go out to collect information that wouldn't be received for four, or five, or six centuries? Received by whom? This was before the invention of the instantaneous communicator; they would be isolated both in space and time. No sane person who has experienced time-slippage of even a few decades between near worlds would volunteer for a round trip of a half millennium. The Surveyors were escapists; misfits; nuts.

Ten of them climbed aboard the ferry at Smeming Port on Pesm, and made varyingly inept attempts to get to know one another during the three days the ferry took getting to their ship, *Gum*. Gum is a Low Cetian nickname, on the order of Baby or Pet. There was one Low Cetian on the team, one Hairy Cetian,

two Hainishmen, one Beldene, and five Terrans; the
ship was Cetian-built, but chartered by the Government of Earth. Her motley crew came aboard wriggling through the coupling-tube one by one like
apprehensive spermatozoa fertilizing the universe. The
ferry left, and the navigator put *Gum* under way. She
flittered for some hours on the edge of space a few
hundred million miles from Pesm, and then abruptly
vanished.

When, after ten hours twenty-nine minutes, or 256
years, *Gum* reappeared in normal space, she was
supposed to be in the vicinity of Star KG-E-96651.
Sure enough, there was the cheerful gold pinhead of
the star. Somewhere within a 400-million-kilometer
sphere there was also a greenish planet, World 4470,
as charted by a Cetian Mapmaker long ago. The ship
now had to find the planet. This was not quite so easy
as it might sound, given a 400-million-kilometer hay-
stack. And *Gum* couldn't bat about in planetary space
at near lightspeed; if she did, she and Star KG-E-
96651 and World 4470 might all end up going bang.
She had to creep, using rocket propulsion, at a few
hundred thousand miles an hour. The Mathematician/
Navigator, Asnanifoil, knew pretty well where the
planet ought to be, and thought they might raise it
within ten E-days. Meanwhile the members of the
Survey team got to know one another still better.

"I can't stand him," said Porlock, the Hard Scientist
(chemistry, plus physics, astronomy, geology, etc.),
and little blobs of spittle appeared on his mustache.
"The man is insane. I can't imagine why he was
passed as fit to join a Survey team, unless this is a
deliberate experiment in noncompatibility, planned by
the Authority, with us as guinea pigs."

"We generally use hamsters and Hainish gholes,"

said Mannon, the Soft Scientist (psychology, plus psychiatry, anthropology, ecology, etc.), politely; he was one of the Hainishmen. "Instead of guinea pigs. Well, you know, Mr. Osden is really a very rare case. In fact, he's the first fully cured case of Render's Syndrome—a variety of infantile autism which was thought to be incurable. The great Terran analyst Hammergeld reasoned that the cause of the autistic condition in this case is a supernormal empathic capacity, and developed an appropriate treatment. Mr. Osden is the first patient to undergo that treatment, in fact he lived with Dr. Hammergeld until he was eighteen. The therapy was completely successful."

"Successful?"

"Why, yes. He certainly is not autistic."

"No, he's intolerable!"

"Well, you see," said Mannon, gazing mildly at the saliva-flecks on Porlock's mustache, "the normal defensive-aggressive reaction between strangers meeting— let's say you and Mr. Osden just for example—is something you're scarcely aware of; habit, manners, inattention get you past it; you've learned to ignore it, to the point where you might even deny it exists. However, Mr. Osden, being an empath, feels it. Feels his feelings, and yours, and is hard put to say which is which. Let's say that there's a normal element of hostility towards any stranger in your emotional reaction to him when you meet him, plus a spontaneous dislike of his looks, or clothes, or handshake—it doesn't matter what. He feels that dislike. As his autistic defense has been unlearned, he resorts to an aggressive-defense mechanism, a response in kind to the aggression which you have unwittingly projected onto him." Mannon went on for quite a long time.

"Nothing gives a man the right to be such a bastard," Porlock said.

"He can't tune us out?" asked Harfex, the Biologist, another Hainishman.

"It's like hearing," said Olleroo, Assistant Hard Scientist, stooping over to paint her toenails with fluorescent lacquer. "No eyelids on your ears. No Off switch on empathy. He hears our feelings whether he wants to or not."

"Does he know what we're *thinking?*" asked Eskwana, the Engineer, looking around at the others in real dread.

"No," Porlock snapped. "Empathy's not telepathy! Nobody's got telepathy."

"Yet," said Mannon, with his little smile. "Just before I left Hain there was a most interesting report in from one of the recently rediscovered worlds, a hilfer named Rocannon reporting what appears to be a teachable telepathic technique existent among a mutated hominid race; I only saw a synopsis in the HILF *Bulletin,* but—" He went on. The others had learned that they could talk while Mannon went on talking; he did not seem to mind, nor even to miss much of what they said.

"Then why does he hate us?" Eskwana asked.

"Nobody hates you, Ander honey," said Olleroo, daubing Eskwana's left thumbnail with fluorescent pink. The engineer flushed and smiled vaguely.

"He acts as if he hated us," said Haito, the Coordinator. She was a delicate-looking woman of pure Asian descent, with a surprising voice, husky, deep and soft, like a young bullfrog. "Why, if he suffers from our hostility, does he increase it by constant attacks and insults? I can't say I think much of Dr.

Hammergeld's cure, really, Mannon; autism might be preferable . . ."

She stopped. Osden had come into the main cabin.

He looked flayed. His skin was unnaturally white and thin, showing the channels of his blood like a faded roadmap in red and blue. His Adam's apple, the muscles that circled his mouth, the bones and ligaments of his wrists and hands, all stood out distinctly as if displayed for an anatomy lesson. His hair was pale rust, like long-dried blood. He had eyebrows and lashes, but they were visible only in certain lights; what one saw was the bones of the eyesockets, the veining of the lids, and the colorless eyes. They were not red eyes, for he was not really an albino, but they were not blue or gray; colors had canceled out in Osden's eyes, leaving a cold waterlike clarity, infinitely penetrable. He never looked directly at one. His face lacked expression, like an anatomical drawing, or a skinned face.

"I agree," he said in a high, harsh tenor, "that even autistic withdrawal might be preferable to the smog of cheap secondhand emotions with which you people surround me. What are you sweating hate for now, Porlock? Can't stand the sight of me? Go practice some autoeroticism the way you were doing last night, it improves your vibes. —Who the devil moved my tapes, here? Don't touch my things, any of you. I won't have it."

"Osden," said Asnanifoil, the Hairy Cetian, in his large slow voice, "why *are* you such a bastard?"

Ander Eskwana cowered down and put his hands in front of his face. Contention frightened him. Olleroo looked up with a vacant yet eager expression, the eternal spectator.

"Why shouldn't I be?" said Osden. He was not

looking at Asnanifoil, and was keeping physically as far away from all of them as he could in the crowded cabin. "None of you constitute, in yourselves, any reason for my changing my behavior."

Asnanifoil shrugged; Cetians are seldom willing to state the obvious. Harfex, a reserved and patient man, said, "The reason is that we shall be spending several years together. Life will be better for all of us if—"

"Can't you understand that I don't give a damn for all of you?" Osden said, took up his microtapes and went out. Eskwana had suddenly gone to sleep. Asnanifoil was drawing slipstreams in the air with his finger and muttering the Ritual Primes.

"You cannot explain his presence on the team except as a plot on the part of the Terran Authority. I saw this almost at once. This mission is meant to fail," Harfex whispered to the Coordinator, glancing over his shoulder. Porlock was fumbling with his fly-button; there were tears in his eyes. I did tell you they were all crazy, but you thought I was exaggerating.

All the same, they were not unjustified. Extreme Surveyors expected to find their fellow team members intelligent, well-trained, unstable and personally sympathetic. They had to work together in close quarters and nasty places, and could expect one another's paranoias, depressions, manias, phobias and compulsions to be mild enough to admit of good personal relationships, at least most of the time. Osden might be intelligent, but his training was sketchy and his personality was disastrous. He had been sent only on account of his singular gift, the power of empathy: properly speaking, of wide-range bioempathic receptivity. His talent wasn't species-specific; he could pick up emotion or sentience from anything that felt. He could share lust with a white rat, pain with a squashed cockroach, and phototropy with a moth. On an alien world, the Authority had decided, it would be useful to know if anything nearby is sentient, and if so, what its feelings toward you are. Osden's title was a new one: he was the team's Sensor.

"What is emotion, Osden?" Haito Tomiko asked him one day in the main cabin, trying to make some rapport with him for once. "What is it, exactly, that you pick up with your empathic sensitivity?"

"Muck," the man answered in his high, exasperated voice. "The psychic excreta of the animal kingdom. I wade through your feces."

"I was trying," she said, "to learn some facts." She thought her tone was admirably calm.

"You weren't after facts. You were trying to get at me. With some fear, some curiosity, and a great deal of distaste. The way you might poke a dead dog, to see the maggots crawl. Will you understand once and for all that I don't want to be got at, that I want to be left alone?" His skin was mottled with red and violet, his voice had risen. "Go roll in your own dung, you yellow bitch!" he shouted at her silence.

"Calm down," she said, still quietly, but she left him at once and went to her cabin. Of course he had been right about her motives; her question had been largely a pretext, a mere effort to interest him. But what harm in that? Did not that effort imply respect for the other? At the moment of asking the question she had felt at most a slight distrust of him; she had mostly felt sorry for him, the poor arrogant venomous bastard, Mr. No-Skin as Olleroo called him. What did he expect, the way he acted? Love?

"I guess he can't stand anybody feeling sorry for him," said Olleroo, lying on the lower bunk, gilding her nipples.

"Then he can't form any human relationship. All his Dr. Hammergeld did was turn an autism inside out . . ."

"Poor frot," said Olleroo. "Tomiko, you don't mind if Harfex comes in for a while tonight, do you?"

"Can't you go to his cabin? I'm sick of always having to sit in Main with that damned peeled turnip."

"You do hate him, don't you? I guess he feels that. But I slept with Harfex last night too, and Asnanifoil might get jealous, since they share the cabin. It would be nicer here."

"Service them both," Tomiko said with the coarseness of offended modesty. Her Terran subculture, the East Asian, was a puritanical one; she had been brought up chaste.

"I only like one a night," Olleroo replied with innocent serenity. Beldene, the Garden Planet, had never discovered chastity, or the wheel.

"Try Osden, then," Tomiko said. Her personal instability was seldom so plain as now: a profound self-distrust manifesting itself as destructivism. She had volunteered for this job because there was, in all probability, no use in doing it.

The little Beldene looked up, paintbrush in hand, eyes wide. "Tomiko, that was a dirty thing to say."

"Why?"

"It would be vile! I'm not attracted to Osden!"

"I didn't know it mattered to you," Tomiko said indifferently, though she did know. She got some papers together and left the cabin, remarking, "I hope you and Harfex or whoever it is finish by last bell; I'm tired."

Olleroo was crying, tears dripping on her little

gilded nipples. She wept easily. Tomiko had not wept since she was ten years old.

It was not a happy ship; but it took a turn for the better when Asnanifoil and his computer raised World 4470. There it lay, a dark-green jewel, like truth at the bottom of a gravity well. As they watched the jade disk grow, a sense of mutuality grew among them. Osden's selfishness, his accurate cruelty, served now to draw the others together. "Perhaps," Mannon said, "he was sent as a beating-gron. What Terrans call a scapegoat. Perhaps his influence will be good after all." And no one, so careful were they to be kind to one another, disagreed.

They came into orbit. There were no lights on nightside, on the continents none of the lines and clots made by animals who build.

"No men," Harfex murmured.

"Of course not," snapped Osden, who had a viewscreen to himself, and his head inside a polythene bag. He claimed that the plastic cut down on the empathic noise he received from the others. "We're two lightcenturies past the limit of the Hainish Expansion, and outside that there are no men. Anywhere. You don't think Creation would have made the same hideous mistake twice?"

No one was paying him much heed; they were looking with affection at that jade immensity below them, where there was life, but not human life. They were misfits among men, and what they saw there was not desolation, but peace. Even Osden did not look quite so expressionless as usual; he was frowning.

Descent in fire on the sea; air reconnaissance; landing. A plain of something like grass, thick, green, bowing stalks, surrounded the ship, brushed against extended view-cameras, smeared the lenses with a fine pollen.

"It looks like a pure phytosphere," Harfex said. "Osden, do you pick up anything sentient?"

They all turned to the Sensor. He had left the screen and was pouring himself a cup of tea. He did not answer. He seldom answered spoken questions.

The chitinous rigidity of military discipline was quite inapplicable to these teams of Mad Scientists; their chain of command lay somewhere between parliamentary procedure and peck-order, and would have driven a regular service officer out of his mind. By the inscrutable decision of the Authority, however, Dr. Haito Tomiko had been given the title of Coordinator, and she now exercised her prerogative for the first time. "Mr. Sensor Osden," she said, "please answer Mr. Harfex."

"How could I 'pick up' anything from outside," Osden said without turning, "with the emotions of nine neurotic hominids pullulating around me like worms in a can? When I have anything to tell you, I'll tell you. I'm aware of my responsibility as Sensor. If you presume to give me an order again, however, Coordinator Haito, I'll consider my responsibility void."

"Very well, Mr. Sensor. I trust no orders will be needed henceforth." Tomiko's bullfrog voice was calm, but Osden seemed to flinch slightly as he stood with his back to her: as if the surge of her suppressed rancor had struck him with physical force.

The biologist's hunch proved correct. When they began field analyses they found no animals even among the microbiota. Nobody here ate anybody else. All life-forms were photosynthesizing or saprophagous, living off light or death, not off life. Plants:

infinite plants, not one species known to the visitors from the house of Man. Infinite shades and intensities of green, violet, purple, brown, red. Infinite silences. Only the wind moved, swaying leaves and fronds, a warm soughing wind laden with spores and pollens, blowing the sweet pale-green dust over prairies of great grasses, heaths that bore no heather, flowerless forests where no foot had ever walked, no eye had ever looked. A warm, sad world, sad and serene. The Surveyors, wandering like picnickers over sunny plains of violet filicaliformes, spoke softly to each other. They knew their voices broke a silence of a thousand million years, the silence of wind and leaves, leaves and wind, blowing and ceasing and blowing again. They talked softly; but being human, they talked.

"Poor old Osden," said Jenny Chong, Bio and Tech, as she piloted a helijet on the North Polar Quadrating run. "All that fancy hi-fi stuff in his brain and nothing to receive. What a bust."

"He told me he hates plants," Olleroo said with a giggle.

"You'd think he'd like them, since they don't bother him like we do."

"Can't say I much like these plants myself," said Porlock, looking down at the purple undulations of the North Circumpolar Forest. "All the same. No mind. No change. A man alone in it would go right off his head."

"But it's all alive," Jenny Chong said. "And if it lives, Osden hates it."

"He's not really so bad," Olleroo said, magnanimous.

Porlock looked at her sidelong and asked, "You ever slept with him, Olleroo?"

Olleroo burst into tears and cried, "You Terrans are obscene!"

"No, she hasn't," Jenny Chong said, prompt to defend. "Have you, Porlock?"

The chemist laughed uneasily: Ha, ha, ha. Flecks of spittle appeared on his mustache.

"Osden can't bear to be touched," Olleroo said shakily. "I just brushed against him once by accident and he knocked me off like I was some sort of dirty . . . thing. We're all just things, to him."

"He's evil," Porlock said in a strained voice, startling the two women. "He'll end up shattering this team, sabotaging it, one way or another. Mark my words. He's not fit to live with other people!"

They landed on the North Pole. A midnight sun smoldered over low hills. Short, dry, greenish-pink bryoform grasses stretched away in every direction, which was all one direction, south. Subdued by the incredible silence, the three Surveyors set up their instruments and collected their samples, three viruses twitching minutely on the hide of an unmoving giant.

Nobody asked Osden along on runs as pilot or photographer or recorder, and he never volunteered, so he seldom left base camp. He ran Harfex's botanical taxonomic data through the on-ship computers, and served as assistant to Eskwana, whose job here was mainly repair and maintenance. Eskwana had begun to sleep a great deal, twenty-five hours or more out of the thirty-two-hour day, dropping off in the middle of repairing a radio or checking the guidance circuits of a helijet. The Coordinator stayed at base one day to observe. No one else was home except Poswet To, who was subject to epileptic fits; Mannon had plugged her into a therapy-circuit today in a state of preventive catatonia. Tomiko spoke reports into the storage banks, and kept an eye on Osden and Eskwana. Two hours passed.

"You might want to use the 860 microwaldoes in sealing that connection," Eskwana said in his soft, hesitant voice.

"Obviously!"

"Sorry. I just saw you had the 840's there—"

"And will replace them when I take the 860's out. When I don't know how to proceed, Engineer, I'll ask your advice."

After a minute Tomiko looked around. Sure enough, there was Eskwana sound asleep, head on the table, thumb in his mouth.

"Osden."

The white face did not turn, he did not speak, but conveyed impatiently that he was listening.

"You can't be unaware of Eskwana's vulnerability."

"I am not responsible for his psychopathic reactions."

"But you are responsible for your own. Eskwana is essential to our work here, and you're not. If you can't control your hostility, you must avoid him altogether."

Osden put down his tools and stood up. "With pleasure!" he said in his vindictive, scraping voice. "You could not possibly imagine what it's like to *experience* Eskwana's irrational terrors. To have to share his horrible cowardice, to have to cringe with him at everything!"

"Are you trying to justify your cruelty towards him? I thought you had more self-respect." Tomiko found herself shaking with spite. "If your empathic power really makes you share Ander's misery, why does it never induce the least compassion in you?"

"Compassion," Osden said. "Compassion. What do you know about compassion?"

She stared at him, but he would not look at her.

"Would you like me to verbalize your present emotional affect regarding myself?" he said. "I can do so more precisely than you can. I'm trained to analyze such responses as I receive them. And I do receive them."

"But how can you expect me to feel kindly towards you when you behave as you do?"

"What does it matter how I *behave*, you stupid sow, do you think it makes any difference? Do you think the average human is a well of loving kindness? My choice is to be hated or to be despised. Not being a woman or a coward, I prefer to be hated."

"That's rot. Self-pity. Every man has—"

"But I am not a man," Osden said. "There are all of you. And there is myself. I am *one*."

Awed by that glimpse of abysmal solipsism, she kept silent a while; finally she said with neither spite nor pity, clinically, "You could kill yourself, Osden."

"That's your way, Haito," he jeered. "I'm not depressive and seppuku isn't my bit. What do you want me to do here?"

"Leave. Spare yourself and us. Take the aircar and a data-feeder and go do a species count. In the forest; Harfex hasn't even started the forests yet. Take a hundred-square-meter forested area, anywhere inside radio range. But outside empathy range. Report in at eight and twenty-four o'clock daily."

Osden went, and nothing was heard from him for five days but laconic all-well signals twice daily. The mood at base camp changed like a stage set. Eskwana stayed awake up to eighteen hours a day. Poswet To got out her stellar lute and chanted the celestial harmonies (music had driven Osden into a frenzy).

Mannon, Harfex, Jenny Chong and Tomiko all went off tranquilizers. Porlock distilled something in his laboratory and drank it all by himself. He had a hangover. Asnanifoil and Poswet To held an all-night Numerical Epiphany, that mystical orgy of higher mathematics which is the chiefest pleasure of the religious Cetian soul. Olleroo slept with everybody. Work went well.

The Hard Scientist came toward base at a run, laboring through the high, fleshy stalks of the graminiformes. "Something—in the forest—" His eyes bulged, he panted, his mustache and fingers trembled. "Something big. Moving, behind me. I was putting in a benchmark, bending down. It came at me. As if it was swinging down out of the trees. Behind me." He stared at the others with the opaque eyes of terror or exhaustion.

"Sit down, Porlock. Take it easy. Now wait, go through this again. You *saw* something—"

"Not clearly. Just the movement. Purposive. A—an—I don't know what it could have been. Something self-moving. In the trees, the arboriformes, whatever you call 'em. At the edge of the woods."

Harfex looked grim. "There is nothing here that could attack you, Porlock. There are not even microzoa. There *could not* be a large animal."

"Could you possibly have seen an epiphyte drop suddenly, a vine come loose behind you?"

"No," Porlock said. "It was coming down at me, through the branches, fast. When I turned, it took off again, away and upward. It made a noise, a sort of crashing. If it wasn't an animal, God knows what it could have been! It was big—as big as a man, at least. Maybe a reddish color. I couldn't see, I'm not sure."

"It was Osden," said Jenny Chong, "doing a Tarzan act." She giggled nervously, and Tomiko repressed a wild feckless laugh. But Harfex was not smiling.

"One gets uneasy under the arboriformes," he said in his polite, repressed voice. "I've noticed that. Indeed that may be why I've put off working in the forests. There's a hypnotic quality in the colors and spacing of the stems and branches, especially the helically arranged ones; and the spore-throwers grow so regularly spaced that it seems unnatural. I find it quite disagreeable, subjectively speaking. I wonder if a stronger effect of that sort mightn't have produced a hallucination . . . ?"

Porlock shook his head. He wet his lips. "It was there," he said. "Something. Moving with purpose. Trying to attack me from behind."

When Osden called in, punctual as always, at twenty-four o'clock that night, Harfex told him Porlock's report. "Have you come on anything at all, Mr. Osden, that could substantiate Mr. Porlock's impression of a motile, sentient life-form, in the forest?"

Ssss, the radio said sardonically. "No. Bullshit," said Osden's unpleasant voice.

"You've been actually inside the forest longer than any of us," Harfex said with unmitigable politeness. "Do you agree with my impression that the forest ambience has a rather troubling and possibly hallucinogenic effect on the perceptions?"

Ssss. "I'll agree that Porlock's perceptions are easily troubled. Keep him in his lab, he'll do less harm. Anything else?"

"Not at present," Harfex said, and Osden cut off.

Nobody could credit Porlock's story, and nobody could discredit it. He was positive that something,

something big, had tried to attack him by surprise. It was hard to deny this, for they were on an alien world, and everyone who had entered the forest had felt a certain chill and foreboding under the "trees." ("Call them trees, certainly," Harfex had said. "They really are the same thing, only, of course, altogether different.") They agreed that they had felt uneasy, or had had the sense that something was watching them from behind.

"We've got to clear this up," Porlock said, and he asked to be sent as a temporary Biologist's Aide, like Osden, into the forest to explore and observe. Olleroo and Jenny Chong volunteered if they could go as a pair. Harfex sent them all off into the forest near which they were encamped, a vast tract covering four-fifths of Continent D. He forbade side arms. They were not to go outside a fifty-kilo half-circle, which included Osden's current site. They all reported in twice daily, for three days. Porlock reported a glimpse of what seemed to be a large semi-erect shape moving through the trees across the river; Olleroo was sure she had heard something moving near the tent, the second night.

"There are no animals on this planet," Harfex said, dogged.

Then Osden missed his morning call.

Tomiko waited less than an hour, then flew with Harfex to the area where Osden had reported himself the night before. But as the helijet hovered over the sea of purplish leaves, illimitable, impenetrable, she felt a panic despair. "How can we find him in this?"

"He reported landing on the river bank. Find the aircar; he'll be camped near it, and he can't have gone far from his camp. Species-counting is slow work. There's the river."

"There's his car," Tomiko said, catching the bright foreign glint among the vegetable colors and shadows. "Here goes, then."

She put the ship in hover and pitched out the ladder. She and Harfex descended. The sea of life closed over their heads.

As her feet touched the forest floor, she unsnapped the flap of her holster; then glancing at Harfex, who was unarmed, she left the gun untouched. But her hand kept coming back up to it. There was no sound at all, as soon as they were a few meters away from the slow, brown river, and the light was dim. Great boles stood well apart, almost regularly, almost alike; they were soft-skinned, some appearing smooth and others spongy, gray or greenish-brown or brown, twined with cablelike creepers and festooned with epiphytes, extending rigid, entangled armfuls of big, saucer-shaped, dark leaves that formed a roof-layer twenty to thirty meters thick. The ground underfoot was springy as a mattress, every inch of it knotted with roots and peppered with small, fleshy-leaved growths.

"Here's his tent," Tomiko said, cowed at the sound of her voice in that huge community of the voiceless. In the tent was Osden's sleeping bag, a couple of books, a box of rations. We should be calling, shouting for him, she thought, but did not even suggest it; nor did Harfex. They circled out from the tent, careful to keep each other in sight through the thick-standing presences, the crowding gloom. She stumbled over Osden's body, not thirty meters from the tent, led to it by the whitish gleam of a dropped notebook. He lay face down between two huge-rooted trees. His head and hands were covered with blood, some dried, some still oozing red.

Harfex appeared beside her, his pale Hainish complexion quite green in the dusk. "Dead?"

"No. He's been struck. Beaten. From behind." Tomiko's fingers felt over the bloody skull and nape and temples. "A weapon or a tool . . . I don't find a fracture."

As she turned Osden's body over so they could lift him, his eyes opened. She was holding him, bending close to his face. His pale lips writhed. A deathly fear came into her. She screamed aloud two or three times and tried to run away, shambling and stumbling into the terrible dusk. Harfex caught her, and at his touch and the sound of his voice, her panic decreased. "What is it? What is it?" he was saying.

"I don't know," she sobbed. Her heartbeat still shook her, and she could not see clearly. "The fear— the . . . I panicked. When I saw his eyes."

"We're both nervous. I don't understand this—"

"I'm all right now, come on, we've got to get him under care."

Both working with senseless haste, they lugged Osden to the riverside and hauled him up on a rope under his armpits; he dangled like a sack, twisting a little, over the glutinous dark sea of leaves. They pulled him into the helijet and took off. Within a minute they were over open prairie. Tomiko locked onto the homing beam. She drew a deep breath, and her eyes met Harfex's.

"I was so terrified I almost fainted. I have never done that."

"I was . . . unreasonably frightened also," said the Hainishman, and indeed he looked aged and shaken. "Not so badly as you. But as unreasonably."

"It was when I was in contact with him, holding him. He seemed to be conscious for a moment."

"Empathy? . . . I hope he can tell us what attacked him."

Osden, like a broken dummy covered with blood and mud, half lay as they had bundled him into the rear seats in their frantic urgency to get out of the forest.

More panic met their arrival at base. The ineffective brutality of the assault was sinister and bewildering. Since Harfex stubbornly denied any possibility of animal life, they began speculating about sentient plants, vegetable monsters, psychic projections. Jenny Chong's latent phobia reasserted itself and she could talk about nothing except the Dark Egos which followed people around behind their backs. She and Olleroo and Porlock had been summoned back to base; and nobody was much inclined to go outside.

Osden had lost a good deal of blood during the three or four hours he had lain alone, and concussion and severe contusions had put him in shock and semicoma. As he came out of this and began running a low fever, he called several times for "Doctor," in a plaintive voice: "Doctor Hammergeld . . ." When he regained full consciousness, two of those long days later, Tomiko called Harfex into his cubicle.

"Osden: can you tell us what attacked you?"

The pale eyes flickered past Harfex's face.

"You were attacked," Tomiko said gently. The shifty gaze was hatefully familiar, but she was a physician, protective of the hurt. "You may not remember it yet. Something attacked you. You were in the forest—"

"Ah!" he cried out, his eyes growing bright and his features contorting. "The forest—in the forest—"

"What's in the forest?"

He gasped for breath. A look of clearer consciousness came into his face. After a while he said, "I don't know."

"Did you see what attacked you?" Harfex asked.

"I don't know."

"You remember it now."

"I don't know."

"All our lives may depend on this. You must tell us what you saw!"

"I don't know," Osden said, sobbing with weakness. He was too weak to hide the fact that he was hiding the answer, yet he would not say it. Porlock, nearby, was chewing his pepper-colored mustache as he tried to hear what was going on in the cubicle.

Harfex leaned over Osden and said, "You *will* tell us—" Tomiko had to interfere bodily.

Harfex controlled himself with an effort that was painful to see. He went off silently to his cubicle, where no doubt he took a double or triple dose of tranquilizers. The other men and women, scattered about the big frail building, a long main hall and ten sleeping-cubicles, said nothing, but looked depressed and edgy. Osden, as always, even now, had them all at his mercy. Tomiko looked down at him with a rush of hatred that burned in her throat like bile. This monstrous egotism that fed itself on others' emotions, this absolute selfishness, was worse than any hideous deformity of the flesh. Like a congenital monster, he should not have lived. Should not be alive. Should have died. Why had his head not been split open?

As he lay flat and white, his hands helpless at his sides, his colorless eyes were wide open, and there were tears running from the corners. Tomiko moved toward him suddenly. He tried to flinch away. "Don't," he said in a weak hoarse voice, and tried to raise his hands to protect his head. "Don't!"

She sat down on the folding stool beside the cot, and after a while put her hand on his. He tried to pull away, but lacked the strength.

A long silence fell between them.

"Osden," she murmured, "I'm sorry. I'm very sorry. I will you well. Let me will you well, Osden. I don't want to hurt you. Listen, I do see now. It was one of us. That's right, isn't it. No, don't answer, only tell me if I'm wrong; but I'm not . . . Of course there are animals on this planet: ten of them. I don't care who it was. It doesn't matter, does it. It could have been me, just now. I realize that. I didn't understand how it is, Osden. You can't see how difficult it is for us to understand . . . But listen. If it were love, instead of hate and fear . . . Is it never love?"

"No."

"Why not? Why should it never be? Are human beings all so weak? That is terrible. Never mind, never mind, don't worry. Keep still. At least right now it isn't hate, is it? Sympathy at least, concern, well-wishing. You do feel that, Osden? Is it what you feel?"

"Among . . . other things," he said, almost inaudible.

"Noise from my subconscious, I suppose. And everybody else in the room . . . Listen, when we found you there in the forest, when I tried to turn you over, you partly wakened, and I felt a horror of you. I was insane with fear for a minute. Was that your fear of me I felt?"

"No."

Her hand was still on his, and he was quite relaxed, sinking toward sleep, like a man in pain who has been given relief from pain. "The forest," he muttered; she could barely understand him. "Afraid."

She pressed him no further, but kept her hand on his and watched him go to sleep. She knew what she felt, and what therefore he must feel. She was confident of it: there is only one emotion, or state of being, that can thus wholly reverse itself, polarize, within one moment. In Great Hainish indeed there is one word, *ontá,* for love and for hate. She was not in love with Osden, of course, that is another kettle of fish. What she felt for him was ontá, polarized hate. She held his hand and the current flowed between them, the tremendous electricity of touch, which he had always dreaded. As he slept, the ring of anatomy-chart muscles around his mouth relaxed, and Tomiko saw on his face what none of them had ever seen, very faint, a smile. It faded. He slept on.

He was tough; next day he was sitting up, and hungry. Harfex wished to interrogate him, but Tomiko put him off. She hung a sheet of polythene over the cubicle door, as Osden himself had often done. "Does it actually cut down your empathic reception?" she asked, and he replied, in the dry, cautious tone they were now using to each other, "No."

"Just a warning, then."

"Partly. More faith-healing. Dr. Hammergeld thought it worked . . . Maybe it does, a little."

There had been love, once. A terrified child, suffocating in the tidal rush and battering of the huge emotions of adults, a drowning child, saved by one man. Taught to breathe, to live, by one man. Given everything, all protection and love, by one man. Father/mother/God: no other. "Is he still alive?" Tomiko asked, thinking of Osden's incredible loneliness, and the strange cruelty of the great doctors. She was shocked when she heard his forced, tinny laugh.

"He died at least two and a half centuries ago," Osden said. "Do you forget where we are, Coordinator? We've all left our little families behind . . ."

Outside the polythene curtain the eight other human beings on World 4470 moved vaguely. Their voices were low and strained. Eskwana slept; Poswet To was in therapy; Jenny Chong was trying to rig lights in her cubicle so that she wouldn't cast a shadow.

"They're all scared," Tomiko said, scared. "They've all got these ideas about what attacked you. A sort of ape-potato, a giant fanged spinach, I don't know . . . Even Harfex. You may be right not to force them to see. That would be worse, to lose confidence in one another. But why are we all so shaky, unable to face the fact, going to pieces so easily? Are we really all insane?"

"We'll soon be more so."

"Why?"

"There *is* something."

He closed his mouth, the muscles of his lips stood out rigid.

"Something sentient?"

"A sentience."

"In the forest?"

He nodded.

"What is it, then—?"

"The fear." He began to look strained again, and moved restlessly. "When I fell, there, you know, I didn't lose consciousness at once. Or I kept regaining it. I don't know. It was more like being paralyzed."

"You were."

"I was on the ground. I couldn't get up. My face was in the dirt, in that soft leafmold. It was in my nostrils and eyes. I couldn't move. Couldn't see. As if I was in the ground. Sunk into it, part of it. I knew I was between two trees even though I never saw them. I suppose I could feel the roots. Below me in the ground, down under the ground. My hands were bloody, I could feel that, and the blood made the dirt around my face sticky. I felt the fear. It kept growing. As if they'd finally *known* I was there, lying on them there, under them, among them, the thing they feared, and yet part of their fear itself. I couldn't stop sending the fear back, and it kept growing, and I couldn't move, I couldn't get away. I would pass out, I think, and then the fear would bring me to again, and I still couldn't move. Any more than they can."

Tomiko felt the cold stirring of her hair, the readying of the apparatus of terror. "They: who are they, Osden?"

"They, it—I don't know. The fear."

"What is he talking about?" Harfex demanded when Tomiko reported this conversation. She would not let Harfex question Osden yet, feeling that she must protect Osden from the onslaught of the Hainishman's powerful, overrepressed emotions. Unfortunately this fueled the slow fire of paranoid anxiety that burned in poor Harfex, and he thought she and Osden were in league, hiding some fact of great importance or peril from the rest of the team.

"It's like the blind man trying to describe the elephant. Osden hasn't seen or heard the . . . the sentience, any more than we have."

"But he's felt it, my dear Haito," Harfex said with just-suppressed rage. "Not empathically. On his skull. It came and knocked him down and beat him with a blunt instrument. Did he not catch *one* glimpse of it?"

"What would he have seen, Harfex?" Tomiko asked,

but he would not hear her meaningful tone; even he had blocked out that comprehension. What one fears is alien. The murderer is an outsider, a foreigner, not one of us. The evil is not in me!

"The first blow knocked him pretty well out," Tomiko said a little wearily, "he didn't see anything. But when he came to again, alone in the forest, he felt a great fear. Not his own fear, an empathic affect. He is certain of that. And certain it was nothing picked up from any of us. So that evidently the native life-forms are not all insentient."

Harfex looked at her a moment, grim. "You're trying to frighten me, Haito. I do not understand your motives." He got up and went off to his laboratory table, walking slowly and stiffly, like a man of eighty not of forty.

She looked round at the others. She felt some desperation. Her new, fragile, and profound interdependence with Osden gave her, she was well aware, some added strength. But if even Harfex could not keep his head, who of the others would? Porlock and Eskwana were shut in their cubicles, the others were all working or busy with something. There was something queer about their positions. For a while the Coordinator could not tell what it was, then she saw that they were all sitting facing the nearby forest. Playing chess with Asnanifoil, Olleroo had edged her chair around until it was almost beside his.

She went to Mannon, who was dissecting a tangle of spidery brown roots, and told him to look for the pattern-puzzle. He saw it at once, and said with unusual brevity, "Keeping an eye on the enemy."

"What enemy? What do *you* feel, Mannon?" She had a sudden hope in him as a psychologist, on this obscure ground of hints and empathies where biologists went astray.

"I feel a strong anxiety with a specific spatial orientation. But I am not an empath. Therefore, the anxiety is explicable in terms of the particular stress-situation, that is the attack on a team member in the forest, and also in terms of the total stress-situation, that is my presence in a totally alien environment, for which the archetypical connotations of the word 'forest' provide an inevitable metaphor."

Hours later Tomiko woke to hear Osden screaming in nightmare; Mannon was calming him, and she sank back into her own dark-branching pathless dreams. In the morning Eskwana did not wake. He could not be roused with stimulant drugs. He clung to his sleep, slipping farther and farther back, mumbling softly now and then until, wholly regressed, he lay curled on his side, thumb at his lips, gone.

"Two days: two down. Ten little Indians, nine little Indians . . ." That was Porlock.

"And you're the next little Indian," Jenny Chong snapped. "Go analyze your urine, Porlock!"

"He is driving us all insane," Porlock said, getting up and waving his left arm. "Can't you feel it? For God's sake, are you all deaf and blind? Can't you feel what he's doing, the emanations? It all comes from him—from his room there—from his mind. He is driving us all insane with fear!"

"Who is?" said Asnanifoil, looming black, precipitous, and hairy over the little Terran.

"Do I have to say his name? Osden, then. Osden! Osden! Why do you think I tried to kill him? In self-defense! To save all of us! Because you won't see what he's doing to us. He's sabotaged the mission by making us quarrel, and now he's going to drive us all insane by projecting fear at us so that we can't sleep or think, like a huge radio that doesn't make any sound, but it broadcasts all the time, and you can't sleep, and you can't think. Haito and Harfex are already under his control but the rest of you can be saved. I had to do it!"

"You didn't do it very well," Osden said, standing half-naked, all rib and bandage, at the door of his cubicle. "I could have hit myself harder. Hell, it isn't me that's scaring you blind, Porlock, it's out there— there, in the woods!"

Porlock made an ineffectual attempt to assault Osden; Asnanifoil held him back, and continued to hold him effortlessly while Mannon gave him a sedative shot. He was put away shouting about giant radios. In a minute the sedative took effect, and he joined a peaceful silence to Eskwana's.

"All right," said Harfex. "Now, by my Gods, you'll tell us what you know and all you know."

Osden said, "I don't know anything."

He looked battered and faint. Tomiko made him sit down before he talked.

"After I'd been three days in the forest, I thought I was occasionally receiving some kind of faint affect."

"Why didn't you report it?"

"Thought I was going spla, like the rest of you."

"That, equally, should have been reported."

"You'd have called me back to base. I couldn't take it. You realize that my inclusion in the mission was a bad mistake. I'm not able to coexist with nine other neurotic personalities at close quarters. I was wrong to volunteer for Extreme Survey, and the Authority was wrong to accept me."

No one spoke; but Tomiko saw, with certainty this

time, the flinch in Osden's shoulders and the tightening of his facial muscles, as he registered their bitter agreement.

"Anyhow, I didn't want to come back to base because I was curious. Even going psycho, how could I pick up empathic affects when there was no creature to emit them? They weren't bad, then. Very vague. Queer. Like a draft in a closed room, a flicker in the corner of your eye. Nothing really."

For a moment he had been borne up on their listening: they heard, so he spoke. He was wholly at their mercy. If they disliked him, he had to be hateful; if they mocked him, he became grotesque; if they listened to him, he was the storyteller. He was helplessly obedient to the demands of their emotions, reactions, moods. And there were seven of them, too many to cope with, so that he must be constantly knocked about from one to another's whim. He could not find coherence. Even as he spoke and held them, somebody's attention would wander: Olleroo perhaps was thinking that he wasn't unattractive; Harfex was seeking the ulterior motive of his words; Asnanifoil's mind, which could not be long held by the concrete, was roaming off toward the eternal peace of number; and Tomiko was distracted by pity, by fear. Osden's voice faltered. He lost the thread. "I . . . I thought it must be the trees," he said, and stopped.

"It's not the trees," Harfex said. "They have no more nervous system than do plants of the Hainish Descent on Earth. None."

"You're not seeing the forest for the trees, as they say on Earth," Mannon put in, smiling elfinly; Harfex stared at him. "What about those root-nodes we've been puzzling about for twenty days—eh?"

"What about them?"

"They are, indubitably, connections. Connections among the trees. Right? Now, let's just suppose, most improbably, that you knew nothing of animal brain-structure. And you were given one axon, or one de-tached glial cell, to examine. Would you be likely to discover what it was? Would you see that the cell was capable of sentience?"

"No. Because it isn't. A single cell is capable of mechanical response to stimulus. No more. Are you hypothesizing that individual arboriformes are 'cells' in a kind of brain, Mannon?"

"Not exactly. I'm merely pointing out that they are all interconnected, both by the root-node linkage and by your green epiphytes in the branches. A linkage of incredible complexity and physical extent. Why, even the prairie grass-forms have those root-connectors, don't they? I know that sentience or intelligence isn't a thing, you can't find it in, or analyze it out from, the cells of a brain. It's a function of the connected cells. It is, in a sense, the connection: the connectedness. It doesn't exist. I'm not trying to say it exists. I'm only guessing that Osden might be able to describe it."

And Osden took him up, speaking as if in trance. "Sentience without senses. Blind, deaf, nerveless, moveless. Some irritability, response to touch. Response to sun, to light, to water, and chemicals in the earth around the roots. Nothing comprehensible to an animal mind. Presence without mind. Awareness of being, without object or subject. Nirvana."

"Then why do you receive fear?" Tomiko asked in a low voice.

"I don't know. I can't see how awareness of objects, of others, could arise: an unperceiving response . . . But there was an uneasiness, for days. And then when I lay between the two trees and my blood was on their roots—" Osden's face glittered with sweat. "It became fear," he said shrilly, "only fear."

"If such a function existed," Harfex said, "it would not be capable of conceiving of a self-moving, material entity, or responding to one. It could no more become aware of us than we can 'become aware' of Infinity."

"The silence of those infinite expanses terrifics me," muttered Tomiko. "Pascal was aware of Infinity. By way of fear."

"To a forest," Mannon said, "we might appear as forest fires. Hurricanes. Dangers. What moves quickly is dangerous, to a plant. The rootless would be alien, terrible. And if it is mind, it seems only too probable that it might become awarc of Osden, whose own mind is open to connection with all others so long as he's conscious, and who was lying in pain and afraid within it, actually inside it. No wonder it was afraid—"

"Not 'it,' " Harfex said. "There is no being, no huge creature, no person! There could at most be only a function—"

"There is only a fear," Osden said.

They were all still awhile, and heard the stillness outside.

"Is that what I feel all the time coming up behind me?" Jenny Chong asked, subdued.

Osden nodded. "You all feel it, deaf as you are. Eskwana's the worst off, because he actually has some empathic capacity. He could send if he learned how, but he's too weak, never will be anything but a medium."

"Listen, Osden," Tomiko said, "you can send. Then send to it—the forest, the fear out there—tell that we won't hurt it. Since it has, or is, some sort of affect that translates into what we feel as emotion, can't you translate back? Send out a message, We are harmless, we are friendly."

"You must know that nobody can emit a false empathic message, Haito. You can't send something that doesn't exist."

"But we don't intend harm, we are friendly."

"Are we? In the forest, when you picked me up, did you feel friendly?"

"No. Terrified. But that's—it, the forest, the plants, not my own fear, isn't it?"

"What's the difference? It's all you felt. Can't you see," and Osden's voice rose in exasperation, "why I dislike you and you dislike me, all of you? Can't you see that I retransmit every negative or aggressive affect you've felt towards me since we first met? I return your hostility, with thanks. I do it in self-defense. Like Porlock. It is self-defense, though, it's the only technique I developed to replace my original defense of total withdrawal from others. Unfortunately it creates a closed circuit, self-sustaining and self-reinforcing. Your initial reaction to me was the instinctive antipathy to a cripple; by now of course it's hatred. Can you fail to see my point? The forest-mind out there transmits only terror, now, and the only message I can send it is terror, because when exposed to it I can feel nothing except terror!"

"What must we do, then?" said Tomiko, and Mannon replied promptly, "Move camp. To another continent. If there are plant-minds there, they'll be slow to notice us, as this one was; maybe they won't notice us at all."

"It would be a considerable relief," Osden observed stiffly. The others had been watching him with a new curiosity. He had revealed himself, they had seen him as he was, a helpless man in a trap. Perhaps, like Tomiko, they had seen that the trap itself, his crass and cruel egotism, was their own construction, not his. They had built the cage and locked him in it, and like a caged ape he threw filth out through the bars. If, meeting him, they had offered trust, if they had been strong enough to offer him love, how might he have appeared to them?

None of them could have done so, and it was too late now. Given time, given solitude, Tomiko might have built up with him a slow resonance of feeling, a consonance of trust, a harmony: but there was no time, their job must be done. There was not room enough for the cultivation of so great a thing, and they must make do with sympathy, with pity, the small change of love. Even that much had given her strength, but it was nowhere near enough for him. She could see in his flayed face now his savage resentment of their curiosity, even of her pity.

"Go lie down, that gash is bleeding again," she said, and he obeyed her.

Next morning they packed up, melted down the sprayform hangar and living quarters, lifted *Gum* on mechanical drive and took her halfway around World 4470, over the red and green lands, the many warm-green seas. They had picked out a likely spot on Continent G: a prairie, twenty thousand square kilos of windswept graminiformes. No forest was within a hundred kilos of the site, and there were no lone trees or groves on the plain. The plant-forms occurred only in large species-colonies, never intermingled, except for certain tiny ubiquitous saprophytes and spore-bearers. The team sprayed holomeld over structure forms, and by evening of the thirty-two-hour day were settled in to the new camp. Eskwana was still asleep and Porlock still sedated, but everyone else was cheerful. "You can breathe here!" they kept saying.

Osden got on his feet and went shakily to the doorway; leaning there, he looked through twilight over the dim reaches of the swaying grass that was not grass. There was a faint, sweet odor of pollen on the wind; no sound but the soft, vast sibilance of wind. His bandaged head cocked a little, the empath stood motionless for a long time. Darkness came, and the stars, lights in the windows of the distant house of Man. The wind had ceased, there was no sound. He listened.

In the long night Haito Tomiko listened. She lay still and heard the blood in her arteries, the breathing of sleepers, the wind blowing, the dark veins running, the dreams advancing, the vast static of stars increasing as the universe died slowly, the sound of death walking. She struggled out of her bed, fled the tiny solitude of her cubicle. Eskwana alone slept. Porlock lay straitjacketed, raving softly in his obscure native tongue. Olleroo and Jenny Chong were playing cards, grim-faced. Poswet To was in the therapy niche, plugged in. Asnanifoil was drawing a mandala, the Third Pattern of the Primes. Mannon and Harfex were sitting up with Osden.

She changed the bandages on Osden's head. His lank, reddish hair, where she had not had to shave it, looked strange. It was salted with white, now. Her hands shook as she worked. Nobody had yet said anything.

"How can the fear be here too?" she said, and her voice rang flat and false in the terrific silence of the vegetable night.

"It's not just the trees; the grasses too . . ."

"But we're twelve thousand kilos from where we were this morning, we left it on the other side of the planet."

"It's all one," Osden said. "One big green thought. How long does it take a thought to get from one side of your brain to the other?"

"It doesn't think. It isn't thinking," Harfex said lifelessly. "It's merely a network of processes. The branches, the epiphytic growths, the roots with those nodal junctures between individuals: they must all be capable of transmitting electrochemical impulses. There are no individual plants, then, properly speaking. Even the pollen is part of the linkage, no doubt, a sort of windborne sentience, connecting overseas. But it is not conceivable. That all the biosphere of a planet should be one network of communications, sensitive, irrational, immortal, isolated . . ."

"Isolated," said Osden. "That's it! That's the fear. It isn't that we're motile, or destructive. It's just that we are. We are other. There has never been any other."

"You're right," Mannon said, almost whispering. "It has no peers. No enemies. No relationship with anything but itself. One alone forever."

"Then what's its function in species-survival?"

"None, maybe," Osden said. "Why are you getting teleological, Harfex? Aren't you a Hainishman? Isn't the measure of complexity the measure of the eternal joy?"

Harfex did not take the bait. He looked ill. "We should leave this world," he said.

"Now you know why I always want to get out, get away from you," Osden said with a kind of morbid geniality. "It isn't pleasant, is it—the other's fear? . . . If only it were an animal intelligence. I can get through to animals. I get along with cobras and tigers;

superior intelligence gives one the advantage. I should have been used in a zoo, not on a human team . . . If I could get through to the damned stupid potato! If it wasn't so overwhelming . . . I still pick up more than the fear, you know. And before it panicked it had a—there was a serenity. I couldn't take it in, then, I didn't realize how big it was. To know the whole daylight, after all, and the whole night. All the winds and the lulls together. The winter stars and the summer stars at the same time. To have roots, and no enemies. To be entire. Do you see? No invasion. No others. To be whole . . ."

He had never spoken before, Tomiko thought.

"You are defenseless against it, Osden," she said. "Your personality has changed already. You're vulnerable to it. We may not all go mad, but you will, if we don't leave."

He hesitated, then he looked up at Tomiko, the first time he had ever met her eyes, a long, still look, clear as water.

"What's sanity ever done for me?" he said, mocking. "But you have a point, Haito. You have something there."

"We should get away," Harfex muttered.

"If I gave in to it," Osden mused, "could I communicate?"

"By 'give in,'" Mannon said in a rapid, nervous voice, "I assume that you mean, stop sending back the empathic information which you receive from the plant-entity: stop rejecting the fear, and absorb it. That will either kill you at once, or drive you back into total psychological withdrawal, autism."

"Why?" said Osden. "Its message is *rejection*. But my salvation is rejection. It's not intelligent. But I am."

"The scale is wrong. What can a single human brain achieve against something so vast?"

"A single human brain can perceive pattern on the scale of stars and galaxies," Tomiko said, "and interpret it as Love."

Mannon looked from one to the other of them; Harfex was silent.

"It'd be easier in the forest," Osden said. "Which of you will fly me over?"

"When?"

"Now. Before you all crack up or go violent."

"I will," Tomiko said.

"None of us will," Harfex said.

"I can't," Mannon said. "I . . . I am too frightened. I'd crash the jet."

"Bring Eskwana along. If I can pull this off, he might serve as a medium."

"Are you accepting the Sensor's plan, Coordinator?" Harfex asked formally.

"Yes."

"I disapprove. I will come with you, however."

"I think we're compelled, Harfex," Tomiko said, looking at Osden's face, the ugly white mask transfigured, eager as a lover's face.

Olleroo and Jenny Chong, playing cards to keep their thoughts from their haunted beds, their mounting dread, chattered like scared children. "This thing, it's in the forest, it'll get you—"

"Scared of the dark?" Osden jeered.

"But look at Eskwana, and Porlock, and even Asnanifoil—"

"It can't hurt you. It's an impulse passing through synapses, a wind passing through branches. It is only a nightmare."

They took off in a helijet, Eskwana curled up still sound asleep in the rear compartment, Tomiko piloting, Harfex and Osden silent, watching ahead for the dark line of forest across the vague gray miles of starlit plain.

They neared the black line, crossed it; now under them was darkness.

She sought a landing place, flying low, though she had to fight her frantic wish to fly high, to get out, get away. The huge vitality of the plant-world was far stronger here in the forest, and its panic beat in immense dark waves. There was a pale patch ahead, a bare knoll-top a little higher than the tallest of the black shapes around it; the not-trees; the rooted; the parts of the whole. She set the helijet down in the glade, a bad landing. Her hands on the stick were slippery as if she had rubbed them with cold soap.

About them now stood the forest, black in darkness.

Tomiko cowered down and shut her eyes. Eskwana moaned in his sleep. Harfex's breath came short and loud, and he sat rigid, even when Osden reached across him and slid the door open.

Osden stood up; his back and bandaged head were just visible in the dim glow of the control-panel as he paused stooping in the doorway.

Tomiko was shaking. She could not raise her head. "No, no, no, no, no, no, no," she said in a whisper. "No. No. No."

Osden moved suddenly and quietly, swinging out of the doorway, down into the dark. He was gone.

I am coming! said a great voice that made no sound.

Tomiko screamed. Harfex coughed; he seemed to be trying to stand up, but did not do so.

Tomiko drew in upon herself, all centered in the

blind eye in her belly, in the center of her being; and outside that there was nothing but the fear.

It ceased.

She raised her head; slowly unclenched her hands. She sat up straight. The night was dark, and stars shone over the forest. There was nothing else.

"Osden," she said, but her voice would not come. She spoke again, louder, a lone bullfrog croak. There was no reply.

She began to realize that something had gone wrong with Harfex. She was trying to find his head in the darkness, for he had slipped down from the seat, when all at once, in the dead quiet, in the dark rear compartment of the craft, a voice spoke. "Good," it said.

It was Eskwana's voice. She snapped on the interior lights and saw the engineer lying curled up asleep, his hand half over his mouth.

The mouth opened and spoke. "All well," it said.

"Osden—"

"All well," said the soft voice from Eskwana's mouth.

"Where are you?"

Silence.

"Come back."

Wind was rising. "I'll stay here," the soft voice said.

"You can't stay—"

Silence.

"You'd be alone, Osden!"

"Listen." The voice was fainter, slurred, as if lost in the sound of wind. "Listen. I will you well."

She called his name after that, but there was no answer. Eskwana lay still. Harfex lay stiller.

"Osden!" she cried, leaning out the doorway into the

dark, wind-shaken silence of the forest of being. "I will come back. I must get Harfex to the base. I will come back, Osden!"

Silence and wind in leaves.

They finished the prescribed survey of World 4470, the eight of them; it took them forty-one days more. Asnanifoil and one or another of the women went into the forest daily at first, searching for Osden in the region around the bare knoll; though Tomiko was not in her heart sure which bare knoll they had landed on that night in the very heart and vortex of terror. They left piles of supplies for Osden, food enough for fifty years, clothing, tents, tools. They did not go on searching; there was no way to find a man alone, hiding, if he wanted to hide, in those unending labyrinths and dim corridors vine-entangled, root-floored. They might have passed within arm's reach of him and never seen him.

But he was there; for there was no fear any more.

Rational, and valuing reason more highly after an intolerable experience of the immortal mindless, Tomiko tried to understand rationally what Osden had done. But the words escaped her control. He had taken the fear into himself, and accepting had transcended it. He had given up his self to the alien, an unreserved surrender, that left no place for evil. He had learned the love of the Other, and thereby had been given his whole self. But this is not the vocabulary of reason.

The people of the Survey team walked under the trees, through the vast colonies of life, surrounded by a dreaming silence, a brooding calm that was half-aware of them and wholly indifferent to them. There were no hours. Distance was no matter. Had we but

world enough and time . . . The planet turned between the sunlight and the great dark; winds of winter
and summer blew fine, pale pollen across the quiet
seas.

Gum returned after many surveys, years and lightyears, to what had several centuries ago been
Smeming Port on Pesm. There were still men there to
receive (incredulously) the team's reports and to record its losses: Biologist Harfex, dead of fear, and
Sensor Osden, left as a colonist.

FALSE DAWN

CHELSEA QUINN YARBRO

Chelsea Quinn Yarbro was born in California and attended San Francisco State University. She has worked with mentally disturbed children and as a statistical demographic cartographer. She began writing professionally in 1961 for a children's theater company; four of her plays have been produced. She is also a trained musician and composer and teaches voice. She is the author of **Save Me a Place by the Rail** (Orangetree Press), a book about opera.

Ms. Yarbro began publishing science fiction in 1967, and her stories have appeared in **If, Galaxy, Infinity, Strange Bedfellows, Planet One** and other magazines and anthologies. She is the co-editor, with Thomas N. Scortia, of the anthology **Two Views of Wonder** (Ballantine). Her work has been nominated for the "Edgar" award given annually by the Mystery Writers of America for the best work published in that field each year. A former Secretary of the Science Fiction Writers of America, she is married to Donald Simpson, an artist and inventor.

"False Dawn" shows us a polluted and devastated future Earth. A young woman, biologically adapted to this environment, travels across this bleak landscape and is a witness to the brutality of survival.

Most of the bodies were near the silos and storage tanks, where the defenders had retreated in the end. Caught between the Pirates and the Sacramento, they had been wiped out to a man. Mixed in with a few Pirate bodies Thea saw an occasional CD uniform. The cops had gone over at last.

She moved through the stench of the tumbled, looted corpses cautiously, carefully. She had not survived for her twenty-six years being foolhardy.

After dark she made her way east into Chico—what was left of it. Here the Pirates had revenged themselves on the few remaining townspeople. There were men, terribly mutilated men, hanging by their heels from lampposts, turning as they swung. And there were women.

One of the women wasn't dead yet. Her ravaged body hung naked from a broken billboard. Her legs were splayed wide and anchored with ropes. Her legs and belly were bloody, there were heavy bruises on her face and breasts, and she had been branded with a large "M" for mutant.

When Thea came near her, she jerked in her bonds and shrieked laughter that ended in a shuddering wail. *Don't let me ever get like that,* Thea thought, watching the woman's spasmodic thrusts with her hips. *Not like that.*

There was a movement down the street and Thea froze. She could not run without being seen and she could not wait if it were Pirates. She moved slowly, melting into the shadow of a gutted building, disappearing into the darkness as she kept watch.

The creatures that appeared were dogs; lean, wretched things with red-rimmed eyes and raised hackles. Thea had seen enough of the wild dogs to know that these were hunting meat. In the woman they found it. The largest of the dogs approached her on his belly, whining a little. He made a quick dash and nipped the leg nearest him. Aside from a long

howl of laughter the woman did nothing. Embold-
ened, the dog came toward her, taking a more decisive
bite from the leg. The response was a jerk and a
scream followed by low laughter. The other dogs grew
bolder. Each began to make quick, bouncing attacks,
taking token bits of flesh from her legs and feet, growing ever bolder when they met with no resistance.

Thea watched stonily from the shadows, fitting a
quarrel to her makeshift crossbow. Then she braced
her forearm and pulled the trigger.

The high sobbing laughter was cut off with a
bubble and a sigh as the quarrel bit into the woman's
neck. There was no sound then but the snarling dogs.

In the deep shadows of the alley Thea moved away
from the dogs. *I'd forgot about that,* she said to herself accusingly. *There will be more dogs. And rats,* she
thought, after a moment.

As she walked she tightened her crossbow again
and fitted another quarrel to it. *She probably wasn't a
mutant,* she let herself think. *Probably she was just
healthy.* She didn't want to consider what the Pirates
would do to Thea herself, genetically altered as she
was.

The sound of the dogs died behind her in the
empty, littered streets. Here and there she saw piles of
bodies, some dead from fighting, others from more
sinister things. The "M" brand was on many of them.
Twice she saw the unmistakable signs of New Leprosy
on the blind faces, skin scaled over and turning the
silver that allied it with the old disease. But unlike
the first leprosy the new variety *was* contagious. And
the Pirates had carried it away with them.

She chafed her dark, hard skin, long since burned to
a red-brown. So far she had been lucky and had re-
sisted most of the new diseases; but she knew that the

luck would eventually run out, even for her. Even if she found the Gold Lake Settlement and they accepted her.

After more than an hour of walking she left Chico behind, striking eastward through ruined fields and swampland. The last crops had been forced from the ground and now the stalks crisscrossed underfoot like great soggy snakes. A heavy phosphorescence hung over the marshland, a light that did not illuminate or warm. Thea did not know the source of it, but she avoided the spot. Since the Sacramento Disaster four years ago the valley had ceased to be safe land. Before the levees had crumbled, it had been a haven from the pollution around it. Now, with the delta a reeking chemical quagmire, the upper river was slowly surrendering to the spreading contamination.

She stumbled and saw a dead cat at her feet. Animals had been at it: the chest gaped and the eye sockets were empty, but the fur was healthy. She shook her head at the waste of it. Bending closer, she noticed with surprise that the front paws were the tawny-orange of regenerated tissue. Maybe it had been virally mutated, as she had been. Or maybe the virus was catching. A lot of other things sure were catching. Shaking her head again, she dragged some rotting stalks over the little carcass, knowing it for the empty gesture it was even as she did it.

The ground grew soggier as she went, the old stalks becoming a vile goo, and sticky. She looked ahead for firmer ground and saw an oily stretch of water moving sluggishly under the wan moon. Beyond was the stunted fuzz of what had been cattails. Sliding the nictitating membranes over her eyes, she dropped to her knees and moved forward, her crossbow at the ready. The river was not a friendly place.

Once she heard a pig rooting along the bank and she stopped. Those pigs that were still alive were dangerous and hungry. Eventually it crashed away up the bank and Thea began paddling again. *One thing to say for the Disaster,* she thought as the stinking water surged around her. *It killed a lot of insects.*

Then she reached the cattails and slipped in among them for cover. There was a kind of protection that would last her until first light, when she would have to find higher ground. She found a hummock and curled up on it for a few hours' sleep.

The dawn brought more animals to the river, and a few foraging Pirates who swept by in their modified open vans. They had rifles and took three shots for two carcasses—the pig from the night before and an ancient horse with broken knees.

"Bring 'em in! Bring 'em in!" hollered the one in the lead van.

"Give me a hand, you snot-fucking Mute!"

The first gave a shout. "Montague gave you hauling this week. Cox didn't change that. *I* didn't have maggots in my pack." He snorted mockingly and revved the engine.

"You know what you have to do if you waste fuel," the one doing the hauling said gleefully.

"Just you shove it!" shouted the first, panic in his voice. "I don't want to hear no threats from you. I could drop you right now."

"Then you'd have to do the hauling," reminded the second laconically, then added, "Cox says Montague's dead, anyway."

"Him and his guard," the one on the bank said, as if it were a curse. "They tried to stop Wilson and me when we got that Mute kid out of the cellar. Said to leave him alone. A rotten Mute! Montague; he was crazy."

They were silent but for the whir of the engines and the sound of the dead animals being dragged through the mud.

Thea huddled in the cattails, hardly daring to breathe. She had seen Cloverdale after they had sacked it, in the days before Montague had organized them under that ironic rallying cry, "Survive!"

"That's one," said the first.

"Lick your cock."

Again there was silence until the one doing the hauling let out a scream.

"What's the matter?" demanded the one at the vans.

"Water spiders!" the other shrieked in terror. "Dozens of 'em!" And he made a horrible sound in his throat.

From her protection in the cattails, Thea watched, crouching, fright in her eyes. Water spiders were nothing to mess with, even for her. She clung to the reeds around her and watched for the hard, shiny bodies with the long hooked mandibles filled with paralyzing venom. Three of them could kill you in less than ten minutes. Dozens, and you didn't have a chance at all.

The voice-rending shouts had stopped, and soon a body drifted aimlessly by, with the spiders climbing over the face toward the eyes. Thea turned away.

Up on the bank there was a cough and the motor whizzed as the Pirate on the van drove off too fast.

Thea waited until the body had slid out of sight around a bend in the river before she moved free from the cattails. Then she ran off through the brushy undergrowth, not pausing to look for Pirates or for

spiders. Her knees were uncertain as jelly and her
fright made her light-headed. She ran frantically until
she was on higher ground; there she stopped and
breathed.

She had come about half a mile from the river in
those few minutes, and had left a wake like a timber
run through the underbrush. There was nothing to
concern her about that: it could easily have been
caused by an animal and would not be investigated.
But the hunting party meant that the Pirates were still
around, maybe camped. She had to get away from
them, or she would end up like the woman in Chico.
Not like that. She shuddered.

She guessed that the Pirates were camped near the
river, within walking distance of Chico, so she started
off to the southeast, keeping to the cover of the trees.
The scrub oaks were gone, but the hardier fruit trees
had run riot. Thea knew that if she had to, she could
climb into the trees and pick off the Pirates one by one
with her crossbow until they killed her. That would
take time. And she needed time.

By midday she had put several miles between herself and the Pirates. The river lay below her, a greasy
brown smudge. The east fork of the Sacramento was
dying.

That was when she found the makeshift silo. Some
farmer in the hills, maybe one of the old communes,
had built a silo to store his grain, and there it stood:
lopsided, rusty, but safe and dry. A haven for the
night, and perhaps a base for a couple of days. It
would be a good place to come back to after scouting
the hills for the best way into the sierra and Gold
Lake.

She walked around the silo carefully, looking for the

door and for the farmhouse it had once belonged to. The farmhouse turned out to be a charred shell. The silo was the only thing left standing where once there had been a house, chicken coops and a barn. She shook her head and swung the door open.

In the next instant she was reeling back. "Stupid, stupid!" she said aloud. "Stupid." For there was a man in the silo, waving something at her. She started to run, angry and frustrated.

"No! No!" the voice followed her. "Don't run away! Wait!" It got louder. "That's my arm!"

Thea stopped. His arm. "What?" she yelled back.

"It's my arm. They cut it off." The words made a weird echo in the corrugated walls of the silo. "Last week."

She started back toward the sound. "Who did?"

"The Pirates. In Chico." He was getting weaker, and his words came irregularly. "I got this far."

She stood in the doorway looking down at him. "Why'd you keep it?"

He drew in a breath. "They were looking for a man with only one arm. So I sewed this in my jacket. I can't get any further without help," he finished.

"Well, you better bury it," she told him, casting a glance at the thing.

He met her eyes. "I can't."

Thea looked him over carefully. He was ten, fifteen years older than she was, with a stocky body made gaunt with hunger and pain. His wide face was deeply lined and grimy. The clothes he wore were torn and filthy, but had once been expensive, she could tell.

"How long you been here?" she asked him.

"I think three days."

"Oh." From the state of the arm that was about right. She pointed to the stump. "How does it feel? Infected?"

He frowned. "I don't think so. Not much. It itches."

She accepted this for the moment. "Where were you going? You got a place to go?"

"I was trying to get into the mountains."

Thea considered, and her first impulse was to run, to leave this man to rot or live as it happened. But she hesitated. Gold Lake was a long way away, and getting there would be hard.

"I got medicine," she said, making up her mind. "You can have some of it. Not all, 'cause it's mine and I might need it. But you can have a little."

He looked at her, his rumpled face puzzled. "Thank you," he said, unused to the words.

"I got parapenicillin and a little sporomicin. Which one do you want?"

"The penicillin."

"I got some ascorbic tablets for later," she added, looking thoughtfully at the stump of his arm as she came into the silo. There had been infection, but it was clearing and the skin was the tawny-orange color of regenerating tissue. "You left-handed?"

"Yes."

"You're lucky."

After releasing the crossbow and storing the quarrel, she shrugged out of her pack, putting it down carefully, not too close to the man. He still had one good arm and he had admitted he was left-handed. "What's your name?" she asked as she dug into the bag.

"Seth Pearson," he said with slight hesitation.

She looked at him sharply. "It says David Rossi on your neck tags. Which is it?"

"It doesn't matter. Whichever one you like."

Thea looked away. "Okay. That's the way we'll do it, Rossi." She handed him a packet, worn but intact. "That's the penicillin. You'll have to eat it, I don't have any needles." Then she added, "It tastes terrible. Here." She handed him a short, flat stick of jerky. "Venison and tough. It'll take the taste away." She put her pack between them and sat on the floor. When the man had managed to choke down the white slime, she said, "Tomorrow I'm going east. You can come with me if you can keep up. There's one more bad river ahead, and you might have to swim it. It's rocky and fast. So you better make up your mind tonight." Then she took two more pieces of jerky out of her pack and ate them in a guarded silence.

The north wind bit through them as they walked; the sun was bright but cold. The gentle slope grew gradually steeper and they climbed more slowly, saying nothing and keeping wary eyes on the bushes that littered the slopes. By midafternoon they were walking over the crumbling trunks of large pine trees that had fallen, victims of smog. The dust from the dead trees blew in plumes around them, stinging their eyes and making them sneeze. Yet still they climbed.

The going got slower and slower until they called a halt in the lee of a huge stump. Rossi braced his good shoulder and held out his tattered jacket to protect them from the wind.

"Are you all right?" Thea asked him when she had caught her breath. "You're the wrong color."

"Just a little winded." He nodded. "I'm . . . still weak."

"Yeah," she said, looking covertly at his stump. The color was deepening. "You're getting better."

His feet slid suddenly on the rolling dust and he grabbed out to her to keep from falling.

She stepped back. "Don't do that."

As he regained his footing, he looked at her in some surprise. "Why?" he asked gently.

"Don't you touch me." She grabbed at her crossbow defensively.

He frowned, his eyes troubled, then his brow cleared. "I won't." In those two words he had great understanding. He knew the world that Thea lived in as well as she did.

With a look of defiance she tightened the crossbow's straps on her arm, never taking her eyes from the man. "I can shoot this real fast, Rossi. Remember that."

Whatever he might have said was lost. "Hold it right there," came the voice from behind them.

Aside from the exchange of quick, frightened glances, they did not move.

"That's right." There was a puff of dust, and another, then a young man in a ruined CD uniform stood in front of them, a rifle cradled in his arms. "I knew I'd catch you," he said aloud to himself. "I been following you all morning."

Thea edged closer to Rossi.

"You people come out from Chico, right?" He bounced the weapon he carried.

"No."

"What about you?" he demanded of Thea.

"No."

He looked back toward Rossi, an unpleasant smile on his face. "What about you . . . Rossi, is it? Sure you didn't come through Chico? I heard a guy named Rossi was killed outside Orland."

"I don't know about that."

"They said he was trying to save Montague when

Cox took over. You know anything about that? Rossi?"

"No."

The younger man laughed. "Hey, don't you lie to me, Rossi. You lie to me and I'm going to kill you."

In the shadow, Thea slowly put a quarrel into her crossbow, keeping as much out of sight as she could.

"You're going to kill us anyway, so why does it matter if we lie?" Rossi was asking.

"Listen," the CD man began. "What's that?" he said, looking squarely at Thea. "What are you doing?" And he reached out, grabbing her by the arm and jerking her off her feet. "You bitch-piece!" He kicked savagely into her shoulder, just once. Then Rossi put himself between them. "Move!"

"No. You want me to move, you'll have to kill me." He said to Thea, without turning, "Did he hurt you?"

"Some," she admitted. "I'll be okay."

"She your woman? Is she?"

Rossi rose slowly, forcing the man with the rifle to move back. "No. She's nobody's woman."

At that the other man giggled. "I bet she needs it. I bet she's real hungry for it."

Thea closed her eyes to hide the indignation in her. If this was to be rape, being *used* . . . She opened her eyes when Rossi's hand touched her shoulder.

"You try any more dumb things like that, cunt, and that's going to be the end. Understand?"

"Yes," she mumbled.

"And what will Cox say when he finds out what you're doing?" Rossi asked.

"Cox won't say nothing!" the CD man spat.

"So you deserted." Rossi nodded at the guilt in the man's face. "That was stupid."

"You shut up!" He leaned toward them. "You are going to take me out of here, wherever you're going. If anybody spots us, or we get trapped, I am going to make both of you look like a butcher shop. You got that? . . . HUH?"

"You stink," said Thea.

For a moment there was anger in the young, hard eyes, then he grabbed her face with one hand. "Not yet, not yet." His grip tightened. "You want some of that, you're gonna have to beg for it, real hard. You're gonna have to suck it out of me. Right?" He looked defiantly at Rossi. "Right?" he repeated.

"Let her go."

"You want her?"

"Leave her alone."

"All right," he said with a little nod. He stepped back from her. "Later, huh? When you've thought it over."

Rossi looked at the CD man. "I'll be close, Thea. Just call."

As the two men stared at each other, Thea wanted to run from both of them, to the protection of the destroyed forest. But she could not escape on an open hillside. She rubbed her shoulder gingerly and went to Rossi's side.

"I'm a better choice," the CD man mocked her. "My name's Lastly. You can call me that, bitch-piece. Don't call me anything else."

She said nothing as she looked up the hillside.

Rossi's voice was soft. "Don't try it now. There's cover up ahead and I'll get him into a fight."

With deep surprise she turned to him. "Truly? You'd do that?"

He would have gone on, but Lastly shoved them apart. "I don't want none of that. You don't whisper when I'm around, hear? You got anything to say, you speak up."

"I wanted to piss," said Rossi.

Lastly giggled again. "Oh, no. Not for a while. You aren't gonna leave a trail. Got that?"

With a shrug Rossi led the long walk toward the trees.

"What was that?" Lastly turned the barrel of his gun toward the sound that surged through the underbrush.

The ululation rose and fell through the trees, lonely and terrible.

"Dogs," said Rossi bluntly. "They're hunting."

In the deep shadows of dusk the scattered trees seemed to grow together, surrounding the three people who moved through the gloom. The sound came again, closer and sharper.

"Where are they?"

Thea looked back at him. "A ways off yet. You can't shoot them until they get close."

"We got to get out of here," Lastly said in fear. "Right? We got to find someplace safe."

Rossi squinted up at the fading sky. "I'd say we have another hour yet. After that, we'd better climb trees."

"But they're rotten," Lastly protested.

"They're better than dogs," Rossi reminded him.

But Lastly wasn't listening. "There used to be camps around here, didn't there? We got to find them. No dogs gonna come into camp."

"You fool," said Rossi dispassionately.

"No talking. I don't want to hear it." Lastly's gun wavered in front of Rossi.

"Then you both stop it," Thea put in quietly. "The dogs can hear you."

All fell silent. In a moment Rossi said, "Thea's right.

If we're quiet, we might find one of your camps in time."

"You get moving, then," Lastly said hurriedly. "Right now."

It had been a summer cabin once, when people still had summer cabins. The view below it had been of pine forests giving way to the fertile swath of the valley. Now it stood in a clearing surrounded by rotting trees, above the spreading contamination of the river. Oddly enough the windows were still intact.

"We can stay here," Rossi said after circling the cabin. "The back porch is screened and we can get the door off its hinges."

"We can get through the window," Lastly said eagerly.

"If it's broken, so can the dogs." When this had sunk in, Rossi went on. "The back is secure. We'll be able to protect ourselves."

"You two get it done," Lastly ordered, pointing the rifle toward the rear porch. "Get it done fast."

As Thea and Rossi struggled with the door, Lastly straddled the remains of a picket fence. "Say, you see what Cox did to that Mute in Chico? Took the skin right off him, hey. Cox, he's gonna get rid of all the Mutes—just you wait."

"Yes," said Rossi as he pulled at a rusted hinge.

"Know what? Montague wanted to save 'em. You hear about that, Rossi? Why would someone want to do that? Huh? Why'd any real man save Mutes?"

Rossi didn't answer.

"I asked you something . . . Rossi. You tell me."

"Maybe he thought they were the only ones worth saving."

"What about you, bitch-piece? You save a Mute?"
He bounced on the fence as he stroked his rifle.

With a look of pure disgust, Thea said, "Just me,
Lastly. I'm saving me."

"What you saving for me? I got something for
you . . ."

"The door's off," Rossi interrupted, pulling it aside.
"We can go in now."

Mice had got into the house, eating the dried fruits
and flour that had been stored in the ample kitchen.
But there were cans left, filled with food Thea could
hardly remember. Pots and pans hung on the wall,
mostly rusty, but a few made of enamelware and
ready for use. The stove was a wood-burner.

"Look at it," Rossi said, his eyes lingering on the
cupboards and their precious contents. "Enough to
take with us for later."

"Damn, it's perfect. I'm gonna have it right tonight.
Hot food, and a bath and all the ways I want it." He
glanced slyly from Rossi to Thea.

"Smoke might bring the Pirates," said Rossi with a
sour smile. "Have you thought of that?"

"It's nighttime, Rossi. They ain't coming up here till
morning."

Thea had wandered around the kitchen. "There's no
wood, anyway. That table is plastic."

They all stood for a moment, then Lastly announced, "You heard the lady, Rossi. There's no wood.
You gonna get it for her, right? Right?"

"I'll go," said Thea quickly.

"Oh, no."

"But he can't work with one arm."

"If he takes his time, bitch-piece."

"What about you, Lastly?" Rossi asked evenly.
"You're able and you've got the gun."

"And let you two lock me out with the dogs? I ain't dumb, Rossi." He moved around the table. "It's you, Rossi. You're it." He shoved a chair at him. "Catch your breath, 'cause you're going out there."

"Not without Thea."

Lastly made his now familiar giggle. "Want it for yourself, huh? She ain't putting it out to you. She wants a man. Not you."

Thea gave Rossi a pleading look. "Let me lock myself in the side room. Then both of you can go."

"Right!" said Lastly unexpectedly. "The bitch-piece is right. We lock her up and we get the wood. Rossi?"

"If that's what you want, Thea."

She nodded. "Yes."

"I'll see you later?" he asked her, his deep eyes on hers.

"I hope so," she answered.

"Come on, bitch-piece. We're going to lock you up." He took her by the arm, half dragging her through the main room of the cabin to the side room. "There you are," he said, thrusting her inside. "Your own boudoir. You keep nice and warm while you wait." And he slammed the door. There was a distinct sound as Thea pushed the lock home.

She sat in the bedroom, huddled on the bare mattress in the center of the room, listening for the sound of the men. She had wanted to run from them, but she felt tired and helpless now. As time passed, she slumped and slid until she stretched on the bed, asleep.

"You were supposed to get ready. I told you to get ready," said the harsh voice above her. "You knew I'd be back." She was pulled roughly onto her back and pinned there by a sudden weight across her body.

Barely awake, Thea pushed against the man, hands and feet seeking vulnerable places.

"Shut UP!" Lastly growled, his hand slamming across her face. When Thea cried out, he hit her again. "You listen, cunt; you're for me. You think I'm letting a Mute-fucker like Montague get you? Huh?" He struck her arms back, catching her wrists in a length of rope. "We taught him and his pervs a lesson at Chico. You hear?" He pulled the rope taut against the bed slats. "This time I'm getting mine. Right?"

With a sob of pure fury Thea launched herself at Lastly, teeth bared and legs twisting.

"No, you don't." Lastly giggled. This time his fist caught her on the side of the head and she fell back, dizzy and sick. "Don't give me a hard time, cunt. It makes it worse for you." Rope looped her left ankle and then her right, to be tied under the mattress. Angrily Thea pulled at the ropes.

"Don't," Lastly said, coming near her. "You do that any more and I'm going to hurt you. See this?" He put a small knife up close to her face. "I got it in the kitchen. It's real sharp. You give me any more trouble and I'm gonna carve you up some, till you learn some manners."

"No."

Ignoring this, Lastly began to cut off her jacket. When he had ripped that from her, he slit the seams on her leather pants. As he pulled these away, she twisted in the ropes.

Immediately he was across her. "I told you." He put the knife to her, catching one nipple between the blade and his thumb. "I could peel this off, you know?" He pressed harder. The knife bit into her flesh. "No noise, cunt. You be quiet or I take it all off."

In the sudden sharp pain the nictitating membranes closed over her eyes.

And Lastly saw. "Mute! Shit! You lousy Mute!" There was something like triumph in his voice. She cried out as he pulled the wrinkled bit of flesh from her. Blood spread over her breast.

With a shout Lastly wiggled his pants down to his knees and in one quick movement pushed into her. Forcing himself deeper, laughing, he said, "Montague's Mute! I'm gonna ruin you." Falling forward, he fastened his teeth on her sound breast.

At that she screamed. He brought his head up. "You do that again, Mute, and this one comes off with my teeth." He hit her in the mouth as he came.

In the next moment he was off her, torn out of her and slammed against the wall.

"You filthy . . . !" Rossi, his hand in Lastly's hair, hit him into the wall again. There was an audible crack and Lastly slumped.

Then he came back to the bed. "Oh, God, Thea," he said softly. "I never meant it to be like this." He knelt beside her, not touching her. "I'm sorry." It was as if he were apologizing for the world. Gently he untied her, speaking to her as he did. When he freed her, she huddled on the bed in silent tears which shook her wholly.

Finally she turned to him, shame in her eyes. "I wanted you. I wanted you," she said and turned away.

In wonder he rose. "I have one arm and a price on my head."

"I wanted you," she said again, not daring to look at him.

"My name," he said very quietly, "is Evan Montague." And he waited, looking away from her.

Then he felt her hand on his. "I wanted you."

He turned to her, holding her hand, not daring to touch her. She drew him down beside her, but pulled back from him. "He hurt me," she said numbly.

"Here I tried to save everybody and couldn't even save you," he whispered bitterly. He looked at her, at her bloody breasts and bruised face, at the deep scratches on her thighs. "Let me get your medicine . . ."

"No." She grabbed at his hand frantically. "Don't leave me."

With what might have been a smile he sat holding her hand while she shivered and the blood dried, until they heard the sound of engines, like a distant hive.

"They're looking for him. Or me," Montague said.

She nodded. "Do we have to leave?"

"Yes."

"If we stay?"

"They'll kill me. Not you, though . . . And you are a mutant, aren't you?"

She understood and shook spasmodically. "Don't let them. Kill me. Kill me. Please."

The terror in her face alarmed him. He pulled her fingers to his lips, kissing them. "I will. I promise, Thea." Then he changed. "No. We're getting out of here. We're going to live as long as we can."

Sighing, Lastly collapsed, his head at a strange angle.

"Come on," Montague said.

With an effort Thea rose to her feet, holding on to his arm until the dizziness passed. "I need clothes."

He looked about the room, to the dresser that was encircled with ropes. "There?" he asked, going to it and pulling the drawers. The clothes were for children, but Thea was small enough to wear some of them. With determination she struggled into heavy canvas jeans, but balked at a sweater or jacket. "I can't," she whispered.

"Shush," he said. They heard the sounds of the motors getting nearer.

"What time is it?" she asked.

"Early. It's gray in the east."

"We've got to go. My pack . . ."

"Leave it," he said brusquely. "Neither you nor I can carry it."

"My crossbow . . ."

"In the kitchen. Put it on my arm. If you load it, I can fire." He bundled a jacket under his arm. "You'll want this later."

The engines grew louder. "I thought that was the way," Montague said ironically. "I was a fool." He went to the window and opened it. "This way. And straight into the trees."

"Evan!" she called as the cold morning air brushed the raw places on her breast. "Evan!"

"Can you make it? You've got to," he said as he came to her side.

"Yes. But slowly."

"All right." He took her hand, feeling her fingers and the crossbow warm in the morning cold. "We'll go slowly for a while."

As they climbed away into the dying forest and the dark, the sounds of the engines grew loud behind them, shutting out the noise of their escape and sending the wild dogs howling away from them into the cold gray light before dawn.

NOBODY'S HOME

JOANNA RUSS

Joanna Russ grew up in New York City and attended
Cornell University, where she received her B.A. in English
Literature, and Yale University, where she studied play-
writing and received her M.A. Her stories have appeared
in **The Magazine of Fantasy & Science Fiction** and the
anthologies **Orbit, Quark, That New Improved Sun, Final
Stage, Again Dangerous Visions** and **Aurora: Beyond
Equality.** She is the author of two novels, **And Chaos Died**
and **Picnic on Paradise** (both published by Ace Books).
Her short story "When It Changed" won a Nebula Award
in 1973. She is Assistant Professor of English at Harpur
College, State University of New York at Binghamton.

"Nobody's Home" takes place in a future world which
has developed a system able to transport a person in-
stantaneously to any place on the earth. Human society has
been transformed by this development; the people in this
story live in a utopian world without scarcity and with a
great deal of freedom. Societal and family structures have
changed as well, but certain problems still remain.

After she had finished her work at the North Pole,
Jannina came down to the Red Sea refineries, where
she had family business, jumped to New Delhi for
dinner, took a nap in a public hotel in Queensland,
walked from the hotel to the station, by-passed the
Leeward Islands (where she thought she might go,

but all the stations were busy), and met Charley to watch the dawn over the Carolinas.

"Where've you *been*, dear C?"

"Tanzania. And you're married."

"No."

"I heard you were married," he said. "The Lees told the Smiths who told the Kerguelens who told the Utsumbés, and we get around, we Utsumbés. A new wife, they said. I didn't know you were especially fond of women."

"I'm not. She's my husbands' wife. And we're not married yet, Charley. She's had hard luck. A first family started in '35, two husbands burned out by an overload while arranging transportation for a concert —of all things, pushing papers, you know!—and the second divorced her, I think, and she drifted away from the third (a big one), and there was some awful quarrel with the fourth, people chasing people around tables, I don't know."

"Poor woman."

In the manner of people joking and talking lightly they had drawn together, back to back, sitting on the ground and rubbing their shoulders and the backs of their heads together. Jannina said sorrowfully, "What lovely hair you have, Charley Utsumbé, like metal mesh."

"All we Utsumbés are exceedingly handsome." They linked arms. The sun, which anyone could chase around the world now, see it rise or set twenty times a day, fifty times a day—if you wanted to spend your life like that—rose dripping out of the cypress swamp. There was nobody around for miles. Mist drifted up from the pools and low places.

"My God," he said, "it's summer! I have to be at Tanga now."

"What?" said Jannina.

"One loses track," he said apologetically. "I'm sorry, love, but I have unavoidable business at home. Tax labor."

"But why summer, why did its being summer . . ."

"Train of thought! Too complicated." And already they were out of key, already the mild affair was over, there having come between them the one obligation that can't be put off to the time you like, or the place you like; off he'd go to plug himself into a road-mender or a doctor, though it's of some advantage to mend all the roads of a continent at one time.

She sat cross-legged on the station platform, watching him enter the booth and set the dial. He stuck his head out the glass door. "Come with me to Africa, lovely lady!"

She thumbed her nose at him. "You're only a passing fancy, Charley U!" He blew a kiss, enclosed himself in the booth, and disappeared. (The transmatter field is larger than the booth, for obvious reasons; the booth flicks on and off several million times a second and so does not get transported itself, but it protects the machinery from the weather and it keeps people from losing elbows or knees or slicing the ends off a package or a child. The booths at the cryogenics center at the North Pole have exchanged air so often with those of warmer regions that each has its own microclimate; leaves and seeds, plants and earth are piled about them. The notes pinned to the door said, Don't Step on the Grass! Wish to Trade Pawlownia Sapling for Sub-Arctic Canadian Moss; Watch Your Goddamn Bare Six-Toed Feet! Wish Amateur Cellist for Quartet, Six Months' Rehearsal Late Uhl with Reciter; I Lost a Squirrel Here Yesterday, Can You Find It Before It Dies? Eight Children

Will Be Heartbroken—Cecilia Ching, Buenos Aires.)

Jannina sighed and slipped on her glass woolly; nasty to get back into clothes, but home was cold. You never knew where you might go, so you carried them. Years ago (she thought) I came here with someone in the dead of winter, either an unmatched man or someone's starting spouse—only two of us, at any rate— and we waded through the freezing water and danced as hard as we could and then proved we could sing and drink beer in a swamp at the same time, Good Lord! And then went to the public resort on the Ile de la Cité to watch professional plays, opera, games—you have to be good to get in there!—and got into some clothes because it was chilly after sundown in September—no, wait, it was Venezuela—and watched the lights come out and smoked like mad at a café table and tickled the robot waiter and pretended we were old, really old, perhaps a hundred and fifty . . . Years ago!

But *was* it the same place? she thought, and dismissing the incident forever, she stepped into the booth, shut the door, and dialed home: the Himalayas. The trunk line was clear. The branch stop was clear. The family's transceiver (located in the anteroom behind two doors, to keep the task of heating the house within reasonable limits) had damn well better be clear, or somebody would be blown right into the vestibule. Momentum- and heat-compensators kept Jannina from arriving home at seventy degrees Fahrenheit internal temperature (seven degrees lost for every mile you teleport upward) or too many feet above herself (rise to the east, drop going west; to the north or south you are apt to be thrown right through the wall of the booth). Someday (thought Jannina) everybody will decide to let everybody live in decent climates. But not yet. Not this everybody.

She arrived home singing "The World's My Back Yard, Yes, the World Is My Oyster," a song that had been popular in her first youth, some seventy years before.

The Komarovs' house was hardened foam with an automatic inside line to the school near Naples. It was good to be brought up on your own feet. Jannina passed through; the seven-year-olds lay with their heads together and their bodies radiating in a six-person asterisk. In this position (which was supposed to promote mystical thought) they played Barufaldi, guessing the identity of famous dead personages through anagrammatic sentences, the first letters of the words of which (unscrambled into aphorisms or proverbs) simultaneously spelled out a moral and a series of Goedel numbers (in a previously agreed-upon code) which . . .

"Oh, my darling, how felicitous is the advent of your appearance!" cried a boy (hard to take, the polysyllabic stage). "Embrace me, dearest maternal parent! Unite your valuable upper limbs about my eager person!"

"Vulgar!" said Jannina, laughing.

"*Non sum filius tuus?*" said the child.

"No, you're not my body-child. You're my godchild. Your mother bequeathed me to you when she died. What are you learning?"

"The eternal parental question," he said, frowning. "How to run a helicopter. How to prepare food from its actual, revolting, raw constituents. Can I go now?"

"*Can* you?" she said. "Nasty imp!"

"Good," he said. "I've made you feel guilty. Don't *do* that," and as she tried to embrace him, he ticklishly slid away. "The robin walks quietly up the branch of the tree," he said breathlessly, flopping back on the floor.

"That's not an aphorism." (Another Barufaldi player.)

"It is."

"It isn't."

"It is."

"It isn't."

"It is."

"It—"

The school vanished; the antechamber appeared. In the kitchen Chi Komarov was rubbing the naked back of his sixteen-year-old son. Parents always kissed each other; children always kissed each other. She touched foreheads with the two men and hung her woolly on the hook by the ham radio rig. Someone was always around. Jannina flipped the cover off her wrist chronometer: standard regional time, date, latitude-longitude, family computer hookup clear. "At my age I ought to remember these things," she said. She pressed the computer hookup: Ann at tax labor in the schools, bit-a-month plan, regular Ann; Lee with three months to go, five years off, heroic Lee; Phuong in Paris, still rehearsing; C.E. gone, won't say where, spontaneous C.E.; Ilse making some repairs in the basement, not a true basement, but the room farthest down the hillside. She went up the stairs and then came down and put her head around at the living-and-swimming room. Through the glass wall one could see the mountains. Old Al, who had joined them late in life, did a bit of gardening in the brief summers, and generally stuck around the place. Jannina beamed.

"Hullo, Old Al!" Big and shaggy, a rare delight, his white body hair. She sat on his lap. "Has she come?"

"The new one? No," he said.

"Shall we go swimming?"

He made an expressive face. "No, dear," he said. "I'd rather go to Naples and watch the children fly helicopters. I'd rather go to Nevada and fly them myself. I've been in the water all day, watching a very dull person restructure coral reefs and experiment with polyploid polyps."

"You mean *you* were doing it."

"One gets into the habit of working."

"But you didn't have to!"

"It was a private project. Most interesting things are."

She whispered in his ear.

With happily flushed faces, they went into Old Al's inner garden and locked the door.

Jannina, temporary family representative, threw the computer helmet over her head and, thus plugged in, she cleaned house, checked food supplies, did a little of the legal business entailed by a family of eighteen adults (two triplet marriages, a quad, and a group of eight). She felt very smug. She put herself through by radio to Himalayan HQ (above two thousand meters) and hooking computer to computer—a very odd feeling, like an urge to sneeze that never comes off—extended a formal invitation to one Leslie Smith ("Come stay, why don't you?"), notifying every free Komarov to hop it back and fast. Six hikers might come for the night—back-packers. More food. First thunderstorm of the year in Albany, New York (North America). Need an extra two rooms by Thursday. Hear the Palnatoki are moving. Can't use a room.

Can't use a kitten. Need the geraniums back, Mrs. Adam, Chile. The best maker of hand-blown glass in the world has killed in a duel the second-best maker of hand-blown glass for joining the movement toward ceramics. A bitter struggle is foreseen in the global economy. Need a lighting designer. Need fifteen singers and electric pansensicon. Standby tax labor xxxxxpj through xxxyq to Cambaluc, great tectogenic—

With the guilty feeling that one always gets gossiping with a computer, for it's really not reciprocal, Jannina flipped off the helmet. She went to get Ilse. Climbing back through the white foam room, the purple foam room, the green foam room, everything littered with plots and projects of the clever Komarovs or the even cleverer Komarov children, stopping at the baby room for Ilse to nurse her baby, Jannina danced staidly around studious Ilse. They turned on the nursery robot and the television screen. Ilse drank beer in the swimming room, for her milk. She worried her way through the day's record of events—faults in the foundation, some people who came from Chichester and couldn't find C.E. so one of them burst into tears, a new experiment in genetics coming around the gossip circuit, an execrable set of equations from some imposter in Bucharest.

"A duel!" said Jannina.

They both agreed it was shocking. And what fun. A new fashion. You had to be a little mad to do it. Awful.

The light went on over the door to the tunnel that linked the house to the antechamber, and very quickly, one after another, as if the branch line had just come free, eight Komarovs came into the room. The light flashed again; one could see three people debouch one after the other, persons in boots, with coats, packs and face masks over their woollies. They were covered with snow, either from the mountain terraces above the house or from some other place, Jannina didn't know. They stamped the snow off in the antechamber and hung their clothes outside. "Good heavens, you're not circumcised!" cried someone. There was as much handshaking and embracing all around as at a wedding party. Velet Komarov (the short, dark one) recognized Fung Pao-Yu and swung her off her feet. People began to joke, tentatively stroking one another's arms. "Did you have a good hike? Are you a good hiker, Pao-Yu?" said Velet. The light over the antechamber went on again, though nobody could see a thing, since the glass was steamed over from the collision of hot with cold air. Old Al stopped, halfway into the kitchen. The baggage receipt chimed, recognized only by family ears—upstairs a bundle of somebody's things, ornaments, probably, for the missing Komarovs were still young and the young are interested in clothing, were appearing in the baggage receptacle. "Ann or Phuong?" said Jannina. "Five to three, anybody? Match me!" but someone strange opened the door of the booth and peered out. Oh, a dizzying sensation. She was painted in a few places, which was awfully odd because really it was old-fashioned; and why do it for a family evening? It was a stocky young woman. It was an awful mistake (thought Jannina). Then the visitor made her second mistake.

"I'm Leslie Smith," she said. But it was more through clumsiness than being rude. Chi Komarov (the tall, blond one) saw this instantly, and snatching off his old-fashioned spectacles, he ran to her side and patted her, saying teasingly, "Now, haven't we met? Now, aren't you married to someone I know?"

"No, no," said Leslie Smith, flushing with pleasure.

He touched her neck. "Ah, you're a tightrope dancer!"

"Oh, no!" exclaimed Leslie Smith.

"*I'm* a tightrope dancer," said Chi. "Would you believe it?"

"But you're too—too *spiritual*," said Leslie Smith hesitantly.

"Spiritual, how do you like that, family, spiritual?" he cried, delighted (a little more delighted, thought Jannina, than the situation really called for), and he began to stroke her neck.

"What a lovely neck you have," he said.

This steadied Leslie Smith. She said, "I like tall men," and allowed herself to look at the rest of the family. "Who are these people?" she said, though one was afraid she might really mean it.

Fung Pao-Yu to the rescue: "Who are these people? Who are they, indeed! I doubt if they are anybody. One might say, 'I have met these people,' but has one? What existential meaning would such a statement convey? I myself, now, I have met them. I have been introduced to them. But they are like the Sahara. It is all wrapped in mystery. I doubt if they even have names," etc. etc. Then lanky Chi Komarov disputed possession of Leslie Smith with Fung Pao-Yu, and Fung Pao-Yu grabbed one arm and Chi the other; and she jumped up and down fiercely; so that by the time the lights dimmed and the food came, people were feeling better—or so Jannina judged. So embarrassing and delightful to be eating fifteen to a room! "We Komarovs are famous for eating whatever we can get whenever we can get it," said Velet proudly. Various Komarovs in various places, with the three hikers on cushions and Ilse at full length on the rug. Jannina pushed a button with her toe and the fairy lights came on all over the ceiling. "The children did that," said Old Al. He had somehow settled at Leslie Smith's side and was feeding her so-chi from his own bowl. She smiled up at him. "We once," said a hiking companion of Fung Pao-Yu's, "arranged a dinner in an amphitheater where half of us played servants to the other half, with forfeits for those who didn't show. It was the result of a bet. Like the bad old days. Did you know there were once *five billion people* in this world?"

"The gulls," said Ilse, "are mating on the Isle of Skye." There were murmurs of appreciative interest. Chi began to develop an erection and everyone laughed. Old Al wanted music and Velet didn't; what might have been a quarrel was ended by Ilse's furiously boxing their ears. She stalked off to the nursery.

"Leslie Smith and I are both old-fashioned," said Old Al, "because neither of us believes in gabbing. Chi—your theater?"

"We're turning people away." He leaned forward earnestly, tapping his fingers on his crossed knees. "I swear, some of them are threatening to commit suicide."

"It's a choice," said Velet reasonably.

Leslie Smith had dropped her bowl. They retrieved it for her.

"Aiy, I remember—" said Pao-Yu. "What I remember! We've been eating dried mush for three days, tax-issue. Did you know one of my dads killed himself?"

"No!" said Velet, surprised.

"Years ago," said Pao-Yu. "He said he refused to live to see the time when chairs were reintroduced. He also wanted further genetic engineering, I believe, for even more intelligence. He did it out of spite, I'm sure.

I think he wrestled a shark. Jannina, is this tax-issue food? Is it this year's style tax-issue sauce?"

"No, next year's," said Jannina snappishly. Really, some people! She slipped into Finnish, to show up Pao-Yu's pronunciation. "Isn't that so?" she asked Leslie Smith.

Leslie Smith stared at her.

More charitably Jannina informed them all, in Finnish, that the Komarovs had withdrawn their membership in a food group, except for Ann, who had taken out an individual, because what the dickens, who had the time? And tax-issue won't kill you. As they finished, they dropped their dishes into the garbage field and Velet stripped a layer off the rug. In that went, too. Indulgently Old Al began a round: "Red."

"Sun," said Pao-Yu.

"The Red Sun Is," said one of the triplet Komarovs.

"The Red Sun Is—High," said Chi.

"The Red Sun Is High, The," Velet said.

"The Red Sun Is High, The Blue—" Jannina finished. They had come to Leslie Smith, who could either complete it or keep it going. She chose to declare for complete, not shyly (as before) but simply by pointing to Old Al.

"The red sun is high, the blue," he said. "Subtle! Another: *Ching*."

"*Nü*."

"*Ching nü ch'i.*"

"*Ching nü ch'i ch'u.*"

"*Ssu.*"

"*Wo.*"

"*Ssu wo yü.*"

It had got back to Leslie Smith again. She said, "I can't do that."

Jannina got up and began to dance—I'm nice in my nasty way, she thought. The others wandered toward the pool and Ilse reappeared on the nursery monitor screen, saying, "I'm coming down."

Somebody said, "What time is it in the Argentine?"

"Five A.M."

"I think I want to go."

"Go, then."

"I go."

"Go well."

The red light over the antechamber door flashed and went out.

"Say, why'd you leave your other family?" said Ilse, settling near Old Al where the wall curved out. Ann, for whom it was evening, would be home soon; Chi, who had just got up a few hours back in western America, would stay somewhat longer; nobody ever knew Old Al's schedule and Jannina herself had lost track of the time. She would stay up until she felt sleepy. She followed a rough twenty-eight-hour day, Phuong (what a nuisance that must be at rehearsals!) a twenty-two-hour one, Ilse six hours up, six hours dozing. Jannina nodded, heard the question, and shook herself awake.

"I didn't leave them. They left me."

There was a murmur of sympathy around the pool.

"They left me because I was stupid," said Leslie Smith. Her hands were clasped passively in her lap. She looked very genteel in her blue body paint, a stocky young woman with small breasts. One of the triplet Komarovs, flirting in the pool with the other two, choked. The nonaquatic members of the family crowded around Leslie Smith, touching her with little, soft touches; they kissed her and exposed to her all their unguarded surfaces, their bellies, their soft skins.

Old Al kissed her hands. She sat there, oddly unmoved. "But I *am* stupid," she said. "You'll find out."

Jannina put her hands over her ears. "A masochist!" Leslie Smith looked at Jannina with a curious, stolid look. Then she looked down and absently began to rub one blue-painted knee.

"Luggage!" shouted Chi, clapping his hands together, and the triplets dashed for the stairs.

"No, I'm going to bed," said Leslie Smith, "I'm tired," and quite simply, she got up and let Old Al lead her through the pink room, the blue room, the turtle-and-pet room (temporarily empty), the trash room, and all the other rooms, to the guest room with the view that looked out over the cold hillside to the terraced plantings below.

"The best maker of hand-blown glass in the world," said Chi, "has killed in a duel the second-best maker of hand-blown glass in the world."

"For joining the movement to ceramics," said Ilse, awed. Jannina felt a thrill: this was the bitter stuff under the surface of life, the fury that boiled up. A bitter struggle is foreseen in the global economy. Good old tax-issue stuff goes toddling along, year after year. She was, thought Jannina, extraordinarily grateful to be living now, to be in such an extraordinary world, to have so long to go before her death. So much to do!

Old Al came back into the living room. "She's in bed."

"Well, which of us—?" said the triplet-who-had-choked, looking mischievously around from one to the other.

Chi was about to volunteer, out of his usual conscientiousness, thought Jannina, but then she found herself suddenly standing up, and then just as sud denly sitting down again. "I just don't have the nerve," she said.

Velet Komarov walked on his hands toward the stairs, then somersaulted, and vanished, climbing. Old Al got off the hand-carved chest he had been sitting on and fetched a can of ale from it. He levered off the top and drank. Then he said, "She really is stupid, you know." Jannina's skin crawled.

"Oooh," said Pao-Yu. Chi betook himself to the kitchen and returned with a paper folder. It was coated with frost. He shook it, then impatiently dropped it in the pool. The redheaded triplet swam over and took it. "Smith, Leslie," he said. "Adam Two, Leslie. Yee, Leslie. Schwarzen, Leslie."

"What on earth does the woman *do* with herself besides get married?" exclaimed Pao-Yu.

"She drove a hovercraft," said Chi, "in some out-of-the-way places around the Pacific until the last underground stations were completed. Says when she was a child she wanted to drive a truck."

"Well, you can," said the redheaded triplet, "can't you? Go to Arizona or the Rockies and drive on the roads. The sixty-mile-an-hour road. The thirty-mile-an-hour road. Great artistic recreation."

"That's not work," said Old Al.

"Couldn't she take care of children?" said the redheaded triplet. Ilse sniffed.

"Stupidity's not much of a recommendation for that," Chi said. "Let's see—no children. No, of course not. Overfulfilled her tax work on quite a few routine matters here. Kim, Leslie. Went to Moscow and contracted a double with some fellow, didn't last. Registered as a singleton, but that didn't last, either. She said she was lonely, and they were exploiting her."

Old Al nodded.

"Came back and lived informally with a theater group. Left them. Went into psychotherapy. Volunteered for several experimental, intelligence-enhancing programs, was turned down—hum!—sixty-five come the winter solstice, muscular coordination average, muscular development above average, no overt mental pathology, empathy average, prognosis: poor. No, wait a minute, it says, 'More of the same.' Well, that's the same thing.

"What I want to know," added Chi, raising his head, "is who met Miss Smith and decided we needed the lady in this Ice Palace of ours?"

Nobody answered. Jannina was about to say, "Ann, perhaps?" but as she felt the urge to do so—surely it wasn't right to turn somebody off like that, *just* for that!—Chi (who had been flipping through the dossier) came to the last page, with the tax-issue stamp absolutely unmistakable, woven right into the paper.

"The computer did," said Pao-Yu, and she giggled idiotically.

"Well," said Jannina, jumping to her feet, "tear it up, my dear, or give it to me, and I'll tear it up for you. I think Miss Leslie Smith deserves from us the same as we'd give to anybody else, and I—for one—intend to go *right up there* . . ."

"After Velet," said Old Al dryly.

"*With* Velet, if I must," said Jannina, raising her eyebrows, "and if you don't know what's due a guest, Old Daddy, I do, and I intend to provide it. Lucky I'm keeping house this month, or you'd probably feed the poor woman nothing but seaweed."

"You won't like her, Jannina," said Old Al.

"I'll find that out for myself," said Jannina with some asperity, "and I'd advise you to do the same. Let her garden with you, Daddy. Let her squirt the foam for the new rooms. And now," she glared around at them, "I'm going to clean *this* room, so you'd better hop it, the lot of you," and dashing into the kitchen, she had the computer helmet on her head and the hoses going before they had even quite cleared the area of the pool. Then she took the helmet off and hung it on the wall. She flipped the cover off her wrist chronometer and satisfied herself as to the date. By the time she got back to the living room there was nobody there, only Leslie Smith's dossier lying on the carved chest. There was Leslie Smith; there was all of Leslie Smith. Jannina knocked on the wall cupboard and it revolved, presenting its openable side; she took out chewing gum. She started chewing and read about Leslie Smith.

Q: What have you seen in the last twenty years that you particularly liked?

A: I don't . . . the museum, I guess. At Oslo. I mean the . . . the mermaid and the children's museum, I don't care if it's a children's museum.

Q: Do you like children?

A: Oh, no.

(No disgrace in *that*, certainly, thought Jannina.)

Q: But you liked the children's museum.

A: Yes, sir . . . Yes . . . I liked those little animals, the fake ones, in the . . . the . . .

Q: The crèche?

A: Yes. And I liked the old things from the past, the murals with the flowers on them, they looked so real.

(Dear God!)

Q: You said you were associated with a theater group in Tokyo. Did you like it?

A: No . . . yes, I don't know.

Q: Were they nice people?

A: Oh, yes. They were awfully nice. But they got

mad at me, I suppose . . . You see . . . well, I don't seem to get things quite right, I suppose. It's not so much the work, because I do that all right, but the other . . . the little things. It's always like that.

Q: What do you think is the matter?

A: You . . . I think you know.

Jannina flipped through the rest of it: Normal, normal, normal. Miss Smith was as normal as could be. Miss Smith was stupid. Not even very stupid. It was too damned bad. They'd probably have enough of Leslie Smith in a week, the Komarovs; yes, we'll have enough of her (Jannina thought), never able to catch a joke or a tone of voice, always clumsy, however willing, but never happy, never at ease. You can get a job for her, but what else can you get for her? Jannina glanced down at the dossier, already bored.

Q: You say you would have liked to live in the old days. Why is that? Do you think it would have been more adventurous, or would you like to have had lots of children?

A: I . . . you have no right . . . You're condescending.

Q: I'm sorry. I suppose you mean to say that then you would have been of above-average intelligence. You would, you know.

A: I know. I looked it up. Don't condescend to me.

Well, it *was* too damned bad! Jannina felt tears rise in her eyes. What had the poor woman done? It was just an accident, that was the horror of it, not even a tragedy, as if everyone's forehead had been stamped with the word "Choose" except for Leslie Smith's. She needs money, thought Jannina, thinking of the bad old days when people did things for money. Nobody

could take to Leslie Smith. She wasn't insane enough
to stand for being hurt or exploited. She wasn't clever
enough to interest anybody. She certainly wasn't
feebleminded; they couldn't very well put her into a
hospital for the feebleminded or the brain-injured; in
fact (Jannina was looking at the dossier again) they
had tried to get her to work there, and she had taken a
good, fast swing at the supervisor. She had said the
people there were "hideous" and "revolting." She had
no particular mechanical aptitudes. She had no particular interests. There was not even anything for her
to read or watch; how could there be? She seemed
(back at the dossier) to spend most of her time either
working or going on public tours of exotic places,
coral reefs and places like that. She enjoyed aqualung
diving, but didn't do it often because that got boring.
And that was that. There was, all in all, very little one
could do for Leslie Smith. You might even say that in
her own person she represented all the defects of the
bad old days. Just imagine a world made up of such
creatures! Jannina yawned. She slung the folder away
and padded into the kitchen. Pity Miss Smith wasn't
good-looking, also a pity that she was too well balanced (the folder said) to think that cosmetic surgery
would make that much difference. Good for you,
Leslie, you've got some sense, anyhow. Jannina, half-
asleep, met Ann in the kitchen, beautiful, slender Ann
reclining on a cushion with her so-chi and melon. Dear
old Ann. Jannina nuzzled her brown shoulder. Ann
poked her.

"Look," said Ann, and she pulled from the purse she
wore at her waist a tiny fragment of cloth, stained
rusty brown.

"What's that?"

"The second-best maker of hand-blown glass—oh, you know about it—well, this is his blood. When the best maker of hand-blown glass in the world had stabbed to the heart the second-best maker of hand-blown glass in the world, and cut his throat, too, some small children steeped handkerchiefs in his blood and they're sending pieces all over the world."

"Good God!" cried Jannina.

"Don't worry, my dear," said lovely Ann, "it happens every decade or so. The children say they want to bring back cruelty, dirt, disease, glory and hell. Then they forget about it. Every teacher knows that." She sounded amused. "I'm afraid I lost my temper today, though, and walloped your godchild. It's in the family, after all."

Jannina remembered when she herself had been much younger and Annie, barely a girl, had come to live with them. Ann had played at being a child and had put her head on Jannina's shoulder, saying, "Jannie, tell me a story." So Jannina now laid her head on Ann's breast and said, "Annie, tell me a story."

Ann said, "I told my children a story today, a creation myth. Every creation myth has to explain how death and suffering came into the world, so that's what this one is about. In the beginning, the first man and the first woman lived very contentedly on an island until one day they began to feel hungry. So they called to the turtle who holds up the world to send them something to eat. The turtle sent them a mango and they ate it and were satisfied, but the next day they were hungry again.

" 'Turtle,' they said, 'send us something to eat.' So the turtle sent them a coffee berry. They thought it was pretty small, but they ate it anyway and were satisfied. The third day they called on the turtle again and this time the turtle sent them two things: a banana and a stone. The man and woman did not know which to choose, so they asked the turtle which they should eat. 'Choose,' said the turtle. So they chose the banana and ate that, but they used the stone for a game of catch. Then the turtle said, 'You should have chosen the stone. If you had chosen the stone, you would have lived forever, but now that you have chosen the banana, Death and Pain have entered the world, and it is not I that can stop them.'"

Jannina was crying. Lying in the arms of her old friend, she wept bitterly, with a burning sensation in her chest and the taste of death and ashes in her mouth. It was awful. It was horrible. She remembered the embryo shark she had seen when she was three, in the Auckland Cetacean Research Center, and how she had cried then. She didn't know what she was crying about. "Don't, don't!" she sobbed.

"Don't what?" said Ann affectionately. "Silly Jannina!"

"Don't, don't," cried Jannina, "don't, it's true, it's true!" and she went on in this way for several more minutes. Death had entered the world. Nobody could stop it. It was ghastly. She did not mind for herself but for others, for her godchild, for instance. He was going to die. He was going to suffer. Nothing could help him. Duel, suicide or old age, it was all the same. "This life!" gasped Jannina. "This awful life!" The thought of death became entwined somehow with Leslie Smith, in bed upstairs, and Jannina began to cry afresh, but eventually the thought of Leslie Smith calmed her. It brought her back to herself. She wiped her eyes with her hand. She sat up.

"Do you want a smoke?" said beautiful Ann, but Jannina shook her head. She began to laugh. Really, the whole thing was quite ridiculous.

"There's this Leslie Smith," she said, dry-eyed. "We'll have to find a tactful way to get rid of her. It's idiotic, in this day and age."

And she told lovely Annie all about it.

OF MIST, AND GRASS, AND SAND

VONDA N. McINTYRE

Vonda N. McIntyre was born in Kentucky and has lived in Massachusetts, New York, Maryland, the Netherlands and Washington. She received her B.S. from the University of Washington with honors and did graduate work in genetics. She has worked as a riding instructor, key-punch operator and as a coordinator of a science-fiction writers' workshop at the University of Washington. Her stories have appeared in **Analog, Quark, The Last Dangerous Visions, Orbit, The Alien Condition, Clarion** and **The Magazine of Fantasy & Science Fiction.** She is coeditor, with Susan Janice Anderson, of **Aurora: Beyond Equality** (Fawcett–Gold Medal).

"Of Mist, and Grass, and Sand," which won the 1973 Nebula Award for best novelette, is a vision of a post-technological world. Its central character is a young woman who heals the sick with the aid of three snakes. The story speaks to us directly; we cannot help ourselves by destroying out of fear the tools we need, but must instead learn to use and understand them.

The little boy was frightened. Gently, Snake touched his hot forehead. Behind her, three adults stood close together, watching, suspicious, afraid to show their concern with more than narrow lines around their eyes. They feared Snake as much as they feared their only child's death. In the dimness of the tent, the flickering lamplights gave no reassurance.

The child watched with eyes so dark the pupils were not visible, so dull that Snake herself feared for his life. She stroked his hair. It was long and very pale, a striking color against his dark skin, dry and irregular for several inches near the scalp. Had Snake been with these people months ago, she would have known the child was growing ill.

"Bring my case, please," Snake said.

The child's parents started at her soft voice. Perhaps they had expected the screech of a bright jay, or the hissing of a shining serpent. This was the first time Snake had spoken in their presence. She had only watched when the three of them had come to observe her from a distance and whisper about her occupation and her youth; she had only listened, and then nodded, when finally they came to ask her help. Perhaps they had thought she was mute.

The fair-haired young man lifted her leather case. He held the satchel away from his body, leaning to hand it to her, breathing shallowly with nostrils flared against the faint smell of musk in the dry desert air. Snake had almost accustomed herself to the kind of uneasiness he showed; she had already seen it often.

When Snake reached out, the young man jerked back and dropped the case. Snake lunged and barely caught it, gently set it on the felt floor, and glanced at him with reproach. His husband and his wife came forward and touched him to ease his fear. "He was bitten once," the dark and handsome woman said. "He almost died." Her tone was not of apology, but of justification.

"I'm sorry," the younger man said. "It's—" He gestured toward her; he was trembling, and trying visibly to control the reactions of his fear. Snake glanced down at her shoulder, where she had been unconsciously aware of the slight weight and movement. A tiny serpent, thin as the finger of a baby, slid himself around her neck to show his narrow head below her short black curls. He probed the air with his trident tongue in a leisurely manner, out, up and down, in, to savor the taste of the smells. "It's only Grass," Snake said. "He cannot harm you." If he were bigger, he might frighten; his color was pale-green, but the scales around his mouth were red, as if he had just feasted as a mammal eats, by tearing. He was, in fact, much neater.

The child whimpered. He cut off the sound of pain; perhaps he had been told that Snake too would be offended by crying. She only felt sorry that his people refused themselves such a simple way of easing fear. She turned from the adults, regretting their terror of her, but unwilling to spend the time it would take to convince them their reactions were unjustified. "It's all right," she said to the little boy. "Grass is smooth, and dry, and soft, and if I left him to guard you, even death could not reach your bedside." Grass poured himself into her narrow, dirty hand, and she extended him toward the child. "Gently." He reached out and touched the sleek scales with one fingertip. Snake could sense the effort of even such a simple motion, yet the boy almost smiled.

"What are you called?"

He looked quickly toward his parents, and finally they nodded. "Stavin," he whispered. He had no strength or breath for speaking.

"I am Snake, Stavin, and in a little while, in the morning, I must hurt you. You may feel a quick pain, and your body will ache for several days, but you will be better afterward."

He stared at her solemnly. Snake saw that though

he understood and feared what she might do, he was less afraid than if she had lied to him. The pain must have increased greatly, as his illness became more apparent, but it seemed that others had only reassured him, and hoped the disease would disappear or kill him quickly.

Snake put Grass on the boy's pillow and pulled her case nearer. The lock opened at her touch. The adults still could only fear her; they had had neither time nor reason to discover any trust. The wife was old enough that they might never have another child, and Snake could tell by their eyes, their covert touching, their concern, that they loved this one very much. They must, to come to Snake in this country.

It was night, and cooling. Sluggish, Sand slid out of the case, moving his head, moving his tongue, smelling, tasting, detecting the warmth of bodies.

"Is that—?" The older husband's voice was low, and wise, but terrified, and Sand sensed the fear. He drew back into striking position and sounded his rattle softly.

Snake spoke, moving her hand, and extended her arm. The pit viper relaxed and flowed around and around her slender wrist to form black and tan bracelets. "No," she said. "Your child is too ill for Sand to help. I know it is hard, but please try to be calm. This is a fearful thing for you, but it is all I can do."

She had to annoy Mist to make her come out. Snake rapped on the bag and finally poked her twice. Snake felt the vibration of sliding scales, and suddenly the albino cobra flung herself into the tent. She moved quickly, yet there seemed to be no end to her. She reared back and up. Her breath rushed out in a hiss. Her head rose well over a meter above the floor. She flared her wide hood. Behind her, the adults gasped,

as if physically assaulted by the gaze of the tan spec-
tacle design on the back of Mist's hood. Snake ignored
the people and spoke to the great cobra, focusing her
attention by her words. "Ah, thou. Furious creature.
Lie down; 'tis time for thee to earn thy dinner. Speak
to this child, and touch him. He is called Stavin."
Slowly, Mist relaxed her hood, and allowed Snake to
touch her. Snake grasped her firmly behind the head
and held her so she looked at Stavin. The cobra's
silver eyes picked up the yellow of the lamplight.
"Stavin," Snake said, "Mist will only meet you now. I
promise that this time she will touch you gently."

Still, Stavin shivered when Mist touched his thin
chest. Snake did not release the serpent's head, but
allowed her body to slide against the boy's. The cobra
was four times longer than Stavin was tall. She curved
herself in stark white loops across his swollen abdo-
men, extending herself, forcing her head toward the
boy's face, straining against Snake's hands. Mist met
Stavin's frightened stare with the gaze of lidless eyes.
Snake allowed her a little closer.

Mist flicked out her tongue to taste the child.

The younger husband made a small, cut-off, frightened sound. Stavin flinched at it, and Mist drew back,
opening her mouth, exposing her fangs, audibly
thrusting her breath through her throat. Snake sat
back on her heels, letting out her own breath. Sometimes, in other places, the kinfolk could stay while she
worked. "You must leave," she said gently. "It's dangerous to frighten Mist."

"I won't—"

"I'm sorry. You must wait outside."

Perhaps the younger husband, perhaps even the
wife, would have made the indefensible objections
and asked the answerable questions, but the older

man turned them and took their hands and led them away.

"I need a small animal," Snake said as he lifted the tent-flap. "It must have fur, and it must be alive."

"One will be found," he said, and the three parents went into the glowing night. Snake could hear their footsteps in the sand outside.

Snake supported Mist in her lap and soothed her. The cobra wrapped herself around Snake's narrow waist, taking in her warmth. Hunger made the cobra even more nervous than usual, and she was hungry, as was Snake. Coming across the black sand desert, they had found sufficient water, but Snake's traps were unsuccessful. The season was summer, the weather was hot, and many of the furry tidbits Sand and Mist preferred were estivating. When the serpents missed their regular meal, Snake began a fast as well.

She saw with regret that Stavin was more frightened now. "I am sorry to send your parents away," she said. "They can come back soon."

His eyes glistened, but he held back the tears. "They said to do what you told me."

"I would have you cry, if you are able," Snake said. "It isn't such a terrible thing." But Stavin seemed not to understand, and Snake did not press him; she knew that his people taught themselves to resist a difficult land by refusing to cry, refusing to mourn, refusing to laugh. They denied themselves grief, and allowed themselves little joy, but they survived.

Mist had calmed to sullenness. Snake unwrapped her from her waist and placed her on the pallet next to Stavin. As the cobra moved, Snake guided her head, feeling the tension of the striking muscles. "She will touch you with her tongue," she told Stavin. "It might tickle, but it will not hurt. She smells with it, as you do with your nose."

"With her tongue?"

Snake nodded, smiling, and Mist flicked out her tongue to caress Stavin's cheek. Stavin did not flinch; he watched, his child's delight in knowledge briefly overcoming pain. He lay perfectly still as Mist's long tongue brushed his cheeks, his eyes, his mouth. "She tastes the sickness," Snake said. Mist stopped fighting the restraint of her grasp, and drew back her head. Snake sat on her heels and released the cobra, who spiraled up her arm and laid herself across her shoulders.

"Go to sleep, Stavin," Snake said. "Try to trust me, and try not to fear the morning."

Stavin gazed at her for a few seconds, searching for truth in Snake's pale eyes. "Will Grass watch?"

She was startled by the question, or rather, by the acceptance behind the question. She brushed his hair from his forehead and smiled a smile that was tears just beneath the surface. "Of course." She picked Grass up. "Thou wilt watch this child, and guard him." The snake lay quiet in her hand, and his eyes glittered black. She laid him gently on Stavin's pillow.

"Now sleep."

Stavin closed his eyes, and the life seemed to flow out of him. The alteration was so great that Snake reached out to touch him, then saw that he was breathing, slowly, shallowly. She tucked a blanket around him and stood up. The abrupt change in position dizzied her; she staggered and caught herself. Across her shoulders, Mist tensed.

Snake's eyes stung and her vision was oversharp, fever-clear. The sound she imagined she heard swooped in closer. She steadied herself against hunger and exhaustion, bent slowly and picked up the leather case. Mist touched her cheek with the tip of her tongue.

She pushed aside the tent-flap and felt relief that it was still night. She could stand the heat, but the brightness of the sun curled through her, burning. The moon must be full; though the clouds obscured everything, they diffused the light so the sky appeared gray from horizon to horizon. Beyond the tents, groups of formless shadows projected from the ground. Here, near the edge of the desert, enough water existed so clumps and patches of bush grew, providing shelter and sustenance for all manner of creatures. The black sand, which sparkled and blinded in the sunlight, at night was like a layer of soft soot. Snake stepped out of the tent, and the illusion of softness disappeared; her boots slid crunching into the sharp hard grains.

Stavin's family waited, sitting close together between the dark tents that clustered in a patch of sand from which the bushes had been ripped and burned. They looked at her silently, hoping with their eyes, showing no expression in their faces. A woman somewhat younger than Stavin's mother sat with them. She was dressed, as they were, in a long loose robe, but she wore the only adornment Snake had seen among these people: a leader's circle, hanging around her neck on a leather thong. She and the older husband were marked close kin by their similarities: sharp-cut planes of face, high cheekbones, his hair white and hers graying early from deep-black, their eyes the dark-brown best suited for survival in the sun. On the ground by their feet a small black animal jerked sporadically against a net, and infrequently gave a shrill weak cry.

"Stavin is asleep," Snake said. "Do not disturb him, but go to him if he wakes."

The wife and young husband rose and went inside, but the older man stopped before her. "Can you help him?"

"I hope we may. The tumor is advanced, but it seems solid." Her own voice sounded removed, slightly hollow, as if she were lying. "Mist will be ready in the morning." She still felt the need to give him reassurance, but she could think of none.

"My sister wished to speak with you," he said, and left them alone without introduction, without elevating himself by saying that the tall woman was the leader of this group. Snake glanced back, but the tent-flap fell shut. She was feeling her exhaustion more deeply, and across her shoulders Mist was, for the first time, a weight she thought heavy.

"Are you all right?"

Snake turned. The woman moved toward her with a natural elegance made slightly awkward by advanced pregnancy. Snake had to look up to meet her gaze. She had small fine lines at the corners of her eyes, as if she laughed, sometimes, in secret. She smiled, but with concern. "You seem very tired. Shall I have someone make you a bed?"

"Not now," Snake said, "not yet. I won't sleep until afterward."

The leader searched her face, and Snake felt a kinship with her in their shared responsibility.

"I understand, I think. Is there anything we can give you? Do you need aid with your preparations?"

Snake found herself having to deal with the questions as if they were complex problems. She turned them in her tired mind, examined them, dissected them, and finally grasped their meanings. "My pony needs food and water—"

"It is taken care of."

"And I need someone to help me with Mist. Someone strong. But it's more important that they aren't afraid."

The leader nodded. "I would help you," she said, and smiled again, a little. "But I am a bit clumsy of late. I will find someone."

"Thank you."

Somber again, the older woman inclined her head and moved slowly toward a small group of tents. Snake watched her go, admiring her grace. She felt small and young and grubby in comparison.

Sand began to unwrap himself from her wrist. Feeling the anticipatory slide of scales on her skin, she caught him before he could drop to the ground. Sand lifted the upper half of his body from her hands. He flicked out his tongue, peering toward the little animal, feeling its body heat, smelling its fear. "I know thou art hungry," Snake said, "but that creature is not for thee." She put Sand in the case, lifted Mist from her shoulder, and let her coil herself in her dark compartment.

The small animal shrieked and struggled again when Snake's diffuse shadow passed over it. She bent and picked it up. The rapid series of terrified cries slowed and diminished and finally stopped as she stroked it. Finally it lay still, breathing hard, exhausted, staring up at her with yellow eyes. It had long hind legs and wide pointed ears, and its nose twitched at the serpent smell. Its soft black fur was marked off in skewed squares by the cords of the net.

"I am sorry to take your life," Snake told it. "But

there will be no more fear, and I will not hurt you."
She closed her hand gently around it, and stroking it,
grasped its spine at the base of its skull. She pulled
once, quickly. It seemed to struggle briefly, but it was
already dead. It convulsed; its legs drew up against its
body, and its toes curled and quivered. It seemed to
stare up at her, even now. She freed its body from the
net.

Snake chose a small vial from her belt pouch, pried
open the animal's clenched jaws, and let a single drop
of the vial's cloudy preparation fall into its mouth.
Quickly she opened the satchel again and called Mist
out. The cobra came slowly, slipping over the edge,
hood closed, sliding in the sharp-grained sand. Her
milky scales caught the thin light. She smelled the
animal, flowed to it, touched it with her tongue. For a
moment Snake was afraid she would refuse dead
meat, but the body was still warm, still twitching
reflexively, and she was very hungry. "A tidbit for
thee." Snake spoke to the cobra, a habit of solitude.
"To whet thy appetite." Mist nosed the beast, reared
back and struck, sinking her short fixed fangs into the
tiny body, biting again, pumping out her store of
poison. She released it, took a better grip, and began
to work her jaws around it; it would hardly distend
her throat. When Mist lay quiet, digesting the small
meal, Snake sat beside her and held her, waiting.

She heard footsteps in the coarse sand.

"I'm sent to help you."

He was a young man, despite a scatter of white in
his black hair. He was taller than Snake and not unattractive. His eyes were dark, and the sharp planes of
his face were further hardened because his hair was
pulled straight back and tied. His expression was
neutral.

"Are you afraid?"

"I will do as you tell me."

Though his form was obscured by his robe, his long fine hands showed strength.

"Then hold her body, and don't let her surprise you." Mist was beginning to twitch from the effects of the drugs Snake had put in the small animal. The cobra's eyes stared, unseeing.

"If it bites—"

"Hold, quickly!"

The young man reached, but he had hesitated too long. Mist writhed, lashing out, striking him in the face with her tail. He staggered back, at least as surprised as hurt. Snake kept a close grip behind Mist's jaws and struggled to catch the rest of her as well. Mist was no constrictor, but she was smooth and strong and fast. Thrashing, she forced out her breath in a long hiss. She would have bitten anything she could reach. As Snake fought with her, she managed to squeeze the poison glands and force out the last drops of venom. They hung from Mist's fangs for a moment, catching light as jewels would; the force of the serpent's convulsions flung them away into the darkness. Snake struggled with the cobra, aided for once by the sand, on which Mist could get no purchase. Snake felt the young man behind her grabbing for Mist's body and tail. The seizure stopped abruptly, and Mist lay limp in their hands.

"I am sorry—"

"Hold her," Snake said. "We have the night to go."

During Mist's second convulsion, the young man held her firmly and was of some real help. Afterward, Snake answered his interrupted question. "If she were making poison and she bit you, you would probably die. Even now her bite would make you ill. But unless you do something foolish, if she manages to bite, she will bite me."

"You would benefit my cousin little, if you were dead or dying."

"You misunderstand. Mist cannot kill me." She held out her hand so he could see the white scars of slashes and punctures. He stared at them, and looked into her eyes for a long moment, then looked away.

The bright spot in the clouds from which the light radiated moved westward in the sky; they held the cobra like a child. Snake found herself half dozing, but Mist moved her head, dully attempting to evade restraint, and Snake woke herself abruptly. "I must not sleep," she said to the young man. "Talk to me. What are you called?"

As Stavin had, the young man hesitated. He seemed afraid of her, or of something. "My people," he said, "think it unwise to speak our names to strangers."

"If you consider me a witch, you should not have asked my aid. I know no magic, and I claim none."

"It's not a superstition," he said. "Not as you might think. We're not afraid of being bewitched."

"I can't learn all the customs of all the people on this earth, so I keep my own. My custom is to address those I work with by name." Watching him, Snake tried to decipher his expression in the dim light.

"Our families know our names, and we exchange names with those we would marry."

Snake considered that custom, and thought it would fit badly on her. "No one else? Ever?"

"Well . . . a friend might know one's name."

"Ah," Snake said. "I see. I am still a stranger, and perhaps an enemy."

"A *friend* would know my name," the young man

said again. "I would not offend you, but now you misunderstand. An acquaintance is not a friend. We value friendship highly."

"In this land one should be able to tell quickly if a person is worth calling 'friend.'"

"We take friends seldom. Friendship is a great commitment."

"It sounds like something to be feared."

He considered that possibility. "Perhaps it's the betrayal of friendship we fear. That is a very painful thing."

"Has anyone ever betrayed you?"

He glanced at her sharply, as if she had exceeded the limits of propriety. "No," he said, and his voice was as hard as his face. "No friend. I have no one I call friend."

His reaction startled Snake. "That's very sad," she said, and grew silent, trying to comprehend the deep stresses that could close people off so far, comparing her loneliness of necessity and theirs of choice. "Call me Snake," she said finally, "if you can bring yourself to pronounce it. Saying my name binds you to nothing."

The young man seemed about to speak; perhaps he thought again that he had offended her, perhaps he felt he should further defend his customs. But Mist began to twist in their hands, and they had to hold her to keep her from injuring herself. The cobra was slender for her length, but powerful, and the convulsions she went through were more severe than any she had ever had before. She thrashed in Snake's grasp and almost pulled away. She tried to spread her hood, but Snake held her too tightly. She opened her mouth and hissed, but no poison dripped from her fangs.

She wrapped her tail around the young man's waist. He began to pull her and turn, to extricate himself from her coils.

"She's not a constrictor," Snake said. "She won't hurt you. Leave her—"

But it was too late; Mist relaxed suddenly and the young man lost his balance. Mist whipped herself away and lashed figures in the sand. Snake wrestled with her alone while the young man tried to hold her, but she curled herself around Snake and used the grip for leverage. She started to pull herself from Snake's hands. Snake threw them both backward into the sand; Mist rose above her, open-mouthed, furious, hissing. The young man lunged and grabbed her just beneath her hood. Mist struck at him, but Snake, somehow, held her back. Together they deprived Mist of her hold and regained control of her. Snake struggled up, but Mist suddenly went quite still and lay almost rigid between them. They were both sweating; the young man was pale under his tan, and even Snake was trembling.

"We have a little while to rest," Snake said. She glanced at him and noticed the dark line on his cheek where, earlier, Mist's tail had slashed him. She reached up and touched it. "You'll have a bruise," she said. "But it will not scar."

"If it were true that serpents sting with their tails, you would be restraining both the fangs and the stinger, and I'd be of little use."

"Tonight I'd need someone to keep me awake, whether or not they helped me with Mist." Fighting the cobra produced adrenalin, but now it ebbed, and her exhaustion and hunger were returning, stronger.

"Snake . . ."

"Yes?"

He smiled quickly, half-embarrassed. "I was trying the pronunciation."

"Good enough."

"How long did it take you to cross the desert?"

"Not very long. Too long. Six days."

"How did you live?"

"There is water. We traveled at night, except yesterday, when I could find no shade."

"You carried all your food?"

She shrugged. "A little." And wished he would not speak of food.

"What's on the other side?"

"More sand, more bush, a little more water. A few groups of people, traders, the station I grew up and took my training in. And farther on, a mountain with a city inside."

"I would like to see a city. Someday."

"The desert can be crossed."

He said nothing, but Snake's memories of leaving home were recent enough that she could imagine his thoughts.

The next set of convulsions came, much sooner than Snake had expected. By their severity, she gauged something of the stage of Stavin's illness, and wished it were morning. If she were to lose him, she would have it done, and grieve, and try to forget. The cobra would have battered herself to death against the sand if Snake and the young man had not been holding her. She suddenly went completely rigid, with her mouth clamped shut and her forked tongue dangling.

She stopped breathing.

"Hold her," Snake said. "Hold her head. Quickly, take her, and if she gets away, run. Take her! She won't strike at you now, she could only slash you by accident."

He hesitated only a moment, then grasped Mist behind the head. Snake ran, slipping in the deep sand, from the edge of the circle of tents to a place where bushes still grew. She broke off dry thorny branches that tore her scarred hands. Peripherally she noticed a mass of horned vipers, so ugly they seemed deformed, nesting beneath the clump of desiccated vegetation; they hissed at her: she ignored them. She found a narrow hollow stem and carried it back. Her hands bled from deep scratches.

Kneeling by Mist's head, she forced open the cobra's mouth and pushed the tube deep into her throat, through the air passage at the base of Mist's tongue. She bent close, took the tube in her mouth, and breathed gently into Mist's lungs.

She noticed: the young man's hands, holding the cobra as she had asked; his breathing, first a sharp gasp of surprise, then ragged; the sand scraping her elbows where she leaned; the cloying smell of the fluid seeping from Mist's fangs; her own dizziness, she thought from exhaustion, which she forced away by necessity and will.

Snake breathed, and breathed again, paused, and repeated, until Mist caught the rhythm and continued it unaided.

Snake sat back on her heels. "I think she'll be all right," she said. "I hope she will." She brushed the back of her hand across her forehead. The touch sparked pain: she jerked her hand down and agony slid along her bones, up her arm, across her shoulder, through her chest, enveloping her heart. Her balance turned on its edge. She fell, tried to catch herself but moved too slowly, fought nausea and vertigo and almost succeeded, until the pull of the earth seemed to slip away in pain and she was lost in darkness with nothing to take a bearing by.

She felt sand where it had scraped her cheek and her palms, but it was soft. "Snake, can I let go?" She thought the question must be for someone else, while at the same time she knew there was no one else to answer it, no one else to reply to her name. She felt hands on her, and they were gentle; she wanted to respond to them, but she was too tired. She needed sleep more, so she pushed them away. But they held her head and put dry leather to her lips and poured water into her throat. She coughed and choked and spat it out.

She pushed herself up on one elbow. As her sight cleared, she realized she was shaking. She felt as she had the first time she was snake-bit, before her immunities had completely developed. The young man knelt over her, his water flask in his hand. Mist, beyond him, crawled toward the darkness. Snake forgot the throbbing pain. "Mist!" She slapped the ground.

The young man flinched and turned, frightened; the serpent reared up, her head nearly at Snake's standing eye level, her hood spread, swaying, watching, angry, ready to strike. She formed a wavering white line against black. Snake forced herself to rise, feeling as though she were fumbling with the control of some unfamiliar body. She almost fell again, but held herself steady. "Thou must not go to hunt now," she said. "There is work for thee to do." She held out her right hand to the side, a decoy to draw Mist if she struck. Her hand was heavy with pain. Snake feared, not being bitten, but the loss of the contents of Mist's

poison sacs. "Come here," she said. "Come here, and
stay thy anger." She noticed blood flowing down
between her fingers, and the fear she felt for Stavin
was intensified. "Didst thou bite me, creature?" But
the pain was wrong: poison would numb her, and the
new serum only sting . . .

"No," the young man whispered from behind her.

Mist struck. The reflexes of long training took over.
Snake's right hand jerked away, her left grabbed Mist
as she brought her head back. The cobra writhed a
moment, and relaxed. "Devious beast," Snake said.
"For shame." She turned and let Mist crawl up her
arm and over her shoulder, where she lay like the
outline of an invisible cape and dragged her tail like
the edge of a train.

"She did not bite me?"

"No," the young man said. His contained voice was
touched with awe. "You should be dying. You should
be curled around the agony, and your arm swollen
purple. When you came back—" He gestured toward
her hand. "It must have been a bush viper."

Snake remembered the coil of reptiles beneath the
branches and touched the blood on her hand. She
wiped it away, revealing the double puncture of a
snakebite among the scratches of the thorns. The
wound was slightly swollen. "It needs cleaning," she
said. "I shame myself by falling to it." The pain of it
washed in gentle waves up her arm, burning no
longer. She stood looking at the young man, looking
around her, watching the landscape shift and change
as her tired eyes tried to cope with the low light of
setting moon and false dawn. "You held Mist well,
and bravely," she said to the young man. "I thank
you."

He lowered his gaze, almost bowing to her. He rose

and approached her. Snake put her hand gently on Mist's neck so she would not be alarmed.

"I would be honored," the young man said, "if you would call me Arevin."

"I would be pleased to."

Snake knelt down and held the winding white loops as Mist crawled slowly into her compartment. In a little while, when Mist had stabilized, by dawn, they could go to Stavin.

The tip of Mist's white tail slid out of sight. Snake closed the case and would have risen, but she could not stand. She had not quite shaken off the effects of the new venom. The flesh around the wound was red and tender, but the hemorrhaging would not spread. She stayed where she was, slumped, staring at her hand, creeping slowly in her mind toward what she needed to do, this time for herself.

"Let me help you. Please."

He touched her shoulder and helped her stand. "I'm sorry," she said. "I'm so in need of rest . . ."

"Let me wash your hand," Arevin said. "And then you can sleep. Tell me when to awaken you—"

"I can't sleep yet." She collected herself, straightened, tossed the damp curls of her short hair off her forehead. "I'm all right now. Have you any water?"

Arevin loosened his outer robe. Beneath it he wore a loincloth and a leather belt that carried several leather flasks and pouches. His body was lean and well-built, his legs long and muscular. The color of his skin was slightly lighter than the sun-darkened brown of his face. He brought out his water flask and reached for Snake's hand.

"No, Arevin. If the poison gets in any small scratch you might have, it could infect."

She sat down and sluiced lukewarm water over her

hand. The water dripped pink to the ground and disappeared, leaving not even a damp spot visible. The wound bled a little more, but now it only ached. The poison was almost inactivated.

"I don't understand, " Arevin said, "how it is that you're unhurt. My younger sister was bitten by a bush viper." He could not speak as uncaringly as he might have wished. "We could do nothing to save her—nothing we have would even lessen her pain."

Snake gave him his flask and rubbed salve from a vial in her belt pouch across the closing punctures. "It's a part of our preparation," she said. "We work with many kinds of serpents, so we must be immune to as many as possible." She shrugged. "The process is tedious and somewhat painful." She clenched her fist; the film held, and she was steady. She leaned toward Arevin and touched his abraded cheek again. "Yes . . ." She spread a thin layer of the salve across it. "That will help it heal."

"If you cannot sleep," Arcvin said, "can you at least rest?"

"Yes," she said. "For a little while."

Snake sat next to Arevin, leaning against him, and they watched the sun turn the clouds to gold and flame and amber. The simple physical contact with another human being gave Snake pleasure, though she found it unsatisfying. Another time, another place, she might do something more, but not here, not now.

When the lower edge of the sun's bright smear rose above the horizon, Snake rose and teased Mist out of the case. She came slowly, weakly, and crawled across Snake's shoulders. Snake picked up the satchel, and she and Arevin walked together back to the small group of tents.

Stavin's parents waited, watching for her, just outside the entrance of their tent. They stood in a tight, defensive, silent group. For a moment Snake thought they had decided to send her away. Then, with regret and fear like hot iron in her mouth, she asked if Stavin had died. They shook their heads and allowed her to enter.

Stavin lay as she had left him, still asleep. The adults followed her with their stares, and she could smell fear. Mist flicked out her tongue, growing nervous from the implied danger.

"I know you would stay," Snake said. "I know you would help, if you could, but there is nothing to be done by any person but me. Please go back outside."

They glanced at each other, and at Arevin, and she thought for a moment that they would refuse. Snake wanted to fall into the silence and sleep. "Come, cousins," Arevin said. "We are in her hands." He opened the tent-flap and motioned them out. Snake thanked him with nothing more than a glance, and he might almost have smiled. She turned toward Stavin, and knelt beside him. "Stavin—" She touched his forehead; it was very hot. She noticed that her hand was less steady than before. The slight touch awakened the child. "It's time," Snake said.

He blinked, coming out of some child's dream, seeing her, slowly recognizing her. He did not look frightened. For that Snake was glad; for some other reason she could not identify, she was uneasy.

"Will it hurt?"

"Does it hurt now?"

He hesitated, looked away, looked back. "Yes."

"It might hurt a little more. I hope not. Are you ready?"

"Can Grass stay?"

"Of course," she said.

And realized what was wrong.

"I'll come back in a moment." Her voice changed so much, she had pulled it so tight, that she could not help but frighten him. She left the tent, walking slowly, calmly, restraining herself. Outside, the parents told her by their faces what they feared.

"Where is Grass?" Arevin, his back to her, started at her tone. The younger husband made a small grieving sound and could look at her no longer.

"We were afraid," the older husband said. "We thought it would bite the child."

"I thought it would. It was I. It crawled over his face, I could see its fangs—" The wife put her hands on the younger husband's shoulders, and he said no more.

"Where is he?" She wanted to scream; she did not. They brought her a small open box. Snake took it and looked inside.

Grass lay cut almost in two, his entrails oozing from his body, half turned over, and as she watched, shaking, he writhed once, and flicked his tongue out once, and in. Snake made some sound too low in her throat to be a cry. She hoped his motions were only reflex, but she picked him up as gently as she could. She leaned down and touched her lips to the smooth green scales behind his head. She bit him quickly, sharply, at the base of the skull. His blood flowed cool and salty in her mouth. If he was not dead, she had killed him instantly.

She looked at the parents, and at Arevin; they were all pale, but she had no sympathy for their fear, and cared nothing for shared grief. "Such a small creature," she said. "Such a small creature, who could only give pleasure and dreams." She watched them for a moment more, then turned toward the tent again.

"Wait—" She heard the older husband move up close behind her. He touched her shoulder; she shrugged away his hand. "We will give you anything you want," he said, "but leave the child alone."

She spun on him in a fury. "Should I kill Stavin for your stupidity?" He seemed about to try to hold her back. She jammed her shoulder hard into his stomach and flung herself past the tent-flap. Inside, she kicked over the satchel. Abruptly awakened, and angry, Sand crawled out and coiled himself. When the younger husband and the wife tried to enter, Sand hissed and rattled with a violence Snake had never heard him use before. She did not even bother to look behind her. She ducked her head and wiped her tears on her sleeve before Stavin could see them. She knelt beside him.

"What's the matter?" He could not help but hear the voices outside the tent, and the running.

"Nothing, Stavin," Snake said. "Did you know we came across the desert?"

"No," he said, with wonder.

"It was very hot, and none of us had anything to eat. Grass is hunting now. He was very hungry. Will you forgive him and let me begin? I will be here all the time."

He seemed so tired; he was disappointed, but he had no strength for arguing. "All right." His voice rustled like sand slipping through the fingers.

Snake lifted Mist from her shoulders and pulled the blanket from Stavin's small body. The tumor pressed up beneath his rib cage, distorting his form, squeezing his vital organs, sucking nourishment from him for its own growth, poisoning him with its wastes. Holding Mist's head, Snake let her flow across him, touching and tasting him. She had to restrain the cobra to keep her from striking; the excitement had agitated her. When Sand used his rattle, the vibrations made her flinch. Snake stroked her, soothing her; trained and bred-in responses began to return, overcoming the natural instincts. Mist paused when her tongue flicked the skin above the tumor, and Snake released her.

The cobra reared, and struck, and bit as cobras bite, sinking her fangs their short length once, releasing, instantly biting again for a better purchase, holding on, chewing at her prey. Stavin cried out, but he did not move against Snake's restraining hands.

Mist expended the contents of her venom sacs into the child and released him. She reared up, peered around, folded her hood, and slid across the mats in a perfectly straight line toward her dark close compartment.

"It's done, Stavin."

"Will I die now?"

"No," Snake said. "Not now. Not for many years, I hope." She took a vial of powder from her belt pouch. "Open your mouth." He complied, and she sprinkled the powder across his tongue. "That will help the ache." She spread a pad of cloth across the series of shallow puncture wounds without wiping off the blood.

She turned from him.

"Snake? Are you going away?"

"I will not leave without saying goodbye. I promise."

The child lay back, closed his eyes, and let the drug take him.

Sand coiled quiescently on the dark matting. Snake

patted the floor to call him. He moved toward her and suffered himself to be replaced in the satchel. Snake closed it and lifted it, and it still felt empty. She heard noises outside the tent. Stavin's parents and the people who had come to help them pulled open the tent-flap and peered inside, thrusting sticks in even before they looked.

Snake set down her leather case. "It's done."

They entered. Arevin was with them too; only he was empty-handed. "Snake—" He spoke through grief, pity, confusion, and Snake could not tell what he believed. He looked back. Stavin's mother was just behind him. He took her by the shoulder. "He would have died without her. Whatever happens now, he would have died."

She shook his hand away. "He might have lived. It might have gone away. We—" She could speak no more for hiding tears.

Snake felt the people moving, surrounding her. Arevin took one step toward her and stopped, and she could see he wanted her to defend herself. "Can any of you cry?" she said. "Can any of you cry for me and my despair, or for them and their guilt, or for small things and their pain?" She felt tears slip down her cheeks.

They did not understand her; they were offended by her crying. They stood back, still afraid of her, but gathering themselves. She no longer needed the pose of calmness she had used to deceive the child. "Ah, you fools." Her voice sounded brittle. "Stavin—"

Light from the entrance struck them. "Let me pass." The people in front of Snake moved aside for their leader. She stopped in front of Snake, ignoring the satchel her foot almost touched. "Will Stavin live?" Her voice was quiet, calm, gentle.

"I cannot be certain," Snake said, "but I feel that he will."

"Leave us." The people understood Snake's words before they did their leader's; they looked around and lowered their weapons, and finally, one by one, they moved out of the tent. Arevin remained. Snake felt the strength that came from danger seeping from her. Her knees collapsed. She bent over the satchel with her face in her hands. The older woman knelt in front of her before Snake could notice or prevent her. "Thank you," she said. "Thank you. I am so sorry . . ." She put her arms around Snake and drew her toward her, and Arevin knelt beside them, and he embraced Snake too. Snake began to tremble again, and they held her while she cried.

Later she slept, exhausted, alone in the tent with Stavin, holding his hand. The people had caught small animals for Sand and Mist. They had given her food and supplies and sufficient water for her to bathe, though the last must have strained their resources.

When she awakened, Arevin lay sleeping nearby, his robe open in the heat, a sheen of sweat across his chest and stomach. The sternness in his expression vanished when he slept; he looked exhausted and vulnerable. Snake almost woke him, but stopped, shook her head, and turned to Stavin.

She felt the tumor and found that it had begun to dissolve and shrivel, dying, as Mist's changed poison affected it. Through her grief Snake felt a little joy. She smoothed Stavin's pale hair back from his face. "I would not lie to you again, little one," she whispered, "but I must leave soon. I cannot stay here." She wanted another three days' sleep to finish fighting off the effects of the bush viper's poison, but she would sleep somewhere else. "Stavin?"

He half woke, slowly. "It doesn't hurt any more," he said.

"I am glad."

"Thank you . . ."

"Goodbye, Stavin. Will you remember later on that you woke up, and that I did stay to say goodbye?"

"Goodbye," he said, drifting off again. "Goodbye, Snake. Goodbye, Grass." He closed his eyes.

Snake picked up the satchel and stood gazing down at Arevin. He did not stir. Half-grateful, half-regretful, she left the tent.

Dusk approached with long, indistinct shadows; the camp was hot and quiet. She found her tiger-striped pony tethered with food and water. New, full water-skins bulged on the ground next to the saddle, and desert robes lay across the pommel, though Snake had refused any payment. The tiger-pony whickered at her. She scratched his striped ears, saddled him, and strapped her gear on his back. Leading him, she started west, the way she had come.

"Snake—"

She took a breath and turned back to Arevin. He was facing the sun; it turned his skin ruddy and his robe scarlet. His streaked hair flowed loose to his shoulders, gentling his face. "You must leave?"

"Yes."

"I hoped you would not leave before . . . I hoped you would stay, for a time . . ."

"If things were different, I might have stayed."

"They were frightened—"

"I told them Grass couldn't hurt them, but they saw his fangs and they didn't know he could only give dreams and ease dying."

"But can't you forgive them?"

"I can't face their guilt. What they did was my fault, Arevin. I didn't understand them until too late."

"You said it yourself, you can't know all the customs and all the fears."

"I'm crippled," she said. "Without Grass, if I can't heal a person, I cannot help at all. I must go home and face my teachers, and hope they'll forgive my stupidity. They seldom give the name I bear, but they gave it to me—and they'll be disappointed."

"Let me come with you."

She wanted to; she hesitated, and cursed herself for that weakness. "They may take Mist and Sand and cast me out, and you would be cast out too. Stay here, Arevin."

"It wouldn't matter."

"It would. After a while, we would hate each other. I don't know you, and you don't know me. We need calmness, and quiet, and time to understand each other well."

He came toward her and put his arms around her, and they stood embracing for a moment. When he raised his head, there were tears on his cheeks. "Please come back," he said. "Whatever happens, please come back."

"I will try," Snake said. "Next spring, when the winds stop, look for me. The spring after that, if I do not come, forget me. Wherever I am, if I live, I will forget you."

"I will look for you," Arevin said, and he would promise no more.

Snake picked up her pony's lead and started across the desert.

About the Editor

Pamela Sargent studied at the State University of New York at Binghamton, where she received her B.A. and M.A. in philosophy. She is the author of over twenty science-fiction stories which have appeared in *The Magazine of Fantasy & Science Fiction, New Worlds, Universe, Eros in Orbit, Wandering Stars, And Walk Now Gently Through the Fire, Fellowship of the Stars,* and other magazines and anthologies. She is also the author of a novel, *Cloned Lives* (Fawcett–Gold Medal). She lives in upstate New York.

0287